Andres & Blanton

MAYBE THIS WEEKEND

Inn Love - The Clairmont Series

Book Five

S. Jane Scheyder

Andres & Blanton
Niantic, Connecticut

MAYBE THIS WEEKEND

Published by Andres & Blanton Publishing, LLC
Niantic, Connecticut

No part of this book may be reproduced or transmitted in any form
or by any means without written permission from the publisher, except in the case of brief quotations for use in reviews. For more information, please contact the publisher: andres.blanton@gmail.com.

This is a work of fiction. Names, characters, businesses, organiza-
tions, places and events are the product of the author's imagination
or are used fictitiously. Any resemblance to actual persons, living or
dead, events or locations is entirely coincidental.

ISBN 978-0-9966721-8-4

Printed in the United States of America

10 9 8 7 6 5 4 3 2 1

For Jessica,
who helped bring this series to life,
and who continues to make Clairmont real for me.

Maybe This Weekend

Andres & Blanton

Prologue

Friday – Noon
Becky

Giant, white flakes drifted innocently onto the windshield, their amazing detail sharpening momentarily before disappearing against the warm glass. Becky Jacobs watched, mesmerized, as each flake gave its final performance and then dissolved. Her eyes drifted toward those that had made better choices, landing in the yard, on the porch railings, on the roof. Those flakes would hang out together, pile up, and no doubt enjoy all of the chaos they were about to cause by having a huge party on the weekend of her wedding.

Wondering if she were actually losing her mind by giving precipitation motivation, she closed her eyes against the peaceful display that could change everything.

No. The wedding would take place as planned. The weather wouldn't keep people from coming. The inn would fill, vows that she had never imagined speaking would be exchanged, and Becky would start a new life with the often moody, sometimes belligerent, and always thrilling Tank Kimball.

Just as soon as he arrived, they'd get started.

Becky opened her eyes and dared the snow to bring her down. It was actually quite beautiful. *Symbolic, really.* She was embarking on a fresh new adventure - clean slate, and all that. The snow was a lovely reminder that she had chosen a new course, a better course. How could something so beautiful ruin everything?

Grabbing her purse and her keys, she ventured out into the cold, stomping on as many of the beautiful, symbolic flakes as she could on her way into the house.

Friday - 1:00 p.m.
Maddy

"So, the Kimballs are really staying here?"

Maddy Fordham referenced the ever-present list on her kitchen countertop. Given the weather, all five guest rooms were clean and ready, but even that might not give her sister the space she needed for these particular guests.

"Yes," Becky sighed. "I guess they finally decided they didn't want to deal with the renovation mess at Tank's house, so *yay*, my in-laws-to-be are going to be underfoot all weekend."

Maddy's eyes danced. "Maybe they heard that this is *the* place to stay in Clairmont."

"One of the two B&Bs in southeast Maine's vacation mecca," Becky monotoned.

"We're the only B&B on the water," Maddy pointed out, ignoring the taunt, and marveling, again, at the miracle of it all.

Two years earlier, the cozy inn in which they currently sat and schemed was a certified dump. It had been no small thing to get it functional, inviting, and commerce-worthy. Maddy reeled her mind back to the subject at hand. Her sister's wedding weekend had finally arrived, and they needed to finalize room arrangements and meals, factoring in an epic snowstorm, and all that *that* might entail.

She absently stroked her dog's head, then realized that it rested on the counter. "Burt! You know better."

The large Irish wolfhound lowered his head in comical submission to his owner, whom he still outweighed, despite her current state. He looked at her with forlorn eyes and slowly wandered off to his mat in the corner of the kitchen.

Maddy sighed as she watched her dog settle in, keeping a protective eye on her. "He's been so clingy, it's getting ridiculous. My own husband can't get near me. I don't know what he's going to do when the house fills up."

"Burt or John?"

Maddy laughed. "The dog. Well, both. I think John's going a little crazy fending him off."

"Yeah, his protective instincts are on overdrive."

"Burt's or John's?"

Becky grinned. "Definitely both. Good luck figuring that out." She leaned her elbows on the counter and rested her chin on her folded hands. "At least we know Tank can handle him - Burt, not John - or at least help to distract him."

"Yeah, if anyone can do it, Tank can," Maddy agreed, choosing to internalize her current views about her brother-in-law-to-be. He should have been home and helping out, not causing her sister all kinds of stress by delaying his return until the day before the wedding. Maddy discreetly looked at her watch. He was due in Augusta soon, if the airport was even open.

She tried her best to mask her concern. "So, back to our list. Why don't we put Tank's parents in the Anchor Room? The less-than-perfect view won't be a big deal this time of year, and that's the best bed, besides the Captain's Quarters." She looked up suddenly. "Oh, unless you don't want to stay there, anymore." She covered the grin that threatened.

Becky rolled her eyes. "Nothing like having your in-laws next door on your wedding night. Why don't you just put them in there with us? They can have the porch."

Maddy giggled. "Yikes. Awkward." She thought for a moment, considering her options. "I still think the Anchor Room is probably best."

"How 'bout that porch?" Becky gestured through the kitchen windows toward the beach.

Maddy considered the howling wind blasting snow around and through what was usually her favorite part of the house, at least a few months out of the year.

"We're in the hospitality business. We have to at least *try* to extend some to your ... interesting in-laws."

"In-laws-to-be, *maybe*. We're not there yet. And leave it to you to come up with the only inoffensive modifier that could possibly apply to them."

"Well, we don't really know them. You might be pleasantly surprised?" Maddy almost laughed aloud at Becky's frown.

"Oh, enough with the endless Pollyanna-tude. You won't be so cheerful when you're up all night, every night, with a howling infant."

Maddy smoothed her hand over her enormous tummy. "Don't say that. He'll hear you!"

"Sorry, kiddo," Becky sort of nodded in the direction of Maddy's abdomen. "Okay. So, anyway, they're supposed to be here in time for dinner. I guess they're planning to stop at the coffee shop first, then Grace and Alex will bring them over. Oh, and since their new place is a bit of a drive, I've offered them a room, in case the roads get any worse."

"Right." Maddy figured Tank's sister and her husband would stay, regardless of the weather. "That shouldn't be a problem. You know," her mind went on a little side-trip, "one of these days, I really have to buy some air mattresses for back-up. I keep meaning to do it, and I just don't ever seem to get around to it." She drew a little design on her pad. "Oh, to have the inn that full off-season, right?"

"Gotta dream," Becky agreed.

The design turned into an air mattress of sorts. "So, how does Alex get along with the in-laws?"

"They're nothing, if not consistent in their determined dislike of ... well, anyone." Becky blew the hair out of her eyes. "They justify disliking Alex because they believe he's unaccomplished, and poor. And not necessarily in that order."

Maddy almost choked on her tea. "Alex? Poor?"

"Yeah, oh, and the fact that he sort of eloped with their daughter."

"Eloped? They didn't elope."

"I know, but the Kimballs didn't have the requisite six-months to clear their schedule. So, as far as they're concerned, their daughter eloped."

"Yikes. And you gave them even less time." Maddy considered that for a moment. "Well, at least they're coming."

"Yes. Go figure." Becky sighed. "Oh, and by the way, we're not supposed to say anything about his business exploits."

"Whose, Alex? Like I know about his business exploits. He's hardly ever around. How would I know what he does?"

"Well, I'm sure you know he travels a lot and he's gotta be super-successful at whatever it is he does, or he wouldn't wear Versace ... socks."

"Versace makes socks?"

Becky paused. "Yes, of course they do."

"How much do you think they cost?"

Becky considered this for a moment. "More than I can afford. Anyway, you've seen how he dresses. But back to the point. Grace was saying the other day that her parents still don't know what he does and she doesn't want it to come up before they have a chance to tell them."

"I can't imagine how it would. And how can they not know?"

"Well, they didn't ask, or didn't ask nicely, so Grace never told them. I guess she was hoping that they'd come around and like him based on who he is and not how much money he makes."

"Think that'll happen?"

"Ha! Doubtful. But I have to hope, or there's not a prayer for me."

"They'll love you. Eventually."

Becky raised a brow.

"I wonder how Grace and Tank turn out so nice?" Maddy ruffled the fur on Burt's head, which now rested in her lap. So much for giving her space.

"Well, it's not like Tank isn't his own social nightmare," Becky replied matter-of-factly. "Grace is great - no explaining that."

Maddy would have liked to argue Becky's assessment of her fiancé, but it was fairly accurate. Once you got to know Tank, you couldn't help but love him, his present absence notwithstanding, but he didn't make it easy.

She returned to her list. "Okay, so that leaves Liz. When is she getting in, again? And she's staying here through Monday or Tuesday, right?"

"Right. She's hoping to get here sometime around dinner, but who knows with this storm?" Becky cast a somewhat anxious look out the window.

Maddy glanced over her shoulder. The snow was coming down hard, and Becky's relatively new friend, Liz Michaels, was traveling from northern Vermont. Mountains and snow - not a good combination. "Think she might change her mind?"

"She texted me that she was getting on the road around noon. Wasn't too bad that far west. Said she'd let me know if she turned back."

"I'm impressed that she's making the trip. I know you bonded enough at Christmas for her to get an invite, but for her to brave this weather? I mean, I love you, but I'm not sure I'd walk to the shed for you in this."

"Ha ha - thanks," Becky returned dryly. "Well, she's coming, but I'm not the only reason. Don't forget that she hit it off with Dr. English Professor while she was here."

Maddy nodded. "The one whose son was supposed to marry her daughter?"

"Yep. They were all worked up because their kids were moving too fast. Then *they* met." Becky smiled at the memory. "That was a crazy week; I'm so glad we decided to stay open over Christmas. I got a front row seat to the whole affair." She paused, and her grin grew wider. "Don't tell Liz I called it that."

"And her daughter is doing okay?"

"Oh, yeah. Kelly's doing great. She'd come to the wedding, but she's covering at the shop so Grace can be here. I suppose if the weather's bad enough that they close down she'll come, but that's its own problem." Becky considered the windows showcasing the storm with a frown. "That reminds me. Did we pick up our order? I should have thought of that when I was out earlier. We won't get through this weekend without more coffee."

"It's all good. John picked it up yesterday." Maddy looked back down at her list. "So, we'll put Liz in the Seashell room, which still gives us one, or possibly two more rooms if we need them." She marked her pad accordingly and glanced at the door leading to the room that Becky used when she helped at the inn. "I can't imagine needing it, but there's your bedroom, too," she added thoughtfully.

Becky glanced over her shoulder. "Yikes, I'd better clean it up, just in case."

"I wouldn't worry about it," Maddy replied. "Seriously, what are the chances?"

Though Becky seemed to be weighing them, Maddy continued. "Pastor Rob is coming for the rehearsal and dinner, but he lives in town, so he should be good, right? How about his wife?"

"Rachel was going to join us tonight, but their little guy is sick. Hopefully, she can come for the wedding tomorrow."

Maddy rubbed her tummy. The baby was kicking up a storm. "I so wish Mom and Dad could be here." She winced and looked up apologetically. Why couldn't she control her maternity mouth?

They'd made their peace with their parents being unable to attend the wedding on such short notice. Still, it was hard. Becky hadn't had a particularly close relationship with them over the years, but that had begun to change. It would have been especially meaningful to have them at the wedding to support her.

"They'll be here soon enough to welcome the newest member of the family."

"I know they'd change their plans if they could."

Becky smiled a little sadly. "This makes the most sense. It was a big deal for them to make the trip at all, and they've planned the one to meet their first grandchild for months."

They were both familiar with the mantra, but it helped to hear it again.

"Tank and I could have had the wedding during their visit, but their window was so short, and we all agreed that it would have been too much at once. Can you even imagine?" She stood up, determined to be cheerful. "They can meet Tank next month. We'll make a production of it. Well, if you having your baby isn't entertaining enough."

Maddy laughed, desperately hoping that the delivery of her first child wasn't entertaining at all.

"I'm not sure we could set him up to look any bigger or more formidable than to present him to Mom and Dad along with your mini-you," Becky mused.

"Tank doesn't need anyone to make him look big and formidable," Maddy observed.

Becky's smile slowly dissolved into straight-lipped resolution. "I'll show him formidable if he ever shows up."

Maddy nodded, determined to believe that Becky would have the opportunity. "Look out, Tank."

Friday - 2:00 p.m.
Becky

Becky checked the ribs that had been slow-roasting since noon, and the garlic, cumin, and onion gently accosted her senses as she opened the oven door. Satisfied with that detail, she looked around the kitchen, further convinced that preparations, as far as the food was concerned, were almost complete.

The house was too quiet. Maddy had gone upstairs to check in with John and do the final walk-through of the rooms. Burt, of course, had followed her. Blake and Parker, John's two young sons, were either 'helping' or tucked away in their family's apartment on the third floor.

Was it possible that the inn could still fill, with all of the players in place, within twenty-four hours? It didn't seem likely.

She had to keep moving. All she really needed to do was put a few final touches on the casual meal they would share, make herself look presentable - a gift, if she had one - and await her fiancé.

All Tank needed to do was show up. He had no responsibilities, other than to keep his parents under control. She groaned inwardly, considering the additional challenge he faced, now that they would be under the same roof for the whole weekend. The Kimballs blamed her for Tank refusing an impressive broadcasting job with ESPN after his football career ended, so their attending the wedding was hardly a show of support. Likely, they were going to make one last, nasty effort to derail everything.

Becky glanced outside and briefly considered the sway that this wealthy and influential couple might have with the weather.

Assimilating into his family was going to be next to impossible, but that was a problem for another day. She and Tank needed to assimilate first, and that wasn't going to happen until the former pro-linebacker-turned-concussion-specialist returned from his latest speaking gig.

He'd become an unwilling expert in the field, and he was on high demand in the high school and college athlete safety protocol circuit. Tank was passionate about his mission, almost as passionate as he had been about playing football. He loved the sport and wanted kids to be able to play it safely. So he flew around the country, speaking about the life-threatening injuries that had upended his career, and educating his audiences about the necessary safety precautions.

He was an imposing presence, having only lost ten to fifteen pounds of his former linebacker self. Every remaining pound was powerfully packed onto his impressive six-foot-four frame. What he lacked in the social niceties, he more than compensated for with his ferocity and football sense. The coaches, players and medical specialists all loved him, despite any intimidation they might feel. That was part of his charm.

Becky sighed. It was important work, and she was proud of him. She wouldn't dream of standing in his way. She would, however, dream of supporting him from less of a distance.

A year and a half ago, Tank had bulldozed into her life, and when they'd stopped fighting and started contemplating a future together, Becky was determined to do it right. There had been a time when simply being alone in a room with a good-looking man had been all the incentive she'd needed to act decisively and let the chips fall where they may. That M.O. had not served her well, and she had resolved to slow down with Tank, even if it killed her.

It was definitely going to kill her.

When Tank turned all of that football passion and energy on her, Becky had no trouble matching it. They quickly found that they'd have to elope or put a continent between them if they were going to wait until they were married to ... explore their relationship further. Since Becky had insisted on a proper wedding, there was more often than not a continent between them.

Becky moved around the kitchen distractedly, setting out what she could for the meal that would all but serve itself in a few short hours. She'd certainly been productive over the last year, her culinary skills reaching new heights as her sister gave her free rein in her gourmet kitchen. Maddy's Inn, perched invitingly on the beach overlooking the Atlantic Ocean, was as much Becky's home as her small apartment in Clairmont. Here, she retreated after engaging, but long days teaching art at the regional high school, occasionally taking over the inn-keeping duties when John and Maddy needed help. It had actually been one of the best years of her life, a chapter she'd look back on with satisfaction and not a little wonder.

She was just more than ready to look back on it from a new perspective, perhaps further down the beach, from Tank's waterfront home.

Glancing, again, at the clock on the stove, assuring herself that it was simply to estimate the remaining cooking time, Becky went to her room to get ready.

§ § §

"Why turn sideways? You're twice as wide that way."

A mild expression of frustration - never an expletive - escaped her sister's lips and got lost in the pile of clean towels that she had carried into Becky's bedroom off the kitchen. Maddy cleared her throat.

"I can't see if I don't turn."

Becky abandoned her bathing plans in favor of harassing her pregnant sister. "They'd be much easier to carry if you folded them, first."

"Yes, brilliant," Maddy almost-snapped, transferring the towels to Becky with more force than was absolutely necessary.

"You were nicer when you weren't so huge." Becky carried the towels in front of her as though pregnant, dodging Burt, who hovered ever near her sister. She tossed the towels with a flourish onto her bed and began folding them.

"At least I was nicer ... ever," Maddy countered, her quick wit and verbal sparring ability diminishing, it seemed, in direct proportion to her increasing girth. "Don't!" She held up her hand, clearly anticipating Becky's latest discourse on the unfortunate effects of pregnancy on the female brain.

Becky picked up another towel. "I'm sorry, it's just so ... satisfying to see you, well, not your usual, controlled self." She added to her neatly folded pile and grinned. "And the waddling is hilarious."

Maddy Jacobs-now-Fordham, experiencing her first pregnancy at thirty-one, was less amused. She plopped down on Becky's bed next to the towels. "I swear I will show no mercy when you start waddling."

"I will never waddle!" Becky countered emphatically.

"Oh, you'll waddle. Trust me. And those long legs won't help you then."

Becky sniffed. "Well, I won't have a reason to waddle if Tank doesn't come home."

Maddy, ever one to forget her own misery when someone else needed comfort, barked a very unladylike laugh. Becky looked up with surprise.

So did Burt.

"This is funny to you? My fiancé, who claims he's been frantic to marry me for the last nine months, falls off the radar the week before our wedding, and you think this is funny?"

Maddy shook her head, her eyes streaming with silent laughter. Becky would have marveled at the emotional spectacle if the subject matter wasn't so painful.

"Yes, I can see that you're really burdened for me," she continued when Maddy obviously couldn't or wouldn't speak a coherent thought. "Tank is probably lying in a ditch somewhere, and oh, ha ha, look at poor Becky, all dressed up for her wedding, and she doesn't even know her fiancé is dead. Isn't that hilarious?"

Maddy fell over on the bed, still in the middle of one seemingly endless giggle spasm, and tried to catch her breath. Burt stood by helplessly, occasionally licking Maddy's ankles and whining.

Becky, resolving to leave her pity party, looked on, concerned. "Maddy, are you alright? I mean, I understand that you're heartless and self-absorbed right now, but this is getting ... weird. Even I wouldn't laugh that hard at someone else's misfortune."

"I'm so sorry, it's not funny," Maddy gasped, and fell into another fit of giggles.

A slow, steady gait in the kitchen turned surprisingly fast when John Fordham approached and saw his wife sprawled on the bed. He launched into the room but managed to put on the brakes before Burt did it for him. The usually gentle dog looked ready to tear his hand off. Maybe his whole arm.

"Easy, Buddy," John said, reaching slowly for the wolfhound.

His relationship with the dog had been hard-won; John wasn't naturally inclined to befriend something that almost matched him in weight and walked on four legs. Still, they'd made considerable progress - until Maddy had become pregnant. Burt now regarded John as some sort of alien, and John was clearly getting tired of fighting for the right to take care of his wife.

Easing around the dog, he sat and gently lifted Maddy into his arms. Burt growled and paced, conceding for the moment.

"Maddy, Honey, are you okay?" John spared a misplaced look of borderline-irritation for Becky. "Is she okay? What happened?"

"Oh, she's fine. I think," Becky mused. "She was laughing at me and the fact that Tank hasn't shown up for our wedding - funny stuff, you know - and it just sent her into a fit."

Maddy snuggled into John's chest and sighed happily. Kissing her forehead, he laid her gently back on the bed. Even a strapping carpenter could only cradle a wife who sported thirty extra pounds for so long.

He turned to Becky. "Tank will be here. He won't let anything stop him from getting home."

Becky swallowed the doubts that had plagued her relentlessly since she'd last heard Tank's voice five days earlier. She managed a nod. "I know."

John looked back with concern at his wife, who now seemed to be on the verge of an unplanned nap.

"She didn't really laugh at you," he insisted, though there was a hint of question in his voice.

Becky offered a small smile. "Maybe not about Tank. But she got something into her head about me and waddling and couldn't let it go."

John considered this for a moment, and wisely decided not to ask. "She hasn't exactly been herself lately, has she?"

"And who can we thank for that?" Becky raised a brow.

John grinned, affection palpable as he looked down at his wife.

Becky sighed. Sandy-haired, tall and strong, John had a perpetual smile for his wife that made him more handsome than ever. It really wasn't fair that Maddy carried all the weight of the pregnancy. John seemed taller and leaner, and Maddy, shorter and rounder, and if they weren't so ridiculously happy, Becky would complain. To someone.

"I should probably try to get her upstairs so she can rest up for tonight," John said.

Becky pondered the thought of John hauling a very pregnant Maddy up two flights of steps. That just might wipe the dreamy, love-sick look from his eyes for a bit.

"Oh, let her rest in here," Becky replied. "It's quiet - for the moment."

John nodded, grateful, and stood. "The rest of the house looks good." He cast her a reassuring look. "I think we're ready."

♬♬♬

The doorbell, which should have been a happy announcement of the party starting, only made Becky more anxious. Grace and her parents weren't due for a while, and Tank would never ring the bell. He'd just storm into the house, bellowing her name. She used to get frustrated with his loud football-player-ness, but she'd give anything to hear him yell for her right now.

Instead, she opened the door to her pastor.

"Hey, Pastor Rob," she said with as much enthusiasm as she could muster.

"Hi Becky," he smiled, stepping into the front hall. "Sorry to get here so early. I visited some folks a couple of blocks from here and wasn't sure I'd get home and back before dinner, or at all. The roads are pretty rough."

"I'm so sorry," Becky replied, giving the small parking lot one more look as she closed the door. "I really appreciate your coming."

"No problem," he replied. "Well, maybe a little problem, but nothing a couple of studded snows won't fix."

Becky simply didn't have the energy to mask her confusion. "Studded what?"

"Sorry, tires. Snow tires. Never mind. What do we hear from our groom? You mentioned that he's been delayed, but not much more than that." Rob's eyes were concerned and comfort-ready.

Becky felt her momentary bravery slipping as she considered her pastor, whose accessibility continued to surprise her. He wasn't that much older than Tank. Not quite as tall and a whole lot leaner, he still had a presence to be reckoned with, and it had a lot to do with his heart.

"Yeah, sorry. I don't know much more than that. Last time we spoke was on Sunday, which is typical, I guess. Tank hates his cell phone and we don't really talk much when he's out of town." She sighed. "He called after the Super Bowl, so you can imagine how much I was on his mind. He told me he picked up an extra speaking event; someone canceled at a conference in New York, and since he's already on the road and his brain is currently, well, always consumed with football..."

"His trips have taken some unexpected turns, haven't they?"

Becky humphed. "He can't ever say no."

"He's doing important work."

"I know." She took Rob's coat. "I received a somewhat curt text on Wednesday saying he'd be here by Friday. I'm assuming he means this Friday."

Rob chuckled. "But this is all fairly normal, right?"

Becky inhaled, smirked. She'd become surprisingly comfortable confiding, on occasion, in this man - another unexpected relationship in her life. She'd also become accustomed to his not coddling her. She usually came away from their interactions a little irritated and a little challenged, but she could never bring herself to doubt what or who motivated him.

"Yes, I guess it is," she finally replied. "But he should be here. He's the one who pushed for this wedding. This weekend. Valentine's Day - woo hoo." Becky waved her hands unenthusiastically.

"*Tank* pushed for a Valentine's Day wedding?" Rob asked.

"I know," Becky said. "It's not like he's all sentimental, it's just that last year on Valentine's Day ... You know what? Never mind. It was just his dumb idea, and now he's not here."

Rob nodded his sympathy.

"And you shouldn't have to be out in this weather. Even if," she caught herself, "even when he does show up, we're just talking through the service anyway, right? No formal rehearsal or anything?"

Talking about the logistics was comfortable territory. It made everything seem more imminent.

"Well, I was hoping to have you rehearse the liturgical dance that will open the service."

Becky's eyes flew wide, and her pastor laughed.

"Sorry, I probably shouldn't do that to you right now." Rob unlaced his wet boots and set them on a rug near the door. "The service will be simple; pretty straight-forward."

Becky nodded, heartily relieved. She didn't even know if liturgical dance was a thing, but if it was, she couldn't begin to imagine Tank's response.

"I wish I hadn't pushed to have a dinner tonight." She thought again about her friends braving the weather for her, and for a wedding that might not even happen. "I don't want people out in this mess for us."

"We're New Englanders," Rob reminded her. "We're not put off by a little snow. Besides, your friends love you and want to support you. And," he added with feeling, "you make the best ribs in Clairmont."

"I make the *only* ribs in Clairmont," Becky laughed, turning and leading him through the house. "Follow me. Otis lost power next door, so he came early. I'm sure he'd appreciate some company."

They entered the sunroom, a bit of a misnomer for the main living area in the house. Just off the kitchen, with its giant fireplace and rows of windows overlooking the ocean, this was where family and friends hung out. It was large enough to accommodate two big couches facing each other over a coffee table, and two comfy recliners at the head of them, facing the fireplace and a TV screen in the corner. There was plenty of room to spare, with game and puzzle tables, and various cozy chairs lining the windows.

Otis, Maddy's eighty-something neighbor, was sitting in one of the recliners, and looked up with a smile. "Pastor, you braved the roads!"

"Please, don't get up," Rob leaned in to shake his hand. "They weren't so bad," he said with little conviction.

Otis nodded, glancing sympathetically at Becky.

The doorbell rang again, and Becky wound back through the old inn as Otis called out, "Well, now. I'll bet that's Tank."

Becky sighed, wishing it were true. While he could potentially arrive at any time, the weather would more than likely cause problems, and he wasn't inclined to communicate about his delays. Why did he have to take on an extra event this week? His conference in Atlanta should have ended on Sunday, and he had planned to be home Monday night, with the whole week ahead to prepare. It's not like he actually would have done anything, but still. He would have been close by, accessible, and not causing so much stress in the final hours. Of course, he couldn't turn down the opportunity that came up in New York, though he was rather evasive about the specifics. That didn't really sit well, under the circumstances.

Becky's steps slowed as she reached the front hall. She had refused to look up the conference to find out when it ended, choosing, instead, to trust that Tank would get back as soon as he could. Of course, he hadn't planned on a snowstorm immobilizing most of New England.

Taking a deep breath, Becky filed her worries away as she prepared to play hostess to more early arrivals. She pasted on a smile and opened the door to Frank Davidson and his father. Frank was John's business partner and he'd worked with John and Tank on building the apartment, or the 'penthouse,' as they liked to call it, on the third floor of the inn. Frank's father, Ed, was a shop teacher at the high school; Becky and Tank knew him well. She was actually very fond of both of them, but wondered why they were both on her doorstep the day before the wedding.

The inflatable, life-sized, party doll should have tipped her off.

Frank, husky, and in his mid-thirties like his business partner, had the decency to look sheepish, but his dad jumped right in.

"He's been gone all week, and we only have one more night with him, Becky. You can't say no."

"No."

For some reason, she still stepped aside as they began to cross the threshold with their bachelor party paraphernalia.

"That goes back to the truck," she gestured decisively at their inflatable friend.

This request didn't seem to surprise either of them, and Frank discharged it with a grin.

"And hold on," Becky said. "You left Anita out there?"

"Yep. She's our excuse for showing up early, so you can blame her," Ed replied with an unrepentant grin.

Becky looked toward the lot, rather concerned that Ed's wife, spry as she was in her mid-seventies, was left to find her way into the house alone.

"Hey Frank," she called. "Help your mom out. She's pulling her third bag out of the truck."

"Anita doesn't like to be pampered," Ed assured her. "She insisted on bringing her food for the reception. Afraid the weather will be too bad tomorrow, and she says you can't have your wedding party without her fruit salad and cannolis."

"Oh, she shouldn't have gone to the trouble. And you," Becky threw her hands up. "You should have had the sense to stop her. Nobody should be out in this."

"Well, you know as well as I do that there's no stopping Anita once she gets something into her head. I didn't want her driving over by herself." Ed switched gears, aiming for a touch of contrite.

Becky almost bought it, until she looked, again, at his armload of party supplies. Nothing about these men and their accessories seemed remotely unplanned.

"Right. You're out doing a good deed in a snowstorm, and you just happened to find Frank and half of a Party Central store on your way over here."

"Well, yeah, that's about how it happened," Ed replied cheerfully. "Wouldn't you say, Frank?"

"Pretty much," Frank agreed, walking up the steps with two of his mother's bags. "And you needed my wheels for this mess." He nodded at the road before turning back to Becky. "You didn't expect me to let John handle Tank's bachelor party, did you? He's a great guy, and I love working with him, but he just doesn't have the tools to make something like this happen."

How Frank found that to be a reasonable argument for taking up Tank's time just hours before their rather last-minute wedding was beyond her. Sadly, her own counterpoint was ready and compelling.

"Tank isn't here, yet. Not sure when he'll show up."

The two men exchanged concerned glances as Becky turned to Anita, who was marching up the porch steps with her fruit salad. Becky smiled. She'd always gotten a kick out of Anita, who probably *would* have snapped at her husband's offer of help. *Still.* Becky held the door and turned again to Ed and Frank with her frown back in place.

"This is supposed to be a rehearsal dinner. My pastor is in the sunroom with Maddy's neighbor, who's even older than you, Ed, if you can imagine that. If you want to throw a bachelor party, they're on your planning committee."

Friday - 3:00 p.m.
Grace

"Are you sure you're ready?"

"What's the worst that could happen?"

"You don't want to ask that question," Grace Mitchell replied, pulling her dark brown hair into a ponytail and turning to face her husband in the small office. Handsome, kind Alex; he really had no idea what was about to hit him.

Her parents had called to let her know that they were half an hour out. There were few things that Grace found daunting anymore, but facing her parents ranked among them. Weathering the emotional turmoil of a difficult divorce, as well as starting a successful coffee shop/sports café, a testament to her determination and business savvy, were simply not enough to ground her confidence where her parents were concerned.

Nothing was ever good enough for them. They had formed a negative opinion of Alex from the start, clinging to the G-rated version of her first husband, though he'd been profoundly unfaithful. They seemed to be holding out for a reunion that would never - should never - happen.

Alex Mitchell, who'd known Grace briefly in high school, had re-introduced himself ten years later, and they'd made a new beginning together that should have thrilled her parents. Nine months into their marriage, she knew a peace and contentment she'd never thought possible.

Unfortunately, those things weren't commodities that her parents valued. They were coming to town for Tank's wedding, but

Grace felt certain they were capable of wreaking havoc in both of their children's lives. She sighed; that wasn't completely fair. Her mother was slightly more reasonable and reachable than her father. She had to stop expecting the worst from them.

"I met them when Tank had his concussion," Alex brought his wife back to the present. "It's not like they don't know me."

Grace considered the man who effortlessly impressed anyone who spoke with him. Except her parents. "Yes, but at the time, you were just the nice guy keeping me out of the way when their prize football-star-son almost died. You hardly registered. Now, you're the one who denied them a proper wedding by eloping with their daughter."

"Eloping? We got married in a church with a pastor who, if you recall, and I know you do because you fought it more than I did, insisted on counseling us for six weeks beforehand."

"That doesn't carry much weight with my parents. For them, the wedding is the big, expensive, impressive reception."

"Which you didn't want."

"Well, yeah, I had one of those the first time and it didn't turn out so well."

Alex pulled Grace into his arms. "You know how many times I've kicked myself for not tracking you down sooner?"

She reached up and silenced his regret. Pulling back a moment later, she placed the tip of her finger where her lips had been, regarding him with her green-eyed, Kimball intensity.

"We can't do that. We're together now and we're making up for lost time. My parents will get on board eventually."

He nipped her finger. "They're gonna love me."

She grinned, drinking in his dark brown eyes and playful confidence. It hadn't always been his way.

"Of course, they will. But we need to make sure they love the right version of you. I don't want them just seeing dollar signs."

"I will charm them with my effervescent personality alone."

Grace laughed. "No doubt. Just don't talk business with my dad."

Alex considered this. "Right. And what is this month's version of what I do for a living? Am I still with the circus?"

"Stop," Grace laughed again. "I'm sorry I never told them. It's just ..." She traced the letters on his T-shirt; he wore her shop's 'Caf-fiend' merchandise well. "Every time I'm ready to set my dad straight, he says something ridiculous and judgmental, and I don't want to end the conversation with the bombshell that they've so completely misjudged you."

"So, when he's ridiculous, you don't want to make him uncomfortable?"

Grace didn't particularly enjoy being called out, but Alex was right. She'd let the misunderstanding go on long enough and it had taken on a kind of life of its own. It was probably time to let her parents know the truth and make an effort to get their relationship on better footing.

"I always figured we'd have this conversation in person, and they've never visited ..."

"And we've never visited."

"Right, but they're retired. We're both running our own businesses. They could have made it a point to come and see us and get to know you."

"That's true. But they're coming now, so here's our opportunity."

Grace sighed. "You're right. We'll try to sort it out this weekend."

Alex covered the hands that were playing with the letters on his shirt. "Do we have time to change before they get here?"

"I hope so. Would you just help me move those coffee bags by the roaster?"

Her husband rolled his shoulders. "You can't move a hundred-pound bag of coffee? Wow. Good thing I'm here."

Grace batted her eyes at him. "Whatever would I do without you?"

"It's too terrible to contemplate."

Grace reached up and pecked him on the cheek. "Just stay on the right side of the counter. I know you like playing with the machinery, but you're out of your league on the barista side."

He pretended to look affronted. "You don't trust me?"

She laughed. "I trust you with anything and everything except my coffee. I've seen you back there, remember. You almost fried the cappuccino frother."

Alex snorted. "It was definitely a frother malfunction. Not an operator issue."

She eyed him doubtfully. "None of the other baristas finds fault with my frother." She delighted in her alliteration for a moment, then tried to regain her stern boss-face. "It's just best if you don't try 'to help' back there." Alex had many gifts, but not one of them seemed to find expression behind her coffee counter.

Her husband looked at her for a long moment.

"Yes, ma'am," he said, then kissed her bossy lips until she forgot about her coffee shop and her parents, and all of the weekend's uncertainties.

$\int \int \int$

Having relocated the unwieldy coffee bags to her satisfaction, Grace took stock of the guest-to-barista ratio and was relieved that she could let the rest of the crew go for the evening. She didn't want to keep anyone out longer than necessary with the storm raging. When her parents arrived, they'd likely have the place to themselves; she could give them a tour of her shop, set them up with one of her specialty coffees, and maybe have a chat. She panicked a little at the thought but was determined not to stress about it. She had plenty to do to get ready to close for the night.

"Would you let Daphne and Jenn know they're good to go?" she asked Alex.

"Sure," he agreed, his eyes lighting up at the idea of playing on the coffee side.

"Never mind. I'll do it."

"I've got it Grace," he called out innocently, scooting behind the counter.

She shook her head and continued straightening the chairs in the front of the store. As her task brought her nearer to the counter, she heard one of her baristas patiently talking to Alex.

"No. This is a fat-free soy latte. I can't use half-n-half. They'll taste the difference right away."

"There's a pound and a half of sugar in that drink. You're telling me they'll taste the extra cream calories?"

Grace was close enough to intervene. "People know what they want, Alex. Quit harassing my employees."

Daphne looked up with a smile as she finished with what was likely the last customer of the day. "We have pretty well cleaned up back here, Grace. You're sure it's okay if we leave?"

Grace tried to ignore Alex poking around behind the counter. "I'm sure. Just give the cash box to that guy lurking behind you. I think he knows what to do with it."

Alex had been a huge help when it came to the financial and marketing side of her business, so while she enjoyed giving him a hard time about the actual coffee part, his help on other fronts was invaluable. She waved to Daphne and Jenn as they headed out the door to the back storeroom, relieved to see her husband following, no doubt heading to the office.

After saying good-bye to the fat-free soy latte guy, Grace finished working her way through the rest of the cafe, tidying chairs and picking up the odd napkin or coffee stirrer. Most of the tables had been wiped down, so the final clean-up didn't take too long. While she worked, she contemplated how she should go about giving her parents a proper introduction to her husband. The fact that they hadn't tried any harder to get to know him stung, but she had to focus on moving forward. She also had to let go of her little fantasy of seeing their surprise and embarrassment when they realized how badly they'd misjudged him. She could have helped their lack of information along the way, but she hadn't. It was not going to reflect well on her, either, when it all came to light.

The only innocent one in the whole business was Alex. There was nothing false or misleading in the fact that he'd never felt the need to impress her parents with his wealth or success. He simply figured that the time would come when he'd be able to explore his shared business interests with her father. His ability to analyze and trouble-shoot made his independent contracting firm highly sought -after, and his income confirmed it. She just wished that he didn't have to travel so much; that was the one down-side. With his traveling, and her shop growing almost beyond her ability to keep up with it, the stress had, at times, been a little tough to navigate. Still, his absences mostly made them more determined to make the most of the time that he was home in Clairmont.

Her mind slipped back a year and a half to when her shop was just a couple of months old. Tank had helped her finance the initial effort, but then he'd dropped off the radar, dealing with his career-ending injury. She'd hardly had time to process his pain while she tried to keep her new business afloat.

Alex had re-entered her life at that point, claiming that she had helped him profoundly in their brief year together in high school. She didn't even know that she'd done it. All she knew was that ten years later, Alex had become a successful businessman, and he'd never forgotten the role she played in his life. Determined to thank her, he'd found her on the coast of Maine and re-introduced himself. He'd continued to visit, and their friendship had blossomed. Before long, he moved his home base from Chicago to Clairmont, and they made a go of it.

Seven months later, they had married in a quiet ceremony, with his parents and family in attendance. Tank had been there for her, and Becky, too. Now it was their turn.

She finished wiping down the last table. It was too bad that her parents hadn't been at her wedding, but she'd made her peace with it. That they were showing up for Tank's on such short notice, she hoped, was good news.

She wouldn't hold her breath.

ſſſ

The bell on the shop door jingled, bringing Grace out of her reverie. Her parents, David and Maryann Kimball, walked in radiating wealth. The quality of their winter accessories and impossibly fine outerwear planted the seed; their carefully bored and rigid expressions brought the impression to life, such as it was.

Grace took a deep breath and walked over to greet them.

"Mom, Dad, glad you made it," she called out as she untied her apron. Her shop attire irritated her mother, and the least she could do was lose the apron with its sticky creamer stains.

"Grace," her mother extended an elegantly gloved hand. "Are you still serving coffee here? I thought you owned this place."

Grace leaned in and kissed her mom's cheek. "I enjoy this part of the job," she explained for what seemed like the hundredth time.

"Hey Dad." She reached up and gave him a hug. Though her father wasn't near Tank's weight, he did have his height and frame. There was no doubt where Tank got his size. There was also no doubt where her father's affections lay.

He received her hug with a pat on the back. "Hello, Grace." He pulled back and looked around the shop. "How's business? Is there any?"

She fought an eye-roll. "Well, we have record-breaking snow this weekend. My customers are very committed, but they're pretty savvy when it comes to whether or not they'll risk their lives for a cup of coffee." She looked around her store with pride. "It was actually a little busier than I expected today."

Her mother followed her gaze, finally settling on the large coffee bags that Grace and Alex had just moved nearer to the roaster. "What on earth is in those bags?"

"That's the coffee, Mom."

"Isn't there somewhere you could store them where they're not in the way?"

"It's part of our decor. And it's helpful if they're close to the roaster." Grace shrugged. "People are used to seeing them around. It's part of the charm."

Her mother grimaced but withheld further comment. At least she seemed to be trying to understand.

Apparently bored with shop talk, her father rubbed his hands together. "Alright, well. Where can we find Tank?"

Grace sighed. "Tank has been delayed. How would you like a cup of coffee? And maybe you'd like to say hello to my husband?"

§ § §

Grace stifled a groan when Alex stepped up to the counter to greet them.

"Hello, Mr. & Mrs. Kimball. It's good to see you."

Cappuccino froth streaked the front of his hunter green apron, a mystery she couldn't begin to explore at the moment. She turned to her parents, whose matching looks of almost-revulsion indicated that they probably thought Alex was one of her employees. Apparently, it rendered them mute.

Alex filled the uncomfortable silence. "I'll bet you could use a cup of coffee after your trip. What can I get you?"

Grace looked on with mixed pride and fear. She loved the fact that Alex wasn't intimidated or put off by her parents' rudeness, but it didn't follow that he had any business trying to make their drinks.

"I don't want any coffee, but I'd like to use a rest room." Her mother glanced around, the idea of using public facilities obviously alarming.

"I'll have one of those macchiato coffees," her father decided.

Grace panicked and tried to catch her husband's eye. "I'll be happy to make Dad's drink, Honey. Come on, Mom, let me show you where the bathroom is."

Alex grinned the heart-stopping smile that sometimes caused her mind to go blank. "Are you sure? I'd be happy to do it."

Grace tried to glare at him, but her own smile won out. "Really, I'd like to do it. Maybe you could start locking up?"

Her father had little patience for their exchange. "If this is a problem..."

"Oh, no, Dad. Not at all. Why don't you have a seat? I'll have your drink out in a minute." She glanced pointedly at her husband, who raised his hands and bowed slightly in deference to her wishes. Grace led her mother to the back of the store.

Crisis averted, but another false impression firmly set. Unwinding the whole mess was going to be interesting.

Friday - 4:00 p.m.
Liz

Liz Michaels coasted - slid, really - into the welcome center's parking lot, almost certain her momentum was not due to anything mechanical. Her car was eerily quiet as she put it into park and tried to restart it.

Nothing.

She sighed and put her head on the steering wheel. It had been crazy to make the five-hour trip to Clairmont, even if her daughter, Kelly, lived there, and their good friend was getting married. Never mind that she'd just met their good friend at Christmas. Becky had been playing innkeeper while Liz stayed at Maddy's Inn, and they'd really connected, despite the fifteen-year age difference. They had stayed in touch and Liz was thrilled that Becky's much-anticipated marriage was about to begin. Becky had tried so hard to wait for the May wedding that they'd been planning, but Tank had worn her down, and they'd agreed, rather last minute, to tie the knot on Valentine's Day. Just a few friends were gathering, and Liz was one of them. Surely this justified tossing caution to the wind and making a less-than-responsible road trip?

Liz tried to start her car again and processed the silence with a groan. She rarely found herself in circumstances like these because she rarely took chances. Her life was predictable, based on reason and facts and figures. Just ask the students who scrambled to excel in, or sometimes just pass, her no-nonsense finance and business courses. Reason was her refuge, and almost always guided her decision-making. It took more than supporting Becky or visiting her daughter to completely sabotage her reasoning power and send her out into decidedly unsavory traveling conditions. She fought a giggle at the teenager-y tremors that took over her forty-four-year-old self as she contemplated what was really driving her through the snow to the coast of Maine in the middle of a February storm. It certainly wasn't her car.

Christopher.

She sighed a happier sigh. Liz had met the quiet and intriguing literature professor almost two months earlier over the Christmas break, and they'd started a tentative, although decidedly passionate relationship. Passionate, that is, by *her* standards. Although married and divorced, Liz was spectacularly reserved, and she didn't share intimacy easily. It had been a big deal to allow Christopher to kiss her.

And, oh, could Christopher kiss her.

Of course, she hadn't seen him since she'd finally ended her extended holiday visit and beat it back home to start the second semester. They'd talked on the phone a lot, but there was a degree of safety in getting to know each other that way. Now, heading to Clairmont to celebrate her friend's wedding, they would meet for the first time since agreeing to attempt a long-distance relationship. Would the magic that swept them off their feet at Christmas still be there?

Liz glanced in the mirror, still not used to seeing herself as girlfriend material. The limited reflection was merciful; the fine lines around them notwithstanding, her deep-set, blue eyes remained her most arresting feature. The rest of her was in good shape; she made the point to exercise - had to, with her smaller frame - though she didn't have the muscle and athletic grace of her gymnast daughter. Still, Liz felt satisfied with her mid-forties' fitness.

She ran her hands over her shoulder length, dark blonde hair, grateful that Kelly had encouraged her to maintain a relatively stylish cut. Liz smiled at the thought. Her daughter had a sharp eye and helped to fine-tune things that weren't even on her radar anymore. She carried herself confidently - that wasn't negotiable when her job involved standing, day after day, in front of a roomful of college kids - but translating that confidence into a dating relationship was another matter. Thankfully, Kelly was ready to help.

She could feel herself beginning to travel the well-worn path of imagining those first few moments with Christopher, how it would be, but her serious, adult self took over the fantasy and dragged it back to reality. Would they simply realize that it wasn't realistic, given the miles that separated them, never mind the fact that they'd only had two weeks together to start the whole business?

Liz grimaced; trust her to call a potentially life-altering relationship 'business'. Still, it would be nothing short of a miracle if they worked it out.

She tried, one last time, to start her car, and came to terms with the fact that she was going to have to ask for help. Could she have it towed on a Friday night in a snowstorm? She glanced at the navigation app on her phone. She was still half an hour out of Clairmont in good weather. Who would brave the roads to rescue her?

Christopher.

Liz hated to ask it of him, but Kelly had been talking of needing new tires, and wasn't crazy about driving in the snow. She'd skate, ski, snowshoe and hike in it, but she didn't like to drive in it. Who did? At least Christopher had both a car and a truck, and the latter would probably take the storm in stride. Liz regretted bothering him; she had hoped their first meeting would be sweet and romantic and erase all the doubts that had surfaced in the six weeks since she'd seen him. She sighed. Maybe some time to talk in the car would be a good way to break the ice.

There was one way to find out. She took a deep breath and picked up her phone.

$\int\int\int$

Sending up another prayer of thanks that she'd broken down at a warm and functioning welcome center, Liz left the building and carefully made her way out to Christopher's truck. She desperately wished that this important reunion didn't have to involve him doing her such an enormous favor. She supposed that this was going to be part of the test of their relationship; seeing each other was not going to be easy. They might as well face that fact from the outset and see if they could weather the challenges.

Christopher Harrison opened his door and stepped out of his truck, and the first thing Liz noticed was his smile. Rather brooding by nature, he didn't smile easily, and the fact that he did for her sent her heart into a happy tailspin. Even after getting a last-minute call to navigate a snowstorm, he greeted her with a smile.

She could feel her own natural reserve give way, and, perhaps unwisely picking up her pace, she slid down the walkway into his arms.

"Thank you so mmmm..." she began, but Christopher covered her thanks with a kiss meant to make up for six weeks of absence. Liz deferred to his better judgment and forgot about the world for a few happy, dizzying moments.

He finally pulled back and looked into her eyes, ignoring the snow collecting on the lashes that framed them.

"I've really missed you," he said.

"Me, too," she replied with great eloquence.

He crushed her in a hug. She'd forgotten how solid he was.

"I guess I should take a look at your car?"

Liz would have heartily preferred to stay wrapped in his arms, but again, she deferred. "That would be great. I'm really so sorry about this." She regretfully pulled back and led the way to her vehicle. "Do you know much about cars?" she asked as she unlocked her door.

"I can probably tell whether it's electrical or fuel-related. Not that there's a lot we can do about it now, but I'll take a look."

Several minutes behind the wheel, and then under the hood, confirmed that the issues were beyond Christopher's abilities with the resources available. Securing her vehicle, they loaded her bag into his truck, and started the snowy, slippery trek to Clairmont.

♫ ♫ ♫

Liz tried not to stare at the man next to her, and then gave up. She watched his eyes crinkle as he felt her gaze.

"So, what have you been up to for the last month and a half?" he asked.

Besides thinking of you? she thought dreamily, then said, "Oh, you know, teaching, shoveling snow, not skating."

"Not skating?" he tsked, glancing over at her, his eyes warm. "Kelly will be so disappointed."

"I know," Liz sighed. "She had such hopes for me."

Christopher shook his head in mock disappointment. "Think we can find time to skate this weekend?"

Liz warmed at the memory of skating with him the day after they'd met. Already, the sparks were flying, utterly dumbfounding the pair of reserved and otherwise focused college professors.

She pulled herself back into the present and to the very real Christopher beside her. "I brought my skates for that very reason."

"And I thought you were coming down for a wedding."

Liz sat back, relaxing as much as she could into the bench seat of Christopher's hardy old truck. At least it seemed to navigate the roads without difficulty. Christopher wasn't doing half-bad, himself.

"You probably think I'm crazy for making this trip. I must be. Who does this?" she pondered aloud.

"Well, I'd probably think you were crazy if you were just coming for the wedding of a friend you'd just met," he agreed matter-of-factly. "But then I'd have to consider how long, or rather, how short it took us to realize that we had something special, and I'd say there's nothing ordinary about the way you connect to people."

Liz thought about this for a moment, and Christopher continued. "So, no, I don't think you're crazy. I think you go to great lengths to take care of the people who are important to you."

"That's sweet. Thank you."

"Especially the handsome professor types."

Liz laughed. "Especially those."

"Singular, of course."

"Of course," she agreed, remembering why she'd fallen so fast for this almost-stranger beside her. "Did we really fall in ... connect so completely in just two weeks?"

"Well, maybe it took you two weeks to fall in...connect," Christopher replied. "I was a goner the night we met."

"Before or after the mistletoe?"

His smile deepened. "Both, I expect."

"And we thought we were going to save the day for our kids."

"Well, we kind of did."

Liz hummed her agreement, marveling, again, at the fact that the man beside her was supposed to have been an in-law, not a love interest. When her daughter and Christopher's son got engaged, Liz and Christopher had spent the Christmas break trying to get them to slow down, concerned that the relationship had developed too quickly. Little did they know that they'd be fighting the same battle between themselves.

No thanks to their parents, Kelly and Cam had come to the mutual conclusion that they were not lifetime-compatible. Liz and Christopher had been left feeling a bit disoriented about what had ended and what had begun, and were now ignoring every bit of advice about slowing down that they'd given their kids.

"How's Cam doing?" she asked.

"Working hard," Christopher replied. "He's planning to intern for Bobby. Not sure how I feel about that."

Liz nodded. She had also met Christopher's brother over the break, and could understand the reservations about Cam interning with his lawyer uncle, even if he was a successful corporate attorney.

"Cam won't come home for the summer?"

"No, he'll stay in Boston with my brother. I'd try to convince him to take a break, but he's not really interested in my advice right now."

Liz cringed a little. Cam had taken the break-up a bit harder than her daughter had, and seemed to be having a more difficult time accepting the fact that his almost mother-in-law could conceivably, someday, *perhaps*, become his step-mother. Liz knew the whole situation was difficult and regretted the toll it was taking on Christopher's relationship with his son.

"Kelly seems to be doing well," Christopher observed. "She's always very friendly when I come into the coffee shop. I wouldn't blame her if she avoided me, but she seems to be okay with us."

"I'm glad to hear it. I'm so relieved to have her support. Well, after the initial shock," Liz clarified. "She's happy for us, though she still can't believe I'm dating, or whatever this is."

Christopher picked up her hand. "I'm looking forward to finding out whatever this is."

"Me, too." Liz squeezed his hand.

Considering how quickly they'd met, connected, and committed, there was no telling what might happen in a weekend.

Friday - 5:00 p.m.
Maddy

"I really should have washed this floor yesterday." Energy sizzled through Maddy as she leaned over to wipe up a spill. Her eyes scoured the area. "It wouldn't have taken that long."

Becky laughed. "I can just see you crawling around, your belly barely clearing the floor." She rested a hand on Maddy's shoulder. "It's fine. The whole house is spotless. Can you try to relax?"

Maddy shrugged as she unbent to almost eye level with her sister. "I have to get things done while I can. I seem to relax without warning these days." She stretched, her hands bracing her back. "I am so sorry I laughed at you earlier. I didn't plan on falling asleep before I had a chance to explain."

Becky arranged some ribs on a platter. "It is amazing to watch you go from ninety to nothing and back again. One minute you're doing laundry and vacuuming, and getting this whole inn ready for my party, and the next minute, you're asleep in the middle of a laughing fit." She wiped up a bit of barbecue sauce. "It's been very entertaining watching you be pregnant. Educational, too."

Maddy rolled her eyes and sat down at the table. "Believe me, it's no party not having control over any of this. And just maneuvering," she sighed. "I'm so ready to hold this little one anywhere but here," she stroked her tummy, wondering, again, at what was going on inside of her. "I wish I didn't have to wait another month for her."

"Now it's a she?" Becky asked, shaking her head. "Why don't you just find out?"

Maddy grinned. "We will, soon enough."

Becky joined her in 'petting the baby,' as John's five-year-old son, Parker, liked to call it. They shared a peaceful, contemplative moment, until Burt nudged his head between them.

Becky rubbed his ears. She wasn't afraid of Burt, and he knew it.

"What are you going to do for the actual wedding? Is he just going to stand next to you the whole time? And really, just any time somebody wants to talk with you? This might actually be a thing." Becky continued to stroke his head, but Burt's attention was fixed on Maddy.

"I've honestly never had an issue with him; not with any of our guests - ever," Maddy mused.

"But you've never been this pregnant before."

"Yes. There's that."

"So..."

"So, we'll just have to lock him in the penthouse if he can't handle people being near me. I don't know what else we can do." Maddy shuddered at the idea and looked away - couldn't look into Burt's eyes and think those thoughts.

"Well, he pretty much knows everybody who's coming. Except the Kimballs." A smile played around Becky's lips. "Oh my, I hope they're not afraid of dogs - big, scary, overprotective wolfhounds," she added, clearly warming to the idea.

Maddy laughed. "Let's hope not." The baby moved, and she grabbed Becky's hand. "Here we go again."

She and her sister stilled as the little one relocated under their fingertips.

Becky sighed a dreamy, almost motherly sigh, then said, "You definitely need to keep that baby right where it is until we get this wedding done." She tapped Maddy's burgundy maternity sweater. "I need you too much to give you up to the whims of a tiny, help-less infant."

Maddy shifted as Burt took his turn and rested his head on her tummy. It wasn't the first time he'd done it, and the shelf was getting easier and easier to find.

"Yeah, the whole nesting thing has worked out well for you. I would never have believed I could have so much energy while lugging all this extra weight around."

"As long as we can keep you from falling asleep in the middle of your chores," Becky reminded her. "I had to fold all those towels, you know."

"Oh, poor baby," Maddy replied with a laugh. "And yet," she sniffed, her powers of smell almost overwhelming in their new precision, "it seems you've had time to bathe in what, like rose petals and ... is it jasmine? And your beautiful blonde locks have that silky shine and that little flip to them, your make-up is flawless, and your nails are manicured." She looked her sister up and down. Her navy sheath was elegant and casual - very Becky. "I'd say you managed well with your dramatically reduced prep time."

Becky preened a little. "You know I have this routine down to a science."

Maddy couldn't argue, though her sister had changed a lot over the last year and a half; she was more grounded than Maddy had ever thought possible. She hoped it was enough to see her through whatever this weekend held. She followed Becky's gaze through the window to the dark beach. The smile had left her face; her brown eyes were troubled.

"I'm so afraid that something's happened to him."

Maddy ached for her sister; couldn't imagine why Tank hadn't been in touch, but it was certainly nothing new. She still hoped that what delayed him was some wonderful surprise he was planning for Becky. She'd held on to that hope tenaciously as the hours slowly and painstakingly passed. Now preparing to serve the meal that was preceding rather than following a still uncertain rehearsal, Maddy was starting to have doubts of her own.

Fighting them, again, she said, "I'm sure it's the weather. The roads are pretty nasty, and even Tank's heavy-duty jeep will have to take it slowly."

"He could call or text."

"You're right. He should. But you know how often he lets his phone die or forgets to have it at all..."

Becky turned back to Maddy, the fear and uncertainty in her eyes finally, completely unmasked.

"This is our wedding," she whispered. "Even thoughtless Tank would be in touch. Something is wrong."

Maddy swallowed, her fears gaining momentum with her sister's. Tank's first-hand knowledge of the dangers of concussions may have made him a sought-after speaker, but it had almost cost him his life a year earlier, and no doubt before that when he actually played. While she knew he was great for her sister and was excited for them to start a life together, the whole family knew that Tank's health issues - or issue - could bring the whole dream crashing down at any moment. She prayed fervently that it wouldn't be this moment - this weekend. It had to be something mundane or circumstantial that kept Tank from calling. She continued to cling to that increasing impossibility for Becky.

"Let's get the food on the table and feed this crew. That much needs to be done. And you should eat." She gestured at Becky's slim frame with a touch of envy. "You'll feel better, and you need something to display that beautiful dress on."

♪♪♪

After a couple hours of who-knows-what-sports on TV, probably more of the endless Super Bowl debriefing, the bachelor party planning committee had apparently decided to plan, or at least field questions from the floor. Otis, Ed, Frank, Pastor Rob, and John's sons, Blake and Parker made for an interesting focus group. Eight-year-old Blake sat quietly on the couch, listening and taking in the undoubtedly new and interesting subject matter. Parker was more determined to have some answers, and, if he had his way, significant input on how this party was going to go down.

Maddy had come in to announce dinner, but no one acknowledged her when she entered the room, so she stopped and waited, watching the proceedings with interest. What were they thinking, turning the rehearsal dinner into a bachelor party? Sure, the dinner was informal; everything had been quickly planned over the prior two weeks, so it was understood that the event would be casual and a bit open-ended. But a bachelor party? Under more normal circumstances it might have been fine, but everything about this wedding had been streamlined. No doubt, Tank would grudgingly appreciate the effort - these were his closest friends in Clairmont - but all Maddy could think of was where she would put everybody if the snow didn't let up. Nothing like a multi-generational bachelor rehearsal dinner slumber party.

"Okay, guys, it's time to break it up for dinner," she finally announced. "You can reconvene, you know, later."

The party planning quickly took a back seat to dinner and she smiled as the unusual group filed to the kitchen.

"Boys, wash up first," she reminded John's sons. "And afterward, too. Especially afterward," she repeated, imagining barbecue sauce all over the surfaces of her clean kitchen.

With this disconcerting thought, she headed to the penthouse for reinforcements.

§ § §

Maddy took her time walking up the steps to the third floor. It wasn't like she had much choice - she wasn't doing anything quickly these days - but she did make it a point to soak up the momentary peace while she made her way to her family's apartment. Burt matched her pace, sighing occasionally, as though he understood her burden like nobody else could.

She ran her hand along the polished banister, amazed at the changes that had taken place in this house - in her life - over the past two years. She had purchased the run-down property, determined to turn it into a cozy seaside inn, and wildly underestimating the amount of work necessary to make that happen.

Stopping on the landing of the second floor, she admired the clean, intact walls, and the striking artwork, thanks to Becky, interspersing the doors to the five guest rooms. The home had been almost beyond repair, which is the only reason she had been able to afford it. Bringing the place back to its glory had taken the whole summer, as well as one very committed and talented contractor with his crew.

Maddy wandered into the Captain's Quarters, the biggest room with a private bath and the best view. She recalled her first walk-through of the house when she'd met John Fordham and he was making a bid for the job.

She'd been unprepared for his visit - they'd crossed wires on the meeting time - and she had no idea he'd be so, well, lumberjack-y. She'd hardly been able to form a coherent thought as she'd walked him through the property, but somehow, they'd managed to come up with a plan. They also managed to fall in love, and John's two sons had been quick to win her heart.

Now, in less than a month, if Maddy had anything to say about it, they were having a baby. She rubbed her tummy in greeting and felt a responding twinge. Bracing her hand on the bed, she waited for the baby to settle. Burt circled nervously, which never actually helped Maddy relax. She closed her eyes and tried to tune him out. In a moment, she could breathe normally, and she exhaled slowly through the shiver that ran through her body.

"Be good for Aunt Becky's party, little one," she whispered. "Then we'll have lots of time to get to know each other."

§ § §

John looked up as Maddy entered their apartment, Burt nervously in tow. "Oh, Honey, why didn't you text me? Do you need something?" He stood and walked over to her, gently enveloping her in a hug. He stared down the dog, who grumbled and dropped unceremoniously at their feet. Alpha points for John.

"I need the exercise," Maddy said a little breathlessly, snuggling the best that she could against him. Her gigantic stomach didn't help.

He gently turned her, as was their new habit, and pulled her back into his chest, his arms encircling her and their baby. He turned a little more so that they could see their reflection in the mirror next to the door. Maddy happily rested her head on his shoulder.

"You are so beautiful," John murmured, stroking her tummy.

"You are so biased," she smiled, trying to look objectively at her reflection as he held her. Wavy, light brown, shoulder length hair framed a face that had not gained the weight that the rest of her had. She supposed she should be grateful for that. She didn't have her sister's height, but she fit just right under John's chin, which made her feel rather perfect, the cumbersome cannonball notwithstanding.

"I can't link my fingers anymore," John grinned into her hair as he made a show of trying to encompass her belly with his big hands. "You must be getting close."

Maddy's own smile faded. "You're not allowed to say that. I've got almost another month," she reminded him, settling his hands on top of her stomach. "I don't see how I can get any bigger. This has to be a boy. A really gigantic boy."

John kissed the top of her head and looked at her in the mirror. "I hope she's a perfect little girl with big blue eyes, just like her mom."

He nuzzled her ear, and Maddy sighed.

Burt whined.

"Anything from Tank?" John asked.

Maddy sobered. "No. Not a word. Becky's really afraid, though she's hiding it well. Honestly, I am, too. I keep trying to encourage her, but I'm running out of things to say."

John nodded, concerned. "He's gotta be concentrating on navigating the roads. It's a mess out there. The drive from Augusta can't be easy."

"If he even made it that far. It would be nice to know. There's no excuse not to be in touch."

"Right. But the technology necessary comes second-nature to you. I swear Tank doesn't even know he's got a camera on his phone. And remember how long it took him to figure out how to access his voicemail? It's just not his thing."

"He is funny that way."

John gave her a gentle, encouraging squeeze. "Until we see or hear otherwise, we have to stay hopeful."

Maddy reached her hand back and stroked his cheek. "That's what I love about you, my gentle, hopeful John." She turned to face him. "If Tank messes this up, you'll make him regret it, won't you?"

She could feel her husband startle at her words. Apparently, he still wasn't used to her sudden and uncharacteristic, pregnancy-induced outbursts. But really, she hadn't said anything so bad. John could fill in the blanks appropriately.

"I'm sure he's going to get here, and a few hours from now, we'll all be laughing about this," John replied. "But if Tank has to answer for something, I have no doubt Becky can handle him. She's the only one who can."

Maddy couldn't argue that. She ran her hands across her husband's rather impressive chest. "Is my big, strong husband afraid to take on the former linebacker?"

John grunted a laugh. "When he drops thirty pounds - *from his shoulders* - I'll think about it."

Maddy giggled. "Are you hungry? I'm supposed to be bringing you down for dinner."

"I've just about wrapped up this project bid. Sorry I've been missing the action. I wanted to get this finished before the weekend really started."

"Well, the weekend really started. Pastor came early to make sure he didn't miss the rehearsal, and the Davidsons stopped by and now they can't leave."

"The Davidsons? Frank?"

"The Davidsons - Ed and Anita. *And* Frank. You missed the bachelor party planning party."

John's brows lifted in surprise.

"Oh yeah. Frank and Ed arrived with all kinds of party supplies."

Those same brows knit together.

"But don't worry, you were well-represented. Blake and Parker are helping."

"They're doing what?" John released her and headed for the door. "Whose idea was that?"

"I think Becky suggested it. Figured it would keep the big boys behaving."

John waited for Maddy and Burt, and then pulled the door closed behind them. "Do I want to know who the big boys are?"

"Well, Otis is here."

John shook his head with a sigh.

"And, of course, Pastor Rob is with them."

"Of course," John replied wryly, though he sounded a little relieved.

"Although he said something that actually made Frank blush. I don't think I've ever seen that before."

Maddy laughed as John hustled down the stairs ahead of her.

"I'll be fine. Don't worry about me!" she called after him. "I'm just pregnant with your giant child!"

John was already on his way down the second flight of stairs that led right into the kitchen. Maddy smiled and waddled down the steps behind him.

Friday - 6:00 p.m.
Becky

Becky was wiping down the kitchen table when the doorbell rang for the third time on the day before her alleged wedding. Having received a text, warning that Grace was on the way with her parents, Becky drew a deep breath and washed her hands. Her dear friend had delayed their coming as long as possible, giving an extended tour of the coffee shop and who knows what else in an effort to give Tank time to arrive at the inn before they did. *Ah well.* Her disapproving in-laws-to-be were arriving for a delayed wedding rehearsal with an MIA groom.

An MIA bride would have suited them much better, and Becky was more than ready to oblige them.

However.

She made her way to the front door, and John was already there, smoothing the way for her. She really did love her brother-in-law. She also loved the fact that Parker was helping. The Kimballs would have to behave in front of him.

"Come on in. Here, let me grab your suitcase." John pulled the door wide and transferred one of their bags inside as the group filed in.

Grace greeted him and started the introductions.

"John, these are my folks, David and Maryann Kimball. Mom and Dad, this is John Fordham - he and Maddy, Becky's sister, own the inn. And this is his son, Parker."

"Hi. I'm Parker!" He stood self-importantly next to his dad.

The Kimballs offered civil greetings and then stiffened when Becky stepped forward.

"Mr. and Mrs. Kimball. Welcome. I'm glad you made it safely."

Mr. Kimball nodded, and Tank's mother delicately cleared her throat. "Thank you. I don't need to tell you it wasn't easy. However, we've already missed one wedding," she sent a pointed look toward her daughter. "We didn't want to miss the other."

Becky offered a cool smile in return. "Well. Let's get you settled in your room." She hugged Grace and then turned to her husband. "Alex, good to see you."

They shared a brief commiserating glance as he leaned in for a quick hug. Pulling back, he said, "Any chance we can get a room tonight? I don't think we want to go back out in this."

"Oh no! I mean, yes, of course! We planned on having you stay." Becky glanced out the window. "Really that bad, huh?"

"You can hardly see the roads, and that's just from here to the shop. Who else are you still expecting?"

Becky drew a deep breath. "Liz is on her way from Burlington. She ran into car problems, but Christopher is picking her up. I'm hoping they arrive soon. And Tank ..."

Silence settled over the foyer while everyone processed the fact that the groom had still not made an appearance.

"Will be here soon," Grace finished. "Nothing will stop him."

"Yeah. Uncle Tank is maybe stuck in the snow. But he's so strong, he's just gonna push right over it. Then he's gonna come and we're gonna have a party for him!"

John took Parker's hand. "Yes. There will be a lot to celebrate when he gets here. Let's help our new friends find their room."

Parker nodded and started up the stairs. "Come on! I'll show you where to go!" he hollered, not waiting for the guests to follow.

"Well," Mr. Kimball said, "I wouldn't blame Tank if he decided to stop somewhere along the way. Nothing is worth being out in this." His glance bounced off his son's intended, his meaning clear.

Grace looked apologetically at Becky, who refused to sink any deeper. Whatever had happened to Tank, she would deal. That was the bottom line.

"Why don't you all follow me? We'll drop off your things and then I'll feed you."

"We've already eaten," Mr. Kimball gruffly dismissed her offer. "Some pancake sandwich at the coffee shop."

"We played with my new Panini maker," Grace explained. "It took a while to figure it out," she said meaningfully, and Becky swallowed a laugh. Nothing about any kind of kitchen appliance would ever stump Grace. She must have allowed her dad to try to unlock its secrets in order to waste time. "We'd still love some of your ribs," Grace continued, and Alex seconded her heartily. "And I've got baked goods to bring in."

Becky smiled at her wonderful friend. "Thank you so much."

Grace waved her off. "It's my pleasure. We'll grab them later - they'll keep in the car 'til we're ready."

Becky nodded and followed Parker up the steps, determination re-asserting itself. So her wedding weekend was falling apart and she may even spend the night she'd been dreaming about for a very long time with two people who despised her, instead of her new husband. There were worse things. She'd dealt with people who despised her before and most certainly would again. Tank was on his way, or he was safe somewhere waiting out the storm. Any other option was unacceptable.

$$\mathcal{SSS}$$

"So I put Grace and Alex in the Ship room. Liz in the Seashell room." Becky thought for a moment. "That leaves the Lighthouse room. We should probably have Ed and Anita stay there."

"What about Frank? And Otis? I can't send him back to his house if he has no power." Maddy looked down at her list.

"I know," Becky sighed. "Power's out all down the beach, according to Grace. They would have just stayed at Tank's tonight, but they can't without heat."

"That means Tank stays here, too."

"If he shows up."

"He will." Maddy looked at her with determination. "Look at us. We still have power - lights - heat. It's a miracle, already. So, now. How do we do this?"

Pastor Rob walked into the kitchen. "You two holding up?"

"Oh shoot! Pastor Rob ..."

Becky cringed at his look of surprise, but before she could apologize, Maddy continued. "People are going to have to double up. Why didn't I pick up those air mattresses?" she moaned, rapping her pen on the counter. "The Anchor room has a daybed, can we put him in there?"

"Wait - but I just ..."

"The Kimballs. Right. That won't work."

Rob approached the two of them slowly. "You need to put me somewhere?"

Maddy looked up. She seemed almost surprised that he had materialized before them.

"It might be best if you stay here tonight," Becky explained. "Alex and Grace barely made it over here with my," she swallowed, "in-laws. They say the roads are just about impossible."

Rob considered what was likely not surprising news. "Hmmm ... I just talked to Rachel. I'll give her a call back and see what she thinks."

Becky nodded. "Hopefully, it will clear up by tomorrow. You okay with spending the night here?"

Rob pulled his phone out. "If I need to stay, I can sleep anywhere - don't worry about me."

He left the room to make his call and Maddy and Becky shared a look of concern.

"I don't suppose we can move the Kimballs - ohhh!" Maddy yelped as her stomach spasmed again.

"Oh, no you don't," Becky panicked. "Breathe or something and keep that baby inside!"

Maddy glared at her as the pain receded. "Thank you so much for your concern." She rubbed her tummy to comfort both herself and the little one who was taunting her.

Becky found herself matching her sister's calming breaths. "I'm sorry," she managed, smoothing the hair away from Maddy's forehead. "You okay?"

Maddy drew another big breath. "I'm good. Now, who are we going to put in the daybed in the Kimballs' room?"

§ § §

Becky looked around at the crowd of people gathered in the formal parlor, sitting in antique chairs and on couches and settees that had been rearranged to form a make-shift chapel. Pastor Rob had suggested that they go ahead and talk through some of the logistics of the wedding service; she could fill Tank in later.

How much later remained to be seen.

Frank, Ed, and Anita sat just inside the room, in varying degrees of discomfort and satisfaction at finding themselves attending a wedding rehearsal instead of a bachelor party. Frank had signed on to be there, Anita seemed delighted to find herself there, and Ed appeared to be making the best of being caught in the middle. Parker and Blake, resigned to being at a boring wedding rehearsal, claimed the small game table near the window. Otis, pleased to be part of the proceedings, tried to get comfortable in a rather stiff-backed chair near the fire, and the two families filled the remaining seats near the pillared plant-stand-turned-lectern.

Rob introduced himself and invited everyone to briefly explain who they were and their relationship to the bride and groom.

"But first," he said, "we need to pray some people here."

$$\int \int \int$$

Becky leaned into the comfort of the prayer business a little more every time she did it, especially if someone who seemed to know what they were doing did it for her. She still wrestled with what it all meant. *It's all about the conversation*, Rob always said. *Just talk to God about it.*

She peeked up at the group and smiled. Clearly, she wasn't the only one who was trying to figure out what had just happened. The Davidson party shifted about, avoiding looking at each other, or anyone else, for that matter. The Kimballs tried to look cynical, but there were tiny cracks in their masks of disdain, as though a bit of hope was trying to break through. John and Maddy, Otis, Grace and Alex all seemed very comfortable with the process, and that, in itself, always made Becky marvel. Blake and Parker had dutifully bowed their heads, but they both popped out of their prayer positions and looked to the front door as soon as they heard, "Amen."

Oh, for that kind of faith.

Maddy shifted slowly to her feet to start the introductions.

"Hello, everybody." She glanced around the room with a big smile. "I'm Becky's sister, Maddy Fordham. Well, I guess you all know that, but, anyway, John and I own this inn, and I guess you know that, too, so welcome, officially! Let me know if you need anything at all."

"Let *me* know if you need anything at all," John, sitting next to her, amended. He held his wife's hand and kept the other firmly on Burt's collar.

"Well, yes, either one of us is fine," Maddy agreed. She rubbed her tummy. "John is a little faster than I am these days, but just know that we're here for you." She looked down at Becky. "We couldn't be happier for you. And I just love that you're going to be close by! Oh, and this little guy is due in a little less than a month," she added, dropping back down between Becky and John, probably with a little less grace than she had planned.

John stood. "Welcome, everyone. We're happy to be hosting Becky and Tank's wedding. Trust that he'll be here soon and then we'll all ... enjoy the storm together." He looked around the room. "It's going to be cozy; we're not exactly sure where everyone's sleeping yet, but this is a big place. We'll figure it out." Burt whined to get closer to Maddy, and John let him pass with what could have been a quiet growl of his own. "This is Burt. He's usually harmless, but right now he's on a mission to protect Maddy, and sadly, you are all threats. Just don't try to come between them and you'll be fine." John sat down with a sigh.

Otis chuckled and stood, directing his comments to the Kimballs, since everyone else pretty much knew each other.

"I'm Otis Jensen, and while I'm old, I'm new to the family," he grinned. "I live next door, and I watched Maddy and John," he paused for a moment and looked over the room, "and Frank and Tank, and Becky, and these fellows, here," he gestured at Blake and Parker, "all work together to transform this old house into 'Maddy's Inn'." He beamed at the group. "I haven't known them all that long, but they're a hard-working bunch and they took me into the family as soon as Maddy and Burt, here, moved in." His gaze landed on Becky. "Becky's been a big help, decorating and running the inn for Maddy. I never would have guessed that she and Tank would hit it off, the way they ..." He hesitated when he saw the look Becky directed at him. "Well, it all worked out just fine, now, didn't it?" He cleared his throat and sat down, and Becky sighed her relief.

Anita stood and spoke for her party. "Hi folks. I'm Anita Davidson. Ed, my husband, works at the high school with Becky, and Frank, my son, works with John in their renovating business. I have my hands full, trying to make them behave." She put her hands on her hips. "I have to say, I'm not one bit sorry that their plans to derail this lovely family gathering have been thwarted."

"In my defense, I am one of the groomsmen," Frank said formally, standing up and bowing to the group. "Don't want to shirk my responsibilities." He sat down again with a grin.

"Dad, can I talk?"

All eyes turned to Parker, who waited for John's nod before launching into his introduction.

"Well, this is my house, and I live way up on the top. Pretty soon Mr. Tank will come, and we'll probably play in the snow. He's a great snow monster!"

He paused and looked around the room, figuring he'd delivered some pretty significant news. Not quite eliciting the reaction he expected, he sat down abruptly and looked at his brother. "This is Blake."

Blake stood to address the group.

"Oh, and I'm five!" Parker yelled.

Blake looked at his brother and waited. At Parker's shrug, he began his introduction. "I'm Blake. I'm eight," another glance at his brother. "I hope Mr. Tank is safe in the snow. I'm glad he's going to be my uncle." He started to sit down, and then straightened as he glanced out the window. "Someone's here!"

Within moments, the front doorknob rattled, and the living room erupted with energy as the group made an awkward surge toward the door. Frank, closest to the action, called out to the new arrivals as the rest of the party bottle-necked in the Victorian obstacle course.

"Hey folks. We're all in here." He caught Becky's eye. "Looks like your friend made it."

Becky received this news with considerable relief for Liz and Christopher, accompanied by the ever-present disappointment that it wasn't Tank. She made her way through the crowd to meet her friends, who were shedding their outer gear in the front hall.

"Hey Liz, Christopher. So glad you made it safely!" She took her friend's coat and wrapped her in a hug.

"Becky! I'm so happy to see you!" Liz returned the hug. "It's wild out there. Good thing this guy knows what he's doing."

She held Christopher affectionately in her gaze, and Becky's heart squeezed with relief and a little envy.

"I'm so sorry you had to drive in this mess." She took his coat and gave him a hug. "Thank you for rescuing Liz."

"My pleasure," he replied, patting her back a little stiffly.

"Come on in and warm up by the fire. We're just doing some introductions." She met Liz's questioning gaze with a brief shake of her head. "Still no groom."

Her phone buzzed and she fumbled to pull it from the pocket of her sweater. She took a deep breath and focused on the screen. She didn't recognize the number, but the source of the punctuation-less message was clear.

"New phone home late tonight sorry"

Friday - 7:00 p.m.
Grace

Grace eased into the front hall in time to see Becky's look of supreme relief morph into irritated determination.

"Is it Tank? What happened? Is he okay?"

Becky glanced up and took a deep breath. "He says he's getting in late tonight."

Grace bear-hugged her friend. "He's okay! Oh, I'm so relieved! I knew he wouldn't let anything stop him from getting here." She pulled back to gauge Becky's response. "Are you okay?"

"Relieved, happy, irritated," Becky sighed. "But that's life with Tank. Well, the last part, anyway."

Grace laughed and hugged her again. "You are uniquely qualified to field his Tank-ness."

"What about Tank?" Maddy, trailed by Burt, squeezed through the crowd to the front hall, demanding an answer.

"He just texted. He'll be in late tonight."

Maddy threw her arms around Becky, and Burt steamrolled his way between them with a growl.

Grace smiled and turned to Liz and Christopher. "Hey - welcome! Sorry for the commotion." She hugged Liz and then shook Christopher's hand. "We're so happy you made it safely."

"Thank you," Liz smiled. "This storm is pretty epic. I hope Tank doesn't have far to travel."

Becky untangled herself from Maddy's arms, shoved Burt aside with her hip, and physically turned her sister to face her friends.

"Maddy, meet Liz and Christopher. Liz and Christopher, this is my very pregnant sister, Maddy. She's usually delightful, but sometimes, yikes! So just, you know, be nice."

They smiled politely as Maddy scowled back over her shoulder at Becky.

"Really nice to meet you, Maddy," Liz said. "You have a beautiful place here."

"Thank you," Maddy replied, shrugging away from Becky, and grasping Liz's hands. "I'm so glad you made it safely." She turned to Christopher, who stepped back when Burt shoved in between them. They shook hands over his back. "Dr. Harrison."

"Please, call me Christopher."

"Where's Mr. Tank?" Parker yelled, squirming into the mix.

"Tank is here?" Grace's mother's voice carried from the parlor. "Why didn't you tell us?" She pushed into the crowded foyer.

"What's this about Tank?" her father bellowed.

Grace turned to update the crowd that hadn't yet managed to sardine itself into the front hall. "He's not here yet, but he just texted Becky that he's on his way."

"He's traveling in this weather?" her father sputtered. "That's ridiculous!"

"Dad, let's just be glad he's okay."

"He'll stay okay if he gets off the road."

Grace glanced at Becky, who seemed remarkably calm in the face of her father's insensitivity. Maddy, however, looked ready to blow. Burt sensed it and paced restlessly.

John called over the crowd. "Please come back in where it's warm. We'll finish introductions while we wait for Tank."

Several moments of commotion ensued as the group rallied around this suggestion and started to move back into the parlor.

Grace gestured for Liz and Christopher to head in and she followed, letting the news that her brother was safe, for the moment, sink in.

♪ ♪ ♪

After settling back in around the fire, Pastor Rob picked up where they'd left off. "Well, our prayers are being answered." He looked to the newcomers, who were finding their places among them. "And, welcome!"

Becky smiled the first truly genuine smile Grace had seen since she'd arrived. "This is my good friend, Liz Michaels and Dr. Harrison," she explained. "Liz, just tell them what you do and how we're connected."

Liz nodded. "Hi everyone. Like Becky said, I'm Liz Michaels, and I'm a professor of finance at St. Vincent's, a small, liberal arts college in northern Vermont. My daughter lives in Clairmont and works for Grace." They exchanged a little wave and she continued. "I met Becky over the holidays when I stayed here at the inn, and, somehow, I managed an invitation to this wonderful celebration." She smiled warmly at Becky. "And I'm especially happy to be here, since my car broke down and I thought I might be spending the weekend at the welcome center." She looked at her friend. "This is Christopher, my rescuer."

He turned to the group. "Christopher Harrison," he said. "Professor of literature at Clairmont Community College."

He settled his arm around Liz, the affection between them obvious. Dr. Harrison was a regular at the coffee shop; he came in several times a week to grade papers with a big cup of whatever they happened to be brewing. That suited Grace just fine; she liked people treating her shop as a second home, or office, as the case may be. The college girls certainly knew his habits, and that didn't hurt her business, either. She even wondered if their tendency to flock around him was part of why he made a point to be available in such a public space. He would stop his work and patiently field their questions but seemed oblivious to their sighs and subtle flirting. She liked him better for it, and remembered her own passing crush when he first started coming into the cafe. There was something about his quiet, almost forbidding reserve, and his somewhat gothic, romantic appearance.

Those poor college girls were going to be heartbroken when they found out his heart was now clearly spoken for.

When Pastor Rob realized that Christopher had said all that he intended to say, he turned to the Kimballs. "Okay, why don't we hear from Grace and Tank's folks?"

Her father stood, and Grace held her breath.

"I'm Tank's dad, David Kimball." His eyes surveyed the room. "We live in Connecticut. I retired from manufacturing management last spring so that my wife and I could travel. I've been doing some consulting work in Hartford since then. Keeping my head in the game, so to speak."

"Goldhearst Manufacturing?"

Grace flinched as Alex reflexively guessed the name. He had worked with a firm in Hartford during the summer, which she remembered only because he wasn't flying back and forth across the country for a few weeks. She squirmed as her father turned slowly toward them.

"What do you know about Goldhearst?"

She'd felt Alex tense momentarily. This wasn't the time or the place to clarify that he was not the barista they imagined him to be, but was, instead, the accomplished businessman they likely couldn't imagine. Alex wisely covered his tracks, at least temporarily. "I've done some reading on business management."

Her dad hmmphed dismissively.

Alex squeezed her hand before she could object to her father. "Goldhearst was featured in an article I read. Sounds like they're changing their approach pretty significantly."

Her dad eyed Alex speculatively. "I've given them some new direction, yes."

Grace hoped he wouldn't say anymore. The company had likely turned around under her husband's recommendations. No one in the room would necessarily know that, but Alex certainly did. While she wasn't really surprised that her dad would try to take credit, she was sad that his behavior was so transparent to the one who mattered most.

Having been so focused on wanting her parents' approval for Alex, she'd overlooked the impression they were making on him. It wasn't a good one, and her failure to set the record straight early on was exposing her father's arrogance.

"Okay, thanks, Dad," Grace interrupted. "We can talk business later. My mom, Maryann Kimball," she waved to her mother.

Her father reclaimed his seat slowly, obviously not appreciating the dismissal. Her mother declined to stand as she acknowledged her daughter's wave with a nod. Was that the tiniest bit of an eye roll? Grace hardly dared hope.

"I'm Maryann. I'm a retired bookkeeper. I'll be in more of a mood to talk when I know Tank's safe." She glanced at Becky, and Grace wished her mother's look didn't imply that she'd prefer her son were safe from Becky, as well.

Grace sighed and stood. "Well, most of you know me, but I'm Grace, Tank's sister." She looked with real warmth at Becky. "I had Tank and Becky pegged from the beginning and will happily take all the credit for having brought them together."

Becky seemed glad for the support.

"Oh, and you all know this, but I own - we own," she gestured at Alex, "Caf-fiend, the coffee shop-sports cafe in town."

Alex waved at the group. "Hi, I'm Alex. Grace and I are excited to be here for Becky and Tank." He nodded at Becky. "We can attest to the whole marriage thing. I recommend it highly."

Grace beamed at him, then turned to face the rest of the room. "Okay, so I think that's pretty much everyone. Now, how is this wedding thing supposed to go?"

Friday - 8:00 p.m.
Liz

Liz tried to concentrate on the wedding rehearsal, such as it was without the groom, but all she could think about was the man sitting beside her. When they weren't holding their collective breath while skidding along the highway, they'd found conversation easy on their way to the inn. Any remaining doubts that she had about their chemistry were erased. She found herself on the same thrilling and unnerving rollercoaster that had taken her breath away when she met him two months earlier.

She shifted on the tiny Victorian love seat that they shared, and Christopher turned and caught her eye. His expression softened as he raised a brow. Liz felt her color rise. Could he read her so easily? Did he know that she was both wishing for and fearing time alone with him to explore this crazy thing that was, apparently, still happening between them?

He gave her shoulder a squeeze and turned back to the group. The pastor was wrapping up a very brief overview of the next day's much-anticipated service.

"So, Becky, we're still planning for 4:00 p.m.?"

All eyes turned to the bride-to-be.

"Assuming that Tank gets in tonight," she replied with tentative enthusiasm.

"We could also move it up, since we're all here," her pastor suggested.

Becky seemed caught off guard by the idea, but then slowly nodded her agreement. "Of course. You all will need to get back to your families when the weather clears." She paused. "I suppose it doesn't really matter."

Maddy fidgeted on the couch next to her. "We can certainly be flexible, but there are still meals to prepare and housekeeping issues," she reminded them. "And I'm sure we'd all like time to be ready for the big event; some of us will need a little more than others." She was trying to be supportive, but clearly panicking in her roles as both host for the larger than expected group and matron of honor for her sister.

Liz glanced between the sisters, hoping she'd be able to help in a meaningful way. Becky obviously shared the burden of hosting and entertaining everyone who was waiting for the party to start. She caught her eye and offered an encouraging smile, which Becky returned bravely. For all of the turmoil, Liz envied her, too. In less than twenty-four hours, she'd be starting her new adventure with the man she loved. What would the next twenty-four bring for Liz?

Pastor Rob was speaking and she tuned in to his final words.

"So we'll leave the wedding at four unless we find a compelling reason to move it up," he concluded.

The group nodded their agreement and Maddy looked visibly relieved. She stood slowly, leaning on John as she did so.

"Thank you, Pastor. If we're done here, you all can make your way to the kitchen. We'll have warm cider and other drinks and snacks out shortly. We can continue to get to know each other on the cozy side of the house."

Before the group could get moving, she turned to Liz. "Are you two hungry? We've got plenty of Becky's ribs left. Oh, but you probably want to get settled in. Let me show you to your room, first."

Liz froze as the group erupted into small pockets of conversation, unconcerned about the bomb that had just been dropped. She felt Christopher's eyes on her and turned slowly, feeling the heat in her face as she met his amused gaze.

"She did encourage us to get to know each other."

The heat in her face spread throughout her body; every part of her now completely thawed from their cold ride to the inn. She cleared her throat.

"Well, I didn't want you to drive home in this," she murmured quietly, "but they've got to have some other options." She hated that she sounded so prudish. Was it really such a big deal to share a room under the unusual circumstances? Liz held one hand over the other to keep from fanning herself. "I'll talk to Becky."

"Don't worry on my account," Christopher replied, apparently enjoying her confusion.

"Stop," Liz fought her own smile.

She watched as Maddy started maneuvering through the room, expecting them to follow. "Okay, well, I'll find Becky at some point and get it sorted out."

They made their way out to the foyer with the others as Maddy was beginning to climb the stairs.

"I'll get your bag," Christopher said.

Liz nodded her thanks as she followed her hostess up to the second floor. Maddy led the way down the hall and opened the door to a cozy room, softly lit by a bedside lamp with a shell-filled base. The antique sleigh bed was enchanting, but Liz had a hard time appreciating its charm.

"So, this is the room we have for you, Liz." Maddy glanced at Christopher. "I'd like to offer separate accommodations, but at this point, we're having to make do. It's going to be a little crowded until this storm clears."

Liz's shoulders sagged a little in relief, simply for being understood. Old-fashioned or not, her feelings were valid.

"The room is beautiful. Thank you." She stepped inside, taking in the creams and blues and understated shell decor. She turned as Christopher entered and set her bag down. The room suddenly felt very small.

Maddy excused herself. "Let me get both of us out of here so you can get settled."

The door closed behind her and Liz turned to her unexpected roommate. "Okay, so, this is nice."

"It is." Christopher walked to the small desk and lowered himself carefully onto the delicate antique chair. "Not sure I'd want to grade papers here, but it's a great period piece." He ran his hand lightly over the dark mahogany and looked up at Liz. His mouth quirked. "So…"

"So," Liz replied, fidgeting for the first time in twenty years. "I know you must think I'm hopelessly old-fashioned. People probably don't even think about this kind of thing anymore, but I just …"

Christopher stood and walked back over to her. "You don't have to apologize to me. Whatever people are doing these days, I haven't been a part of it."

He touched her cheek gently. She shivered, and he lowered his hand. "Although, it's been a long time since I've had that effect on a woman."

Liz touched her cheek. "That you know of."

The corner of his mouth hitched as he shook his head.

"I feel like such a child," she said. "I know this isn't how I behaved at Christmas." She sighed. "Don't get me wrong, if we ever get to that point, I'm going to be so ready to engage - fully, enthusiastically," she faltered at the new look on his face.

Perhaps she'd said too much.

Christopher cleared his throat. "I don't want you to think that I have any agenda here, Liz." He paused. "Well, I didn't until you said you were ready to engage - fully, enthusiastically …"

Liz laughed nervously. "Right. We don't need that much honesty right now." She took a step back. "I'm all over the place. Part of me wants to run, and part of me wants to forget about the wedding and the snow and all the complications and just hide out in this beautiful room for the rest of the weekend with you."

Christopher rubbed a hand over his jaw. "It might be smart if we joined the others right now."

Liz nodded. "That's a good idea."

She jumped at a knock on the door.

"Come in," she called.

Maddy poked her head in. "Sorry for the interruption. I just wanted to drop off these towels. The bathroom is down the hall. Sorry about that. Private baths are next on our to-do list. John can't wait!"

Her face was flushed as she shifted her sizeable load in reverse and started to back out of the door.

"Thank you," Liz replied. "We'll be right down."

There. Now they were committed.

"Wonderful. You'll enjoy ... ohhhh!"

Liz knew that sound well, even if it had been over twenty years since she'd made it. "Maddy?" she hurried into the hall.

Breathing as she'd no doubt been trained to do, Maddy braced herself against the wall, giving a slight nod as she focused on getting through what could well be the first of many contractions.

Liz gave her space but stayed close. "Christopher, would you mind tracking John down?"

§ § §

"Please let me know if there's anything else I can do," Liz said. "I'm happy to help, and I'm a light sleeper, so don't be afraid to knock on my door if you need me in the middle of the night," she added in a whisper to John. Maddy was denying the whole labor thing, but Liz had been there, and suspected that they'd be celebrating more than a wedding over the weekend.

"Thank you," John replied. "I won't hesitate if," he cast a look over his shoulder at Maddy, who relaxed, for the moment, in a recliner in their apartment, "if the excitement picks up again." He smiled at Liz, but concern was clearly etched across his features.

"Good," Liz replied. "And please don't worry about the crowd downstairs," she added. "We'll be fine."

Friday - 9:00 p.m.
Maddy

Maddy prepared a reassuring smile as John closed the door and turned. She was sure that the houseful of people and all the excitement had simply gotten the best of her, and she'd be good to go in the morning. She might even be able to check on the room situation one more time, if ...

"Oh, no, you don't," John covered the space between them in a rather impressive leap and braced his arms on either side of her in the recliner. "You need to take it easy now. What do you need? I'll get it."

Sighing, Maddy looked up into his handsome, concerned face. Then she punched his shoulder.

"I can't just lie here with all these people in the house! Who's sleeping in the daybed? Did anyone clean the kitchen? I've got to let Burt out!"

She made the mistake of turning too fast, and came nose-to-nose with her pet, whose expression gave her more pause than her husband's. He was, of course, hovering uncomfortably near - that made two of them - and Burt's occasional scowl at John did not bode well. It was enough to make her calm down just a little.

Shifting slowly, she gave Burt a reassuring pat and turned back to her husband. Apparently, her right hook hadn't scared him off, and she watched as John pulled up a nearby foot stool, sat down next to her, and picked up her hand.

"Sorry," Maddy said, squeezing his fingers. "This must be so exhausting for you."

"I think it's probably a little harder on you," John conceded, gently massaging her hand.

Maddy closed her eyes and tried to relax. "You are so patient," she sighed, shifting slightly to her side. "Are the boys in bed?"

"Working on it," John replied.

Maddy could just make out the sounds of giggling in the bathroom, though Burt's panting over her head muffled most of it.

"Go ahead and finish tucking them in." She opened one eye. "I won't go anywhere. Burt will make sure of that."

John slowly stood. "Promise?"

"I won't leave before you come back."

"No need to leave at all. Everything is under control." He eyed her sternly. "Becky texted me - she's got the room assignments all worked out, and she said Anita has the kitchen as clean as it's been since the turkey fire."

"You just had to bring that up."

John tucked the velvety-soft blanket in around her. "We've got a great group of people here, Maddy. Everyone's working together, and nobody's expecting five-star treatment. Relax. Please."

Sighing, Maddy shifted again. The baby was using her ribs for some sort of resistance training. Surely this little one wasn't trying to make an appearance at his aunt's wedding? She practiced her breathing and smiled weakly at her husband. The baby wasn't due for another month, or almost. She needed that time to help her sister get married and then finish preparing the little nursery nook that John had built.

The baby simply couldn't come any sooner.

$$\mathit{SSS}$$

The knock on her door, or Burt's answering growl, brought Maddy out of a brief, but welcome nap. She opened her eyes and turned as Becky let herself into the apartment.

"You doing okay?" she asked quietly.

"I think so," Maddy replied, assessing her tummy, her breathing, and most of all, the look of momentary calm on Burt's face. "I think all of the excitement just overwhelmed me." She tried very hard to believe what she was saying as unnerving twinges started up again. "How are you doing?"

"I'm good," Becky responded, putting her own bright face on the concerns she was processing. "Everyone's got a spot for tonight. I tried to give away the Captain's Quarters, but no one would take the 'honeymoon suite', so I put Otis in my room, and I'll sleep there." She paused for a minute, then giggled. "Not in my room, in the Captain's Quarters. Rob and Frank will camp out in the sunroom when everyone else goes to bed."

Maddy tried to concentrate on the report as her child hurled itself around her abdomen.

"If only I'd picked up those air mattresses ... " She sighed. "Would you help me up? I think it would be better if I could walk this off."

"This? What's 'this'?" Becky did her best to guide Maddy out of the recliner. "Shouldn't you try to rest?" The panic in her voice didn't particularly help.

Burt didn't like it, either.

"I'm fine, really," Maddy replied. "I just need to stretch and give this baby room to move, that's all." She walked tentatively across the living room and focused on breathing. Burt followed on her heels.

"John said you said Anita cleaned up the kitchen?" Nothing like the subject of housework to dull the senses.

"Yep, like a champ. Wouldn't even let me in there. Liz helped her, and then helped me make sure everyone had bedding and towels. Then she started a thousand-piece jigsaw puzzle with Christopher." Becky joined her and matched her step. "I think she's afraid to go back to her room."

Maddy smiled. "I'm sorry this is awkward for them. I don't know what else we could have done ... except buy air mattresses."

"Okay, you really have to let that go. I promise we'll pick some up, or order some next week."

Maddy continued to waddle. "Thanks."

"And Liz and Christopher will be fine. It'll be good for them. Who knows? Maybe they'll get married tomorrow, too."

Her sister's forced cheer helped Maddy to focus on something other than her discomfort for a moment. "Oh, Becky, just think. Tomorrow at this time, you'll be married, and ..."

"And celebrating my first night of wedded bliss with my in-laws," Becky completed her sentence with a snort. "And that's the best-case scenario."

Maddy managed a laugh. "Maybe the power will be back on by then and you can, um, have some privacy at Tank's place."

"Oh, if the power's back on at Tank's, I'm sure his folks will follow us right on down there," Becky replied with a groan. "I'm sure they won't leave us alone together for a minute. Then they'll work on getting the marriage annulled due to lack of consumma-tion."

Maddy giggled, and her whole tummy bounced. "I definitely think Tank would have something to say about that."

"I can't imagine them catering to anyone, even Tank."

"Well, they can hardly stay here forever," Maddy pointed out, silently counting her breaths.

"They can if it keeps snowing."

"Well, it's bound to let up by ... April for sure."

"Ugh! Please!" Becky dropped into the abandoned recliner and considered the fluffy slippers that completed her rehearsal dinner ensemble. "Maybe they'll just move in with us."

Maddy's laugh turned into a rather alarming howl. Burt danced in a circle around her, and Becky tried to scramble back up again.

"Are you okay? Should I get John?"

"I'm here," John bolted into the room, decisively pushing Burt out of the way. "Why are you up?"

"I'm alright," Maddy wheezed. "That one was - *ow* - that one hurt, but it's passing." She rubbed her tummy with one hand and Burt's head with the other as she caught her breath. "Really. Sorry I yelled. I just wanted to walk a bit, maybe get distracted."

She could feel Becky and John exchanging glances around her. "Please. I won't go far. It's just hard to breathe when I sit with this ... cannonball pressing on my lungs. I'll stretch right here - maybe turn on the news and see how long this storm is supposed to last?"

Before they could argue, she picked up the remote and aimed it at the TV, tuning in the sports channel that inevitably lit the screen.

All three of them paused as an unmistakable form appeared in front of them. The volume was muted, but the picture was crystal clear.

"Hey, that's Uncle Tank!"

Maddy and her baby jumped at Parker's voice.

John herded the boys, who had materialized right along with their uncle-to-be, back toward their room. "I just tucked you in. Let's get back to bed, guys."

"But Uncle Tank's on TV! Can't I watch?" Parker squirmed to get a better look, but John's grip was firm.

"It's just a quick news clip. You've seen him on TV before."

"Yeah, but who's that lady?"

The door clicked quietly and Maddy and Becky were left alone, staring at the screen. The picture changed, and the reporter moved on to other news. Maddy turned the television off and looked at her sister.

"Becky, I'm sure..."

"Don't. Please." She drew her own shaky breath. "I'm sorry, Maddy, but there's only one person who can explain, and he's not here." Blinking back un-Becky-like tears, she said, "Right now, we need to make sure that you're okay. That's all that matters."

"No, Becky, that's not all that - ohhhh, I'm so sorry!" Maddy doubled over. "This baby is definitely not waiting for her nursery to be ready," she ground out, bracing her hands on her knees.

She wondered for a moment if she'd make it until breakfast.

Friday - 10:00 p.m.
Becky

The Italian coastline looked warm and inviting, and Becky decided it belonged on her bucket list. She looked around Christopher's shoulder as he and Liz sorted out the border to the puzzle with the intensity of a surgical team.

Liz felt her gaze and looked up. "Oh, Becky! How's Maddy?"

Christopher turned, and Frank muted the volume on the TV. Pastor Rob popped up from where he'd apparently been prone on one of the couches, and Becky reeled back in surprise.

Regaining her footing, she said, "Doing okay for the moment." She headed over to the fireplace, where the crackle and snap of the logs promised warmth through the endless storm. She soaked up its comfort, letting her weary bones relax a little.

"I'm so relieved," Liz replied. "I really thought she might be going into labor early."

Becky turned and considered the unusual group - Liz sharing the storm with three men whom she really hardly knew - Frank, not a particularly religious person, camping out with Pastor Rob, and Christopher, stuck at the inn with relative strangers because he'd rescued Liz ... All because they thought they were coming to a wedding. Becky pulled herself back into the moment. Her sister wasn't out of the dark, yet.

"Honestly, she might be, but for right now, she's resting again. John's itching to take her to the hospital to get her checked out, but, of course, that's not happening. We may still have an interesting night ahead of us."

The group quietly processed the news, Liz, no doubt thinking about how she could help, and the men likely contemplating how far away from the action they could reasonably stay.

"Any more from Tank?" Rob asked.

Becky took a deep breath and crossed her arms. She was glad that not everyone had seen the news clip that she'd seen, and yet ... She glanced up at the TV screen: Sports, of course. Maybe they had.

"Nothing new from him," she replied. It was mostly true. He certainly hadn't called to say that he'd been spending enough time with a woman who wasn't his fiancée to have it be newsworthy. "I think I'm going to try to get a little sleep. I want to be ready in case Maddy needs me." She looked around at the silent group. "Do you all have what you need for the night?"

No one had the nerve to ask why she wasn't planning to wait up for Tank and she was relieved. Whatever they knew or didn't know, she wasn't up for discussing any of it with her guests.

"We're all fine," Liz answered, walking over to give her a hug. "Get some rest. Tomorrow's a big day."

Becky hugged her friend. Tomorrow would be a big day. The birth of a baby was a lot to celebrate.

It was enough.

♫ ♫ ♫

Becky noted the clean kitchen with real gratitude as she walked toward the front of the house. She hadn't been in the parlor since the 'rehearsal' and she figured she'd use up some energy reorganizing the furniture. She certainly wasn't tired and couldn't even think about sleeping. Maddy had managed a few minutes without a contraction and was determined to believe that things were going to calm down for her. John was far from convinced. Becky wasn't so sure, herself, for all that she knew about such things, but she figured they needed some time alone. John would get her if he needed her.

Becky looked around the parlor, surprised. If only all of their guests were so thoughtful and inclined to clean up after themselves. Every chair, ottoman and love seat was back in position. Even the pillows had been returned to their respective spots. The fire screen was in place and the last of the embers hissed softly. The plant stand/podium was off to the side, ready for use. Becky's heart constricted.

Used for what?

She turned away from the mental image of Pastor Rob cheerfully leading them through their vows. Heading back through the room, she blocked out the memory of the happy, expectant faces that had filled it just hours earlier. Well, *mostly* happy faces. Those that weren't happy before were likely to be thrilled before long.

The stairs suddenly seemed unscalable, and Becky hefted leaded feet, one after the other, up the steps. She may not be able to sleep, but maybe she'd take another long bath and try to block out the world for a while. She considered checking in with John one more time, and then silently groaned at the thought of the second staircase leading to the penthouse. She'd let him text if he needed her.

The only thing she knew for sure was that she didn't want to be around when Tank finally arrived. She agonized over his safety, but she just didn't have the energy to deal with him. She needed what little she apparently had left for her sister.

The front door rattled and Becky's heart stopped cold. Longing and anger warred within her as she contemplated the last, few, remaining steps to seclusion.

Longing won out and she turned.

Tank stepped over the threshold and the breath left her body. He was always overwhelming, especially when she hadn't seen him in a while. Still six-foot-four, still well over two hundred pounds.

Why did he shrink in her imagination when she was separated from him? Was she trying to make him more manageable?

Like that could ever happen. Every single pound was accounted for and standing in her sister's foyer. A myriad of emotions rolled through her, and Becky braced herself on the banister as the blood rushing through her head worked its mayhem and finally began to settle down. Tank was here, standing in front of her, dripping snow and dragging mud. Hale and healthy, his intense green eyes found her and didn't leave her face. They should be hugging, kissing, celebrating; well, except for the snow that covered him. In their normal reunions, her feet would be off the ground for a full minute before he remembered to put her down and let her breathe again.

Instead, they stood, warily facing each other.

"You're here," Becky finally found her voice.

Tank nodded, eyes still searching.

"Thank you for your text earlier. I was pretty sure you were dead the night before our wedding. It was nice to know that you weren't."

A muscle worked in his jaw. "I'm sorry."

Becky considered him. "You mentioned that in your otherwise very brief and uninformative text."

Tank inhaled, and half of the air seemed to leave the foyer. She wondered if she should wait for him to put some of it back before she drew her own next breath, curiously aware that most of the time she didn't have to remind herself to breathe.

"We saw you on the news."

Tank shifted, waited, dripped.

"No, not the news. It was one of those sports channels. And it wasn't the usual boring news conference. This was an unexpected treat; to see you with - who was it, Tank? An old girlfriend?" Becky considered the silent man she had been planning to marry. There were so many questions.

He nodded slowly.

"Very kind of you to reach out to her during the days - hours - before our wedding."

Tank said nothing, of course.

Apparently, he hadn't given a lot of thought to explaining his absence. She would never understand him, and wondered why she put up with his unwillingness to communicate, pretty much across the board. Forget the phone, he was standing right in front of her and had nothing to say for himself.

Becky descended the stairs, giving up the comfort of looking down at him as she continued the one-sided conversation.

"When I saw her ... in your arms ... I was crushed. I stared at that screen and silently cursed you for making me love you. But then you know what I did, Tank?"

She stepped closer, reached up and touched his jaw. His cheeks were red and cold. She'd imagined this first touch a thousand different ways, and none of them included the present scenario.

"I want you to know, that for the first time in my life, I consciously made the choice to believe. I looked at you, standing with a beautiful woman who, just maybe, you used to love, and I said, 'but he's my man, and he's coming home to me, and we're going to get married.'"

She dropped her hand, searched his eyes, and noted his Adam's apple bob as he swallowed. "The last half hour has been the longest of my life. Trying not to worry, trying to hope. I'm exhausted, Tank." She stepped back from him; his nearness was always unsettling. "I think, deep down, I knew, or hoped, it would all be okay when I saw you again." She took a deep breath, hating that tears had sprung to her eyes. "And you walked through the door just now," her voice dropped to a whisper, "and I don't know."

Tank reached for her.

"I trusted you," she choked out, backing up again. "I waited for you, and I never waited for anyone."

His face began to blur through her tears.

"Becky," Tank's voice was hoarse. "Please."

She swiped in frustration at the tears. She was done feeling sorry for herself. It was time for a little anger to take charge of this one-woman show. Tank might be ready to start talking, but she didn't have to listen until she was good and ready. He was safe; that much was good. His parents and friends would be happy.

Let them celebrate.

"You've missed a lot here, tonight," she said, amazed that her voice sounded even by the end of the short sentence. "It's really not about us, anymore. I need to check on my sister, and you need to get cleaned up - I'm sure you'd like to get warm. There's a fire in the sunroom, and plenty of company out there. I'm not sure where you're going to sleep." She felt the first twinge of guilt over his cold, wet state.

"What's wrong with Maddy?"

Becky refused to let the deep, gruff tones of the voice that she'd missed so much move her, and found new energy to climb the stairs. She turned halfway and looked down at her would-be fiancé.

"Maddy is quite possibly in labor. She's not due for another month. It's too early, and we can't get her to the hospital." She drew another breath, picking up momentum. "You missed your bachelor party, though your buddies are still here. It's a packed house, Tank. Everyone but the groom." His shoulders dropped a little at that. "I've spent a scintillating evening with your parents, whose concern for you was probably outweighed by their relief that you might not marry me, after all."

Fairly sure she'd covered the highlights, Becky started back up the stairs. One more thought occurred, and she turned.

"But the good news is, there *is* an open bed in the house - a lovely, frilly, daybed, and it's in their room. You know the one - the Anchor room? Go ahead and join them when you're ready. They'll be thrilled to see you."

Friday - 11:00 p.m.
Grace

Grace couldn't say what exactly propelled her out of her very cozy room with her very attentive husband, but it had to be compelling to pull herself out of their bed and toward the door. They hadn't really planned on turning in early, but getting her parents settled into their room and extracting herself from her mother's dramatics had been exhausting. Alex had coaxed her into their own room, rubbing the knots out of her neck, and providing much-needed distraction. Her response to his sweet and selfless concern, well, it made her forget that the inn was full of people and that her brother was still missing.

"I'm so sorry, Honey," she said, fumbling for anything that could serve as her non-existent robe. "I think I might have heard Tank's voice." Garbed in her husband's T-shirt and her own yoga pants, she dashed out into the hall, and bounded toward the staircase.

"Tank! You made it!"

She flew down the steps and immediately regretted the bear hug she tried to give her brother. Though he'd taken his coat off, there was still plenty of damp, cold surface that she'd just thrown herself against. She stepped back and shivered. "What did you do, walk from New York?"

He grunted a small smile - typical Tank-to-Grace greeting - and she smacked his arm with affection. Then it occurred to her that Becky wasn't involved in this important reunion, and she looked around in concern, finally glancing back toward the staircase. Alex stood at the top, bless his heart, but there was no sign of the bride-to-be.

"Wait. Where's Becky?" she asked.

Alex looked around the empty landing with a shrug. Taking the stairs at a more dignified pace, he greeted his brother-in-law. "Hey Tank."

They shook hands. "Alex." Tank turned to his sister. "Maddy's having her baby?"

Grace whirled on him. "*What?!* How could you possibly know that? When did this happen?" She looked in confusion from him, to Alex, up the stairwell, and back to Tank again.

He cleared his throat but said nothing.

"Okay, well, I'm glad you're safe, and I want to know everything, but I need to go check on Maddy. Alex, would you ... ?" She gestured helplessly at the mess Tank was making as he continued to drip in the foyer.

Alex smiled. "Come on, Tank. Let's get you something to eat."

Relieved and somehow newly overwhelmed, Grace ran up the steps, wondering what she'd missed while hiding out with her husband.

$$\mathcal{S} \, \mathcal{S} \, \mathcal{S}$$

She met Becky halfway up the steps to the penthouse. "How's Maddy?" Grace asked breathlessly. "And you know Tank made it, right? Well, you must, because ... Maddy first. Is she okay?"

Becky lowered herself to the steps with a sigh. "She's okay for the moment. Convinced she's not in labor, but John's not so sure."

"When did it start? I can't believe I missed this!"

"Yeah, where have you been?" Becky looked up, her eyes more tired and sad than curious.

Grace sat down beside her, wondering what could have happened to explain Becky's state. Maddy's early labor was certainly a concern, but would it so totally overshadow Tank's safe homecoming? Her mind whirled with the possibilities as Becky repeated her question.

"Seriously, where have you been?"

A bit of Becky's spark resurfaced, and while Grace was happy to see it, she wasn't particularly anxious to answer the question.

"It took a while to get my parents settled in. Well, my mom, anyway. Dad was pretty chill, I guess, but still complaining about being trapped in a - 'frilly boarding house' - I believe he called it." Grace rolled her eyes. "Anyway, I was trying to convince them to go to bed and not wait up for Tank. They had a long day traveling, and it wouldn't help anyone for them to be prowling around being all grumpy."

"Thank you for that," Becky leaned over against the wall with a sigh. "Guess that took a while, huh?"

Grace met her gaze, only to find that Becky was considering her clothing, specifically her rather large T-shirt. She didn't say a word, just looked up with a raised brow.

"Well, yeah, it took a while. And then Alex was great about, you know ..."

"Actually, no, I wouldn't know."

"I was just stressed, and he helped me relax."

"Here - now? With everyone here? Now?"

Grace squirmed.

Becky sighed. "Where did you put Tank?"

Grace huffed a small laugh. Like anyone could 'put' Tank anywhere. "Alex took charge of him. Probably feeding him. Do you, um, know where he's supposed to sleep tonight?"

"I told him to sleep in the daybed in your parents' room."

Grace laughed aloud at that. "I guess I should let them know he made it back safely."

The thought of returning to her mother's room sobered her. The fact that Becky was so disinterested alarmed her.

"I'm sorry I disappeared for so long. I should have been here for you." She touched Becky's arm. "Are you okay? What else happened?"

Becky looked up, unmistakable pain in her eyes. "Any significant redheads in Tank's past?"

Grace reeled back at the question. "Alicia?" Why would Becky be asking about the only woman Tank had ever seriously dated? That begged the bigger question: Where had Tank been for the last few days, and how did Becky know he'd been there? "Tank was with her?"

The pain on Becky's face revealed the carelessness of the question. "I'm sorry. I didn't mean 'with her'. Is that where Tank has been?" New anger surged that this was how her brother had spent the week before his wedding, leaving the family worried about his traveling in the storm.

The glazed look returned to Becky's eyes.

Grace fought the anger that she needed to be saving for her brother. "He told you this?"

"I saw them on one of those sports channels."

Grace caught her breath and processed the information with a new wave of fury. She stood. "I'm going to beat him senseless."

Becky got up and followed her down the steps. "Don't, Grace. I need to figure this out with him. I just need time. And I need my energy for Maddy."

Grace stopped at the bottom of the staircase and turned. "Oh, I'm so sorry. I really did come up to help. I just can't believe ..." She tried to refocus so she could be the friend that Becky needed, and not the sister that Tank had better fear.

They stepped out onto the landing of the second floor. All was quiet, which was nice for the few who had elected to try to get some sleep.

"John will call me as soon as anything changes. All we can do is be ready to help if her labor actually kicks in," Becky whispered.

"When did it start?"

"After she took Liz and Alex to their room. Kind of on and off since then, I guess."

"And when is she due?"

"Mid-March. She always wondered if the date was right. Turns out she might have had good reason."

"Yikes."

"Yeah."

They stopped at the top of the back staircase leading down to the kitchen.

"Okay, so, do you want to talk to Tank while he's still conscious?"

Becky managed a smirk. "You have a violent streak when it comes to your brother."

"How do you think I survived growing up with him?"

Becky bent her unfocused gaze toward the stairs. "I just can't imagine what he can possibly have to say to me. After all of the waiting and worrying ... I don't have anything left for anyone but Maddy right now."

"But tomorrow - the wedding. You have to hear him out before then." Realization dawned, and Grace sagged against the wall. "Becky, don't let this ruin everything. He may have made a mistake, but you two are so perfect for each other. Please give him another chance."

The dull look in Becky's eyes didn't bode well. Grace would rather have seen fire and fury than this broken version of her friend.

"I didn't ruin anything," she answered quietly. "I've messed up plenty in the past, but this one is on Tank. We can't start our life together ..." her voice caught a little and Grace's heart squeezed. "I'm going to go get some rest in case Maddy needs me."

Becky turned and walked toward the Captain's Quarters, the room they had decorated as the honeymoon suite. She stopped at the door and considered the "Just Married" sign. Grace ached for her friend as she pulled it down and entered the room, quietly closing the door behind her.

♪ ♪ ♪

Grace found Tank at the island in the kitchen, staring at the food Alex had pulled out like it was a calculus problem that needed solving. She felt a twinge of sympathy for his dejected state, then remembered Alicia, and the sympathy flew right out the window into the stormy night.

"Alicia, Tank?" she demanded quietly as she approached him. Her husband had joined several others who were still up in the sunroom, but she only glanced long enough to make sure they were occupied.

Tank turned his head slowly. "It's not what you think."

"I haven't had time to think anything. I just left a heart-broken almost-bride and I want to know why I shouldn't throttle you."

Tank's mouth tried to quirk and failed. "She hates me."

"Should she?"

Tank looked down again.

"Whatever you did, Tank, you'd better fix it. Now. Becky loves you. She's good for you. She's the only one who could ever put up with you. Don't you dare mess this up."

"And if I already did?"

Grace drew a deep breath. "This is a conversation you should be having with Becky. Not me."

"Where is she?"

"She's in your honeymoon suite, the Captain's Quarters, probably tearing down all the nice decorations Maddy and I put up for you."

Tank snorted, clearly not regretting the demise of their handiwork. Then he sobered, again. "Don't know what I'll do without her, Gracie."

Grace got good and close to her big brother. "Then don't find out."

Friday - Midnight
Liz

Liz tidied up the remaining puzzle pieces and stifled a yawn. She and Christopher had enjoyed the interesting group of wedding guests over the past several hours, but enough was enough. She was tired. After her long, stressful drive, she desperately needed to reset.

She glanced at Christopher across the room, nodding at something Frank was saying. She sighed. There was no more delaying the fact that they were going to be sharing a room, *a bed*. At least they were too tired to do anything but sleep.

Probably.

Liz headed toward the kitchen and confirmed that it was empty. Grace and Tank had been having a rather intense conversation earlier, and she hadn't wanted to disturb them. She'd been so relieved when he'd walked in with Alex sometime after eleven, but was surprised that Becky hadn't joined them.

The conversation between the siblings wasn't exactly a happy, 'welcome home' conversation. Something was definitely not right. If the groom had arrived, everyone should be relieved and ready for a party. Liz hoped that Becky's absence from the reunion had more to do with Maddy than any problems with Tank.

She supposed she'd find out soon enough. If Maddy went into labor, Liz was the woman with the most recent experience with childbirth, even if it was two decades in the past.

One didn't forget that particular skill set.

Liz waved good-night to the others and ducked through the kitchen into the back stairwell, hoping to make her escape before their new pastor friend returned. He didn't seem to be the disapproving sort, but his presence was a constant reminder that she'd be sharing a room with a man who wasn't her husband. Whether he had an opinion on the matter or not, she did. She would continue to remind herself of her very valid convictions right up until she lay down next to the very handsome and intriguing English professor, who would very soon follow her up to their room.

She climbed the steps up to the second floor, her heart beating much faster than the effort required.

$$\int \int \int$$

"Oh, Liz. I'm so glad you're not in bed, yet!"

Liz dropped her cosmetic bag inside the door and pulled it shut. At least she'd brushed her teeth.

"Hey, Becky. Is Maddy okay?"

"Her contractions are starting up again, and she's beginning to panic a little. She doesn't want to bother you, or anyone, of course, but I think it would help if someone experienced was nearby."

Liz tried to smile reassuringly. "Well, I've been there, anyway. I'll be happy to do whatever I can."

Becky's nod in response did not hide the distress that went beyond her sister's early labor. Liz touched her arm as she turned to lead the way to the apartment upstairs.

"Are you alright? Have you seen Tank?"

Becky paused and her shoulders slumped. "Yes."

"And? What happened? Is everything okay?" Liz wasn't normally so pushy, but there was nothing normal about this weekend. She figured that any of the snowbound guests had a right to know what had kept Tank from joining them. More than anything, she wanted to ease the look of quiet despair on her friend's face.

Becky sighed. "He's here. He's safe." She started up the steps again. "Maddy is my priority now."

Liz could hardly argue that. As curious as she was about Becky and her elusive fiancé, the answers to those questions would have to wait. She followed Becky to Maddy's apartment and hoped she'd be able to help at least one of the sisters through this unexpectedly complicated weekend.

$$\mathcal{SSS}$$

John's relief was palpable when Liz entered the cozy living area of the owner's loft on the third floor. Apart from her brief stop earlier in the evening, she'd seen the apartment once before during her Christmas visit and had admired the inviting and efficient use of the space. John's handiwork was evident all over the inn, and one day she would tell him how impressed she was. At the moment, he needed a different kind of reassurance.

"Thank you for coming up," he said quietly, gesturing for her and Becky to follow him into the kitchen. Maddy seemed to be resting, for the moment, in the same recliner that Liz had left her in earlier, and John glanced at her anxiously as they gathered at the island to talk.

"I can't really make sense of what's going on," he said in a low voice. "She seems to be resting peacefully, and I think she might actually sleep, then a contraction hits, and I'm sure she's starting her labor." He ran a hand through his hair, then rested both hands on his hips.

"When was her last doctor's visit?"

"Monday. Everything was fine. The doctor seemed to think we were on track for the baby's arrival next month."

Liz nodded. "So, she's at thirty-six weeks or so?"

"Could be thirty-seven. The doctor said the baby was a good size."

Liz tried not to smile at John's discomfort. She didn't suppose he was used to feeling helpless.

"I'm sure the baby is healthy and strong." She decided to affirm the medical decision about which she actually knew nothing. "If he or she is determined to come soon, the best we can do is be ready. Do you think Maddy would like a little more privacy? Maybe we could have her move into your room?"

John swallowed and braced himself on the island counter. He'd apparently hoped to be assured that an early delivery wasn't possible. Although it might not be imminent, being unprepared was irresponsible. If she did nothing else, Liz would make sure that Maddy had a reasonable facsimile of a delivery room set up.

"How about if you show me your room?" she suggested, figuring John would prefer action to fretting.

"Sure." He seemed to shake off his bemused state. "This way."

He led them into a small, but comfortable bedroom. Liz was relieved that the bathroom was close by.

"Okay, here's what we're going to do," she said, her professor's voice commanding attention and action. "We're going to get this space ready to receive a baby. Then, if Maddy continues to rest, we'll just tuck her in and let her sleep. If she goes into real labor, we'll be as ready as we can be."

She looked between John and Becky, ready to quell any objection. They wore matching looks of bewildered determination, and Liz nodded. They'd do their best to create as comfortable a birthing room as could be arranged on the third floor of a seaside inn during a February nor'easter.

♫ ♫ ♫

Liz opened the door quietly, assuming that Christopher had returned to their room and likely gone to bed while she was helping Maddy. She still wasn't sure which way it would go; Maddy had had several more contractions over the last hour, but had rested fairly comfortably, otherwise. Becky had checked back in and offered to hang out in the recliner for a while, so Liz figured it was safe to get some sleep, herself. She felt better knowing that her hostess was, at the very least, settled in a private, comfortable space, for whatever the next few hours held.

Her own room was dark - really dark - and Liz found herself both disappointed and relieved. She was exhausted, and pretty sure she wanted nothing more than to climb into bed and recover from the long, stressful day.

She tried to listen for Christopher's breathing or anything that would indicate that he was in the room, but the heating system had kicked on, and its gentle pings and creaks created its own interesting concert. She was familiar with old heating systems and found a strange comfort in the odd sounds her own generated at home. At the moment, she would gladly do without the distraction. It would be nice to know beforehand if she was climbing into bed with another person.

She sighed as she felt along the wall for the suitcase rack which held her bag. Liz hadn't shared a bed with a man in more than five years, and even then, her bedmate was disinterested, at best. She wondered, again, how easy it would be to shake the difficult memories of her first marriage and really contemplate a second effort. Christopher had planted that seed in December, asking her to consider the prospect of a life together.

There. She opened what she hoped was her bag. Christopher had mentioned packing an overnight bag, himself, and had probably brought it up at some point during the evening. Liz removed her lounge pants and cotton shirt that she'd packed for pajamas. Glancing toward where she knew the bed was, she again made an effort to discern any kind of shape. Apparently, the Fordhams had invested in really effective light-blocking shades; absolutely no light came in through the window. Maddy had pointed out a nightlight earlier but had noticed that the bulb was out. Replacing it had become lost in the turmoil surrounding her early labor. At the time, Liz hadn't given it a second thought.

Oh, what she'd give for a little light right now.

As she considered where to change, the lack of light turned out to be convenient. She eased out of her jeans and sweater and pulled on her pajamas. Folding her clothes and neatly tucking them back into her bag, *she hoped*, she straightened and contemplated climbing into bed. Should she feel around and hope that she didn't touch him? Hope she did? What if he woke up? What if he didn't?

Realizing she was too tired to be coherent, Liz tip-toed carefully across the room and gently reached for the spread. It had been pulled back, and she cautiously ran her hand along the sheets until she felt the pillow. Slowly, she spread her hands toward the center of the bed. He'd left the closer side open for her, bless his heart. She took a deep breath and climbed in.

Liz waited for movement, breathed a quiet 'hello', but felt and heard nothing. She stared at the ceiling and began to make out the light fixture overhead. Moving her right hand ever-so-slowly, she inched along the mattress, figuring she'd feel warmth, at least, before her hand met with Christopher's ... what, his *thigh*? She yanked her hand back and held it with the other.

Trying to still her pounding heart, which she was sure would wake Christopher if her attempts to grab his leg hadn't, she tried hard to tune in between the pings, but couldn't discern a sound. Was he really that quiet of a sleeper? Deciding she couldn't stand the suspense anymore, she quietly said his name.

Nothing.

A little louder. "Christopher?"

Silence.

Sighing, she began to suspect that she had unnecessarily put herself through a crazy amount of stress. Turning on her side, she stared at what she was now fairly sure was an empty pillow.

She huffed a quiet laugh, reached over boldly, and rested her hand square in the middle of Christopher's solid chest.

Saturday - 1:00 a.m.
Maddy

Maddy turned on her side and considered the man lying next to her. The glow from the small nightlight gently touched his face. Had he fallen asleep? Poor John, he'd been so concerned for her, he didn't realize how exhausted he was, himself.

She adjusted her position for their little one, who seemed content to rest for a while between them. Breathing a quiet sigh of relief, she gently laid her hand on the baby, wondering what it would be like to have him or her actually lying in the bed between them. Maddy thought about the sweet array of clothing from her recent baby shower and tried to imagine dressing her son or daughter - *a real baby* - in the little, white, onesie pajamas with the tiny lamb on the front.

It all seemed so impossible, and yet, after the past few hours, it all seemed terribly imminent. She frowned at the thought. Terribly wasn't the right descriptor, but imminent fit the bill. Could the baby really be coming so early?

She breathed carefully and arched ever so slightly to give her ribs a little more room. It was enough to bring John around, and he turned to her with concern. It also brought Burt's head popping up from her own side of the bed.

"Are you alright?" John whispered.

"I'm fine. Sorry for waking you." Maddy reached back and patted Burt's head, hoping it was enough. Turning to face her dog and greet him properly was out of the question.

Her husband covered a yawn. "No problem. Not really sleeping."

"Thank you for taking such good care of me."

John reached over and cupped her cheek. "It's my pleasure."

She turned her head and kissed his palm. "You used to say that when we were first getting to know each other. *It's my pleasure.*' It sounded so old-fashioned and endearing."

"Great. Really charmed you, didn't I?"

"You know you did."

"And look where it got us."

Maddy could hear the affection warring with concern over the burden she carried that he couldn't share.

"It's been a great adventure," she replied. "And it's only beginning."

He nodded, trying to maintain a somewhat hopeful look.

Maddy laughed a little, and the baby kicked in response. Her hand went reflexively to the spot. "You are being so brave."

"Who, the baby or me?" John asked.

Maddy laughed again. "Both, I guess." She moved her hand to John's face. "I know this is driving you crazy - not being able to get me to the hospital or take the pain away."

"You know I would if I could."

"I know." Maddy shifted again. "What a crazy time for this to be happening. Do you think I overdid it getting ready for the wedding?"

She shouldn't have asked. John had made his feelings on that issue perfectly clear. She glanced up and could make out the confirmation on his face.

"I'm sorry I didn't try harder to take it easy. There was just so much to do, and I felt perfectly fine before, well, whenever this started."

"Maybe if you get some sleep, things will calm down."

"Is that your way of telling me to 'shut up' so you can rest?"

John snorted a laugh. "Because I always talk to you that way." He gave her the look that had been making her heart do a little dance for almost two years.

She giggled and tried to turn onto her back. *Big mistake.* She glanced at Burt, who had been remarkably quiet on his side of the room. He was probably tired, too. Maddy rolled back to face John.

"Okay, I'll try to rest. You too, okay?"

He touched her cheek. "Yes, ma'am."

Maddy closed her eyes. "The storm is really crazy, huh? Good thing you replaced all the windows last fall."

"Hmmm," John was obviously ready to sleep and not particularly inclined to discuss home repairs.

She listened for a few more minutes and then jumped up, or tried to. The baby slowed her efforts considerably.

"Did Tank ever get here? Oh, how could I have forgotten?"

John had jumped up with her, and reached out to calm her. "He's fine, Maddy. He's here. Relax."

Maddy leaned back against the pillows and breathed a sigh of relief. "I'm so glad." She rested her hands on John's arm, which was now stretched protectively across her belly. "Is Becky okay? Did they work everything out?"

John sighed. "Becky's in our recliner right now, trying to stay close in case we need her." His arm tightened gently as he felt Maddy start to move out of bed in response. "She's fine. They'll be fine. She's more concerned about you than anything, right now."

Maddy settled back into the pillows, new concern for Becky washing over her. "Who was that woman on TV with him?"

"Try not to worry about them, Maddy. You need your sleep. They'll be fine."

"If Tank has messed this up, I'll ..."

John's quiet laugh was not the response she expected. "Save your threats for Tank and concentrate on taking care of yourself." He slid his hand over her tummy. "This one needs you right now."

That argument was compelling. Maddy tried to relax but hated the thought of Becky trying to sleep in her recliner.

"John?"

Sigh. "Yes?"

"Would you please tell Becky to go to bed? I think I'm okay. She needs her rest, too."

John made an admirable effort to stifle the groan he undoubtedly wanted to release at this suggestion.

"Probably a good idea," he conceded. He pulled himself out of the bed and headed toward the door. "You," he pointed at her with mock severity. "Sleep."

Maddy smiled and saluted. Then she blew him a kiss and snuggled down into the pillows. Becky and Tank were going to be okay. Tomorrow they would get married. Her baby would settle down and allow her to celebrate with her sister. She repeated this hopeful mantra and tried to put her baby to bed.

Saturday - 2:00 a.m.
Becky

Becky considered the wrinkled navy sheath that had felt and probably looked fairly chic seven or eight hours earlier. *That long?* Where had the time gone, and why hadn't she changed?

Relieved that she'd thought to pack some clothes and a toothbrush before giving Otis her room, she also felt a tug of concern, and decided to check on him before going to bed. While Maddy's neighbor seemed pretty self-sufficient, he'd never spent the night. What if he woke up disoriented and wandered out, needing help? She decided to loop through the inn one more time to make sure that everyone was settled.

The thought that she might stumble on Tank sleeping on a settee somewhere also occurred.

Arriving at the bottom of the main stairwell, Becky braced herself and peered into the parlor. It was just as she'd left it earlier, or at least what she could see of it, the fire having died down to a few determined coals.

She tiptoed down the hall, through the dining room and into the kitchen, where she could see that the sunroom was dark. The door to her bedroom off the kitchen, where Otis was sleeping, remained closed. She stopped and listened for a moment and could hear nothing beyond the howling wind of the storm. She hoped people were finding a way to sleep through it.

Relieved, and more than a little curious about where Tank had ended up, she made her way back upstairs. The second floor was as quiet as the first, the storm notwithstanding. If Maddy managed to sleep through the rest of the night, then all three floors of would-be wedding attendees would actually get some rest before ... before what? The baby arrived? The news hit that there might not be a wedding?

Becky let herself into the Captain's Quarters and tried not to see the evidence of Grace and Maddy's handiwork. It helped that the room was dark; only a nightlight in the bathroom gave her any orientation. She fought the despair that she'd been able to keep at bay while she focused on her sister. She should have insisted on remaining in the apartment upstairs; anything rather than return to what should have been the honeymoon suite.

Following the nightlight beacon into the bathroom, she started running water in the tub, opened her hastily packed bag, and pulled out what she needed for what was left of the night. She brushed her teeth, focusing disinterestedly on the towel patterns, and avoiding her reflection. She didn't need any reminders about the toll this day had taken.

Finished with that small but critical detail, Becky reached back to unzip her dress and stopped breathing. She didn't need what the mirror angle revealed to know who had materialized in the doorway. She felt him and she froze.

"Please talk to me," Tank said, his gravelly voice sounding like he'd allowed himself to rest while he waited for her.

Becky dropped her arms and pivoted to face him. His rumpled button-down and dress pants confirmed the theory. She'd walked right past him sleeping on the bed?

"What are you doing in here? You're supposed to be with your parents."

The look on his face told her what he thought of that idea.

She turned off the water, straightened, and crossed her arms. Summoning stamina from some unfathomable source, she looked him in the eye. "You need to find a place to sleep. It's not here."

Tank nodded almost imperceptibly.

"So?" She wanted to march past him and show him the door, but he blocked her path out of the bathroom pretty comprehensively. She didn't trust herself to touch him, so she stayed at the sink and raised a brow.

"I need to talk to you."

"You didn't feel this need for the last five days."

"You know I hate the phone."

"That's pretty clear to everyone who's been waiting and wondering and worrying about you, Tank."

"I'm sorry."

He looked as vulnerable as a former linebacker could possibly look, and Becky felt a twinge of conscience. Wherever he'd been, he still fought a terrible storm to find his way back home. He had to be exhausted, whatever else he was feeling.

With a sigh, Becky approached the door. When Tank didn't move, she waited until he made room, then slipped past him and planted herself in the rocking chair by the window. She immediately regretted her choice. Sitting in a rocker hardly set her up to be the formidable prosecuting attorney in this particular courtroom.

The defendant followed and paced in the dark. Becky decided against turning on the light, preferring, for the moment, not to see his face so clearly. Itching to pepper him with questions, now that she had the opportunity, she breathed deeply and waited. It was time for Tank to step up and explain where he had been, without her drawing him out.

She'd be ready with cross-examination.

Tank cleared his throat and stopped by the giant poster bed. It was tall enough that he could lean against it without actually sitting. Becky refused to think about any other application for that particular piece of furniture. For now, it was simply a Tank-holder-upper.

"The second conference," he paused, collecting his thoughts. "You know I met an old friend there."

Old friend - *ha!* She didn't look like just a friend, and she certainly wasn't old. Becky held her tongue.

He drew in a big breath and blew it out. "I knew, going into it, that I would see her."

Somehow, Becky knew this, but hearing it made her heart hurt. She couldn't speak if she wanted to, so she waited.

"Alicia is on the board for the group that asked me to fill in last minute."

Becky felt Tank's eyes on her but couldn't meet his gaze. She stared out at the storm, wishing she could see the waves crashing on the shore. She imagined she could hear them above the howling wind. Maybe it was just the blood pounding in her ears.

When Tank didn't continue, she allowed her gaze to slide over to him. He watched her, probably waiting for her to guess what happened next or at least make a stab at who this woman was to him. She wasn't about to do either.

She looked back out at the storm.

He cleared his throat. "Her son was in the hospital. Got a concussion playing football in some sort of indoor camp."

Becky spun back to Tank. "Football? How old is he?"

Tank shook his head. "He's just a little guy. They have these teams - they're so young ..." He ran his hand over his bristly crew cut and sighed heavily.

"Is he okay?"

"I think he will be." Tank started pacing again. "Last night he turned a corner, and by this morning, the doctors said he was out of danger." He rubbed a hand over his jaw. "It's all a blur. I felt responsible; I had to make sure he'd be okay."

Becky took some time to make sense of this new and unexpected information. It must have hit Tank hard. Injuries like this were why he did what he did.

However, the connection with the boy's mother also played into the story.

"I understand that you were concerned," she finally said, "but what made you think you were responsible for him?"

The jury waited, not terribly anxious for this particular piece of evidence. Tank continued to regard her; Becky felt it more than saw it.

"Alicia and I went out a long time ago, but she ended up marrying another guy on the team." He paused a beat. "It didn't last," he finally continued. "He retired early when his knee gave out and he couldn't handle it. It was ... messy." He breathed a humorless laugh, obviously recalling his own final injury. "She reached out to me when all of that went down. Jimmy was little - I don't know - younger than Parker, anyway.

"We tried, again, for a while, and Jimmy got attached. After we broke up," another pause, "I guess he watched me play on TV." Tank blew out a breath. "He loved football - wanted to be like me - so Alicia let him start playing with a local youth flag team."

"Maybe he wanted to be like his dad."

Tank paused. "I guess I'm the one he latched onto."

Becky processed that for a moment.

"I'm sorry that he got injured and that you feel responsible." She could see how Tank could get lost in this family's heartache for a few days, even the days before his own wedding. What remained unspoken was just how much of his relationship with Alicia was rekindled in the process.

"Alicia told me that Jimmy's dad ..."

Becky looked up and held her breath.

"Yes?" she prodded dully.

"Wasn't her ex."

This, Becky had begun to surmise.

She rocked in her chair a bit. It really was a soothing motion. She could see why grandmas enjoyed doing it. However, she also noticed that her body suddenly felt very cold, and she thought a blanket would be nice. It would certainly complete the picture.

Becky was surprised when she heard her own voice. "Are you telling me that you rediscovered your family, Tank? That you found your long-lost son? And just in time, too. Think how complicated this would have been a few days from now."

Tank walked over and hunched down beside her. She couldn't look at him.

"He's not my son, Becky."

She glanced at him, unable to make out his features in the dark room. His voice sounded sincere, but she hardly felt like an impartial judge. She continued to rock, feeling older by the minute.

"I don't know what to say, Tank. Do you want me to dig for information? Maybe ask why your friend wanted you to know? Try to do the math and see if she has reason to believe that you should know?"

Tank tired of perching on his haunches and looked around for another chair. Becky watched him unfold and walk across the room to grab the delicate chair near the desk. She cringed a little when he brought it back and lowered himself onto it.

"I won't pretend that Alicia wasn't hoping I'd be interested in the job."

Becky closed her eyes and rocked. "That's a double negative at two in the morning, Tank. Give me a minute." The storm raging outside didn't hold a candle to Becky's inner turmoil.

"I see," she finally said. "And why did she pick you? I mean, I get it. I would. *I did.*" She glanced up at him. "Did you happen to mention that you were getting married, and that maybe this wasn't a good time to take on another family?"

Tank stopped her rocker. "Of course, I did."

Becky tried unsuccessfully to get her chair in motion again.

"And yet you still spent the week before our wedding with her. When was the picture taken? You two looked very cozy."

"She hugged me when she found out Jimmy was going to be okay."

Oh. Well.

"Her sister took the picture and shared it, I guess."

Becky didn't have the energy to feel convicted. If she recalled correctly, and she likely did, because the stupid photo was burned into her memory, there was more than relief on the beautiful red-head's face.

Exhaustion hit, and she stood.

"I'm really tired, and you need to go." She walked toward the bed, then changed her mind and headed back to the bathroom. "When you figure out your story, you can let me know how it ended, and maybe even, how it really began. Right now, I need to sleep in case Maddy needs me."

He followed her and they found themselves back where they started, Becky by the sink and Tank in the doorway. Perhaps the judge should take a seat during closing arguments. She had a wild urge to laugh at the picture, but there was nothing funny about this conversation occurring the night, or morning, before the wedding that just might not happen after all.

"The truth is, there was unfinished business with Alicia. But I wouldn't have taken that gig or seen her if her son wasn't injured."

Becky looked up at Tank, the nightlight in the bathroom a veritable spotlight after their conversation in the dark, showcasing his haggard appearance. It probably didn't do her any favors, either. She allowed his words to sink in for a moment, and realized that there was very little comfort to be drawn from them.

"So, just to clarify. You still have unfinished business with an old girlfriend, but her son, who is not also your son, is recovering, so we're good."

Did he look momentarily hopeful?

Unbelievable.

"She was going through a scary time with her kid this week, and I felt responsible because he looked up to me. I lost track of time at the hospital."

That bit of evidence had already been admitted. Perhaps it was time to render judgment.

"I'm glad for Jimmy, was it? I'm glad he's okay," Becky said. "And I understand your concern for him. But Tank? This was the week of our wedding. The wedding that you insisted we move up three months because you didn't want to wait. Believe it or not, it took a lot of work to make that happen." She stepped closer to him. "And you not only missed the action, you caused a lot of worry. And why? Because you were reconnecting with an old girlfriend with whom you have 'unfinished business'."

He swallowed.

"Nothing about that is okay."

Saturday - 3:00 a.m.
Grace

Grace nestled more deeply into her husband's side. His breathing had changed and she suspected that he was awake, too.

"Did you hear something?" she asked sleepily.

"Above this howling wind?" he whispered. "Just you snoring."

She gasped and shoved him. He gathered her in his arms again and laughed quietly.

"I do not snore." She could feel him laughing beneath her and tried to stay irritated. "I would know if I snored," she insisted.

Alex stilled long enough to say, "Why do you think I travel so much?"

Before she could adequately decry this accusation, Alex made quick business of shifting her onto her back. He leaned over her with what she knew would be an infuriating smile.

She glared up at him as best she could in the darkness. "It took you nine months to share your dissatisfaction?"

"Who said I was dissatisfied?" His grin was audible.

"If you heard me snoring over this wind, there's a problem."

He laughed again. "You don't snore, Grace."

Relieved, she relaxed a little and reached up to touch his stubbly jaw. "Troublemaker."

Alex leaned down and kissed her lightly on the nose, then lowered himself back onto his pillow.

Patting her leg and yawning, he said. "Not much, anyway."

Saturday - 4:00 a.m.
Liz

A surprisingly deep and welcome sleep kept the occupants of the Seashell room contentedly resting, despite the raging storm. No one snored or argued, there were no labor pains or restless dogs. Neither tension nor temptation kept Liz or Christopher from surrendering to the unusual circumstances and getting a decent night's rest.

Saturday - 5:00 a.m.
Maddy

The same peace that pervaded the Seashell room seemed to drift upward toward the apartment on the third floor of the inn. For several very precious hours, all five members of the Fordham family, including one exhausted Irish wolfhound, managed to tune out the world and get some much-needed sleep.

They would need it for the day ahead.

Saturday - 6:00 a.m.
Becky

Her head pounded relentlessly, and Becky gave up trying to sleep. Easing herself out of bed, she found her way into the bathroom, thankful that one of her blinding headaches at least kept her from processing the events and revelations of the night, or the hours, before.

It occurred to her that there wouldn't likely be any sort of pain reliever in the medicine cabinet, but she had to check. She hadn't thought to pack anything like that before giving Otis her room. It had been a long time since she'd had one of her headaches.

Her knees almost gave way in relief when she found a bottle of acetaminophen next to a travel-sized tube of toothpaste. The rest of the contents of the shelf went unnoticed as she grabbed the medicine and her water bottle.

She walked slowly back into the bedroom, every step sending a new shock of pain through her head. She crawled into bed and took a deep breath, then set all her energies on opening the child-proof bottle. That feat accomplished, she shakily poured the medicine into her hand. Her mind skittered to her conversation with Tank and her head pounded anew. Maybe she'd been a little bit unfair. Maybe it really was all about the boy. But why throw in that great big question about who his father was? It was too much to think about, and her head would likely burst if she tried. Sinking into the pillows, she once again focused on the pills in the palm of her hand. She sighed, washed them down, and prayed for oblivion.

Saturday - 7:00 a.m.
Grace

Grace heard her parents in the hallway, and silently groaned. Why couldn't they have slept a little longer? She contemplated her sleeping husband, wishing she could stay tucked in with him for a while. Then she recalled the snoring conversation and briefly considered some sort of revenge. Sighing, she slid out of bed and let him sleep. Dealing with her parents, or at least her father, was punishment enough.

She dressed quickly and quietly and eased into the hallway, relieved that her folks had apparently gone downstairs. They hadn't been particularly quiet, and she didn't want anyone else waking unnecessarily early.

Grace found them in the dining room, looking around in frustration for coffee and breakfast fare. As she paused in the doorway, it occurred to her that neither Maddy nor Becky would likely be in a position to play host for breakfast.

She was happy to find a way to help. She knew coffee, and the scones she'd brought the day before just needed to be warmed a bit.

"Morning, Mom and Dad. How did you sleep?" Grace entered the room with as much cheer as she could muster, knowing there would be little attempt to match it.

"Alright, I suppose," her mother replied.

Grace could almost imagine a momentary, unguarded affection in her mom's eyes, but it was just as quickly covered. She would never understand that transformation, and by force of habit, buried the hurt.

"It would be nice to have some coffee," her father chimed in. "Who's running this place?"

"Well, Dad, Maddy and John are a little distracted right now because Maddy started having labor pains last night. If they're not down here, it's because they're either getting some much-needed rest, or maybe they're having a baby."

Her mother's brief show of concern gave way to more immediate needs. "She's having her baby now?" she asked. "Didn't they think about that possibility when they planned this event?"

There was so much wrong with that response.

"She's not actually due for another month," Grace said, garnering her patience. "This 'event' was moved up, as you know, for Tank and Becky, at Tank's request." She couldn't resist reminding her mother that Tank and Becky were very much in love and anxious to get married. At least she hoped that was still the case. "Anyway, I don't know for sure where Maddy is with her labor, but we need to be ready to help." She gestured toward the kitchen. "I'll make some coffee and get breakfast started. You know Tank got in safely?"

"Yes, and it would have been nice to know when he arrived," her father grumbled.

"Well, I told him there was a bed in your room," Grace replied. "He probably didn't want to wake you."

"He's in there now, and he looks ridiculous."

Grace almost laughed aloud. She didn't know what was funnier, the thought of Tank in that daybed or how disgusted her father was by the mental picture.

"I got up about an hour ago," he continued, "and found him in that parlor out front. I told him to use that silly bed in our room and he was tired enough to do it."

"He looked awful," her mother tsked.

"But he's safe and healthy and here, so that's good," Grace reminded them quietly as she started the coffee. "Just keep in mind that there are people sleeping out there," she nodded toward the sunroom. "We need to keep our voices down."

$$\int \int \int$$

Grace was definitely in her wheelhouse, getting a simple breakfast ready for a small crowd. Her folks started to come around a bit when they had mugs of coffee in their hands.

"Well, at least they have decent coffee," her father conceded.

"That's my coffee, Dad," Grace reminded him. "We roast it at the shop - you saw the big roaster - and we grind it right before we brew it. Makes a difference, don't you think?"

He grunted his approval, and her mother sighed. "We just always thought you'd use your business degree for something a little more ..." she hesitated.

"Impressive?" Grace supplied. "Sorry that you're disappointed." She refused to allow their unsurprising lack of support to continue to take a toll. "I love what I do, and it makes a lot of people happy." She pulled the white chocolate cranberry scones out of the oven and breathed deeply. "And I'm making a good living at it, so I feel really blessed."

"You get what you deserve when you work hard," her father corrected her. "So, you didn't mention that your husband works for you."

"I didn't mention it because ..." She looked toward the door with a relieved smile. "Morning, Honey."

Alex walked into the room, relaxed and cheerful. Grace looked on with pride as he made his way over to her. Her husband carried himself with the confidence of a man who had worked hard and proven himself. Her dad would much rather he grovel, and it drove him crazy that Alex wasn't intimidated.

He kissed her cheek and poured himself a cup of coffee. Leaning against the counter, he asked. "How's everybody doing?"

"I was just asking Grace about what you do at her shop," her father answered, narrowing his eyes on his son-in-law.

Alex glanced at Grace. Circumstances hadn't lent themselves to having 'the conversation' the night before, and now the silent question passed between them. The decision was made when they heard Frank and Rob greeting each other in the sunroom. They wouldn't be alone in the kitchen for long.

"Well, I pretty much do whatever Grace needs me to do," Alex finally replied. "I do some of the bookwork, and I've had some ideas about marketing and promotion that she's used."

It was all true, and his ideas for a sports-themed area in the back of the shop had been forward-thinking and well-received by the community. Of course, he wasn't about to go into the real details of his involvement at the moment. Hopefully, they'd have the opportunity to do that before the weekend was over.

"Well, you'll never get anywhere if you don't make a plan and apply yourself," her father pointed out, and then launched into a lengthy barrage of unsought advice on how to succeed in the business world.

Alex inclined his head, as though riveted by her father's discourse on corporate management. Grace made a monumental effort to keep from interrupting and setting her father straight. How much more would he embarrass himself before he knew the truth? She looked at her husband and realized that there was nothing false in the way he listened to her father. She supposed that it was part of what made him so successful; he was always willing to learn. With a sigh she sipped her tea and admired her husband and listened to her father preach.

Saturday - 8:00 a.m.
Liz

The raging wind shook the windows, blowing endless snow around the centuries-old inn, and wrenching Liz out of a very deep and restful sleep. As wakefulness slowly edged out slumber, she listened to the howling storm and felt her body tense for the inevitable shiver. Apparently too languid to follow through, it relaxed again, and she burrowed deeper into the warmth of her wonderfully cozy bed.

She froze when her pillow moved.

"Morning," said a rather deep, sleep-tousled voice, sort of next to, but also alarmingly beneath her.

Liz resisted the urge to leap from the bed and Christopher's exceedingly comfortable embrace.

Now thoroughly awake, she tentatively evaluated the shoulder and chest that supported her head, moving gently as Christopher breathed. Further observation revealed that her pillow was encased in a T-shirt. She held her breath as she considered the placement of her own body, praying fervently that she hadn't wrapped herself around her new friend while she slept. A brief analysis assured her that her head and left hand were the only things that had violated Christopher's space. While she'd made a pillow of his chest, her hand rested gently on his rib cage, rather than his abdomen, which somehow seemed a little less invasive.

She finally noted, with profound relief, that she hadn't drooled. Daring to breathe, she eased her head back to look at him.

"Morning," she whispered, sliding gently off his shoulder and onto her own pillow.

Oh, he was handsome in the early morning light. His brown, silver-streaked hair, which was never particularly tidy, was especially unruly. His dark brown, sleepy eyes regarded her with affection, and something she thought it best not to explore. His unshaven jaw broke into an irresistible smile.

She grinned a little sheepishly. "Well, we slept together. Whatever will people think?"

He turned more fully, regarding her with interest. "I'm much more concerned with what you think."

She sighed and touched his jaw. "You were amazing."

He growled quietly. "Liz..."

The playful severity of his tone did something funny to the nerves already on full alert throughout her body. She pulled her hand back, losing herself a little in his eyes before closing her own against the overwhelming emotions passing between them.

"I'm sorry. I shouldn't tease - this is difficult enough."

"Marry me, Liz."

Her eyes flew open. He was smiling, but he wasn't teasing.

"Why? So that we can really sleep together?"

"Well, sure."

She laughed and pushed his shoulder. "You probably shouldn't ask me when we're in such a compromising position."

"You doubt my motivation?"

"You just made your motivation perfectly clear."

Christopher smiled, raising himself up and bracing his stubbled jaw with his left hand. "*I am influenced - conquered; and the influence is sweeter than I can express; and the conquest I undergo has a witchery beyond any triumph I can win.*" He touched her cheek gently, drawing his finger along her jaw.

Liz melted into the pillows. "I may be a numbers person, but I know my Jane Eyre."

He grinned. "Busted."

"I see I'm going to have to brush up on my reading so I know whether or not your material is original."

"Well, how about, *'When you trip over love, it is easy to get up. But when you fall in love, it is impossible to stand again.'*"

Liz processed that for a moment, her heart beating irrationally in response to the 'love' talk. Choosing the safe route, she said, "I can see I've got a lot of reading to do."

Christopher merely smiled.

Liz squirmed. "Okay, seriously, who said that?"

"I did."

"Quoting whom?"

He huffed in disappointment. "You're not even going to try to guess?"

"I don't read a lot of romantic literature. I'm sorry. That may be an irreconcilable difference."

"Albert Einstein."

"I'm sorry?"

"That's who said that. Besides me. Well, he said it first."

"You're kidding."

"Nope." Christopher traced the side of her jaw again.

Liz sighed. "You are full of surprises."

"Okay, then marry me."

She laughed helplessly, marveling at the playfulness she never would have suspected of him. "Again, we need to think beyond ... this ... here ... now." She propped herself on her own elbow, trying desperately to create a less intimate setting between them. Considering that they were sharing an antique sleigh bed in a romantic inn during a storm that left them feeling very much secluded, nothing really helped.

"The present inducements aside," his smile deepened at her reaction, "I want to marry you even more for all of the reasons that we talked about last night after you accosted me."

Liz laughed. "Accosted you? I probably spent ten minutes feeling around on the bed, worrying and whispering your name. I tried very hard *not* to accost you."

"Well, whatever it was, the conversation that followed was well worth the attack."

Liz threw herself back on her pillow with another laugh. "Oh, please." She turned and eyed him, thinking it might be awfully fun to wake up to him every day. "Can we please talk about this after I brush my teeth?"

He leaned over and planted a kiss on the side of her mouth. "We can do whatever you want."

More suggestive than acquiescing, his response had Liz moving decisively out from under the warm covers.

$$\mathcal{S}\,\mathcal{S}\,\mathcal{S}$$

The knock came after she'd dressed and brushed her teeth, and Liz was relieved to see that Christopher had at least pulled on his jeans before she returned to the room. The fact that he had, and that he'd also sort of made the bed, helped her feel a little less like they were almost-lovers and more like necessary roommates.

Content to believe that the rest of the household, or whoever cared to think about it, was equally deceived, she dropped her hairbrush into her bag as Christopher answered the door. He greeted John, but made way for Liz to intercept his inevitable request.

"How's Maddy?" she asked, hoping her calm tone would ease some of the obvious strain on John's face. He clearly hadn't slept much. He almost certainly wasn't the least bit concerned about what had transpired between her and Christopher during the night.

"She's being a trooper, but the contractions are coming more regularly. She dozed on and off throughout the night, but she's definitely awake now. She probably had ten in the last hour." He swallowed. "They're not letting up."

"Six minutes apart," Liz concluded, waving good-bye to Christopher and following John along the now familiar path to the third-floor apartment. It was clear from what she'd seen of the storm that there was no way they'd be making the attempt to drive to the hospital. Keeping Maddy as comfortable as possible would be paramount. There was no telling how quickly her labor would progress, of course, but confirming the pace of her contractions would definitely help them be prepared.

They arrived at the apartment door, and John, still a gentleman despite his obvious stress, opened it for her.

"Thank you," Liz tried to smile encouragingly up at him. "I'm no doctor, John, but I'll do everything I can to help." She paused. "I know it's a mixed blessing, but it might be comforting to remember that this could still take a while. Maddy just might make it until the storm clears enough for you to get her to the hospital." She touched his arm gently. "If there's any way that you can turn off for a bit, it would help you both. I'll get you if Maddy needs you."

"Thanks." John sounded both resigned and relieved. "I'll just check on her and then hang out here and listen for the boys. Please don't hesitate if anything ..." Dark circles framed his worried eyes and her heart ached for him. He'd need some sleep if he was going to be able to navigate the day ahead.

"I promise."

He nodded and disappeared into the bedroom, returning before Liz had a chance to fully contemplate the unexpected direction the weekend had taken.

"She'd be happy if you'd sit with her," he said. "I really can't thank you enough."

"I'm glad I can help," Liz replied. "Rest if you can."

She slipped past him and into their room where Maddy sat propped on the pillows. Liz had hardly crossed the threshold when their formidable dog stood, regarding her with concern.

"She's a friend, Burt, let her in," Maddy said quietly. Her dog slowly sat, eyes still glued to the intruder.

Liz approached, reaching out to him carefully. "Hey Burt, just coming to help you sit with Maddy."

Her very pregnant host regarded her tiredly from her pillowed throne. "Thanks for being brave enough to pass the guard."

Liz nodded as she reached the bed, Burt having grudgingly approved her passage. She picked up Maddy's hand. "How are you holding up?"

"They're coming more regularly." Maddy sucked in a breath as the next contraction began. Fighting the panic, she closed her eyes and concentrated on breathing.

Liz silently applauded her determination. "I'm right here. Just breathe through it."

The years fell away and Liz remembered bringing her daughter Kelly into the world. Many things had likely changed in the medical world to help the process along, but all of that was stripped away while Maddy lay in her own bed at home, trying not to fight the inevitable progression. Liz held her hand and counted the exhalations with her as the baby continued its determined course to join the wedding party.

Saturday - 9:00 a.m.
Maddy

Surprisingly comforted by the presence of the relative stranger who had relieved John, Maddy finished counting through the contraction and laid her head back on the pillows. She closed her eyes and willed her body to relax.

She took her time before opening them again, relieved that she wasn't expected to make any kind of conversation. "Is John going to rest?" Maddy was convinced that her husband had hardly slept while she'd dozed during the last few hours.

Liz nodded. "He's in the living room, listening for the boys."

Maddy glanced at her clock, worried now that the boys weren't up and about. While it had been a late night for them, they never slept past eight.

"I should check on them." She shifted toward the side of the bed.

Burt whined and she sighed. Why couldn't her silly dog have slept in?

"I'll go." Liz stood, and Burt lumbered up with her.

It really was a miracle that she didn't seem bothered by the pony-sized animal. When had her dog gotten so big?

"I'm glad you're okay with him. He's so protective - it can be intimidating."

Liz considered the wolfhound. "I'll admit I was a little overwhelmed when I first met him, but he's not so scary anymore."

"That's a big deal. You haven't had that much time with him, so it's great that he trusts you." Maddy considered her dog with mixed affection and frustration. "He's always been a gentle giant, but if he takes a disliking to you ..."

"I'll behave," Liz smiled. She managed to ruffle the scraggly fur on his head and he allowed it, though his stance remained guarded.

"Thank you so much for being here. I hope you'll come back when I can return the favor. Well, not help you have a baby necessarily, but, you know, take care of you and be a host and everything."

"Please don't worry about it. I'm just glad I can be here for you now," Liz replied.

Maddy could feel her eyes getting heavy. *Oh, for a little more sleep.*

"Do you want me to take him with me?"

Maddy managed a giggle which seemed to set off another contraction. "You can try," she gritted her teeth and tried to control the flow of air and relax her body. "He ... hasn't ... left ... my side..."

"Don't talk," Liz was next to her again. "Just breathe. I'll check the boys when we get through this one."

The *we* helped a little, and Maddy tried very hard to fight the panic. She could survive the next minute. That's all that mattered.

The contraction finally subsided, and she let go of her new friend's hand, which she'd been gripping rather tightly.

"Okay. I'm okay. Would you check the boys?"

"Of course." Liz stood and quietly left the room.

Maddy hardly had the energy to consider where this angel had come from and why she was so attentive. She closed her eyes and tried to rest up for the next contraction. It was time to make her peace with the baby's decision to come early.

It wasn't like she had a lot of say in the matter.

She felt herself dozing for a few seconds - or minutes - it was difficult to tell how much time really passed. Burt rested his head lightly on her arm and Maddy opened her eyes.

"It's okay, Buddy," she whispered. "You're going to have to let me holler a little. It's how this works, I guess." She pulled her hand free and ran it over his concerned face. "How are we ever going to move you out of here when this business gets serious?" She smiled a little as she considered who would end up with the job of physically hauling Burt out of the room. Maybe John and Tank together could do it? Where would they put him?

The answer to that perplexing question got lost in another contraction. She was relieved when Liz returned and vaguely processed her assurance that the boys were awake and playing quietly in their room. The rest was lost in the momentum of the contraction. She gripped the hand held out to her and breathed.

$$\mathcal{SSS}$$

"I need to get up and walk."

Liz jumped at her side. Had she dozed between contractions, too? Maddy felt the angel's eyes assessing her.

"I'd like to convince you to rest, but I know it's hard to lie still if you can't." Liz stood and reached out to Maddy. "Let's loop the room and see how you feel."

Maddy gratefully took her hand and eased her legs over the side of the bed. "How far apart are my contractions?" She felt like she should know, but she was still fighting the stupor of on-and-off sleep between baby attacks.

"You're holding at about six minutes," Liz replied.

"How long..."

"Any time now."

"And you're letting me up?"

Liz laughed a little. "Your body knows what it wants. I say we listen to it."

The next contraction came before she stood, and Maddy sat back down on the bed, breathing and counting and trying to fantasize about all of the things she planned to do during the coming pain-free blocks.

She stood with determination when she was able. "I need to find Becky."

Liz absorbed this unexpected announcement with admirable calm. "Would you like me to go look for her?"

"No, I want to take my five minutes and find her. I need to see if she's alright. She's getting married today." Maddy started moving toward the door, stopping to pull her robe from the hook beside it. She really didn't have time to argue.

"We'll have to walk past your husband. How do you think that's going to go?"

Maddy paused. "I have to keep moving. I have a list ..."

She felt a gentle hand on her arm. "Have you tried texting or calling her?"

Maddy's shoulders slumped. "No." She turned to Liz. "I just really need to see her."

Eyes filled with compassion, Liz gently guided Maddy back to the bed. "Let's try texting her first. See if we can get her to come up here." She picked up Maddy's phone from the bedside table and brought it over.

Maddy sighed; Liz was right. She picked up her phone and typed, *'Happy Wedding Day!'* She looked at the text for a moment and then erased it. *'How are you doing? Ready for your big day?'* She considered this message and then erased it with a frustrated sigh. *'Hey Becky - come see me?'* This she sent, and then sat on the bed and waited, wondering how many contractions it would take before her sister walked through the door.

Two contractions was plenty of time to answer a text, Maddy decided with a groan. She pulled herself up from the bed, Liz lending her a hand as she stood.

"I'm going to call her. If she doesn't answer, I want to use my next contraction break to find her." She looked at Liz with determination. "I know you're here to help me, and I'm telling you I really need to do this."

Liz considered her plea and nodded. "It'll have to be a straight shot. No detours. We'll find Becky, make sure she's okay, and hustle right back up here. We're not having the baby in the stairwell."

Maddy stifled a laugh. "Yes, ma'am. Thank you."

Liz squeezed the hand that Maddy was still gripping, and then walked over to the door. "I'll just see what John's doing while you call."

Maddy dialed her sister and watched Liz ease the door open. She peeked out into the living room and pulled her head back into the room. She gave a thumbs-up, and Maddy nodded while she waited for Becky to answer. After six rings, she dropped her phone on the bed. "We're going down."

"Okay," Liz replied quietly. "The boys are up. They're in the kitchen. John seems to be sleeping." She looked questioningly at Maddy.

Maddy quickly did her contraction math. "We'll check the boys and I'll try to get into the stairwell before I have my next contraction. Don't want to freak them out. Then we'll find Becky, have a contraction, and then come back up. That's about twenty minutes. Hopefully John will sleep."

Liz shook her head, resigned, but also seemed to be fighting a smile. "And Burt will be okay with this?"

The dog stood resolutely at Maddy's side. She ruffled the fur on his head as she walked to the door. "He'll just follow. He never barks or whines, well, loudly. We'll be fine."

Easing quietly into the living room, Maddy blew out a relieved breath when she saw John stretched out in the recliner. Then her gaze moved to the kitchen where she saw Blake and Parker quietly trying to make their breakfast. She hurried over, relatively speaking, to help them.

"Morning guys," she whispered. "I'm glad you're letting your dad sleep. The baby and I kept him awake last night." She rubbed her tummy and the real culprit.

"Was he crying?" Parker asked, then stopped and really looked at her. "Did you hear him?"

Maddy smiled. "No, he wasn't crying, just moving around a lot. Here let me pour the milk."

Liz was right behind her and helped get the boys set up with cereal and orange juice.

"Is Uncle Tank here?" Blake asked. Maddy's heart broke a little at the concern in his voice.

She rested a hand on his shoulder. "Yes, Blake, he made it."

His answering smile helped Maddy to forgive Tank a little for what he'd put them all through. John's boys adored their uncle-to-be because he really took time with them and invested in them. She wished she'd get to see their reunion.

Parker threw his arms up in the air. "Yes! Now we can," he clamped a hand over his mouth, and then continued, muffled, "we can have his party."

Maddy smiled. "Okay, guys, I'm - ohhhhh," she swallowed her wail. There was no way she was getting out in the hallway for this one. She turned away from them and leaned against the counter, trying to make the contraction look as unalarming as possible. Liz, bless her, chatted away with Blake and Parker to distract them.

When it ended, Maddy simply said, "Becky."

Liz nodded, finishing her quick instructions to the boys to let their dad sleep as much as possible. Maddy glanced at her husband as she opened the door of the apartment. Surprisingly, he hadn't stirred, and she was relieved. He certainly needed the rest. With luck, she'd be back in her room in less than three contractions, and he'd never know she left.

$$\int \int \int$$

The steps were a bit more challenging than she expected, but with the help of her new, wonderful friend, Maddy got to Becky's room before the next contraction hit. Burt paced at her side while she tapped on the door of the Captain's Quarters.

"Becky?" she whispered-called.

She heard nothing, so she tapped again. When her third tap went unanswered, she put her hand on the knob, then hesitated.

"Oh, do you know if ... did Tank sleep in here?" She didn't want to barge in if they'd made up on the night before their wedding and had, well, made up.

"I don't know," Liz whispered.

"Okay, well, I'm going in," Maddy decided, determined to be inside the room before the next contraction hit.

Another door opened in the hallway and Maddy spun around, smile frozen in place.

Tank stood in the door of the Anchor room, looking disoriented, but somehow, still overwhelming. He'd clearly slept in his clothes. The three of them stood awkwardly for a moment, regarding each other.

Maddy finally spoke. "Hey, Tank. I'm glad you made it home safely." Her tone of voice probably didn't match her words.

He nodded in response.

"I was just checking on Becky," she explained.

Concern replaced disorientation. "Is she okay?"

At that moment, the door to the penthouse opened, and another disoriented and formidable man entered the conversation.

"Maddy, what are you doing down here?"

"Checking on Becky."

"What's wrong with Becky?" Both men closed in on the Captain's Quarters.

For all Maddy knew, Becky was down in the kitchen making breakfast. She hadn't really thought beyond her concern that her sister wasn't answering her phone. She was just about to explain this new theory when she felt the telling twinges of a coming contraction.

John knew the signs. "Let's get you back upstairs."

"I just wanted to check on her," she ground out while she was able. "She was so sad last night. And with the wedding today ..."

"We've got more important things to think about right now," her husband said, pushing her through the door as Burt followed nervously.

Maddy heard Liz and Tank talking quietly as the door closed. She figured that, between them, they'd make sure Becky was okay. She'd text Liz after her contraction was over.

"Think you can manage the steps?" John hovered and rubbed her back.

Maddy tried to slow her breathing. "Maybe the boys should ..."

"I'll ask Liz to take them downstairs for us."

"Oh good," Maddy wheezed, trying to navigate the stairs with Burt on one side and John on the other.

She stopped again, realizing that she didn't know if Becky or anyone was getting food and coffee on.

"Breakfast?" she asked in a panic.

"Are you hungry?"

Maddy almost pushed her thoughtful husband back down the steps. "For ... the ... guests ..."

"Right. Well, I can smell the coffee. Somebody must be on it. I'll find out as soon as I get you settled. Let's just focus on our baby right now."

Maddy stopped, breathing through her contraction while Burt and John glared at each other and waited. A few moments later, she took her cleansing breath and looked up at her husband.

"I'm sorry I left."

"Let's just get you back upstairs."

The affection and concern in his eyes released a rush of gratitude, relief and hope. "We can do this, right?'

"Absolutely." He followed as Maddy pushed her way to the top of the steps and into the apartment.

"I should have had a back-up plan for breakfast," she sighed.

John walked with her into the bedroom and fluffed the pillows. "We never could have anticipated this. You have to trust that people will understand, and figure out how to feed themselves, if necessary."

She did not like the way that sentence ended and drew breath to protest.

"Maddy." John's voice was slightly sterner, which was the extent of his temper. "They're friends. They'll be alright. Please try to relax."

Maddy sighed and settled into the bed.

"Now, what can I get you?"

She managed a weak smile. "A healthy baby?"

Her husband stroked her cheek. "That's the plan."

Saturday - 10:00 a.m.
Becky

Why had she worn the rumpled blue dress for her wedding?

Becky looked down in confusion. Maddy should have helped her make a better choice. And where was her sister, anyway?

She heard a cry and turned to see Maddy in the wedding dress, holding three squirming babies.

"Do you take this man to be your lawfully wedded husband?"

Becky glanced over at her groom and then looked down into his face. He seemed so young.

At least he was out of the hospital.

"Becky!"

She jerked back to the pastor. Why was Otis doing the service? Where was Rob?

Suddenly, she was floating up and over the room full of wedding guests, and the only faces she recognized were Tank's parents, who smiled and waved as she floated higher and higher and further out of reach.

"Becky!"

Otis meant business.

She fought to pull herself out of her crazy dream world into the semi-dark reality around her. Someone was right in her face, and it wasn't Otis. Only one person could loom like that, and honestly, waking up to that behemoth was a little terrifying.

She scrambled back. "What are you doing here? You weren't supposed to sleep here!"

"I didn't."

"What are you doing in this bed? Why are you breathing like that?"

"I'm not in it, I'm sitting next to you. Relax." Tank's directive did not match his delivery. He backed up a little, but still hovered. "Maddy couldn't get a hold of you and she was concerned."

"So she sent you to terrify me out of a perfectly good sleep?"

Tank shrugged his massive traps and Becky woke up enough to be irritated.

"Well, I'm fine. Please go away so I can get dressed. I need to check on Maddy."

She back-burnered her irritation for a moment and considered him. He was breathing unevenly, and the look in his eyes said he'd been concerned, too.

"Seriously, Tank? I was sleeping. I was really tired. I *am* really tired. I woke up earlier with a pounding headache and took something for it, and now I've slept way too long. I need to get up. And you look terrible." Becky tried to make a little more distance between them. "You should know better than to take Maddy too seriously right now," she added, a tiny bit convicted by the fear in his eyes that was finally starting to abate. "I'm sorry you were worried. Now please move."

Tank gave her a little more room.

Becky eased out of bed with a sigh, smoothing the blue dress, which she now planned to burn as soon as she got it off her body. To think that she'd thought to impress her fiancé in it. What a joke.

"I'm going to shower," she said, giving Tank a wide berth as she passed him. "Why don't you go find your parents or something? I'm sure they'd like to know you're okay."

"They know."

She ventured a look at him from a safer distance. "What about Grace? She was worried sick, too."

"I talked to Grace."

Tank-speak again. Becky rolled her eyes.

"Well, go somewhere ... else. You have lots of friends stuck in this house." Lots of friends who probably needed breakfast, or at least coffee. Why hadn't she set an alarm?

"We need to talk."

Becky stepped into the bathroom. "I need to clean up, check on my sister, and figure out how and what to feed all of these people who are stuck here for the wed ... weekend. We'll talk later." She closed the door and leaned against it.

She couldn't begin to process 'later', or she'd set off another one of her blinding headaches. Maddy and her baby and all of their snowbound guests had to be the focus.

Tank had held the party up the day before. It was his turn to wait.

Saturday - 11:00 a.m.
Grace

Grace cleaned up from the breakfast-turned-brunch, not surprised that Maddy's Inn was well-stocked and able to provide for the crew that ended up being snowed in together. Once she helped herself to the kitchen and all of its resources, she found that she enjoyed working in the space and the whole innkeeper drill. Kind of like her shop, the buzz of people enjoying coffee and food, talking and laughing, was a great backdrop for her work making a big vat of scrambled eggs with leftover scallions and an orange bell pepper sitting forlornly in the vegetable drawer of the fridge. There was a lot to celebrate - potentially. Tank had arrived, and if all went well with Maddy and her baby, they could still be celebrating a wedding.

Of course, Becky would have to agree to marry Tank, so the 'ifs' were a bit complicated.

"Well, my fruit salad worked for breakfast," Anita observed, tucking the leftovers back into the fridge. "We still have enough food to feed an army. I guess I can stop contemplating sending Ed out into the storm for reinforcements."

Grace laughed. "I'm not sure if anything would be open if you did." She had a skeleton crew on at her own shop, but that was only because Kelly and Drew lived right in town and could come and go pretty easily. When she checked in earlier, she heard that a couple of hardy coffee drinkers had braved the storm, but they'd still agreed to close up around noon.

"That's true," Anita agreed. "Well, he's behaving for the moment. I guess I'll let him be."

"Why don't you relax with the others? I think we can close the kitchen down for a while."

Anita looked around the room with a nod. "I'm getting spoiled in here. I'm not going to want to go back to my own little space."

Grace agreed. "This is an amazing facility. And you can't beat the view. Well, usually."

They both looked outside and considered the blinding white of the storm. Inside, the kitchen remained bright and cheery, the light cupboards reflecting the bright morning light that spilled through the windows despite the weather.

"Okay, well, I'll go see what all those boys are up to."

Anita warmed up her coffee and walked out into the sunroom where Ed, Frank, and John's boys were playing some sort of board game by the fire. Otis relaxed in a recliner, talking with Pastor Rob and Christopher, and Alex and Tank stood at the windows, coffee mugs in hand, deep in conversation.

Grace was grateful that her parents had gone back up to their room an hour earlier. They had been up since seven, pacing and grumbling, and barely being civil to the others who'd joined them throughout the morning. She was especially relieved that they'd left before Tank showed up. He looked to be in pretty rough shape, and she was glad he had a chance to breathe a bit before they descended on him again. She'd watched Parker and Blake all but maul him when he entered the kitchen, and was happy to see how that softened him up a bit. He had spent a few minutes greeting his friends, and she was proud of him for making that effort. There was a time when he would have simply stormed into the room and brooded, letting people address him if they dared.

Becky brought out a lot of good in her brother. Grace hoped that her parents would begin to see and appreciate that before the weekend was over.

As if on cue, Becky ducked into the kitchen, somehow looking elegant in her yoga pants and oversized knit sweater, the pale blue complimenting her complexion. The woman could dress down all she wanted, but something about her bearing demanded attention and, in Grace's case, a little bit of awe.

It also demanded protection. Becky did not wish to be seen.

"Hey there," Grace whispered. "Coffee?"

Becky, haggard underneath the stylish veneer, nodded gratefully. She glanced toward the sunroom with trepidation. No doubt she could hear the voices but couldn't identify all the occupants from her particular angle in the kitchen.

Grace followed her gaze and confirmed that everyone seemed settled in their conversations for the moment. She nodded at her friend reassuringly and poured the coffee. As much as she was anxious for the bride and groom to reconcile, she didn't envy them having an audience while they worked things out. This group was ready for a party that Tank and Becky weren't ready to host.

"John and Liz, too," Becky quietly pulled a tray from a corner cupboard. "Oh, wait. Liz doesn't drink coffee. I'll need to make some cocoa."

"Already done," Grace replied. "Special order for the boys."

"Oh good. Thank you. And they could use a bite to eat upstairs. I'm sure they have something in their kitchen, but this would be easier." She sighed. "I think Maddy's really in labor."

"Oh, wow, okay." Grace piled scones on a plate and got bowls out for fruit salad, trying to catch up with this latest development. Liz had looked fairly concerned when she delivered John's boys mid-morning, but the kitchen had been buzzing with people and food preparation, and they hadn't really spoken before Liz disappeared again.

"I can't thank you enough for taking over here this morning," Becky said quietly. "I'm not sure what I was thinking. I knew Maddy would be in no shape ..."

"Please," Grace interrupted. "Don't even think about it. We're family, right?" She desperately hoped so, anyway.

Becky lifted the tray. "Well, this is above and beyond. Really, thank you."

"You're welcome. And don't worry about dinner. Anita and I helped ourselves to the stores here and made a plan." She smiled encouragingly. "We're having fun with it, so don't even give it a thought. Just take care of your sister."

Becky nodded, a suspicious sheen in her eyes.

Grace swallowed. "Oh Becky, are you okay?"

"I'm fine," Becky replied, glancing toward the sunroom. Hearing commotion indicating that someone was likely heading toward the kitchen, she shifted the tray and backed into the dining room door. "I need to go. I can't deal with Tank right now."

Grace watched the door swing shut with concern. She wasn't used to seeing Becky anything less than composed and in control. The woman who just refused to face Tank less than five hours before their wedding didn't have a lot of time to get her head together, put Tank in his place, and get this wedding back on schedule.

Never mind that Becky's sister was probably going to have her baby at home in the middle of a snowstorm. Grace sighed as her mind wandered off in another direction altogether.

Abruptly brought back to the present by the person who was the source of most of the weekend's turmoil, she caught her brother's arm.

"Let her go," Grace said as he tried to follow Becky through the door. Reconciling on the way to the birthing suite wasn't going to happen. "Seriously, Tank, leave her alone. She's got other things besides you on her mind right now. She's taking food to John and Liz."

Tank paused momentarily, but the tension in his arm indicated that he didn't plan to hang around.

Grace tried to be patient. "You know Maddy's in labor, right?"

That brought him around. "I just saw her an hour ago. She was fine." He seemed to stop and think about that for a minute. "Well, she was upset, and I guess she's pretty huge."

Grace rolled her eyes. "I wouldn't lie about this."

"Shouldn't she be in bed somewhere?"

"I don't know." Grace wasn't much more informed about the process than her brother was, but she wasn't about to second-guess a ritual she didn't yet understand. "So, what's going on with you and Becky? Have you two talked at all?"

He breathed deeply. "We talked some last night. We need to finish." He looked behind her at the door.

Grace didn't have nearly the answers she was looking for, but she did know that Becky needed space. The version of her friend who had just stopped in the kitchen for coffee looked ready to bolt and never return.

"Well, right now, you need to let Becky focus on her sister."

"I need to talk to her."

"You can do it later."

"We're getting married today. We need to talk now."

There was the slightest uncertainty in her brother's voice, and Grace ached for him, even though the whole mess was his fault.

"Let her check in on Maddy. There's only so much she can do, and then she'll probably be back down."

Tank looked at her hopefully, in his owlish way. Grace took advantage of the silence.

"It's not like she can go anywhere. You'll have your chance to talk. But Tank," she looked at him pointedly. "This has to be on her terms. You put her through - well, all of us, really, have paid for your choices and no communication. If I were you, I'd concentrate on taking care of the people who are stuck here because they came to celebrate with you. Becky will come to you when she's ready."

Doubt rolled down over his hope like an old-fashioned window shade.

"Tank, I'm not kidding. Give her space."

His shoulders heaved with a sigh. He looked toward the door where Becky had disappeared with her tray.

"I'll give her an hour."

Grace threw up her hands and turned away. If it came to it, she'd get his buddies to distract him or lock him in a closet somewhere. One way or another, she was going to protect her friend from her brother.

Saturday - Noon
Liz

"Well, that certainly complicates things."

Liz considered what Becky had shared with her. They'd had a few minutes to catch up in the penthouse kitchen, and she hardly knew how to comfort her friend.

"And it's not like you have time to talk to each other, with the baby on its way."

"I know," Becky sighed with concern and glanced toward the bedroom where John was taking his turn breathing with Maddy. "I should probably at least tell people that things are on hold. We can blame it on Maddy for now."

"Can I help?"

"I should get Tank to do it. Somehow. Without seeing him." Becky got lost in thought for a moment. "That might be tricky. Yeah, maybe you could just let people know about Maddy and the baby. She could use the prayers."

"Sure. I can do that."

"Thank you," Becky sighed. "I'm so sorry you made that awful drive for nothing." She traced the lip of her mug with her finger, then looked up. "But I'm really glad you're here - for Maddy, for me." She set the mug aside. "And Christopher sure is happy."

Liz smiled. "It's really good to see him."

"So, how's that mistletoe magic, without the mistletoe?" Becky managed a bit of a smile at the rather memorable launch of Liz and Christopher's relationship. "You sure looked cozy last night." She perked up. "I forgot to ask you about sharing a room with him. Was that okay?"

"It was fine; a little awkward, but we got over it."

Becky met that with a full-blown grin. "Yeah?"

Liz replied with a full-blown blush.

"Oh Liz! Are you kidding?"

Liz regained her composure enough to derail Becky's imagination, which was taking hers right along with it.

"Yes. No! We slept in the same bed - that's all." She cleared her throat and tried to sip her cocoa casually, then put her mug down and sighed. "But it sure was nice to wake up next to him."

Becky hummed her delight. "I'm glad you both were okay with it. We tried to come up with another option, but unless one of you wants to sleep with Tank's parents ..."

Liz shuddered. "No thanks."

"Yeah, we thought not." Becky tilted her head. "Why don't you and Christopher get married today?"

Liz almost choked on her scone.

"Seriously! How happy would that be?" Her friend warmed to the crazy idea. "You're clearly in love with each other - you make each other so happy. Why wait?"

Liz could think of quite a few reasons to wait to start a potentially life-long relationship with someone. She hardly knew where to begin.

Becky's dreamy look had become rather steely. "It's not like you're ever going to find a simple solution to where you're going to live or how you'll handle your jobs. You might as well be married while you're sorting it out. Life's too short."

Her mind fairly exploding with the direction the conversation had taken, Liz could only stare at Becky in wonder. "Okay, sure. I'll let Christopher know."

Becky laughed aloud at that, which was a wonderful sound to hear.

"Great! I'll stay here and relieve John when he surfaces." She stood and stretched. "You go propose to Christopher."

Liz stood with her. "He did ask me again, this morning."

Becky paused and looked at her speculatively. "And?"

"I told him I wanted to brush my teeth first, and then John came knocking."

Becky laughed. "Well, then. Run along and say 'yes'." She sobered a little. "Someone should definitely get married this weekend."

♪ ♪ ♪

"Oh, hey Liz, I'm glad you're here." Grace closed the dishwasher and hit the power button. "Kelly and Drew are on their way over - snowshoeing - not driving. I hope you're okay with that?"

Liz set her mug on the kitchen counter, her head still spinning with the idea of taking Christopher up on his offer, and sooner rather than later, if Becky had anything to say about it. The fact that her daughter and her friend were heading out into a dangerous snowstorm should probably alarm her, but she was used to Kelly's winter sports daring.

Trying to lose what was undoubtedly a silly grin, Liz composed her face into an appropriate look of concern. "Well, she'd hoped to get to the wedding, and I guess this is the only way that could happen. I hadn't even thought to touch base this morning with everything going on here." She reached for her phone and realized that she didn't have it on her.

Grace smiled. "Yes, she tried to get a hold of you. I told her I'd let you know."

"My phone must be in my room. I'll have to go grab it." Liz refilled her mug from the cocoa carafe she'd come to appreciate over her Christmas holiday at the inn. "I hardly knew whether to hope we'd see each other this weekend, but I didn't consider the

Kelly fearless factor." She sighed, concerned, but mostly glad that she would get to see her daughter after all.

"Yeah, she's something else," Grace agreed. "They just closed up the shop a few minutes ago. Drew had to finish with the coffee; nothing stops him from keeping his roasting schedule." She wiped the counter and continued. "Anyway, they're loading up a bunch of baked goods to bring over here. The storm isn't supposed to let up until tomorrow afternoon, so I'm not even going to open in the morning." She shrugged. "Might as well not waste all that food."

"So they'll snowshoe through a blinding snowstorm with pastries piled on their backs? That's the plan?"

Grace laughed. "Something like that. They'll figure it out. We need half 'n half, too, so they're really saving the day."

"How long do you think it will take?"

"It shouldn't take much more than an hour. And Liz, Drew grew up around here, and is just as fearless as Kelly. Well, not that *that's* a comfort, necessarily, but they'll have their phones and navigation apps. They'll take good care of each other."

Liz nodded. Drew Brookner was a fellow athlete and probably Kelly's best friend. With time, they'd probably figure out that they were more than that, but after her daughter's broken engagement in December, she was probably in no hurry to commit again. Drew, on the other hand, if Liz had read him right during her short visit at Christmas, was quietly and completely taken with Kelly. Liz had no doubt he'd be watching out for her daughter.

"Okay, so, how's everyone doing down here?"

"Well, Anita and I have been feeding people all morning. Everyone's hanging out in the sunroom now, except my parents and Tank. They're in the parlor, I think. I'd definitely stay on this side of the house."

"Thanks for the tip."

"How is Maddy doing?" Grace asked. "Are we going to have a baby this weekend?"

Liz warmed her hands on her mug. "Maddy's doing okay. Labor is steady, so that baby is definitely coming. There's no telling how long it will last - it's different for everybody - so all we can do is keep her as comfortable as possible. And wait."

Grace considered this information. "Okay, so who's our medical team?"

Liz tapped a finger to her lips. "I'm more insurance and billing."

Grace laughed. "And I'm the cafeteria."

Liz smiled. "Well, I basically know the routine and I'm ready to be on the front lines if Maddy wants me there. I figured I'd check with Anita and see what kind of wisdom she can bring to the table."

"Good idea." Grace agreed. "I wish I could say that my mom would help, but she was never very good with anything ... messy." She grimaced. "But you know what? I'm pretty sure Drew is studying sports medicine. I wonder if he could help?"

Liz tried to imagine the quiet coffee-roasting hulk helping to deliver Maddy's baby. "Hmmm ... maybe."

"Just an idea. We need any medical expertise we can get."

"For sure. I just can't picture ..." Liz shrugged. "But what do I know?"

Grace giggled a little. "It is a bit of a stretch. But who knows? There's always the chance that Maddy will make it until the storm clears."

Liz nodded with little conviction. Apart from her doubts that Maddy would last that long, prolonging the process was also the last thing she'd wish on anyone in the throes of labor.

"Possible, but not likely."

Grace considered this. "Right. Okay, so how is Becky?"

"Her spirits are okay, all things considered."

Grace sighed. "I'm trying to get Tank to give her some space. He's frantic to talk to her."

"I think they'll need more time than they have. Becky's asked me to let people know about Maddy, and essentially announce that the wedding's on hold, under the circumstances."

"I guess that makes sense," Grace replied slowly, clearly disappointed. "And we need to be praying for Maddy and that baby, and, well, everyone."

"That's what Becky said." Liz paused. "So, any ideas for how I should approach this?"

Grace thought for a moment. "We should let the boys know first, don't you think? And then we can tell the others."

"That's sweet. Of course, they should be the first to know."

Grace nodded. "Would you like me to do it?"

"Oh, would you mind?"

"No problem. I'll make the announcement and then people can check in with you for details while I go tell my family." She grimaced. "I hate to say it, but my parents will be relieved. Don't know what Tank will do."

"Well, you said we need to be praying for everyone."

"That's for sure."

They stood to go deliver the news and Grace glanced at her watch with a sigh. "We've got a little over three hours. What do you think it would take to make a wedding happen today?"

Now there's a question.

"I honestly don't know."

♫ ♫ ♫

The fire roared, the wind howled, and the boys cheered a significant victory at the game table by the window as Liz and Grace entered the sunroom. Frank was contesting whatever the boys were cheering about, and Ed and Anita were talking with Rob and Otis while a basketball game buzzed quietly on the TV screen. Christopher and Alex stood at the puzzle table, talking and moving pieces around, but clearly not terribly invested in the picture taking shape in front of them.

Grace walked over to John's sons and pulled them aside. She crouched down and spoke to them quietly. Liz smiled as their faces reflected the news they were hearing. Blake looked concerned, but he nodded, and Parker's eyes went wide.

Grace rose to her feet and put a hand on each of their shoulders as she turned to face the group.

"Hey everybody," she called out. "The boys and I have an announcement."

The group turned and quieted in expectation.

"We want to update you on Maddy and the baby." She paused and looked around the room. "It turns out, she's definitely in labor. There's a good chance the baby will be born here at home this weekend."

There was a rumble of surprise throughout the room.

"Becky's with her and John right now. Needless to say, the wedding is on hold until Baby Fordham arrives safely."

The guests processed this news, and Grace continued. "I don't suppose we have anyone with a medical background here?"

The group quieted again and exchanged glances. No doctors, surgeons, nurses or midwives stepped forward.

"Okay, well, no surprise there." Grace patted the boys' shoulders and made her way back over to Liz. "So, Liz has been with Maddy for a good bit of the morning, trying to keep her comfortable. If you have any questions, you can talk to her. We'll keep you updated as best we can."

Grace and Liz exchanged a glance while Pastor Rob made his way over with Anita on his heels.

"What can I do?" they asked simultaneously as the four unlikely storm mates came together.

"Well," Grace replied, "Anita, Liz can update you so the moms can unite and figure out a plan to help Maddy. Pastor Rob, would you come with me while I share the news with my family? We can go from there to check in on the Fordhams."

"Of course," he replied.

They left the room and Liz turned to Anita.

"Alright, fellow mother. Looks like this bond uniquely qualifies us for service. You game?"

"Oh, you bet I am," Anita replied with determination.

Liz waved briefly at Christopher, who lifted his hand with a look of concern.

"Your boy looks a little lost there," Anita observed, following her gaze. "Better make some time with him over this crazy weekend, too. I'll do my part to help Maddy."

"Thank you. It will definitely be a team effort," Liz replied. "And I'll be sure to get some time with my boy."

"You do that," Anita said, suddenly sounding in charge. "Now, what's going on with Maddy? How far apart are her contractions? Is she comfortable?"

Relieved to be sharing the burden, Liz returned her attention to Mrs. Davidson. "Why don't we step into the kitchen? I'll give you the rundown there."

Saturday - 1:00 p.m.
Maddy

"You're doing great, try to rest now."

Maddy didn't really need John's directive, but she appreciated the sentiment. She closed her eyes, trying to make the most of her non-contraction moments.

"I think someone's at the door," he said quietly. "I'll be right back."

John left the room and Maddy heard a murmur of voices. He came back a few minutes later. "You up for visitors?"

Maddy shifted in her bed, trying not to let vanity determine her answer. Part of her really welcomed the distraction. "Who's here?"

"Grace and Rob, and Becky, of course. They're assembling the 'Baby Team', and would like to consult with you."

He looked at her hopefully and Maddy nodded. She and John could both use a baby team.

"Okay, how about I freshen up and meet them out there? I'm done trying to 'rest' between contractions. I think I'd rather move around a little."

Her husband eyed her with concern. "May I request that you not leave the apartment this time?"

Maddy smiled again, twice in one contraction break, she noted with some hope. "Yes, sir. Would you grab my robe and help me deal with my hair?"

$$\int\int\int$$

Feeling slightly more human, and one contraction closer to delivery, Maddy stepped into the living room with Burt on her heels. She glanced hopefully at her 'team', whose looks of encouragement masked various stages of alarm. She could hardly blame them.

"Hey everybody," she greeted them. "You've come to help me figure out how to have this baby?"

They murmured their assent, giving the recliner a wide berth so she could settle there as soon as she could waddle into position.

"Please, relax," she said. "I think I'll stand for now. Or maybe pace." She wanted to erase the looks of borderline dread from their faces. "How's it going downstairs?"

Grace seemed relieved to have a reason to talk. "We've got everything under control. Brunch is done, the kitchen is clean, and our dinner plan is made. Don't worry about a thing down there; we've got it covered."

"Thank you," Maddy replied, genuinely relieved to hear it from the source. She leaned against the recliner she'd declined.

Pastor Rob also found his tongue. "We're all praying for you and the baby. Everyone's on standby to help."

Maddy pondered the somewhat alarming picture of the wedding guests filing through her apartment to help - Otis, Frank, Ed, Tank, the English professor - *what is his name again?* Her determined cheer faltered.

"I think the best thing you can do is to keep everybody happy downstairs while we figure things out up here." She touched John's arm. "This guy could use a break, and at some point," she glanced down at her dog doubtfully, "someone is going to have to move Burt." She looked back up at the group. "Good luck with that."

They all smiled nervously at Burt, who didn't smile back.

"We'll get it figured out," Becky assured her. "And I'll hang out with you while John rests for a while."

"Liz is ready to come back whenever you need her, and Anita will help, too," Grace added. "Oh, and Drew and Kelly are on their way over - snowshoeing - and I'm pretty sure he's studying sports medicine, so we'll have somebody with a medical background."

"The coffee roaster man is the closest thing we have to a doctor?" Maddy asked, feeling the onset of another contraction. "Oh dear."

John was at her side. "Breathe, Maddy."

She obeyed, forgetting about her team and concentrating on the count. When she could finally look up and make eye contact again, their matching stunned faces made her laugh with what little energy she had remaining.

"Okay, you are all going to have to get used to that if you want to help me." She eased into the recliner with John's help, determined to use the next few moments of clarity to give some instructions. "Becky, I'll take you up on your offer. John, please go rest for a bit. I have a feeling I'll be doing this for a while." She shifted her baby, and Burt danced nervously at her side. "Grace, if you wouldn't mind sending Anita up, I'd like to talk to her. Pastor Rob, please keep praying for this little guy, oh, and for my doctor. For some reason, we can't get a hold of him. I hope he's okay, but I'd really like to talk to him."

Everyone murmured their acceptance of the various directives and started to disburse.

John squeezed her hand. "Are you sure you're comfortable out here? Would you rather go back to our room?"

"I'm good," she replied. "Please go rest. Becky will get you if we need you."

He leaned down and kissed her. "I love you. You're amazing."

"I know," she grinned. "Love you back. Now go."

Maddy and Burt watched with satisfaction as the room cleared. She could feel her dog relax beside her as the threats to her person lessened. Apparently, he was okay with Becky.

"So, exciting twist to the weekend, huh?" Becky dropped down on the foot stool next to her.

Maddy looked at her sister with concern. They hadn't had a minute alone since Tank had returned and Maddy's labor had begun in earnest.

"I need to know how you're doing and what's going on with Tank."

"I'm okay." Becky took her hand, ignoring Burt's gentle growl. "Tank and I still have some things to work through. I don't want you to worry about us."

"I'm not worried. Well, I am, but right now, I need to breathe, but then we'll figure everything out."

"What can I do?"

"Count with me."

$$\int\int\int$$

She'd always thought that her 'penthouse' apartment was plenty big, but that was likely because there was a huge house to roam whenever she had the desire to leave it. There would be no more roaming today. The incredible ocean view from windows on three sides usually made the space seem endless, but the driving snow took care of that. For the first time, Maddy felt confined in her happy space, and it didn't help her perspective.

She sighed, detouring around the coffee table to change up the path a bit. Burt, undeterred, maneuvered his large body along the altered course behind her. Becky had stopped caboosing three contractions earlier and sat in the recliner, following the parade with concerned eyes. Maddy was glad for her sister's company but felt her time would be better spent with her fiancé.

"Okay, so you really need to go find Tank and work this out."

"I'm not leaving you alone."

Maddy glanced at the beast on her heels. "Like I'm ever alone."

"Burt is a great companion and protector, but he's not going to deliver your baby."

"And you are."

Becky's eyes widened a bit at the possibility, then she shrugged. "If I have to. Burt and I will figure it out."

Maddy laughed and swallowed the fear that continued to surface. "Maybe I'll just try calling my doctor again."

Becky glanced at her watch. "It's been fifteen minutes. Maybe he's 'back'," she quoted with her fingers.

"Yeah. He probably ran out for coffee."

Becky nodded. "Ran a few errands. Got a pedicure."

Maddy let out a belly laugh that had them both glancing at the bedroom door. "Played a round of golf ... with his pretty toes." She stopped and braced herself at the kitchen counter.

Becky snickered. "Are you sure you want this man delivering your baby?"

Maddy's giggle began taking the shape of a contraction and she sobered very quickly. "He's probably too busy to deliver my baby," she gasped as she tried to get centered to breathe. "But I would sure take some advice right now."

Becky was on her feet and at her side. "We'll call him after this one and we'll find out everything we need to know."

Maddy nodded her thanks. "Go find Tank," she ground out.

"Right after this contraction." Becky's arm around her shoulders steadied her. "Then I'll send him to the golf course to find your doctor."

Maddy collapsed against her sister in an overwhelming, giggling contraction.

Saturday - 2:00 p.m.
Becky

Becky pulled the door gently closed behind her and paused to breathe. She found herself counting as she exhaled, and managed a quick laugh. Maddy had another capable breathing buddy in Anita, who seemed to be a gentle, yet confident presence. Her sister was in good hands.

Not entirely sure where she was headed, except to go anywhere Tank was not, Becky descended the stairs slowly, considering her options. If he was any kind of host, Tank would be socializing in the sunroom with the people who had gathered in his honor and were now snowbound at the inn. Of course, hosting wasn't high on Tank's list of priorities, being taciturn to a fault, and finding the social niceties, well, silly. Tank was neither nice nor social and everybody knew it. Somehow, he still managed to keep some friends - very hardy and resilient friends. Whether or not he could keep a fiancée remained to be seen.

Lost in thought, she arrived at the second-floor landing, stumbling to a halt when she saw someone sitting in one of the chairs clustered under her painting of the Gloucester coast.

Profoundly relieved that it wasn't Tank, she composed herself, wondering vaguely if anyone ever really stopped to observe her handiwork that decorated the hallway of the second floor. *Probably not.* Her seascapes were nothing to the reality just outside the inn. She sighed. It wasn't a good habit to continually marginalize her skills. That was one thing the man in front of her had taught her.

"Becky." Pastor Rob rose gratefully, his tall form obviously less than comfortable in the Victorian balloon-back chair. Apparently, he wasn't just hanging out in the second-floor gallery for her art-work, either. "I was hoping to find you."

"Well, you weren't really looking very hard."

He smiled. "I figured you'd have to pass by here on your way out of Maddy's apartment." He twisted and stretched his back. "I thought Anita would relieve you sooner. I should have brought my sermon to work on."

"Maddy and I were having way too much fun. Hard to leave." Becky dropped into the other chair, and Rob, somewhat resignedly, claimed his own again.

"How's she doing?"

"Pretty much the same. She actually laughed through one of her contractions. Don't know if that really helps the baby, but I think it was good for Maddy."

Rob chuckled. "And probably good for you, too."

"Yep," Becky agreed. "So, you wanted to talk to me?"

She had no doubt he was all about her reconciling with Tank, which was his job, of course, but she felt too spent to do the math with another person. She and Tank would either work things out eventually, or they wouldn't. She was surprised at how removed she felt from the process on the day of their supposed wedding. That had changed, of course. Surely Tank wasn't under any kind of illusion that they'd solve all of their issues and exchange vows in the next couple of hours. Surely their pastor wouldn't recommend rushing the process. Becky manufactured as pleasant a face as she could manage and tried not to drum her fingers on the table be-tween them.

Rob glanced around the empty hallway and seemed to accept it as a passable counseling room. He faced her again.

"Well, I wanted to know how you're doing, of course. And I want to know how I can help with Tank."

"And you probably want to know if you've been stuck here all weekend for a reason, or if the wedding's off," Becky replied.

His gaze was unwavering. "Is that the direction you're heading?"

Becky dropped hers. "I honestly don't know."

"I spoke with Tank for a while. He's pretty devastated. He'd really like a chance to talk to you."

Becky looked at the Gloucester coastline. Her visit to that city had been interesting, definitely a memory that belonged in her past.

"Do you know why he was delayed?"

"He told me."

"It's not okay." She paused. "I mean, I get the part about the boy, but not the part about his mother. And the fact that he didn't communicate at all about it just makes it all more ... complicated."

"It does," Rob agreed. "Forgivable, though?"

She sighed. "I guess so, but that's not the point right now. He needs to figure out what he wants."

"I think you know the answer to that."

"Honestly, I'm not sure I do." Becky looked at her pastor. "We just moved this whole thing up too quickly. There's so much we don't even know about each other." She stood again. "You know he never even told me his real name?"

Rob considered this revelation. "There are ways to find that out."

Becky rolled her eyes, wondering only briefly if that was an acceptable response to a clergyman. "I know. But it's something that *he* should tell me, just like this whole business with whatever-her-name-is. There are too many unanswered questions. And I don't think there's time to answer them. Not this weekend."

"You don't have to get married today. Everyone here will understand if you need more time."

"Except Tank."

"Will you talk to him? Try to come to a better understanding?"

Becky squirmed a little. "Maddy's my priority right now."

"And you just left her in very capable hands," Rob reminded her. "It's okay if you take care of yourself, Becky." He stood with her. "I'm not suggesting that you give Tank a chance to explain just for his sake. It's for yours, too."

Becky didn't know if she had the emotional energy to hear Tank out and still be fully available for Maddy. Although, if she was honest with herself, she knew that her sister would be very much relieved if they were reconciled. That was fairly compelling.

"Tell you what," Becky finally said. "If Tank and I can find a way to talk in the middle of this weekend's chaos, I promise I'll listen to what he has to say."

§ § §

The back stairway seemed like a good idea as Becky tried to escape her concerned pastor and also avoid her fiancé. She disliked the cat and mouse game - really didn't care to be the mouse - but she needed some time to think. She figured that the likelihood of seeing Tank before he saw her was greater if she approached the lower level through the kitchen.

Unless, of course, Tank was lurking in the back stairwell.

Surprise and dismay paralyzed her momentarily, but the need for escape soon loosened her limbs. Becky didn't stop to question why her fiancé was sitting in that stairwell, directly in her path to the kitchen, she simply devoted her energy into back-pedaling up the steps. This was not an easy maneuver, made even more difficult by Tank's subsequent grip on her ankle from his unlikely perch on the steps below her.

"Oh, nice," she ground out, trying to dislodge her heart from her throat. "That's really mature, Tank. Let me go."

She could see it cost him to release her. If he wanted her to stay put, he could make it happen. The fact that he didn't throw his strength around that way made her slightly more inclined to listen to him. Pausing her retreat on her own terms, she processed the rather odd fact that he really was just sitting in the stairwell.

"Why are you here?"

Tank sighed. "I was on my way upstairs when I heard you and Rob talking."

"You heard our conversation?"

"No, just your voices, so I started back down."

"And you what, stopped to rest?"

Tank looked a little sheepish, an interesting phenomenon. "My parents are in the kitchen."

Enough said. It certainly changed Becky's plans. She turned to head back up the steps.

"Becky."

She wasn't accustomed to hearing vulnerability in Tank's voice.

"Please talk to me."

With a sigh, Becky turned to face him again. Apparently, this conversation was happening.

She'd just promised her pastor she would listen if they got a chance to talk. How could she be called out so quickly? She'd hardly had a chance to decide if she really meant what she said. Resigned, she leaned against the wall and crossed her arms. The fact that this conversation was happening in a cold, dark stairwell, while the rest of the house was brimming with activity and her sister was probably about to give birth, should have registered as odd, or funny, or something. Instead, she just felt empty.

"You're the one that needs to do the talking."

"Will you at least sit down?" Tank sounded relieved and bewildered, another twist of the knife in her already battered heart.

She sighed, lowering herself onto a step.

"How's Maddy?"

Becky considered the man that everyone expected her to marry. He was either being evasive, or uncharacteristically empathetic.

Of course, he cares about Maddy.

"She's okay. She finally got a hold of her doctor, so we have a better idea of how to handle things if ... well, not if, *when* the baby comes."

Tank blew out a breath. "That's good."

"Yep. She's brave, and she has John, and lots of support." This assessment was as much for herself as for Tank.

He nodded, then stood, bracing his hands on the walls.

Becky stood right along with him. She wasn't about to let him do his towering thing, not when she could leverage the steps in her favor. "I thought you wanted to sit."

He dropped his arms. "It's not comfortable."

"Well, I was just passing through. Wasn't planning to hang out here."

"We need to talk, and there are people everywhere."

This, she knew. The Captain's Quarters was available, but that was a really bad idea. She'd rather stand in the stairwell.

He seemed to read her mind. "Can we go ..."

"Absolutely not."

He nodded slowly, looking at her intently.

She would not soften under that penetrating gaze. "So, the last thing you said was that you took on a speaking engagement because an old girlfriend appealed to you."

Becky immediately regretted her word choice.

"She's on the board." Tank corrected her, but maybe not for the right reason.

"Tank. She used her position to get you to New York, and you agreed to delay coming home - during the week before our wedding - so that you could see her. And her son, I know, but still."

He had the decency to look down. "Timing was bad, I know." He rubbed the back of his neck. "I felt a responsibility to see Jimmy." He dropped his arm as he looked back up at her. "And the conference was important to me. I had a chance to address the issue of young kids playing football. To see him in a coma because he wanted to do what he sees, or saw me doing on TV," Tank shook his head. "I had to say my piece. I felt like I owed it to him."

"I can understand that, Tank. But why didn't you just tell me? When you called on Sunday, you said you were filling in at another conference. And you didn't stay on the phone long. You just expected me to absorb that huge change of plans and roll with it. We can't operate that way."

"I know. I'm sorry." Tank kicked at a piece of peeling paint on the steps. "I didn't want to go into it all. It was complicated."

"Obviously."

"As the week wore on, I knew that if I talked to you - heard your voice - I would come straight home."

"Well, Tank. That's sweet. But you still chose another woman and her son. What am I supposed to do with that?"

Of course, he didn't have an answer.

"You said you had unfinished business with her."

"I don't." His intense green eyes found hers in the dark stairwell. "I shouldn't have called it that. I was curious, but that was the extent of it. I told you I wouldn't have seen her if Jimmy hadn't been injured, and I meant it." His gaze didn't waver as he continued. "Whatever we had is long past. That was more clear when her son came around and she immediately started pushing for us - for me to be his - well, to get back together." He paused and drew a breath. "I know the timing was terrible. What I did to you - and to everyone here - was ... I'm just really sorry." He reached as though to touch her but then dropped his hand. "You have every right to delay, postpone ..." He stopped mid-sentence, as though unwilling to complete the thought.

"Cancel?" she suggested.

His face fell and Becky's heart twisted.

"Tank, it wasn't just that you worried me or inconvenienced our guests. Your head was in a whole different place just days before our wedding. And you were completely out of touch. What was I supposed to think?"

"I should have called. I was back and forth between the conference and the hospital and lost track of time."

"I get that. But can you imagine how that felt on this end? It's not like you haven't done this before, but that's also part of the problem. If I can't trust you to make coming home for your wedding a priority, I'm not sure what will ever bring you home. Once you get out there on the road, you get so distracted. Football is everything. It was a novelty for a while, but this week, I started to wonder just how or *if* I really fit in to your life."

This concern hit its target. Tank ran both hands over his head, clasping them behind his neck. He looked at her helplessly. "Please help me figure this out. I can't lose you." He swallowed. "I'll give up the traveling."

This concession surprised her, although it was more a result of desperation than deliberation. "I wouldn't ask that of you, Tank. I know what you do is important. I just need to know that I'm important, too." Becky glared at him so she wouldn't start to cry. "And this whole week? I couldn't just be angry with you; I was so worried."

His eyes softened as his own fear dissolved in the face of hers. He dropped his arms and shoved his hands in his pockets. "Ah Becky, I'm so sorry."

"Why couldn't you at least have let us know when you were on your way home?"

He found something really interesting to look at on the step next to her feet. "I left my phone at the hospital."

She sighed. "Of course, you did." And she believed it. He had a strange and resistant relationship with his series of phones.

He looked back up. "By the time I got to the airport, my flight to Augusta was canceled. I found one to Boston and barely made it. I picked up another phone when I landed and texted you."

Becky was a little convicted about the fact that she had no idea how he'd ended up getting home. She'd been too angry to ask. "So you, what, rented a car and drove from Boston yesterday - in all that snow?"

"Yeah. An SUV. It handled the snow pretty well, but it was slow going."

"Couldn't you have updated me along the way? At least once?"

He sighed. "I got mad at the stupid navigation app and pitched the phone behind me. It went all the way to the back of the vehicle. I didn't want to stop driving to find it."

Becky wanted to laugh and smack him at the same time. "You are such a mess."

The hope playing around his eyes grabbed a hold of her heart.

"No. Stop. And go away. I need time to think about what to do with you."

His face grew serious again. "I love you, Becky. Please believe me. I *will* work on communicating."

Her heart softened a little more. She had to get away and clear her head. Any reconciliation in their future wasn't happening in a dark and unromantic stairwell. "I know, Tank. Just give me some time to think. It's been … a weekend."

She slipped past him and started down the steps. He didn't try to stop her. It was only when she opened the door into the kitchen that she realized why he let her go so easily.

$$\mathcal{SSS}$$

"Oh hey, Mr. and Mrs. Kimball. Hi Grace."

Becky tried to recalibrate, and made a beeline for the coffee. "How is everyone weathering the storm down here?"

She could tell that she'd interrupted a significant conversation, but for once, Becky didn't feel like the target of their disgust. Lucky Alex; he was likely the one currently being roasted. She sipped her coffee, longing to get Grace alone for a few minutes to talk about her dumb brother. Or maybe she didn't want to think about him at all. She was almost surprised when Grace answered.

"We're hanging in. How's Maddy?"

Good question. It seemed like hours since she'd seen her sister.

"Pretty much the same. Her spirits are pretty good, which is amazing."

"That's good to hear."

An awkward silence followed, as everyone studied their mugs and avoided eye contact.

"Oh, Kelly and Drew made it through the storm," Grace informed her. "Apparently they had an interesting trip over - haven't heard the story, yet."

"Are they in the sunroom?" Becky welcomed any excuse to leave the kitchen.

"I think Kelly's up with Liz, putting dry clothes on. Drew is probably sitting as close to the fire as he can get."

"Well, I'm glad they made it. I don't know what we would have done without more half-n-half."

Grace grinned. "They're definitely the ones to call in a coffee emergency."

"Well, I'll just go check in with the rest of the group." Becky made a point to look at the Kimballs. They met her gaze with studied disinterest, and she couldn't help a sigh of regret.

Was it terrible that a little part of her hoped her marriage to Tank worked out just so she could make their lives a little more miserable?

Probably.

She smiled at them, in spite of them, and left the room.

Saturday - 3:00 p.m.
Grace

"Why can't you at least make an effort to be civil to her?"

Her mother had the decency to look slightly embarrassed. Her dad stood and looked at his watch.

"She's not the type of woman we envisioned for Tank," he replied.

Grace almost choked on a disbelieving laugh. "Well, Dad, it's entirely possible that you don't know what's best for Tank."

Both of her parents stiffened at her challenge. She rarely confronted them, and while it was uncomfortable, she had no doubt it was necessary, and long overdue.

Her dad's eyes narrowed. "We spent a lot of time and money investing in that boy."

"Believe me, Dad, I know very well where your focus has been all these years."

It felt good to finally say it. Alex would be proud. He'd been wonderful about helping her deal with her feelings of inadequacy when it came to her parents. It gave her the courage to confront them - an opportunity she had imagined might come up on any other day than the day her brother was supposed to get married.

This weekend was full of surprises.

Her father stared, Tank-like, and her mother filled the void.

"Then you can understand why it's so important that Tank has someone to support him in the ... larger opportunities we'd like to see him enjoy."

Dumbfounded, Grace turned to her mother. Perhaps the way she confronted their favoritism lacked clarity. Her mother glanced at her and then turned to her husband for support.

Grace wasn't about to wait. "You have no idea - either of you - what you have in Becky, or in Alex, or in me, for that matter. Your obsession with Tank makes you absolutely blind."

Funny, she didn't resent her brother. It had always just been a matter of fact that Tank was their favorite. Throughout her childhood, he'd been the source of her heartache and oddly, her only comfort.

She pulled a teabag from a canister on the counter, not bothering to see how her comment landed. Silence reigned as she added hot water to her mug. It was broken a moment later when the dining room door opened.

Grace looked up and didn't fight the smile that seemed to be her auto-reply to her big brother. He still had a lot to answer for, but deep down, he was a good guy and she loved him.

For someone who was used to commanding a room, however, he looked ready to run, and Grace wasn't going to let that happen.

"Well, here's that boy, himself." She walked up to Tank and patted him on the arm. "Mom and Dad were just talking about you. I'll leave you to chat."

With that, she ducked out of the kitchen into the much happier, commotion-filled sunroom. She wasn't going to change her parents' minds in a weekend or begin to unravel the world of hurt that accompanied their rejection. She could, however, keep helping to mend the relationships that seemed open to healing. Grace took in the noisy room and made a beeline for Becky.

$$\mathcal{S}\,\mathcal{S}\,\mathcal{S}$$

" ... their Labradoodle, Charlie, had him pinned - flat on his face - in the McDermott's yard."

Kelly Michaels collapsed against her mother in a fit of giggles.

It still amazed Grace how much mother and daughter looked alike - same sleek, dark blonde hair, and same petite build. She felt certain that no one ever said that about her and her own mother, whose false platinum curls contrasted so completely with Grace's straight, dark brown hair.

"You were pinned by a Labradoodle?" Frank asked with a grin.

Drew Brookner scowled from his spot on the couch next to Kelly. "They're bigger than you'd think." It would take something big to pin Drew, a twenty-something former college athlete.

Having caught her breath, Kelly jumped back into her tale. "Of course, all Charlie really wanted was the pack of muffins strapped to Drew's back, so when I stopped laughing long enough to help him get a nice, fresh, lemon poppy seed ..."

"Took you long enough," Drew mumbled, affection still evident to the close observer, which, of course, Grace was. She knew both of her employees well and had watched their not-quite-romance not quite develop with interest.

Kelly laughed again with no remorse. "So, anyway, he trotted off with his treat, and after about five minutes of digging Drew out of the snow drift ..."

"Like you helped. You were laughing too hard."

"I warned you not to cut through. Charlie's always out."

"What kind of idiot leaves their dog out in a snowstorm?"

"Are you kidding? He was having a blast out there. Especially after we dropped in." Kelly clearly enjoyed keeping Drew riled up.

Liz sighed. "Well, I'm glad you both made it safely. It was a little crazy to take that on."

"Yeah," Frank agreed. "What kind of id ..." he tapped a finger to his mouth. "Never mind."

Drew shook his head. "I know it was crazy, but Kelly wanted to come to the wedding, and see her mom, so ..." He glanced at the culprit and she leaned into him.

"You were very brave. Thank you, Drew." Kelly looked up at the group and shrugged. "I didn't want to miss the party."

Grace could tell that she was itching for a wedding update. Instead, Kelly wisely asked, "How's Maddy?"

"Well, she's definitely going to have that baby," Becky replied, stiffening a little as Tank entered the room.

He wisely stopped at the puzzle table and stood with folded arms. Grace wondered briefly where her parents were and figured they must have retreated to their room again. She watched Becky process where Tank planted himself and then turn back to Kelly.

"She's hanging in there. Tends to get very busy between contractions, so if you happen to see her wandering around the inn, redirect her to the penthouse."

"The penthouse?"

"Their apartment on the third floor."

"Oh, cool. But she's really having her baby? Wow!"

"So," Otis entered the conversation, his concern for Maddy evident as he fiddled with the buttons on his sweater. "What can we do? Is there any way to transport her to the hospital?"

Frank had the biggest truck, and he was doubtful. "I can get through most things, but the way the wind is blowing this snow around, I'd be afraid I'd lose the road. And then ..." He shuddered, and in the ensuing silence, everyone completed the mental picture of a roadside delivery.

"John would definitely kill me," Frank decided. "I think Maddy's better off here. And by extension, so am I," he grinned. "Of course, Kelly and Drew could always help her snowshoe the five or so miles to the medical center."

The room erupted in a much-needed laugh.

"I agree with Frank," Liz replied. "Well, not about the snowshoeing, the part about Maddy being better off here. She seems to be comfortable in her space, which we've prepped with all of the supplies we can think of."

"And she finally got in touch with her doctor," Becky assured everyone. "He's on stand-by, and he gave John some good directives. He was bringing Anita up to speed when I left them."

"Anita will be a big help," Ed piped in, clearly proud of his wife. "Nothing throws her. Last year, when one of our horses ..."

"Let's save that story for another time," Frank interrupted his father. He turned back to the room with a slight grimace. "Suffice it to say, my mom will take good care of Maddy."

"She'll deliver that baby, tend to Maddy, and re-upholster the sofa while she's doing it," Ed agreed, turning Frank's much-needed comfort into something rather less-so.

Becky jumped back in, obviously familiar with Ed's unpredictable input. "Anyway, the doctor's just a phone call away. So that's good." She took in the crowded room and smiled a little. "Thank you all for being here. I know this isn't the party you expected, but it sure is nice to be surrounded by friends right now."

There were murmurs of support, and Grace realized that this was the first time that the group had seen Becky and Tank together since the wedding weekend started. She looked again from one to the other; could the other guests feel the stress reverberating between them?

"I know you all had a great brunch earlier," Becky continued, "but we have plenty of food for a second round. We'll work on having that ready in the next hour or so."

"Can we have Uncle Tank's party now?" Parker asked.

All eyes turned to the five-year-old, who had moved from the block fort he'd been building to his uncle-to-be by the puzzle table.

Tank colored slightly, and Grace was perfectly happy to see her brother sweat a little. He ruffled Parker's hair, looking around the room for help.

"Well, now that Tank's here, and Maddy seems to have the help she needs, we'll have that wedding after all, won't we?" Otis piped in cheerfully.

There was Grace's answer.

Silence met this optimistic prediction, and Grace could feel her friend powering down beside her. Pastor Rob looked like he might try to bridge the gap, when a throat cleared across the room.

"Becky and I are waiting until Maddy has her baby," Tank said firmly, fielding the question on everyone's minds. "When we know that they're okay, we'll decide about the wedding."

There was a murmur of disappointed assent as people turned to gauge Becky's response. She nodded, briefly returning Tank's gaze.

"I'm sorry, but I'm sure you understand that our priorities have shifted," she added.

Parker sighed with disappointment, and after a moment, Becky said, "You could probably still have your party, Parker." Apparently warming to the idea, despite Tank's obvious discomfort, or maybe because of it, she continued, "Why don't you use the parlor? Frank? Ed?" She turned to them. "How does that sound?"

They squirmed at the idea of having their bachelor party in such a feminine venue, but once again, it was Tank who surprised the room by responding.

"Great idea." He picked Parker up, threw him over his shoulder, and started toward the kitchen with his giggling burden. "I'd like to see what kind of party you planned for me, Buddy." He stopped and turned. "Blake, we need you, too."

Blake lit up at the invitation and hurried to join them.

"You're next, you know," Tank told him, nodding his head at Parker, who flailed happily down his back.

"I'm too big," Blake protested with a grin.

"Oh, Buddy," Tank laughed. "Challenge accepted."

Grace marveled at the side of Tank that the boys brought out in him. She wasn't sure she'd ever seen a playful Tank before, or at least not for a very long time. She also suspected that none of them would be seeing this light-heartedness unless Tank had made some headway with Becky.

"I'm gonna go dump this load in the snow, then I'm coming back for you," Tank growled. He looked up at the bemused crowd watching the show. "And the rest of you ... wedding planners ..." he eyed his buddies with a shake of his head, "party's in the parlor."

$$\mathcal{S}\,\mathcal{S}\,\mathcal{S}$$

Becky turned to Grace, her surprise evident. "Well."

Grace nodded. "He's trying."

There was a bit of commotion as most of the guests left to go to the front of the house, leaving the much larger, more comfortable room to those remaining. Christopher wisely stood his ground with Liz and her family, which, for the moment, included Drew. Alex was the last of the crew to leave.

Grace raised a brow as he approached her. "I'm surprised you weren't a part of this."

He smiled. "I can't wait to watch Tank field Frank and Ed's party maneuvers in front of his nephews." He took a hold of her hand and kissed her cheek. "I'll let you know how it goes."

"I look forward to it."

"Someone should probably invite John," Becky observed. "He could use the break. And he was definitely concerned about Blake and Parker's involvement, so ..."

Alex shifted, clearly not comfortable with the idea of knocking on the door of the birthing suite.

"You know what? I'll just text him." Becky smirked at Alex's obvious relief. "I'm sure he'll join you when he can."

"Sounds good," Alex replied, squeezing Grace's hand before following the others.

Grace turned to Becky. "I think the kitchen's free. Shall we?"

Saturday - 4:00 p.m.
Liz

Liz smiled at Kelly, curled up in the middle of the pillows on the opposite couch. Relieved that she'd packed extra clothes so that her daughter was now dry, Liz cringed at the memory of those first moments in the room she shared with Christopher.

Her daughter had looked around, wide-eyed. "You're sleeping in the same bed as Cam's ... as Dr. Harrison? Talk about moving fast, Mom." It was more disbelief than censure, but Liz, ever the conservative where intimacy was concerned, couldn't correct the impression fast enough. Of course, in doing so, she fumbled over her explanation and only sounded like she was covering up something she was desperately trying to lay bare.

Her daughter had glanced at her wryly while changing out of her wet clothes. "Mom, you kissed him within hours of meeting him. You're on a whole different timeline with this guy. You don't have to explain it to me, I'm just surprised."

Eventually, Liz had made her case, and Kelly's disbelief had turned into amusement.

"So my ultra-prudish mom ..." Liz had taken issue with that word, but it only made her daughter laugh, "is sleeping with a man ..." Liz had also taken issue with that phrase, and her daughter amended, "is sharing a bed with a man she's wildly attracted to, but would never sleep with, unless ..."

Liz had finally shut the conversation down, insisting that the group below was waiting for them, and Kelly had followed her out of the room, laughing all the way. Thankfully, plenty of distraction awaited them in the sunroom, and Kelly had quickly launched into their snowshoe adventure. Now, exhausted from their trek, having apparently laughed her way through most of that, as well, she was warm, dry, and fighting to stay awake.

"Why don't you close your eyes for a few minutes, Honey?" Liz suggested. "We'll catch up when you've had a chance to rest."

Kelly covered a yawn. "It was an early start to the day. And this guy," she nudged Drew's foot with hers, "was up even earlier, roasting." She yawned again. "I don't know how he does it." Her lids shuttered closed.

Liz glanced at Drew, who looked ready for his own nap but was doing a better job of fighting it. Poor guy could hardly curl up into the corner of the couch like her daughter could.

"Drew, you're welcome to rest in my room for a while. Unless you'd like to join the bachelor party," Liz offered with a smile.

"I'm fine here, Ms. Michaels."

"Well, I can't thank you enough for coming over with Kelly. Once she sets her mind on something, she can be pretty determined."

He shifted away from Kelly, stood and stretched. "She didn't really need me. She could easily have made it on her own." Moving to the recliner, he added, "I think I might just stretch out here for a few, if that's okay."

"Good idea," Liz agreed, noting how quickly he relaxed into the chair and closed his eyes.

She leaned into Christopher's side and looked into the fire. "I didn't realize how worried I was. Now that Kelly's here ..." She sighed, and he tightened his arm around her.

"You've had a busy morning," he replied, matching her quiet tone. "You haven't had a chance to think about anything else."

Liz fought her own battle with weariness. She was glad for the role she'd been able to play, but it had been more taxing and less relaxing than she'd budgeted for this weekend. Still, her daughter was safe, Maddy was in good hands, and Liz, herself, was nestled into Christopher's side for a few precious moments. She wasn't about to complain.

"I think Anita will be good for Maddy," she observed. "For all of Ed's terrifying commendation, she does exude a confidence that I'm sure will comfort the crew upstairs."

Christopher stroked her arm. "Think you can rest for a bit?"

Liz yawned. "And keep you from the bachelor party? Wouldn't dream of it."

She felt his quiet laugh.

"I'm good." He kissed the top of her head. "This is exactly where I want to be."

Liz sighed happily as she gazed into the fire. "Becky said she thinks we should get married today."

Apparently, she'd said that aloud, because her pillow stiffened into a firm wall that was less comfortable, but inviting in its own way.

"Did she?"

Liz laughed quietly, glad that Kelly and Drew both seemed to be sleeping, or at least safely tuned out.

Trying for lightness, she replied, "She thinks someone should get married. You know, keep the crowd happy."

Christopher's chest relaxed a little. "We could finish our respective semesters and have the summer together to work out the logistics."

Liz stilled. Was he serious? And thinking that far ahead? Sure, they'd teased about the possibilities ... Well, more than teased, but, really, hadn't there been enough surprises in the last twenty-four hours?

She turned to look up at him. The firelight reflected in his eyes for a moment before he turned his gaze to her. Everything inside of her rearranged itself at the look on his face.

"That was supposed to be a joke," she whispered.

In reply, he leaned down and kissed her. He made a compelling argument.

When he lifted his head, there was steeliness in his gaze. "Let's do it, Liz. Let's get married and figure the rest out later."

Stunned, she let out a small giggle. "That's crazy."

"I know." His gaze didn't waver.

"So, isn't that a bit of a red flag for you?"

He shifted so that he could see her more fully. "I've been careful and predictable my whole life."

"So have I." Liz tried to remain focused and calm. "It's served us well."

"It has. So I think the decision-makers in both of us have the capacity to cut through the nonsense and see that we've found something special, something worth being a little crazy for."

She looked into his beautiful brown eyes. "I'm ready to consider the possibilities, but ... today?"

Christopher laughed quietly. "When is it going to get any easier? We're never going to be able to date casually. Time isn't going to slow down for us, Liz."

That was certainly true.

"We talked almost daily for the last six weeks. We may know each other better for all of those conversations that weren't distracted by ..." he touched her cheek, allowing her to surmise where his mind had gone.

"Being in the same state?" Liz supplied, determined to bring him back.

"Something like that."

"So, we get married and I go back to Vermont and see you again, say, at spring break, and then maybe for the summer?" Liz couldn't believe the direction of the conversation, and how much she suddenly longed for him to convince her that getting married today was a really good idea.

Christopher smiled, tracing the line of her chin. "If the weather allows, I can drive up every weekend. I don't have classes on Fridays."

Her heart skipped a beat, which was actually fine, because it had been seriously over-working itself. "Okay ... and what about this summer? And more importantly, next fall?"

He looked into the fire and thought for a moment. "Can you come here for the summer? I'll re-visit the job offer I have in Vermont."

"That's still available?"

"My friend has been hounding me for years. If he even smells interest on my part, he'll make it happen."

"You would do that for me?"

He looked at her intently. "I would."

"And what about your farm?" When he'd all but proposed in December, he'd mentioned that the farm had been in the family for years. There was no mortgage payment, which meant Christopher had options, but would he just abandon it for most of the year?

"It'll be here."

"This is crazy," Liz said again, starting to imagine Christopher in her home in Vermont. She had invested well when she had the opportunity years earlier, and owned a sweet little spot with its own charm; a narrow blue-grey two-story situated on a fairly private lot, uncommon in Burlington. She could see Christopher there, grading his papers in the little dining nook. As long as Kelly was settled ...

Reality slammed back into her consciousness. *Kelly!* Her sweet daughter, sitting just a few feet away, hadn't figured into this unbelievable conversation. How had *that* happened? Kelly was always her first consideration. Liz was definitely losing ... something. She didn't know what it was, or if it was safe to let it go.

She turned back to Christopher and tilted her head toward her daughter, as though they suddenly had cause to be discreet.

He looked at Kelly and raised a brow. Liz followed his gaze.

Kelly eyed her mom with a sleepy smile. "Do it, Mom."

$$\mathcal{S} \, \mathcal{S} \, \mathcal{S}$$

A roar of laughter from the front of the house filtered back to the sunroom. Someone must have opened the door to the dining room from the kitchen at just the right moment, or else that particular party had really taken off.

Liz appreciated the brief distraction from the party planning in the sunroom. Had her daughter really just told her to get married?

She opened her mouth to speak but could only watch as Kelly rearranged herself in her pillow pile until she was more sitting than reclining. Newly propped, she glanced around the room, noted that Drew rested in the recliner, and with a small nod, looked back at Liz. The sleepiness was gone.

"Mom, you've been working so hard for so long, taking care of everybody around you. Can you think, for a minute, about what would make *you* happy?"

"Well, yes, but ..."

"I have never heard your voice as upbeat and positive as I've heard it when we've talked over the last couple of months." Here Kelly glanced at Christopher. "I'll admit, I was pretty freaked out when it started - and *how* it started - I mean, honestly," she rolled her eyes. "But you're light-hearted for the first time that I can remember. That has to mean something."

Christopher picked up her hand, but Liz couldn't take her eyes off of Kelly. Had the change in her life been so noticeable that her daughter had seen it, even across the miles?

"You've been carrying the load alone for a long time. I'd love to see you share it - and have a little fun in the process." Kelly hugged the pillow in her lap.

"You've been sharing it with me for a long time," Liz reminded her daughter. "We've been a good team."

Kelly smiled affectionately. "We have. But I think it's time for a different kind of teammate." She glanced again at Christopher, and Liz was moved by the acceptance and warmth in her eyes. He had to feel it, too.

"What do you say, Mr. Harrison? Will you make an honest woman of my mother?"

Liz gasped and Kelly continued with a giggle. "And do you promise to take really good care of her? Make sure she gets out skating regularly?"

Christopher's laugh rumbled beside her. "I do. It will be my pleasure."

At this point, Liz had to look at the man who was suggesting that they share their life together. The look of tenderness on his normally stoic face took her breath away. He took both of her hands in his.

"Liz Michaels, will you marry me?"

A sigh and a giggle from the other couch almost derailed her attention, but Liz held firm.

"Yes, Christopher Harrison, I think I will."

Saturday - 5:00 p.m.
Maddy

"I can't believe you got John to go down to the party," Maddy gasped after a particularly grinding contraction. "How did you do it?"

Anita dabbed Maddy's brow with a cool cloth. "I told him he needed a break, and when that didn't work, I assured him that his boys would keep my boys in line." She tilted her head. "He took off like a shot."

Maddy gritted her teeth and shifted, resting her eyes, and her body, for a precious, few moments. She drew a shaky breath. "I think these are coming faster."

"Yep," Anita replied matter-of-factly. "I imagine we will have that baby before too long."

Both terrified and encouraged by this assessment, Maddy gathered her energy for another contraction. "We need to get Burt out of here." Her dog paced purposefully behind Anita, ensuring that she didn't leave Maddy's side. It was a miracle that he didn't scare her current labor coach. "I don't think he's even been out since - well, it's been too long."

"John knows to bring his buddies up to get him." Anita said calmly, taking Maddy's hand. "You just breathe, now."

Maddy complied, and when the contraction ended, she knew with a strange and frightening certainty that it wouldn't be much longer. "He needs to come back *now*."

Anita nodded. "I'll text him."

Commotion in the living area, indicating that he had already arrived, had Anita pocketing her phone. Burt growled and stood in the doorway as he approached.

"It's okay, Buddy," John's voice preceded him.

Her husband appeared and immediately seemed to understand that something had changed. "Maddy?"

"Time to move the dog," Anita said evenly. "Now would be good."

Maddy barely processed John's response. She concentrated on breathing and vaguely heard his conversation with someone outside the room. The only thing she knew for sure at the end of her contraction was that Burt was still in the room growling at John and whomever he'd brought with him.

"Tank," Maddy gasped. "Get Tank."

She could now make out Frank's voice, and in her brief window of clarity, observed that Burt was having none of their cajoling to remove him. It would have been entertaining, under any other circumstances, to hear two grown men trying to negotiate with her giant wolfhound.

The apartment door closed as Frank, she supposed, went after Tank, and John tried to re-enter the bedroom.

"Don't even try," she warned as John hovered in the doorway, frustration and a healthy residual fear of her dog warring with his concern for her.

His subsequent effort to side-step her guard was met with a growl that none of them had ever heard before.

"Best wait for reinforcements," Anita observed. "Maddy needs you in one piece when you get in here."

The next contraction hit particularly hard, and Maddy forgot about her dog and clung to Anita's hand like a lifeline. When it was over, she gradually tuned in to the sound of more voices, too many voices, and the much closer rumble of Burt's intensifying growl. Why hadn't she insisted that they deal with this earlier? If the baby arrived while half a dozen men man-handled her dog in the next room, she'd never forgive her husband.

"Sounds like they moved the whole party up here," Anita said with a shake of her head. "Bunch of yahoos can't move a dog."

Maddy tried to smile, but fear for what Burt might be capable of if he were threatened - if *she* were threatened - effectively took the humor out of the situation. So did the fact that she was about to give birth. A little privacy would be nice.

"Just Tank," she whispered. "He needs a friend, not an army."

At that moment, John reappeared in the doorway, which Burt continued to block resolvedly. Maddy wasn't sure what frustrated her husband more - the dog in front of him or the unruly group behind him.

"Maddy," he said again, much more calmly than she expected. His voice soothed her, but Burt was unmoved.

"I'm okay," she whispered back. "He just needs ..." she fumbled as she tried to prop herself on her elbows.

"Just Tank," Anita clarified. "All those men are making him nervous."

Burt validated her comment with another fierce growl.

"And I will take care of my wife on my own terms," John growled back, thankfully, more to Burt than to Anita. He straightened to his full height and stared down the dog. Before Burt could decide how to respond, John pushed past him into the room.

Maddy looked on with wonder as Burt lay down in the doorway with a sigh. Soon after, Anita left the room, stepping over him like she was navigating a pile of laundry.

"Well done," Maddy whispered. John lowered beside her as the next contraction gained momentum. "I'm not sure I would even have attempted that."

John made an effort to slow his breathing, which was a really good idea for both of them.

"Breathe, Honey," he managed, gently brushing her hair back.

Vaguely processing Anita directing Burt's successful removal, Maddy clung to John's hand and let the next contraction roll over her.

$$\mathcal{S}\,\mathcal{S}\,\mathcal{S}$$

The effort to relax her body while their precious child fought its way into the world gave exhaustion a whole new meaning. At some point, Maddy realized that Burt was, indeed, gone, and the sound of his growling had been replaced by quiet instrumental music. John sat at her side, holding her hand, and just beyond him, Anita entered the room purposefully.

John squeezed Maddy's hand a little. "We're getting ready now, Honey. Anita and I have both spoken to the doctor and Liz has him on the phone right now. He's going to talk us through it."

Maddy managed a nod as the next contraction took all of her energy and attention. When it was over, she heard Becky respond to one of Anita's directives, and suddenly the room was bright with light.

Maddy closed her eyes and shifted obediently as pillows were rearranged behind her. Newly propped, she opened her eyes again and looked gratefully at her delivery crew.

"Okay," Anita said calmly, "after the next contraction, we're going to start thinking about this differently. Time to help this little one along."

Maddy's gratitude wavered as she bit back a groan. If she had not been helping her little one along this whole time, then her prenatal classes had been a bust.

The contraction hit and John gripped Maddy's hand.

"Jesus, we trust you to bring this baby safely to us. And keep Maddy strong and safe."

The softly-spoken prayer unleashed a surge of peace and determination, and Maddy offered her own silent prayer of thanks for the sister who prayed it, the husband who held her, and the baby team who would surely see it answered.

§ § §

Maddy took in the scene around her, dazedly trying to navigate the waves of euphoria and exhaustion that buffeted her. She smiled weakly as her baby team hustled around, making sure that she was warm, clean, and comfortable. The only person not moving was John, who stood just outside the door, staring into the bundle of blankets in his arms. Maddy's heart almost burst at the sight. That tiny, seemingly helpless child had fought valiantly through an unexpected home delivery, and John finally had his opportunity to carry the precious load. Maddy leaned back into the pillows in quiet awe.

"Alright, come on back in," Anita said briskly. "Mama needs some time with her baby."

John looked up and locked eyes with Maddy. He walked back into the room, cradling his precious bundle carefully. Sitting down on the bed beside her, he gently laid the baby in her arms.

"She's perfect," Maddy whispered, feeling like she might start crying and never stop.

"She is," John agreed. "And you were amazing. So brave." He kissed her temple. "How are you feeling?"

"I hardly know," Maddy replied. "Relieved, I suppose, beyond anything. How can I be anything but wonderful, when she's here, safe and sound?"

John hummed his agreement. "Straight up miracle."

"And what a team," Maddy marveled, leaning into him. "You all knew just what to do." She gently stroked her daughter's tiny cheek, the baby turning toward her touch.

"Anita should consider going into business as a midwife," John replied. "She ran the show and we all just followed her lead."

"We were too afraid not to," Becky said, re-entering the room. "I'm done cleaning up. Let me see that baby."

Maddy laughed and her insides seized up. "Oh, wow, *ow* ..."

John jumped beside her. "Are you okay? What can I do?"

"It's perfectly natural," Anita announced, following Becky in. "Your insides are just reorganizing themselves after your ordeal. It will feel like contractions, only not as bad, and they'll get less painful."

Maddy settled back against John as the pain ebbed. She'd kind of hoped she was done with the contraction bit, but was glad that, once again, Anita seemed able to explain what was going on.

Becky approached the bed. "Is she a keeper?"

John laughed quietly. "Yeah. Take a look."

Becky leaned in and caught her breath a little. "She's perfect. Good work, you two." She laid her hand on the blanket gently and then pulled back. "I do expect to hold her later, but I'll let you all bond right now."

Maddy looked up at her gratefully. "Thank you for all of your help." She paused and thought for a moment. "Did we really laugh in the middle of all this?" The last hour was a little blurry, but she seemed to remember Becky trying to keep things light.

"Of course, we did," her sister replied, her light tone belying the tears in her eyes. She backed away quickly. "Should I go get the boys and send them up?"

"That would be great," John and Maddy replied together.

Becky sighed dramatically. "Please. Will you two ever stop?" She headed for the door. "Anita, can I get you anything? Or are you about ready for a break from this needy crew?"

Anita laughed. "I'll take a break when you get back."

"Good idea," Becky nodded. "I'll be back soon with a couple of brothers."

§ § §

Nestled in John's arms as they marveled at their tiny daughter, Maddy willed her body to settle down so she could absorb the miracle. It seemed every part of her demanded attention; some parts were obviously preparing in earnest for the next phase, while others were working hard to reclaim the status quo. Her entire lower half shook uncontrollably.

"You're cold," John said, holding her more tightly.

"I don't really feel cold, I just can't stop shaking," she replied, watching her legs quake under the blankets with more fascination than concern.

Anita buzzed through, once again anticipating Maddy's needs as she tucked a warm blanket around her legs.

"Your body's been through a trauma," she explained, although they were all fairly well aware of the fact. "It'll settle down in a bit." She patted the blanket in place and then stood with her hands on her hips, apparently ready to go save the world in another part of the house.

"Thank you, Anita." Maddy closed her eyes with a happy sigh as warmth spread throughout her lower body. She willed her eyes to open again. "How can we ever thank you for all that you've done for us?"

Anita brushed off the thanks with a wave of her hand. "Handy that you have a dryer up here. I just tossed this in to warm it up."

Maddy smiled; as if blanket-warming were the extent of Anita's efforts. "I don't know how we could have done any of this without you." She shifted her baby; her body and her child's seemed to be communicating that it was time to figure out the nursing thing.

"Oh, you would've done just fine," Anita said, matter-of-factly. "But an extra set of hands never hurts." She nodded at the baby. "I think she's hungry."

Maddy nodded, determined to revisit thanking her friend when she was a little more rested. "I thought we'd introduce her to the boys, first."

"Probably a good idea," Anita replied. "Sounds like they've just arrived."

"Slow down, guys," Becky called unsuccessfully as the brothers made tracks to the bedroom door.

Blake arrived first and paused; Parker didn't and ran smack into his back. They both yelped, and John got up to untangle them.

"Okay, guys, take it easy. Let's wash up, first."

The boys craned their heads to see into the room as their dad walked them around the corner to the bathroom. A few minutes of giggling and splashing accomplished the task, and they appeared in the door a moment later.

John stood with a hand on each of their shoulders. "We need to be nice and quiet now, okay? Let's go meet your sister."

"We got a sister?" Parker shrieked, ignoring the directive.

John slowed their momentum as he walked with them into the room. "Easy now. Stand here by the bed and you can say hello."

The boys managed to stand fairly still as Maddy turned their sister toward them and pulled back the blanket.

Blake looked serious and very relieved. "Wow," he simply said.

"Let me see!" Parker pushed around his brother's shoulder.

"She's so small," Blake observed.

"Her face is scrunchy," Parker giggled.

Blake laughed with his brother, then looked apologetically at Maddy. Her heart squeezed at the look of protective concern on his young face.

"It is a little scrunchy," she agreed, trying not to grimace at the leftover contraction ebbing through her. "I imagine she'll fill out and have chubby baby cheeks before long."

Parker giggled again. "Can I touch it?"

"Her," John corrected him. "Gently, now."

Blake patted the blanket tentatively while Parker went straight for his sister's face. John guided his hand and gentled the contact.

"What's her name?" Blake asked.

"We're still deciding," John replied.

"Can I pick?" asked Parker. "How 'bout Buttercup?"

Maddy smiled and John covered a laugh with a quiet cough.

"We've already narrowed it down to two names, remember? Now we just have to see which one fits."

Parker rolled his eyes. "Those are boring."

John ruffled his hair. "Well, we're going to give it some more thought. We've got time."

"Ichabod?"

Blake giggled.

"Remember from that one book?" Parker continued. "It's a good name."

"But it's a girl," Blake countered, as though that was the most compelling argument against the alarming suggestion.

"Yeah, but it's so funny," Parker giggled back.

Blake joined him. "We'd have to call her Ichabella," he decided, uncharacteristically committing to the silly conversation. Parker fell on the bed laughing.

Maddy shifted her legs, laughing along with them. John pulled Parker off the bed and began to herd them back out of the room.

"Ichabella is hungry right now, so let's let Maddy-mom feed her while we go share the good news."

The boys erupted in a new fit of laughter, making the exodus a little more complicated. John turned back in the doorway.

"I'll be back up soon."

Maddy blew them a kiss, and Dr. Anita materialized a moment later.

"Are you ready to nurse your little one?"

"Oh, yes," Maddy replied, allowing Anita to help her arrange her gown and blankets.

"Hopefully, you'll have a bit of peace and quiet. This is important bonding time." Apparently convinced that Maddy and her daughter could navigate the mysteries of nursing alone, she turned to leave. "Becky's your new doorkeeper. She knows that John's the only one allowed in for a while."

Maddy smiled. "I hope you can rest. You must be exhausted."

Anita smiled with determination. "I'm going to head down and see how badly they've trashed my nice clean kitchen, though I suppose Grace and Liz have got things under control."

"Oh, Liz!" How had Maddy forgotten about her other labor angel? "Did she get to see the baby?"

"She sure did. She helped me give the little one her first bath," Anita replied, her voice softening.

"Wow, okay, I'm glad," Maddy replied, trying to sort out who was doing what around the actual birth. It was a bit of a blur and would undoubtedly remain so.

That was probably okay.

Anita left the room, promising to check in later, and Maddy settled into her throne of pillows with a happy sigh. She looked at her daughter in wonder, unable to comprehend the miracle in her arms.

Saturday - 6:00 p.m.
Becky

"Becky?"

She paused her tidying up of the penthouse kitchen. Had Maddy just called her? Becky hustled toward the bedroom and stopped at the door.

"There you are. Why aren't you in here with me? With us?" Maddy corrected herself with an unearthly smile.

Becky swallowed at the sheer beauty of it.

"I was trying to give you that 'peace and quiet' that Anita was talking about," she explained. "It was killing me, but I've learned over the last few hours to do whatever Anita says."

Maddy laughed a little. "Compliant Becky? I don't think I want to live in that universe."

Becky's grimace turned into a smile as she entered the room. "Me neither. But every once in a while it serves." She sat down on the side of the bed and marveled at the bundle in her sister's arms. "I can't believe you had - have - your beautiful baby." She sighed as Maddy shifted her little girl to her shoulder and gently patted her back. "Way to steal my show."

Maddy laughed. "Yeah, sorry about that." She leaned her cheek against her daughter with a sigh. "Okay, not really."

"Didn't think so." Becky stroked the tiny back, unable to fully comprehend what she'd just helped to bring about.

Maddy sobered and focused on her sister. "So, what's happening with you and Tank?"

"Well, that whole compliant Becky thing can only go so far if I'm going to manage him." She slid her eyes to meet Maddy's and they shared a grin.

"Oh, Becky, I knew you were going to be okay. I just knew you would work it out! You're so good for each other."

A delicate, but decisive burp erupted from somewhere in the middle of Maddy's bundle, and they laughed.

"Well, if that isn't an appropriate response, I don't know what is," Becky observed. "You and your scary uncle will get along just fine."

Maddy shifted her daughter to continue to nurse her. "So what now? When will you get married? Am I still in the wedding? And when can I go to the bathroom?"

Becky laughed, glad that her sister was recovering somewhat from her wonderful trauma. "Well, that last question is probably the most important, but I don't have any directives from Anita, so I'm not really sure ..."

Both women stilled momentarily at the idea of taking Maddy's personal needs into their own hands. Becky considered the baby, who had lost interest in feeding and was dozing peacefully in her mother's arms.

"Okay, here's what we're going to do. We're going to put that baby in that beautiful cradle John made for her, and I'm going to walk you into the bathroom." She stood to prepare for the daunting task. "Ready?"

Maddy nodded, significantly motivated to address the problem. She re-swaddled her baby and held her out. "Can you put her in her bed?"

Becky swallowed. "Of course. I would love to."

She picked up her niece and pulled her close, delighting in the smell of her soft baby head. She kissed it gently, suddenly overwhelmed by the reality of the new life in her arms. Not sure how to process all of the mind-blowing emotions, Becky decided it was best to stick with the plan of helping her sister into the bathroom. She tucked the baby carefully into her crib next to the bed, knowing she'd have time to bond when no one would see her cry.

Maddy slid her legs over the side of the mattress, and Becky jumped in front of her.

"Oh, no you don't. We're taking this slowly. If something happens to you, Anita will kill me!"

Maddy laughed. "Well, we can't have that. We need our bride. Here, give me a hand."

Becky gently pulled her sister to her feet and walked her to the bathroom. "Be careful. I have no qualms about coming in there after you."

Maddy giggled again and held her stomach. "Ow, and yes doctor. Stay close."

"Of course." Becky leaned against the wall as her sister closed the door. "You okay?"

"I'm good," came the tentative reply.

"So, guess what happened while you've been up here having your own party? Christopher officially proposed to Liz."

She heard a gasp that she hoped was related to the news and not to whatever was happening within. Maybe this wasn't exactly through-the-bathroom-door conversation.

"Sorry, that could have waited. You okay?"

A moment's hesitation almost had Becky barging in.

"Christopher, that's his name. I'm so happy for them."

Becky breathed a sigh of relief. "Who knows? Maybe they'll get married today - keep the crowd happy."

Another gasp, and Becky really began to question her judgment. "Okay, seriously, do you need me in there?"

"No, no, I'm good. It's not like this is new territory, it's just ... ow! Wait, okay. No, I'm good. I'll be ... hang on."

Becky was sure that she'd be answering to Anita for this particular lapse in judgment. The idea was slightly terrifying.

"Maddy, just let me help," she began, when a flush signaled at least some success on the other side of the door. A few moments later, the water was running into the sink, and Becky opened the door. "Are you okay?"

Her sister was calmly washing her hands and looked over her shoulder, a slightly puzzled look on her face. "Do you really think they'll get married? Here? Today?"

"Honestly, I don't really know. We can't rule it out. Not this weekend."

Becky took Maddy's hand and walked her back into her bedroom. "Liz filled me in once the baby had safely arrived. I pretty much suggested it – I told her they should get married when we talked earlier today. Apparently, my opinion carries some weight," she concluded airily.

She was kidding, of course; she wasn't used to being taken seriously. Interesting, how finally taking herself seriously seemed to play out in her relationships. The thought warmed her heart a little, until she considered the trouble her weighty opinion could cause for Liz and Christopher. While it was terribly romantic for them to get married this weekend, it wasn't terribly practical. Had she overstepped?

While Becky managed her inner turmoil, Maddy sat down on the bed, leaned over the crib, and stared at her baby. Her look of bemused joy was something to behold.

She looked up with a happy sigh. "Well, I think they should do it. As long as it doesn't keep you and Tank from getting married," she qualified. "How does that work?"

"Well," Becky sat on the bed next to her sister and watched the miracle baby for a moment. "I'm not getting married until you can stand next to me, so ..."

Maddy met her gaze thoughtfully, and then with a determined and growing smile.

"How does a Sunday wedding sound?"

ʃ ʃ ʃ

A lively crowd milled around the kitchen, and Becky wove her way through the bodies with a surreal kind of peace. She was especially relieved to see Anita sitting and eating, and not scrubbing the kitchen floor like she half-expected. She smiled, thinking of John returning to his wife with a huge plate of food that she suspected Maddy wouldn't begin to touch. Her sister was in very good hands.

"Becky, here you are," Liz gave her a hug. "How's our mama? And how are you?"

"I'm fine - she's great," Becky replied, settling onto a bar stool and breathing in the comforting aroma of something fresh-baked. "I'll definitely need some of whatever that is." She considered the kitchen and the wonderful array of food. "This is amazing. Thank you for pulling it all together."

Liz waved a hand. "It's the least we can do, and really, Grace has been running the show."

Becky helped herself to leftover barbecue and some of Anita's fruit salad. "Well, we sure invited the right people to this wedding-turned-baby celebration. What's baking?"

"Grace made rolls. They smell heavenly, don't they?"

Becky smiled in agreement, appreciating the normalcy of people eating good food, laughing and enjoying each other's company. She couldn't help but glance into the sunroom to see if the groom was out there. Well, *her* designated groom, anyway.

Grace buzzed in from the dining room. "There's more food in there," she informed Becky, nodding back toward the door she had just used. "It's such a beautiful set-up, but everyone keeps coming back in here to eat."

Becky and Liz shared a glance. They'd had a lot of interesting conversations in the kitchen when Liz was a guest in December.

"Yeah, that pretty much seems to be the way it works," Becky agreed. "How are you doing? And thank you for taking over here."

Grace rinsed a plate. "This is what I know. I'm happy to do it." She turned off the water and wiped her hands on a towel. "I can't wait to see the baby. Is she so beautiful?"

"Of course," Becky replied.

"Not *so* beautiful," Parker piped in. "She's wrinkly."

"I'm betting that she looks just like our Maddy," Otis offered proudly.

Parker giggled. "No way!" He turned and yelled into the family room. "Hey Blake!"

"No yelling," Becky reminded him. "And just wait; your sister is gonna be a heartbreaker."

Parker turned a confused look on her. "Why?"

A quiet chuckle rippled through the room, and Becky tried to keep a relatively straight face. "I just mean that she'll grow into her wrinkles and be a cute baby. You'll see."

Parker giggled and took off for the sunroom.

"No running," she called half-heartedly as he dodged the adults like a tiny running back.

"How's our new mama?" Anita asked, tuning in to the conversation. "Is she getting a chance to sleep, yet?"

"Not yet. I'm sure John will see to that," Becky replied, wondering, again, where the linebacker was.

Rob walked into the room, looking for seconds and news. "So, we have our baby," he said to Becky. "I trust you'll let me know when I can go up and see the family?"

Apparently, her gatekeeper responsibilities followed her down into the kitchen.

"She needs her rest," Anita piped in. "I think we should wait until morning, at least."

"That's probably a good idea," Becky agreed. "I'm sure they'll text if they're up for company."

"Sounds good," Rob replied, giving Burt plenty of room when the wolfhound growled.

Becky looked over to see Maddy's dog planted in front of the door to the stairway. Somebody was taking his gatekeeper responsibilities very seriously.

"He really is harmless," she pointed out. "Well, I'm pretty sure, anyway. No telling what he's making of being separated from Maddy right now."

She looked at the dog with new concern, but then relaxed a little when she saw him do the same, having settled back onto the floor after the danger of the wandering minister had passed.

Becky turned back to Rob. "How is your family doing in this storm without you? And is your son feeling better?"

"Yes, he is," Rob assured her. "And Rachel's a tough cookie. If I were home, I'd likely be hiding behind her, anyway."

Another laugh circled the room at the thought of their fearless pastor hiding behind his tiny-ish wife.

"Who made the ribs? They're amazing," Kelly chimed in as she and Drew made their way into the kitchen. "He wants seconds but he won't ask." She nodded at him and laughed when he scowled down at her. "I know you do. I'd have more if I could fit anymore. I'm stuffed." She walked over and draped an arm around her mom.

"There are plenty of ribs. Becky made them," Liz said.

"Really?"

Becky shrugged off Kelly's surprise. Most people didn't expect her to be so proficient in the kitchen. "It's not a hard recipe - just takes time."

"Well, I'd love to have it," Kelly replied cheerfully. "How's the baby doing?"

"She's busy being beautiful and adored," Becky sighed.

"Just like me," Frank responded from the fridge.

Anita rolled her eyes. "You're such a child. Still."

Frank laughed, walked over, and kissed his mother's head. "It's your fault, Ma. You're the one who spoiled me - adoring me all these years."

Anita leaned away from his kiss and swatted his arm, 'though there was no hiding the affection in her eyes. "Somebody had to do it. Where's your father?"

" 'Watching' the game. Looking very comfy in the recliner with his eyes decidedly more closed than open."

"Figures. Did he eat?"

"Yep. I'm surprised there are any ribs left for Kelly."

Becky smiled as the conversation flowed throughout the room. She looked down at her plate, but found she had no appetite for the delicious spread in front of her. *Gotta be Tank's fault.* Glancing around the kitchen, she caught Grace's eye and raised a brow.

Apparently on the same wavelength, she nodded toward the door to the porch. Becky followed her gaze. Tank was outside in the storm? She turned back to Grace, who nodded. Becky picked up her plate and walked over to the fridge. Grace joined her.

"Why is he outside?" Becky whispered.

"I think the crowd was getting to him," Grace said quietly. "He was happy about the baby news and all. I wish you could have seen his smile." She shook her head in a kind of wonder. "Anyway, Mom and Dad wouldn't leave him alone, and I guess he figured they wouldn't follow him into the snow."

Becky tilted her head. "I, however, have no such reservation."

Grace's relief was evident. "You should eat first."

"I know. But I'm a little preoccupied."

"Let me cover that for you," Grace offered. "Can you sneak out the front?"

"My room has outside access. I'm good."

"Well, good luck," Grace hugged her.

"We've had some interesting moments in snowstorms." Becky embraced the idea that was blossoming. "I think I'm going to go find me a snow monster."

§ § §

Becky stepped into the storm and shivered down to her toes. *Figures, Tank prefers this to socializing.*

Following the porch around to the beach side, she noticed no other tracks. Not surprisingly, Tank had used the front door.

She carefully navigated the steps, the blowing snow and overall darkness making it almost impossible to see. A few steps onto the beach, she made out a mountain of a shape ahead. It moved and turned when she called out to him. It took three yells, but he eventually heard her.

"Hey," she sort of hollered.

"Hey," he rumbled back. He took her in his arms, then stilled. "Is this okay?"

"No," Becky replied. "I need you to lie down in the snow."

His arms remained frozen around her, then tightened. "No."

"I'm serious, Tank."

His hold loosened and he took a step back. "You okay?" He probably thought she'd lost it after helping Maddy deliver her baby.

"I'm good. Can you just trust me?"

She could barely make out his head shaking as he lowered himself to the ground. He sat, resting his elbows on his knees, and then reached up a hand. She took it, and with a not-so-subtle yank, he pulled her down on top of him as he fell back in the snow.

Becky yelped, caught her breath, and then took a moment to nestle on top of him. So he anticipated her plan; that was okay. He couldn't possibly have forgotten that he'd poured his heart out to her in a snowstorm a year earlier, only she'd been the one trapped beneath him. She smiled at the memory of Parker's snow monster chasing her down and then transforming into a very rare, vulnerable Tank. They seemed to be coming full circle.

My turn.

She took his face in her mittened hands. "I'm glad you cared enough to stay with Jimmy."

Tank exhaled; she could feel his body relax beneath her.

"It was the right thing to do, even though the timing was terrible." It was awkward to half-yell this important conversation, but she was determined to have it.

Tank blinked the snow out of his eyes and nodded.

"And I'm glad you have closure with Alicia." She raised a brow and he raised one back. She smacked him with her mitten. "What does that mean?"

"I told you we were done and I meant it. I was just letting you talk."

She narrowed her eyes at him. "This is not very satisfying."

"Sorry."

"Yeah, right."

Becky pushed herself back so there was more distance between them. She needed him to pay attention to this part.

"But *I* am."

"You're sorry?"

"Yes. I was so quick to tell you that when I saw your picture on TV I refused to give up on you, on us, and it took me, like, half an hour to write you off." She sighed. "I'm sorry. I can do better. I *will* do better."

"I will, too," Tank rubbed his cold glove along her cheek.

Becky swallowed. "I want to make us work. I know it will be difficult sometimes. I won't quit so easily next time."

She was just about to brush the snowflakes off his cheek when he tightened his hold and rolled her over. She gasped as her waist-length ski jacket left her yoga-pants-clad lower half exposed to the cold snow.

That wasn't part of the plan.

"Oh, we can make this work," was his determined reply.

She shoved against his chest. "You jerk! Get off me! It's cold!"

"I know."

She shivered. "You're the worst."

He hovered closer. "But I'll keep you warm."

She pushed his face away. "We're not there, yet. This is going to take both of us. We have to work on our communication. *You* have to communicate," she said with feeling.

He kissed her soundly then. It was less of romance and more of relief, but it was a kiss of commitment and happiness and Becky rather enjoyed it, cold as she was.

He pulled back. "So you'll marry me?"

Becky considered her infuriating fiancé. "I'll marry you, Tank."

"You're really ready for this?"

She was increasingly unable to think of anything else. However, there was no point in giving him the satisfaction of knowing he had that effect on her.

"Yes, Tank. I'm ready," she replied evenly.

"How soon?" Her gentle and patient fiancé cut to the chase, as expected.

"Not today."

"What? The baby's here. Maddy's fine."

Becky couldn't help a laugh. "Seriously, Tank. 'Fine' is relative. She just gave birth! And she's my matron of honor; she needs a little time so she can literally stand up for me."

"We'll get married in their apartment," he proposed.

"We'll get married tomorrow. *If* Maddy can make it downstairs, and *if* we can hold on to our pastor that long."

Tank sighed and flopped over on his back in the snow. Becky followed, climbing on top of him and making use of his significant cold-blocking presence. She grinned down into his face.

"Don't be a baby. It's not like we really thought it would happen today."

"You can't tell me you're ready to be my wife and then expect me to be okay with waiting an hour, much less a whole day."

"You made me wait all week, Tank."

He sighed again and then clamped her in his arms. "I'm gonna spend the next twenty-four hours making you regret this."

"Regret marrying you?"

"Regret waiting."

Intrigued, Becky leaned down and kissed him. It was less of relief and more of romance.

"I can hardly wait."

Saturday - 7:00 p.m.
Grace

Grace nestled next to Alex on the couch, tired but happy after the successful feeding of, and subsequent cleanup after, the snowbound wedding party. She was looking forward to enjoying some calm after the storm and couldn't think of a better place to do it than tucked into her husband's side.

The company, however, was a bit daunting.

She glanced at her parents, who sat side-by-side in the recliners as though reigning over the other inhabitants of the sunroom. She fought an eye roll and looked over at Tank, who took up way too much of the opposite couch. He'd shoved all of the pillows to the far side and sprawled in his corner like there wasn't a houseful of people who might also like to relax after the long, eventful day they'd shared. It could be argued that he deserved a little slack since his wedding was postponed. She looked more closely to see if she could discern any clues about his talk with Becky. If anything, there was a spark of mischief in his eyes as he argued with Alex about the reffing flaws in the college basketball game playing quietly on the television. It both encouraged and concerned her.

Becky's voice carried into the room as she laughed with Liz and Kelly, Christopher and Drew, who were sitting at the table in the kitchen. Tank's eyes followed her as she entered the sunroom, clearly appreciating how she sported her skinny jeans and chunky grey sweater. Grace smiled at the thought of what might have happened out in the snow to necessitate a wardrobe change.

Becky stopped to talk with Rob, who stood near the fireplace watching Frank play some sort of card game on the floor with the boys. Rob listened attentively as Becky informed him that it was a good time to visit the baby and family upstairs. He nodded and headed out of the room.

"Oh, and use the front staircase," she called after him. "You'll have to unlatch the gate, or just climb over it. And don't make eye contact with Burt; you don't want him guessing your plans."

Rob laughed. "Thanks for the warning."

Becky turned again, her gaze resting briefly on Otis and Ed playing chess at the game table before falling on the recliner-couch set. Grace could see her bracing herself as she considered the seating options. She walked over and stood in front of Tank, whose smile deepened as she neared. He patted the cushion next to him.

"Nice," Becky said, ignoring his invitation and leaning over to relocate the pillows.

She grabbed an armful and dumped them all in Tank's lap. He immediately tossed them back, with more force than was strictly necessary to arrange decorative pillows. Predictably, one skipped over the top of the couch and landed in Blake and Parker's game.

"Hey!" Parker, Blake, and possibly Frank yelled.

Tank smirked unapologetically. Becky leaned over the couch to assess the damage.

"Sorry boys, it's your Uncle Tank's fault. Why don't you come over and make him pay for ruining your game?"

Tank reached an arm around Becky's waist and pulled her onto his lap. "Come and get me, guys," he called over her shoulder, his protective shield rolling her eyes and preparing for battle.

Wisely sensing her pending resistance - to him, and not his opponents - Tank clamped her more tightly, ducking into the couch as the pillow came sailing back through the air. It hit Becky squarely in the head, the velocity of the missile suggesting that neither of the boys had thrown it.

Becky launched herself into a full-scale escape attempt while Grace grabbed the pillow, assuming the necessary role of grown-up amidst the chaos. Laughing, she glanced at her parents, whose disapproval was palpable. They'd obviously not gotten the memo that Tank and Becky had worked things out.

Tank's room-rattling "Oof!" marked Becky's successful escape, aided by what was likely a well-placed elbow to his ribs, and the boys, peeking over the couch, jumped up and cheered.

Tank rubbed his side with a grin while Becky caught her breath with a scowl. Surprisingly, she turned to Grace's parents and invited their opinion on the debacle.

"So, any idea when your son might grow up?"

The room stilled at her inquiry, though Tank's grin only slightly abated. There was a sparkle in his eyes as he watched her take their folks on, even at his own expense. Grace could hardly imagine their response. Even Alex stiffened beside her.

Her father, of course, spoke first. "I'm not accustomed to seeing him behave this way. I would imagine you'd be in a better position to explain it."

A beat passed and her mother added, "I'm not accustomed to seeing him at all."

I wonder why? Grace sighed, saddened and embarrassed. What a time for them to force a confrontation. Considering how to intervene, she glanced at Becky to see the damage they'd inflicted.

She was calm and cool; it would probably take a lot to rattle her after the day she'd had. Becky simply nodded and sat down by Tank. The pillow pile placed her at an odd angle, but she embraced her position with dignity and looked up at her fiancé.

"Well, Mr. Kimball? Care to weigh in? Whose fault are you, anyway?"

Tank looked down at her with unmasked affection. "My own," he admitted freely. "But you've made me a better person, Ms. Jacobs. There's no doubt about it."

"Your parents suggest otherwise."

"They're wrong." His voice was determined and the rest of the room remained silent, waiting. He turned to them.

"Dad, Mom, Becky is an amazing, kind and generous woman and I'm lucky to have her in my life. I'll be luckier when she finally marries me." He slid her a pointed look before turning back to face them. "I need you to get on board with this marriage, or it's probably best that you leave."

Grace was stunned. She'd never heard anyone take on her father so ... point blank, much less the son he adored.

Her father sputtered and her mother looked a little baffled.

"We can't leave in this storm!"

Tank sighed, directing a look at her. "You know what I mean, Mom. This has gone on long enough." He pulled Becky in closer and continued. "She has put up with your disdain for a year, now. Enough. Please."

Grace inwardly applauded his brave confrontation and considered her own approach to getting her parents to approve of Alex. She began to wish she'd been more direct and wondered if she'd further regret not having been honest with them early on.

"We just want what's best for you, for both of you." Her father had the decency to include Grace, but she wondered at his motivation.

"And we've found it. Both of us," Tank replied. "Why can't you be happy?" He looked over at Alex and nodded. "You couldn't ask for a better man for Grace, especially after all that she's been through."

"I could ask for a man in a better position to take care of her."

If it was possible for the room to get any more quiet, it did. Grace met Tank's gaze a moment before he ... laughed?

"You're kidding, right?"

Tank was genuinely amused, and Becky seemed to be covering her own smile. In the corner, Frank cleared his throat and knelt back down, quietly directing John's sons' attention away from the melee.

Beside her, Alex shifted slightly and rubbed her arm. "I can assure you, Mr. and Mrs. Kimball, that Grace is fully able to take care of herself. She's a competent, no, a very successful businesswoman. You should be proud of her."

"We are," her father conceded without conviction. "It may not be what we envisioned for her, but she's making a reasonable go of it."

Alex stiffened and Grace knew he prepared for battle. Across from her, Tank's look of amusement had faded. Grace drew in a breath, hardly knowing how, or when, to intervene.

"She built her business from the ground up in less than two years. The people of Clairmont have fully embraced her, and she provides a valuable service to them," Alex said calmly, though his voice had adopted the steel that likely caused his business associates to stop and listen to what he had to say.

"Coffee," her father grumbled.

"Yes, coffee, and a place to gather and build community. It's a fine business with an expanding market. Grace is finding exciting ways to connect with people."

She was touched by his defense of her, especially in the face of her parents' lack of support. Alex had always believed in her and in the coffee shop. That meant more than she could say.

"No offense, Grace," her father said, fully bent on causing offense, "but it's the whole sports bar thing Tank designed that's the big draw. You've done a nice job, but you couldn't have done it without him."

Tank laughed outright at this, looking between his parents and her. She raised a hand to keep him from jumping in.

"You're right, Dad," Grace said. "I could never have opened my shop without Tank's help. He's been a huge financial support from the beginning."

Her father nodded, apparently happy to have one of his points land.

Tank had held his peace long enough. "I was happy to help her get started, but she hasn't needed me since."

Grace watched her father turn to his son.

"Of course she has. That sports area is brilliant. You can't tell me she came up with that on her own."

Marveling at her father's complete lack of faith in her, she fought the rising panic that growing up with his constant devaluation caused. She could only watch as the truth came out, hardly regretting the humbling he was about to receive.

Tank looked at Grace with some confusion, and then back to their father. "I don't doubt that she could have, but it wasn't my idea. Alex came up with that."

Her father turned slowly to Grace. "The coffee server?"

Tank snorted a laugh. "Since when does he serve coffee?"

Grace looked up at Alex, who was rubbing his jaw and covering a smile. "Yeah, I wish. Grace won't let me behind the counter."

"You were behind the counter yesterday," her father insisted.

"No," Tank and Becky objected simultaneously, and Grace almost laughed.

Tank turned back to his dad. "Alex gave Grace the direction for the sports cafe idea, and though Grace ran with it, he's been helping her the whole way. They make a great team."

"Well, then perhaps she should give him a raise," her father muttered.

Tank stilled, considering his father, then swung his gaze back toward Grace. "What am I missing?"

Grace squirmed a little. "I haven't been completely clear about Alex's work."

Tank glanced between them again. "Why?"

"We were hoping they'd want to know him based on who he is, not what he does."

"What does your husband do?"

"Alex, Dad. His name is Alex, and he can answer for himself."

Her father glared as Alex stood.

"With all due respect, sir, I don't owe you an explanation. I can, however, assure you that I'll honor my vow to love and care for your daughter."

Grace stood and held his hand, and he nodded at her before continuing. "I'll do that in the best way I can, whether that's giving her ideas for her business ..."

"Or buying her an island with a coffee plantation on it," Becky finished, standing herself. "I'm sorry for interrupting, Alex, Grace, but I can't listen to this anymore." She walked toward the kitchen and Tank rose to follow, shaking his head.

Grace's father stood, as well. "An island? What is she talking about?"

"Becky, Dad. Her name is Becky."

He glanced at Grace, his bullying posture beginning to crumble a bit.

Beside her, Alex maintained his carefully relaxed stance, although Grace could feel the energy thrumming through him.

"Grace is doing just fine on her own, but she can depend on me for financial support," he wrapped an arm around her, "of any kind."

"How? You come from old money or something?"

Grace caught her father's first flicker of genuine interest, and was repelled by his ever-present regard for wealth. There was so much she wanted to say, but she didn't trust herself to speak. She willed patience for Alex, even as she longed for someone to finally put her father in his place.

Alex rubbed her arm and considered his father-in-law for a long moment. Then he simply said, "I trouble-shoot, primarily for manufacturing firms. They call me in to analyze their management, finances, and operations. I make suggestions and help them get on the right track." He paused. "My services are not inexpensive, but I have a record of getting the job done. My client list is extensive."

Her father considered him with an increasingly humble interest that Grace had never seen before. It was a few moments before he managed, "You were the one they brought in to Goldhearst."

"I was."

"Which is why you knew about their success."

"Yes."

Her father cleared his throat. "And were largely responsible for it."

"It was a team effort."

Grace watched her father swallow the last of his pride.

"That was fine work." His shoulders slumped noticeably as he looked at her. "Why didn't you tell us?"

She sighed. "You were so determined to dislike Alex for who he wasn't, you never asked me who he was."

Saturday - 8:00 p.m.
Liz

Liz looked up as Becky and Tank entered the room. The energy in the sunroom had changed, and while they couldn't hear all the details, they had felt it in the kitchen. She raised a brow, figuring it wasn't likely any of her business, but knowing Becky would fill her in as necessary.

Becky deflected. "So, how's the party going in here?"

Liz watched Tank walk over to the fridge and take out a water bottle. He looked frustrated, and from the bits of conversation she had overheard, she knew it wasn't with Becky.

"Oh, we're just trying to get Mom and Christopher to get married," Kelly replied. "*Tonight*," she added with a grin. "You're good with that, right, Becky?"

Becky smiled big, happily embracing the direction of the conversation. "Am I good with that? I suggested it!"

Liz felt Christopher pick up her hand, and she turned to him. "Who's getting married?"

The question from the general vicinity of the refrigerator refocused their attention on the original bride and groom.

"Liz and Christopher," Becky replied cheerfully. "It makes perfect sense. Who knows when Liz will be able to get back to Clairmont?"

She looked, undaunted, into Tank's face as he closed in and towered over her. Liz smiled at her friend's courage. Anyone else would have fled the room.

Tank stared at Becky for a moment, breathed deeply, and then had the good grace to turn and nod at Liz and Christopher. Apparently, that was the extent of his congratulations. He turned back to his bride-to-be. The party at the table couldn't help but watch the drama play out.

Tank touched Becky's cheek gently and ran a finger along her jaw. She braced her hand on the counter as he continued his surprisingly gentle, unspoken appeal in front an unapologetically fascinated crowd. Liz held her breath, and she wasn't even the target of his interest.

"Any chance we can get on that list?" he asked quietly, lifting Becky's chin.

Liz had never seen Tank be anything but stiff and gruff. She figured there had to be another side to him, but she didn't expect to see it - maybe ever - and certainly not in front of an audience.

Becky stood transfixed, and Liz, herself, still wasn't breathing.

Kelly gasped, "Oh my!" and slumped dramatically down in her chair.

Drew coughed uncomfortably, and Christopher reclaimed Liz's attention with another squeeze of her hand.

"Maybe we should let them have some time alone?"

Becky snapped out of her trance and put a little distance between herself and Tank. "Of course, we can. It's looking good for tomorrow. I talked with Maddy." She patted his chest. "Oh, didn't I tell you?"

His momentary charm faded into a growl, which, rather surprisingly, put the room more at ease. *This* Tank, they knew.

He slowly leaned down and whispered something that brought healthy color to Becky's cheeks, and a new reason to squirm for the people at the kitchen table.

Liz turned to Christopher, her own cheeks starting to warm. The knowing look and accompanying quirk of his lips did nothing to settle her heart rate. Desperately wishing she wasn't sharing this moment with her daughter and the coffee roaster, she did her best to focus on something mundane in order to reset her brain.

"So, what's the latest word on the storm?"

Kelly laughed, easing the tension. "Nice, Mom. Let's talk about the weather."

Drew, who had been looking for any reason to focus on his phone, was quick with the update. "It should stop snowing in the next hour or so."

"Really?" more than one person responded.

"Yeah, then it starts up again around eleven."

A collective sigh reverberated around the room.

"Well, as long as it stops for an hour, we can still get home to-night," Kelly replied, ever the optimist.

"You'd snowshoe at night?" Liz asked with concern.

Kelly looked at Drew and he gave her a brief nod.

"Sure," she confirmed, her bright eyes sparkling. "We've got flashlights. It'll be fun! Besides, where would we even sleep here? You're all packed in like sardines." She grinned at Liz, wiggling her brows. "Which means," she concluded, "that you have an hour to get this wedding done, so we can get out of here when the snow clears."

§ § §

All traces of the bachelor party, such as it was, were cleared from the front parlor when the snowbound group reconvened for a wedding they didn't expect to attend. Liz stood with Christopher in front of the plant-stand-turned-podium, and Pastor Rob beamed at them from behind it. She was a little surprised at his willingness to perform this ceremony on such short notice. Nothing seemed to throw him, however, and he appeared delighted to play a role in securing their future together. Whether that made him a romantic or a little crazy, Liz wasn't entirely sure.

She'd made her peace with the balance of romantic and crazy that she and Christopher had embraced to make this decision on this weekend. Their time together was too limited for a relaxed exploration of their relationship, and even with months of planning, they weren't likely to want anything but a small ceremony. Neither one of them particularly enjoyed the attention, so a quickly planned event, sanctioned, *no, actually insisted-upon*, by her daughter, was the only kind of second wedding Liz was ever likely to want. There would likely be all kinds of disapproval and second-guessing from well-meaning family and friends, but they would field it, together, when the time came.

They'd talked briefly when Pastor Rob had returned from visiting Baby Fordham, bringing the report of a happily resting family up in the penthouse. He'd listened to Christopher's request and nodded thoughtfully, then pointed out that while he could marry them before God and their friends, there would be civic details to take care of when the town opened up again. Christopher had promised that they'd follow through. Rob had then informed them that he always did premarital counseling, but was ready to streamline the process for them.

"Christopher, Liz, you sure you can make this work?"

He'd looked between the two of them as they nodded with a touch of uncertainty.

"You understand that living five hours apart might cause some undue stress?"

They'd managed a nervous laugh.

"And you know that if you truly invite God into this relationship, He'll help you deal with the ... unusual path you've chosen?"

Here, they both assented with more determination.

"Well, then," he'd said. "If you don't mind an unshaven pastor in wrinkled clothes running the show, let's get started."

And so, here they stood. At least the bride and groom had a new wardrobe. Christopher wore a clean oxford and some superbly fitted slacks, and had taken a razor to his ever-present shadow. He looked so handsome, Liz had a difficult time holding his gaze. Of course, the appreciation in his eyes didn't help her composure. He seemed to find the beige sweater dress she'd planned to wear to Becky's wedding a more than suitable gown for her own.

Kelly stood to her right, garbed in the same borrowed clothing from earlier, and interestingly enough, Drew completed the bridal party, standing to Christopher's left. Less than two months earlier, Kelly had been planning to marry Christopher's son, and Drew had kept his distance from the professor, who was a regular at the coffee shop. Now, apparently, there was a new relationship forming, and Liz couldn't help but wonder if they might find themselves in a similar wedding party sometime in the future, with the roles, of course, slightly, but significantly altered.

Her daydreams for her daughter were brought to a close when Pastor Rob began to speak. With warmth and humor, he acknowledged the unexpected change in the main characters of the weekend's drama, at least for the present hour. He looked around the room and, settling on Frank, suggested he prepare for his upcoming lead role in whatever interesting turn the weekend might take.

Everyone laughed, except Tank. Liz glanced at the linebacker who was supposed to have played the role of groom earlier in the day. He stood with his arms crossed, glowering, and Becky looked up and elbowed him. He didn't meet her gaze, but did make an effort to soften his features, although minimally. It was enough for his not-quite-yet-bride, and she turned and caught the eye of the current one. She winked and Liz turned back to the pastor. The lighthearted introduction finished, he embraced the opportunity to preach commitment, forgiveness and love as he launched into the wedding vows.

In less time than it took to have Becky oversee her hair, makeup and wardrobe in preparation for her last-minute wedding, Liz Michaels became Christopher Harrison's wife.

§ § §

The wedding reception consisted of champagne, tea, cookies, and a lovely chocolate cake with an amazingly light whipped icing, that Grace had somehow found the time to start before and then finish after the wedding. The group gathered in the kitchen, enjoying the faire and marveling at the new turn of events.

Liz toasted everyone and then set her champagne glass away for a few minutes while she collected her wits. She had truly just married the handsome man beside her. How were they going to make it work? How many personal days might she be able to take in order to have something of a honeymoon? Christopher, standing close, nodded at Frank, who was soliciting bets over what the next surprise might be.

"So, what do you think? An engagement?" He glanced at Kelly and Drew, who both squirmed and turned various shades of red. "No? Okay, then I'm putting ten in the hat that somebody's going to announce a pregnancy," he decided, "and it isn't me, or, I mean, Linda, my wife, so ..."

A hush came over the room as he looked around, waiting for somebody to confirm or deny his theory. All eyes seemed to follow his path, resting briefly on Becky, who said frankly, "Not possible," and eventually stopping on Grace, who was busy wrapping the remainder of the cake. She paused as she realized that she was the center of attention.

"Don't look at me," she said, color hinting at her cheeks. "Coffee's my baby right now." She glanced at Alex, who smiled - a little wistfully - Liz thought.

"Hey, maybe I'll get a little sister or brother out of this deal," Kelly concluded, finding a way to keep the awkward attention off of her by directing it at her mother. "Wouldn't that be sweet?"

Liz felt her own face flame as all eyes turned toward her and Christopher.

He stiffened slightly, then she heard the rumble of his chuckle. "Well, there's some pressure. I guess we deserve that, given what we've asked you all to witness this evening."

The conversation then turned toward the unlikelihood of their having any success in the effort, considering the houseful of people. Every new conjecture caused Liz untold mortification, and she hardly knew where to turn for comfort. She studiously ignored her new husband, who seemed to take it all in with good humor, based on his occasional hum of laughter.

Becky finally had mercy and redirected the group's attention.

"Okay, enough teasing the newlyweds. Save some of your inappropriate innuendo for Tank and me. We haven't been alone together in … ever. You can bet we'll be kicking you all out of the house tomorrow afternoon, whatever the storm is doing."

She gave Tank a cheeky look, but his thunderous mien covered any embarrassment he might be experiencing. Liz couldn't believe Becky was willing to take on the unwanted speculation and teasing, but she was incredibly grateful that she did.

Beside her, Christopher drew a deep breath, as though recovering a little from the onslaught. She dared to look up at him, and he looked into her eyes, then down at her lips, and then slowly back into her eyes.

Warmth spread throughout her body.

"Well, this conversation is not for my tender ears," Kelly decided with a laugh, apparently ignoring the fact that she'd started it. "And we need to get going, anyway." She looked up at her friend. "What do you say, Drew? Shall we get out of here before this raunchy group targets us again?"

Drew turned crimson at the suggestion, reinforcing the speculation that he felt something for her daughter. Liz wondered how long it would take before the two of them finally figured it out.

Kelly bounced over and hugged Liz and then reached up and pecked Christopher on the cheek.

"Well, I guess you were meant to be a father to me, one way or another," she decided with a tilt of her head. "I'll take step-dad with pleasure." She pulled them both into a hug and then backed up. "Time for us to move out. *Yes, Mom,*" she said before Liz could interrupt. "I'll call or text as soon as we're home." She paused, a little disconcerted. "Well, when *I'm* home. Drew won't be far behind, going, you know, home - to his own home."

Liz smiled as Kelly stumbled through her explanation. "Okay, don't forget. I won't be able to sleep until I hear from you." Realizing that she'd issued an invitation to reopen the previous conversation, she immediately went on. "So, okay, be safe. Stay warm. Here, take a cookie."

Kelly giggled. "Thanks, Mom."

"Oh, do you want your bracelet back?"

Kelly had made a sweet production of giving Liz a very special gift right before the ceremony. The bracelet was one of a pair that they'd made out of embroidery floss when Kelly was a child. One hadn't made it through the years, but Kelly still wore the second one faithfully. Her willingness to part with it had been a sweet and tearful moment before the wedding.

Kelly smiled at the offer. "You keep it for now."

Liz fingered the delicate string, interspersed with beads. "I'll protect it with my life."

Kelly laughed. "You'd better." She turned to Drew. "Ready to go?"

At his nod, she turned again to Liz. "Have a great night. I'll be in touch."

Liz heaved a sigh of relief when her daughter turned away to say her other good-byes.

Beside her, Christopher reached for her glass. "A little more champagne?"

"That would be lovely."

Saturday - 9:00 p.m.
Maddy

Maddy struggled out of a fog of sleep at the sound of a deep sigh. It took a moment to get oriented, but soon her new reality unfolded around her. By the soft light of the bedside lamp, she could see her husband sitting on the other side of the cradle he'd made, his labor of love now embracing their little daughter. His elbows braced on his knees, John sat with his head bowed against his folded hands. Another sigh, tiny and from an entirely different source, caused him to lift his head and gaze into the cradle. Maddy watched his almost haunted look transform into one of quiet joy.

He stretched his big, carpenter hand and rested it on the tiny, sighing bundle, and Maddy couldn't stop the tears that welled. Before she could close her eyes and leave her husband and daughter to their bonding, John looked up, his look pensive as he met her gaze.

Concern took over again. "Are you okay? Did I wake you?"

Maddy slowly shifted into a more upright position. "It's okay. I have a feeling I'll be sleeping more lightly from now on."

"You were out cold," John countered. "One minute, we were talking about names and the next, you were gone." He moved to sit next to her. "It was a little unnerving." He reached over and gently tucked her hair back, wiping a tear with his thumb. "You've been through so much; I wondered if you were going to just collapse."

Maddy leaned into his touch. "Sorry I scared you. I guess I am a little tired." She turned and kissed his hand. "And I guess I'm going to need some backup if I'm going to hear this little one at night."

They both turned to look at the quiet, sleeping bundle, wondering how she would ever make a noise loud enough to wake anyone. It took less than a minute for their daughter to manage a yowl that was unexpectedly piercing and effective.

Their surprised laugh quickly gave way to action, John jumping to pick her up. She was so tiny in his hands as he held her and smiled into her sweet little face. The sweet little face managed another peal of distress, and John quickly handed her to Maddy, who scrambled to arrange her night gown so that she could nurse her. Anita had assured her that it would become as natural as breathing. Maddy continued to cling to that promise and settled in to feed her daughter, happy that one of them seemed to know exactly what she was doing.

John sat next to her again and Maddy looked up to meet his look of quiet wonder.

"Amazing how God works it all out, isn't it?" he asked.

She fought more happy tears. "Amazing."

"Well," he paused, apparently not sure how he fit into the present moment. "I should probably get the boys. It's getting late." He stood and stretched. "No telling what kind of shenanigans they've been up to under Frank's watch."

"*Shenanigans?* Really?" Maddy giggled and winced. "But, yeah, that's probably a good ... oh, wait! Where's Burt? And how did you ever get him out of here?"

John sighed at the obviously stressful memory. "It wasn't pretty. We had to drag him down two flights of stairs. He's probably still camped out in the kitchen, guarding the door to the stairway."

"Yikes - dragged him?"

"No. Well, sort of. Tank coaxed him out of the apartment, but then he kind of freaked out. Burt, not Tank. Well, both." John shook his head. "Tank had to get pretty scary to get Burt's attention and then the rest of us helped push, pull and cajole him down the steps."

"Oh, wow. I think I'm glad I didn't see that."

"Me, too. I saw a whole new side to both of them. I won't be messing with either of them any time soon."

Maddy giggled again. "I'm sorry. You didn't need to deal with that while the baby was coming."

"Yeah, your whole labor thing was a picnic in comparison."

She laughed. "Probably true."

John grinned. "Anyway, we got him outside, but then he was determined to find his way back up here, so we had to block off the front staircase. He finally plunked down by that door in the kitchen. Not sure if anyone's gotten him to move in the last ..." John looked at his watch, "four hours."

"He used to hang out there during renovations, remember?"

John stifled a groan. "I remember being very grateful that he wasn't allowed upstairs while we were working."

"He didn't want to miss the action." Maddy looked down at her daughter nestled in her arms. "I think you can bring him up. He needs to meet the one he's been protecting so fiercely for the last nine months."

"Oh, he knows her very well," John replied. "But I suppose it's time for him to meet the newest member of the family." He leaned over and gently stroked the baby's head. "We really need to decide on a name."

Maddy nodded. "Who knew it would be so hard? She doesn't seem to fit the names we picked."

John straightened. "You know the longer we wait, the more engrained 'Ichabella' will be."

Maddy laughed again and held her side. "Okay, I'm motivated! We'll choose a name when you get back."

John grimaced. "We'll have plenty of help." He walked toward the door. "You're sure you're ready for this?"

Maddy considered her baby domain and nodded. "Bring them up."

♪♪♪

Expecting a fair amount of commotion when the door to the apartment opened, Maddy was surprised when just one set of footsteps quietly approached her room. The mystery was solved when Becky peeked her head in a moment later.

"Hey, Mama."

"Hey, Becky," Maddy beamed, delighting in the title.

"John's letting the boys finish their movie. They should be up soon." Becky approached the bed and sat down. "She's still beautiful." Stroking the blanket surrounding her little niece, she grinned at her sister. "How can you even stand it?"

Maddy sighed. "I don't know. I had no idea these feelings were even possible." She kissed her baby's head. "How are you holding up?"

"Well, it's certainly been a busy day," Becky replied. "I think I'm good. Everything seems to be under control for the moment. And we heard that the storm might actually break by morning."

"That's a relief. I imagine there are a few people who would like to see their families."

"Yeah, and put clean clothes on," Becky shuddered. "Good thing we weren't all piled in the same space in the heat of summer."

She wrinkled her nose and Maddy laughed.

"What's Tank up to?"

"He's next door looking at Otis's generator with Frank and Ed while there's a break in the storm. If they can get it running, Otis can go back home and maybe take Frank and Rob with him. He's got a couple of extra beds, and I'm sure they'd appreciate not having to sleep on the couches again." She folded her hands in her lap.

"And that means I can go back to my room and Tank can have the Captain's Quarters."

"Where did he sleep last night?"

"Who knows? I think he ended up in the daybed in the Anchor Room with his parents." She smiled. "Would love to have seen him crammed in there with his head on a frilly pillow."

Maddy giggled at the thought, then processed the news Becky had shared. "It would be great if they could get that generator going. It's funny to think that my neighbor's been living in my house, and I've hardly even talked to him."

"Your neighbor and half the town of Clairmont."

Maddy laughed again, shifting the baby to her shoulder. "How is everyone else doing?"

"Oh, fine. Liz and Christopher got married. That was cool."

"What?! They really got married?" Maddy's hand froze on her daughter's back. "You tell me this *after* the generator report?"

Becky looked a little sheepish. "Sorry. I guess I'm not prioritizing my gossip very well."

"Wow. Seems like I should've been at the first wedding I hosted."

"Well, honestly, you didn't really do much," Becky pointed out.

Not even giving birth protected her from her sister's unique brand of sass. "Nice. Anything else I should know about?"

Becky thought for a moment. "Well, Tank's folks are no longer in the dark about Alex. That was a pretty sweet reveal."

"Oh my. Is Grace okay?"

"Yeah. She's tough as nails."

"Wow, I really missed a lot."

"Yeah, you didn't plan very well," Becky replied, leaning over to touch the wispy hairs on her niece's head.

Maddy sighed happily. "I guess I'll have to make my peace with it." She looked up suddenly. "Where were Blake and Parker during all of this?"

"Well, they've mostly been with Frank. They did hang out with us for the wedding, though Parker was a little put out at the idea of 'church at night'. Once he found out that there would be cake afterward, he was fine."

"They really got married. That's so romantic!"

"I know. Part of me is still surprised, and yet it makes perfect sense. They were bound to do it sometime. Why get bogged down with the planning?" Becky stood. "Anyway, you should have seen it when everyone started teasing them about having private space for their wedding night."

"Oh no. They didn't!"

"Oh yeah, they did. It's a merciless crowd down there. Don't forget how long they've been cooped up together." Becky tucked her hands into the back pockets of her jeans. "Maybe the newlyweds can stay next door with Otis."

Maddy laughed, and then winced when her tummy seized up. She took a minute to breathe. "What a weekend. We have to remember to have people sign the guest book. We should probably start that soon."

Becky headed for the door. "Right. I'll run it over to the guys while they're working on the generator. Or maybe I'll get Liz's take on what it's like to anticipate her wedding night trapped in a house with a dozen strangers."

"You have to stop making me laugh. It hurts!" Maddy held her stomach with her sort of free hand. "And before you go, please tell me you're still planning to get married tomorrow."

Becky stopped in the doorway and tilted her head. "You're going to be up and on your feet? Able to walk downstairs?"

Maddy nodded furiously. "I'm not missing another wedding," she said with feeling.

"Well," Becky replied with a smile. "Let me see what I can do."

$$\mathcal{SSS}$$

The next time Maddy heard commotion at the apartment door, it was decidedly different. She listened with interest as John tried to control Burt's entrance, while keeping the boys calm. They apparently thought the dog's frantic desire to get into the apartment was hilarious - John, not so much.

"Okay, guys, go get your pajamas on while I take Burt in. I'll let you know when you can come in to see your sister."

"Ichabella!" Parker shrieked and Blake giggled.

"Yeah, that's changing soon. Go get undressed now, and brush your teeth."

"Can't we watch Burt get the baby?"

Maddy smiled a little nervously, tucking her daughter snugly into her side.

"Burt is not going to *get the baby*, he's just going to say hello. Go change. Now."

Maddy heard John sigh as the boys obeyed, and then there was an interesting scuffle as Burt likely pulled him toward their room. She tried not to laugh at the sight of her strong and capable husband being dragged through the door by her determined pet. It was actually pretty impressive how he held firm to Burt's collar as they approached the bed, locking him in an iron grip when Burt was close enough to nose the baby with his big snout.

"Hey Burt," Maddy said quietly, reaching out to pat his head.

Burt fairly quivered with curiosity, but stopped straining when she touched him.

"It's okay. I'm okay. And here's the one you've been so worried about."

She carefully shifted her precious bundle, confident that Burt would be gentle in his assessment of the newest member of the family.

John didn't share her confidence. "Burt, sit."

Burt complied with surprising alacrity, and John clamped his thighs on either side of him, his hold on the collar unwavering.

Maddy bit her lip. "You look like one of those cowboys at a rodeo," she giggled. "Riding the crazy bull."

John's serious, focused demeanor faltered momentarily. "Don't mess with my concentration. This is taking everything I have." He tightened his grip as the dog leaned in to sniff the bundle of new life. Burt was surprisingly gentle as he nosed around, determined to unwrap the mystery of blankets.

Maddy was equally determined to limit the introduction, and kept the baby's face covered.

"Sorry, Buddy. We're going to do this gradually. You're just going to have to trust me." She pulled the baby back to the middle of the bed, away from his inquisitive nose.

Burt stood suddenly, throwing John off balance, and Maddy watched helplessly as he flailed briefly before regaining his equilibrium. Thankfully, Burt had stilled in the process; he probably didn't want John falling on top of him anymore than John did. The two finally separated safely, and Maddy released the breath she'd been holding, admirably stifling the giggle that came with it.

John, fighting his own battle with wanting to laugh and throttle her dog at the same time, quickly shook off his brush with humiliation and refocused on controlling Burt's curiosity. He held firm as Burt sniffed around Maddy, searching out the bundle of baby. A few beats passed, and then Burt sighed and laid his big head on the bed. John sighed and eased his grip.

"I think you can let go. He won't jump up here," Maddy said.

John considered the dog for another moment and then slowly released his collar. When Burt didn't move, John finally relaxed.

"Well. That went well," he conceded.

"That was a Herculean effort. Thank you."

"Think I can leave him in here while I go check the boys?"

Maddy brushed her dog's head. "I'm pretty sure it's our only option." She looked back up at John. "We're good. Go get those boys and let's name this baby."

♪ ♪ ♪

Blake and Parker stood just outside the door whispering, and Maddy smiled as they schemed about how to sneak in. Burt blew their cover as he lumbered up to greet them, his approach suggesting that they weren't a significant threat - good news all around.

"Come on in, you guys," Maddy said. "Your sister is sleeping but you can come and take a peek."

They walked in and Maddy marveled as they passed Burt with a nonchalance that most adults couldn't fathom. He pushed his nose into Blake's shoulder, reminding him that some attention was appropriate, and Blake patted him as he passed. Burt followed the boys as they approached the bed, standing patiently in line for his chance to see what was inside the mysterious bundle.

Parker, accustomed to scampering up into the bed, seemed to understand that some restraint was necessary. Hopping from one foot to the other, he danced quietly near the side of the bed, waiting for Maddy to unwrap his new sister. Blake was uncharacteristically antsy, as well, bouncing up and down on the balls of his feet. Maddy was impressed by the way they contained their energy. John had prepped them well.

"We washed our hands," Blake offered helpfully.

"Yeah, just in case we touch the baby," Parker added.

"That's great," Maddy replied, pulling the blanket back so they could get a good look at their sister. Her breath caught, again, at the sheer beauty of the sleeping face of her daughter.

"She's sleeping again?" Parker asked, disappointed. "I want to see her eyes." He leaned closer, peering into the little one's face and then up at Maddy. "Can we wake her up?"

"She's had a busy day," Maddy replied. "I think we need to let her sleep." She shifted the baby so her brothers could see her better. "I promise you'll have lots of time to get to know her tomorrow."

"Look at her little fingers," Blake said reverently, pointing at the tiny hand that had stretched out from beneath the covers.

"Oh, man!" Parker said in awe.

John appeared at the door, looking happy and a little haggard. "So, what has the council decided?"

"What's a council?" Parker asked, his eyes still trained on his sister's face.

John walked into the room. "The council is our family, and we're deciding on a name for the newest member." He sat on the bed and put his hand on the baby's head. "I think we have it narrowed down to anything but 'Ichabella'."

Blake and Parker giggled.

"Well, we haven't entirely ruled it out," Maddy teased, immediately regretting it when she saw Parker's face light up.

"Yes! We can call her 'Ich' when we don't have time to say the rest."

John chuckled and moved his hand to Parker's head, ruffling his hair. "Sorry, Buddy, Ichabella's out. I think we can do better."

"Aww ... It's a cool name."

"How about just 'Bella'?" Blake asked quietly.

Maddy startled and locked eyes with John. They both smiled.

"That's it," he replied. "Isn't it?"

"I think maybe so," Maddy agreed with growing delight.

She glanced at Blake, who looked self-conscious, but mostly pleased. Parker frowned, apparently wondering why they had removed the only interesting part of the name.

"Beautiful," John reached over and gently lifted the baby out of Maddy's arms. "That's what Bella means. It's perfect."

He held the baby up as though, somehow, she'd be in a better position to receive her new name. They all looked in wonder at the little life that had just joined the family.

"Bella Fordham," Maddy mused aloud.

John closed his eyes and swallowed.

"Does she get another name?" Parker asked. "Like I have two names, can she have two names?"

John tucked his daughter into his side and considered his son. "Well, Parker David, I suppose that would be fair."

Maddy could tell that he controlled the urge to ask for a suggestion.

Parker offered one, anyway. "Maisie is good."

Maddy smiled and pondered the name for a moment. It certainly wasn't what she expected him to suggest, but it did have the advantage of being an actual name. She let "Bella Maisie" bounce around in her head a few times, tickled at John's look of distress.

"Where did you hear that name?" she asked Parker.

"She's a girl in my class. We're getting married."

John almost dropped his precious load as the poignant naming ceremony took an unexpected turn. He tucked Bella into Maddy's arms and they exchanged an amused glance. At least Maddy's was amused.

"I don't remember you mentioning Maisie before," John replied carefully.

"We just decided this week."

"I see." John looked helplessly at Maddy, who could only offer a shrug in response. "Well, I think we did really well choosing Bella's first name. Why don't we sleep on the middle name?"

"I think that's a great idea," Maddy agreed. "I think we all need some rest."

"Delilah was mad. She wouldn't play with us."

"You have a girl named Delilah in your class?" John asked.

"Yeah. She's mean."

"Okay, well, why don't we get a good night's rest and we'll finish discussing this tomorrow? Hug Maddy-Mom gently," John reminded Parker, who had closed in for his nightly hug.

Maddy kissed his head. "Night Parkerpants. Sleep tight."

He backed up and let Blake in for his modified hug.

"Night Blake," Maddy said. "Thanks for giving your sister such a lovely name."

He smiled shyly. "Welcome."

John corralled the boys and directed them toward their room across the hall. Maddy watched them leave, then turned her gaze on Bella.

"You're a lucky little girl," she whispered. She kissed her head and then nestled her into her cradle. "Sleep well, Bella. Welcome to the family."

Saturday - 10:00 p.m.
Becky

Becky climbed over the dog gate blocking the main staircase, smiling at the thought of Burt finally getting to meet Maddy's baby. She made a mental note to move the gate when she confirmed that the introduction had been made. She glanced into the parlor and saw that it was empty; Tank's folks must have gone on to bed.

She wondered how they were processing the news about Alex. It was undoubtedly humbling for Mr. Kimball, who had misjudged him so completely. While she hoped they started treating Alex better, it would hardly reflect well on them if they did. A tiny part of her felt sorry for the Kimballs, knowing well that facing your pride and changing your perspective was no small thing.

Happy to shake off these thoughts, she made her way through the house, curious to find out if the generator crew had returned, and praying they'd been successful. While she did want Otis to be able to return to his house, she mostly wanted more room in this one. Tank needed someplace to sleep that was somewhere not near her. After her visit with Maddy, she'd spent a few minutes tidying up the Captain's Quarters, figuring that he'd be using the room and wouldn't appreciate the evidence of the bridal prep she'd done with Liz.

There was a lot to celebrate, and Becky wanted nothing more than to be in her own bed, with time to process everything that had happened in the last twenty-four hours. She was pretty sure that somewhere in the midst of her niece being born and her friend getting formally engaged and actually married, she'd made up with her fiancé and agreed to marry him. All of that needed sorting out.

Somewhere far away from him.

The kitchen still smelled of the wedding cake, and candles lent their own calming and yet festive scent. Grace was apparently enjoying the hosting business. She and Alex sat at the table with Anita and the newlyweds, and they all looked up when Becky entered the room.

"Any word from Kelly and Drew?" she asked.

"They made it back," Liz replied, obviously relieved. "She just texted a few minutes ago."

"That's great." Becky peeked into the sunroom as she pulled a chair up to join them. Otis and Rob sat by the fire, no doubt talking about the incredible day and likely both ready to put it behind them. "How 'bout the generator boys?"

"No word, yet." Anita sounded matter-of-fact, but she looked a little troubled. She had to be exhausted, and probably wished her men were done playing mechanics in a snowstorm and were tucked in, safe and sound for the night.

"Are you hungry?" Grace asked. "You hardly ate at all before. I saved your plate - I can heat it up for you."

"No, thanks. I'll just snack here." Becky gestured at the tray of veggies, cheese and crackers on the table, another thoughtful Grace effort. "Thanks for doing all of this - you're amazing."

Her friend nodded, but her concern was still evident. As Becky turned to chat with the cozy-looking newlyweds, the door rattled and burst open. Ed stomped his boots on the mat and made way for Frank and Tank, who followed and did the same.

Everyone looked up expectantly, and Ed happily filled them in. "We got it running. Once his place has a chance to heat up a bit, Otis can head back home."

His booming voice easily reached the men in the sunroom, and Rob and Otis joined them in the kitchen.

"Well, what do you know about that?" Otis said with a grin. "I can't thank you enough. Don't know why I didn't think to ask you all to look at it sooner."

"Would have been hard to see anything, the way the snow has been blowing," Ed replied. "But it's running now."

Otis rubbed his hands together. "That's great news. And like I mentioned earlier, I've got two extra beds over there, and a lumpy couch if anyone needs it." He glanced at Tank, the only one who's landing spot for the night wasn't particularly clear.

The idea of Tank being in another building entirely appealed to Becky, but she decided to be kind and save him. "Thank you, Otis. I'm sure Rob and Frank will appreciate real beds tonight. I think the rest of us are good."

She spared a glance for the man she planned to marry the following day, and the look he returned almost made her forget her name.

"Well, okay, if you're sure," Otis replied. "I think I'll just head over now and beat the next wave of snow. I don't mind a little cold in the house." He looked at Rob and Frank. "You boys can head over any time."

"I just have to pack," Frank said, pulling his jacket back on. "And, done!" he announced with a grin.

Rob smiled. "I'll grab my coat and brief case and I'll be right behind you." He glanced at Otis. "Can I get your coat?"

"I'll just follow you and pick one out," Otis quipped as the two headed toward the front of the house.

Frank walked over to Anita and kissed her on the head. "You had a busy day, Ma," he said quietly. "Isn't it time you got some rest?"

"Look who's sending his mother to bed?" Anita yawned and pushed her chair back. "I suppose you're right. Now that you and your father are done horsing around in the snow..." She stood and looked over at her husband. "How about it, Ed? You ready?"

Ed finished lining his boots against the wall and stood, making way for Tank, who moved past him into the room.

"Suppose I am. Big day tomorrow and all." He looked around the kitchen. "For someone. Gotta be, right?" His gaze landed on Becky.

"Yeah, what's the schedule?" Frank chimed in. "Who's getting married when?"

Becky paused her tracking of Tank's progress toward the fridge while the laughter ebbed around her. Hadn't they worked out that little detail?

"When is the storm supposed to clear? Does Pastor have to get back for church?" Grace asked.

Tank approached and stood behind Becky. "The snow's supposed to let up by dawn, but they won't get the roads cleared in time," he said. "Especially out here."

Everyone processed what was probably not a big surprise.

"So, we have Pastor Rob for another day. Lucky him!" Grace smiled as he and Otis re-entered the room.

"I just couldn't be happier for the two of you," Ed chimed in, looking at Becky and Tank with a smile. "There was a time I didn't think you'd figure out what was going on between you."

Becky glanced up at Tank as his gaze shifted to Ed. A muscle twitched in his jaw, then relaxed. She felt his hands on her shoulders and he rubbed them; an uncharacteristic show of affection in front of the others. She had good reason to be concerned.

"Nah. She was pretty obvious. I finally had to give in."

Becky shrugged out from under his hands and stood up next to him. The maneuver was less graceful than she would have liked, but she managed to get out of his clutches. "Oh, please. Whose idea was it to 'fake date'?"

"Now that was good," Ed cheerfully joined the fray that he'd started. "You sure had me fooled that day in the teachers' lounge." He smiled at the memory. "Although I do remember thinking you looked awfully stiff, standing there together. Figured it was 'cuz of those other clowns at the table."

"He completely blind-sided me with that little announcement," Becky asserted to the snow-and-spell-bound crowd. "I walked into the lounge, loathing the sight of him, and walked out his girlfriend. I'm still not sure how or why that all happened." She looked up at Tank, whose mask of innocence didn't fool her, or anyone else.

He pulled her into his side and grinned. "You never loathed me."

"Oh, believe me, I did."

"Not even for a minute."

"Now see, this is what I'm talking about," Ed pointed out with a smile. "Becky was all stiff and angry-looking while Tank clamped her to his side like that. No going anywhere, was there, Becky? See? Same thing here."

The unhelpful crowd looked on, amused, as Becky tried to slip out from under Tank's heavy arm.

"Yeah, isn't he charming? How could I resist him?" She finally gave up and tried to glower at her fiancé.

Unaffected, he leaned down and kissed her forehead.

"I remember a scene like that in this kitchen," Frank joined in. "Made sense of it later when I realized that you two weren't actually going out."

"How long did this go on?" Liz asked, amused. This was part of Becky's story that she hadn't heard.

"Too long - not long enough - who knows?" Becky blew her hair out of her eyes and tried to lean away from Tank. "It was just supposed to be for a week, but then everyone started finding out, and the students got invested ..."

"Started picking sides," Tank added. "Mostly mine."

Becky ineffectively tried to elbow him. She'd have to figure out how to control him when he went all football player on her.

"Really?" Liz laughed. "When did it become real?"

"Hard to say," Becky replied. "Soon, maybe."

Tank barked a quick laugh. "It was always real for Becky. I finally gave in when she invited me to that dance at the school."

"No. They needed chaperones," Becky amended.

"She avoided me all night..."

"Until Tank begged me to dance."

That earned her a growl.

"And then he scandalized the students by kissing me."

"Didn't kiss you."

"Well, not while they were there."

The people in the room faded away as Becky and Tank recalled their first brush of a kiss at the Valentine's Day dance. Her heart sped up at the thought of it.

"And then we got yelled at by the principal," Becky continued, and they both grinned at the memory.

"You *what*?!" This from Grace.

"She accused us of making out in front of the students at the dance," Becky explained airily.

"You didn't!" Grace looked back and forth between her friend and her brother.

"Of course not," Tank grunted.

"But he was thinking about it," Becky pointed out, smiling at Tank. "Even the kids could read you like a book."

He growled again.

"Well, it all turned out just the way it was supposed to," Ed concluded their trip down memory lane. "We just need to get you married tomorrow."

Frank looked between the two of them. "Yeah, that'll be hours and hours away. Tank, I'm thinking you probably shouldn't be in the same house as the bride the night before the wedding. Got a lumpy couch with your name on it next door."

"Nope."

"Aren't there rules about this kind of thing?" Frank countered.

Becky enjoyed Tank's bristling beside her, and readily affirmed Frank's concern. "He does have a point."

"*You* sleep on his couch."

She grinned up at him. "No way. I'm back in my own bed tonight." She turned to Frank. "I don't know, Frank. Unless you can figure out how to move him over there, you may just have to trust us."

Frank considered his friend. "Out of my league," he decided, zipping his jacket again and walking over to join his new housemates. "They're lining up here, Reverend. Got another gig for you tomorrow, unless you can fit them in tonight."

Rob smiled. "Tomorrow's good, I think." He glanced down at his phone. "We definitely won't be having church in the morning. I guess we could have a service here, and," he looked up at Becky and Tank, "maybe I can fit you in."

"We'll take it," Tank said decisively.

Becky looked up and Tank dared her to disagree. She smiled and turned to her pastor.

"What time should we be ready?"

Saturday - 11:00 p.m.
Grace

"What a day," Grace sighed, finding herself back on the couch in the sunroom, trying to rally the energy to debrief about the day. Tank and Becky had lost their steam for bickering and sat cozily together, looking at the fire. Everyone else had finally gone to bed and the four of them were enjoying a few minutes of peace.

"Unbelievable," Becky agreed. "Was it just this morning that I called my folks and told them that the wedding was postponed and that their grandchild was on the way, a month early?"

"Don't know why we had to postpone," Tank mumbled. "The baby didn't stop Liz from getting married."

Becky didn't even bother looking up at him. She just patted his knee as she stared into the flames. "We've got eleven hours to go. I think you can make it."

Tank grumbled something no one could understand and Grace felt Alex chuckle beside her.

"I can't wait to meet that baby," Grace said. "Have they picked a name, yet?"

"Haven't heard anything," Becky replied, "although 'Ichabella' seemed to be getting some traction with the boys."

The men laughed quietly and Grace asked, "I wonder if any of them will sleep tonight?"

"I sure hope Maddy does. She's exhausted," Becky remarked. "John, too, but, just - *wow* - Maddy worked really hard today." She paused, then said, "I hope John won't hesitate to call us for back-up. Anita's idea to layout a tag-team schedule was really smart. I hope it makes it easier for him to take us up on the help."

"Me too. I'm on from 2-4 a.m. I hope he texts. I hope I hear it if he texts," Grace amended, also hoping she'd remember to turn up the volume on her phone.

"I'll hear it. I'm a light sleeper," offered Alex.

Grace narrowed her eyes at him.

"I'm on at midnight," Becky yawned, rerouting their attention to the other couch. "I should probably try to stay awake in case they need me."

"You must be exhausted, too," Grace observed. "Do you want to switch shifts?"

"Thanks, but we'd better not. Anita said no switching - that it would get too confusing in the middle of the night. I don't want to mess with her rules."

"Yeah, we should probably do what she says."

"I don't know what we would have done without her," Becky mused. "She was amazing. We all just kind of attached ourselves to her confidence and ran with it."

Grace had wondered what had gone on upstairs while she took care of the guests below. She had a few very pointed questions for her friend but decided not to ask them in the present company.

Becky answered them, anyway.

"She stayed so calm. Maddy, I mean. You could tell that she was afraid - who wouldn't be? But she just kept calmly following directions. Poor thing," she continued with a shudder, "there's no privacy when you're giving birth, and Maddy's a very private person."

Tank shifted nervously beside his talkative fiancée. Grace felt Alex stiffen a bit.

"Liz was great, too," Becky affirmed. "I guess it helps if you've been there, done that. I had no idea what was going on. Well," she amended, "you know, I had an idea, but until you really ..."

The hand that had been gently stroking Becky's arm lifted and turned her face into the impressive chest that had been her pillow. Her voice muffled and then quieted. Tank let her up.

"Very funny," she said, sitting back and straightening her hair. "Fine. Enough said. But just so you know, I'm significantly motivated to never, *ever* find myself in that particular state."

Grace knew Becky was kidding, but it was entertaining to consider Tank's reaction. His face grew very serious.

"But you're good with that, right?" Becky asked, reaching up and patting his cheek. "It's not like we haven't gotten really good at, you know, waiting, and waiting, and waiting. We'll just wait some more. A really long time. We'll be fine."

Alex cleared his throat beside her and Grace remembered that she wasn't watching the little drama alone. She could hardly wait to hear Tank's response, awkward as it was to hear her brother discuss this particular subject.

Apparently, Tank was able to show a little more restraint than his wife-to-be, which wasn't all that surprising. No way he was having that conversation in front of anyone, much less his sister. He looked down at Becky, his eyes narrowing as she batted hers.

"I'm going to bed." He stood abruptly and reached a hand out to where Becky lay semi-sprawled without her pillow. "Coming?"

"Not with you," she waved his hand away with a smirk.

He took her hand, anyway. "I'll walk you to your room." He pulled her up and Grace wondered what Becky made of his physicality. Although she went along with him this time, Grace had no doubt that Becky wouldn't put up with anything that didn't suit her. Tank had better watch out.

"Aren't you the gentleman?" Becky patted his chest. "But it's not necessary. I know my way."

Tank scooped her up and started to make his way around the couch. Grace sighed. Her brother was really going to have to learn some manners.

Becky settled in fairly quickly, saving her energy, no doubt, for a future battle.

"Good night, you two," she called as they entered the kitchen. "See you in the morning!"

"I so called that a year and a half ago," Grace observed. "Back when you first came to Clairmont." She snuggled happily into her husband's side. "I knew she could handle Tank, and look at them now."

"Yep," Alex replied. "As blissfully happy as ever."

Grace laughed as they listened to the rumble of the other couple arguing their way to Becky's room behind the kitchen.

"I'd like to see Tank 'blissful'."

"Think they'll actually get married tomorrow?"

"They'd better. I can't imagine what would stop them now," Grace mused, immediately regretting giving voice to the thought.

§ § §

The fire burned down to its embers, and Grace watched, transfixed, while her mind swirled through the events of the day. For all of the drama that the two Jacobs sisters had survived, she and Alex had managed some of their own.

She looked up at his handsome profile as Alex considered the coals giving off the last of their warmth. Was he contemplating his new status with his in-laws? What would it mean for all of them?

Grace reached up and touched his jaw. "How are you holding up? We've hardly had a chance to talk since your barista cover got blown."

Alex laughed quietly, capturing her hand, and pressing a kiss into her palm. "Yeah, that was something."

Her husband's kiss sent her senses in another direction, but she soon sobered again. "I hate how my mother started to look at you afterward, like she was trying to calculate your net worth."

"She was just thrown off. She'll come around."

"Yeah, I'm just afraid that she'll come around flattering and kissing up to you. It won't be pretty."

"Maybe you'll be surprised."

"Maybe you'll be mortified. You hate it when people do that."

Alex grinned at her. "I'll be brave."

"I hope so," she replied. "And who knows what my dad's going to do with this?" She thought for a moment. "At least he recognized your part in essentially saving the company he was consulting for."

"That was more than I expected."

"That's actually both hopeful and sad," she acknowledged. "I haven't given you much reason to expect more from him, have I?"

"*He* hasn't given me much reason," Alex amended. "I'm not going to let you take responsibility for his treatment of me. Just because you expected it and prepared me for it, doesn't make it your fault."

"Yeah, I guess. I just wish I'd been wrong."

"Well, for better or worse, they know me a little better now. Even if they change their tune for the wrong reason, at least that's a start."

"You are an amazing man."

He breathed deep, as though contemplating her simple statement. "I know."

Grace laughed and leaned into him. "Good for you. You were the last one who needed convincing."

"You convinced me when you agreed to marry me."

"Well, that's sweet." She turned so she could look at him more fully. "That's what convinced you that you were amazing? Not all of your business acumen and the long list of companies saved from disaster?"

"I know I'm good at my job," he shrugged off his considerable success. "But I knew I was special when Grace Kimball agreed to spend her life with me." He smiled the smile that had won her heart in the space of seven days.

She smiled, herself, and reached up for a taste of his. "Thanks for coming back into my life, Alex Mitchell."

"My pleasure," he said against her lips, clearly warming to the idea of smile-tasting. He pulled back and looked around the empty room. "Think it's safe to leave this party for a while?"

"I guess I've been doing my share of hostessing. Feeling neglected?" She rubbed his nose with hers, the tiredness beginning to fade.

"I am," he replied, pulling her to her feet.

"Not going to carry me up to our room?"

Alex looked her up and down. "I could probably manage it," he mused. "Might be easier if I slung you over my shoulder. Not quite as romantic, but it would get the job done."

Grace laughed and took his hand as they headed up to bed. "I think I'll walk, thank you very much."

He squeezed her hand and in the quiet moment that followed, they heard voices in Becky's room.

"Uh-oh," Grace whispered. "Somebody didn't make it all the way to the Captain's Quarters."

They walked quietly through the kitchen on their way through the house.

"I'm sure Becky will send him packing before long."

They walked up the steps together. "You're probably right."

"Poor Tank," Alex said.

"He'll survive."

They made it to their room and Alex surprised her by scooping her up into his arms. "Carry you over the threshold?" he whisper-asked.

Grace giggled and fumbled for the door handle. "Take me in, Romeo."

Saturday - Midnight
Liz

Liz yawned and glanced at her phone. She didn't want to bother Becky, but they'd agreed to stick to the schedule if John called them in. He'd been so apologetic when he caught her and Anita an hour earlier. He had come down from the penthouse, figuring he'd only ask for help if he found someone awake. Liz was just saying good night to Ed and Anita when John appeared, so she hardly had time to consider the commencement of her unexpected wedding night when it became clear she'd be otherwise occupied. One look at Anita, who'd signed on for the ten to midnight shift, told Liz that she should step in, herself. Anita needed to sleep after leading the charge to help bring Baby Fordham into the world.

Liz had gripped her new husband's hand and felt his answering squeeze. "Anita, I'll take this first shift," she said. "We're going to need you well-rested tomorrow, and you have already done your share of miracle-working today." She smiled up at the new daddy. "Give me a minute to grab a few things and I'll be right up."

Anita drew breath to argue, but Ed stepped in and accepted the offer. "That would be wonderful, Liz. We both thank you." He put an arm around Anita out of affection, and, perhaps, to hold her back. "I, for one, wouldn't want to wake up when she comes back from her shift in the middle of the night." He grinned at his wife. "This works for me."

"Oh, Ed," Anita protested without her usual fire. She turned to Liz. "I want to fight this; I'm the one who said no switching schedules, but since we're just starting, I think it'll be okay." She glanced apologetically at Christopher. "I'm sorry, Dr. Harrison. I can't believe I'm stealing your new wife on your wedding night, but I am tired and would welcome the rest."

John had looked newly concerned, as though he'd forgotten that Liz and Christopher were now married, but Liz anticipated his objection.

"It's all good," she said. "Christopher and I will have our time together." She'd surprised herself with her boldness in making that statement. The thought had sent a rush of happiness through her and she'd turned to her new husband. "See you in an hour," she whispered, pecking him on his shadowed cheek.

He'd been gracious, of course, and she'd heard him reassuring the group as she'd slipped into the room to get her book.

Now, an hour later, Liz glanced, again, at the precious little life sleeping quietly in the bassinet beside her. Once John made the decision to give their tiny daughter into the care of another, she had done nothing but sleep quietly. Liz had hoped to be needed more - would love to have had a reason to hold the little one and walk with her, but she'd apparently been tired after her busy day.

The shift was over, and it was time to send for reinforcements. Liz, herself, was scheduled from four to six a.m., so she was going to need the sleep.

If she slept.

She texted Becky and waited for relief.

$$\mathcal{SSS}$$

"Did you take Anita's shift?"

"Yes - she was exhausted."

"Isn't this your wedding night?"

Liz was not about to enter into a wedding night conversation with No Boundaries Becky.

"Did that really happen today?"

"Sure did. I'll be right up so you can go take care of your husband."

Liz smiled. 'Her husband'. She liked the sound of that.

"Thanks. I'll be here."

A few minutes later, Becky tip-toed up the steps and greeted Liz with a sleepy hug. "I just looked at Sergeant Anita's schedule. Aren't you on again at four?"

Liz ushered her in. "Yes. But I just couldn't let Anita take this shift. You'd have done the same."

"Thanks for thinking that." Becky walked over to where the baby was sleeping. "So this is Bella." She stood gazing into the bassinet. "A perfect name for a perfect little girl."

Liz joined her. "It is. John didn't tell me her name, and I wasn't going to pester him about details. He was pretty tired, too."

"Maddy texted me at some point, but for some reason, I didn't see it until just a little while ago."

"Well, I didn't get a chance to use it myself," Liz observed. "She's been sleeping soundly since John asked for help."

"Of course," Becky said, her face bemused as she looked at her sleeping niece. She finally turned to Liz. "Go try to 'sleep'."

Liz ignored the implication. "Please don't hesitate to text me if you need back-up. You have a big day tomorrow."

Becky waved her off. "I'll be fine." She nudged Liz toward the door. "I'll get you if she gets out of hand."

"Really. Please do," Liz insisted.

"I will," Becky replied. "Now go. See if your husband waited up for you."

"I hardly know what to hope for."

"You know exactly what to hope for."

Liz stalled at the door, not wanting to invite any more speculation, but oddly unwilling to leave. "Who would have thought ..."

"I know! It's crazy. How did you get married first? Tank is not a happy camper."

"Yikes. Sorry about that."

"Please. This is good for him. After what he put us through? I hope this is the longest night of his life."

Liz considered her friend. "How are you doing with the delay?"

"Me? I'm too tired to care. Honestly."

Liz raised a brow, but Becky held firm.

"In fact, since he's in the Captain's Quarters tonight, you'll be right next door to him. Do me a favor and make lots of noise. That should really frustrate him."

Liz knew she should have left when she had the chance. She started down the steps laughing. "Good night, Becky."

"Lots of happy, infuriating noise!" Becky called after her in a loud whisper.

Liz picked up her pace and slipped through the door to the second-floor landing. She closed it quietly and leaned against it, trying to slow her heart rate a little before going in to greet her new husband.

$$\mathcal{S}\,\mathcal{S}\,\mathcal{S}$$

Like the night before, Liz Michaels, finance professor, quietly opened the door into the dark room that she shared with Dr. Harrison, literature professor. Unlike the night before, she was now married to the man. *Married.*

The extraordinary vibe running through the inn on this Valentine's weekend had gotten a hold of her careful and reserved self and changed her life forever. She was not accustomed to making forever changes without a reasonable amount of thought and planning. Liz Michaels should have been absolutely terrified.

Liz Michaels-Harrison, she did like the sound of that, felt new life and energy pulsing through her veins. It was rather a delightful thrumming.

Of course, it was likely due, in part, to some wedding night jitters, however unlikely they were to actually consummate their hasty marriage, surrounded by an inn-ful of inquisitive people. Becky's suggestion unequivocally put the kibosh on that possibility. The very idea that Tank or anyone would hear them ... Liz shuddered, unable to finish the thought, even in the privacy of her own mind.

Still, limitations to the expression of their affection notwithstanding, climbing into bed on this night would be very different from the night before.

Unless Christopher was sleeping, which he probably was.

Closing the door behind her, she listened for his breathing, and like the night before, she heard nothing above the creaky heating system. At least he wasn't a crazy-loud snorer. She hoped. That 'get-to-know-you' detail hadn't quite made the cut over the last six weeks' conversations. Who would have thought it would become relevant knowledge on the weekend of her friend's wedding?

Liz walked into the room quietly, wishing, again, that the nightlight worked. Deciding she didn't need or want the bright glare of her phone's flashlight, she felt for the dresser to orient herself, and leaned over to slip off her shoes. Just beyond the dresser was the luggage rack with her bag, and she felt around for her pajamas. Slipping out of her dress was not going to be easy; the decorative hooks and buttons had to be negotiated before the zipper down the back of the dress could be accessed. She'd had Becky's help before the wedding and thought that she might have Christopher's help afterward.

She listened again.

"Christopher?" she whispered.

No response.

Sighing, she reached for the top fastener on the back of the dress. The bracelet that Kelly had given her managed to snag on the first hook and Liz stopped. She didn't want to break this bracelet, too. She still planned on returning it to Kelly, with the wonderful memory it carried, intact. She reached over her head and then up her back with her other hand, but to no avail. Her right arm was trapped over her head, her wrist snuggly attached to the top of her lovely wedding dress.

"Christopher?" she repeated, a little louder. She walked carefully over to the bed and used her left hand to feel around for him. This time she was a little bolder, and a little less terrified of the possibility of making contact with his person.

At first touch, she only felt the bed spread. Was he even in the room?

"Christopher?" Using her normal voice, she made one more attempt to wake him.

The door behind her swung open, and Liz jumped in surprise. Losing her precarious, one-armed balance, she face-planted onto the bed with a muffled squeal.

Sadly, instead of absorbing his new wife's undignified plunge, Christopher observed it in its full glory from behind, as he stood in the doorway. Liz groaned and tried to turn over, but her free arm was momentarily trapped beneath her.

"Are you okay?" Christopher did a terrible job of covering a laugh as he crossed the room. He eased onto the bed beside her and seemed to assess what he could of her awkward arm positioning before pulling the hair out of her face so she could explain.

"Can you roll me over?" she grunted, a little louder than she'd intended. "Carefully, please."

She was about to explain that her bracelet was caught when another voice entered the fray.

"You know your door is wide open, right?" Becky whispered loudly from the hallway.

Liz groaned again, and this time Christopher laughed out loud.

"Come on in," he called. "Maybe you can help."

"If you two need my help, I'm definitely not coming in there," Becky informed them, her voice drawing nearer. "Liz forgot her book and I thought I'd run it down before, well, you know ..." Her voice sounded like it hovered in the doorway.

"Please help me," Liz ground out. "My bracelet is stuck."

She could hear Becky entering the room. "Okay if I turn on a light?" The grin in her voice was obvious.

"That would be great," Liz replied, more than ready for the humiliation to end. *Speaking of which* ... "Maybe you should close the door first."

Becky giggled. "That'll give people something to think about."

Liz buried her face in the spread.

The soft lamplight must have allowed Christopher to see the source of her entanglement. "Ouch! How did you manage to hold your position when you fell?" He moved the hair away from her neckline, and Liz tried to focus on the problem, rather than his hand in her hair.

"I didn't really think it through." Her voice was still somewhat muffled, although quieter this time. "I'm assuming the bracelet is intact or I wouldn't still be stuck?"

Becky leaned over her. "I need more light."

The bedside lamp came on.

"Wow - how did you manage this?"

Liz felt her friend carefully maneuvering the bracelet and hook, while Christopher continued to gently move her hair out of the way. She tingled beneath his touch, and wondered what Becky was making of his help.

"Got it!" Becky finally managed the detangling, and Liz's arm fell limp above her head.

"Alright, you two. I've done all I can do to help. You're on your own now."

Becky headed to the door as Liz turned over with a sigh. Christopher gently pulled her up to his side.

"Thanks, Becky," Liz managed. "Please don't hesitate to text. I'll have my phone."

Becky stopped at the door. "We'll see." She winked and disappeared, closing the door behind her.

$$\int \int \int$$

"So," Christopher said when they were alone again. "I'm missing something."

Liz raised a tired brow.

"Why were you standing in the dark when I came in just now?"

That must have seemed fairly odd.

"I thought you were asleep. At first, I was trying not to wake you ..."

"You thought I'd be asleep on our wedding night?" Christopher raised a not-so-tired brow.

Liz could feel her face heat up. "It's been a long day - for all of us."

He shook his head with a smile.

"So, anyway, I started to get undressed and then got stuck. I was trying to wake you, well, find you first, and then ask for your help. I think I lost a year of my life when you walked in behind me."

"Sorry about that," Christopher rubbed her back gently. "After you left to help John, I went downstairs to call Cam and Amy. I figured they should know what their dad was doing on Valentine's Day."

"Oh my, how did that go?" Liz had a few people to call herself, but at least her own daughter had been able to attend. She knew Christopher's son, but had never met Amy. What must they think?

"Amy was surprised, but happy. I know I've told you that she's been supportive from the beginning. She's determined to have a party for us in the spring. She can't wait to meet you."

"That's amazing. I can't imagine why she's so willing to give me a chance," Liz replied.

"The truth speaks for itself." Christopher moved his hand to her face, tucking her hair behind her ear.

"Thank you." Trying to focus on the conversation despite how her new husband was regarding her, she ventured, "And how about Cam? Was he upset?"

Christopher thought for a moment. "Not upset. He was surprised, but guarded. I'm not sure he knows what to make of it."

"Did you talk to Bobby?"

Christopher's brother had tried to warn her away from him over the Christmas holiday when they'd all been together. He was convinced that Christopher would never stop grieving the wife he had lost to cancer ten years earlier. She could hardly imagine Bobby's response to their last-minute wedding.

"He was out, but Cam promised to fill him in," Christopher replied, a wry look on his face. "I'm sure I'll be getting an earful from him, but I'm not really worried about that right now."

Liz smiled, then thought about the calls she'd be making the following day. "My mom will be delighted, I think. My brothers still think I'm thirteen, so they've never taken me very seriously. I'm not sure they even believe that I'm a college professor," she mused. "Anyway," she smiled up at her husband, "I sure am looking forward to giving them a little surprise."

"And how long do you think we'll have for a honeymoon?"

She tilted her head in thought. It was amazing what they hadn't yet worked out. "Well, I took Monday off, and I only have two classes on Tuesday. I might be able to manage some extra time."

"And when are you checking out of the inn?" he asked with an admirably straight face.

"I guess that depends on whether I have a place to go when I leave," she pointed out, just as seriously.

"Well, I haven't really cleaned my house," Christopher replied thoughtfully. "That's usually a weekend thing, but I haven't been home since I went on a rescue mission yesterday."

"That was yesterday?" Liz was genuinely dumbfounded.

"Indeed," he replied, stopping to marvel for a minute with her. "Anyway," he continued, "if you don't mind the mess, I'd love to have you visit."

His eyes crinkled on the sides and Liz fell a little more in love with the man she married. "So, we'll see how the literature professor really lives, hmm?"

"If you dare."

She grinned. "I'll check out as soon as the snow clears. Or after Becky and Tank get married," she amended. "I don't imagine they'll waste any time."

"I don't suppose so."

They exchanged a long look, and Liz finally stood. "Okay, well, I don't want to be too forward, Dr. Harrison, but I'm going to need some help getting out of this dress."

Christopher stood, nodding seriously. "I would love to offer you some assistance, Professor Michaels."

"Thank you," she replied, turning her back. "And you forgot part of my name," she said over her shoulder. "I rather like the 'Harrison' I attached to it earlier today."

"Do you?" Christopher asked low, unzipping the back of her dress.

"Yes," Liz replied, trying to remain cool. "And I'll thank you to address me properly next time."

Christopher pulled her back against his chest. He leaned down and kissed her neck. "Did you really marry me today?"

Liz turned in his arms and gave him a better target. "I believe I did," she replied against his lips.

"Well. Happy Valentines Day," he whispered, leaving conversation for another day.

Sunday - 1:00 a.m.
Maddy

Maddy rolled to her side, and out of habit, rubbed her tummy, which felt ... different. A rush of joy immediately followed, and she reached for the crib.

"John!"

She felt her husband's body roll into her. "Are you okay?"

"The bassinet's gone! Where's Bella?"

John rolled back onto his own pillow and exhaled. "She's in the living room, sleeping."

Maddy continued to try to untangle herself from the sheets and covers. John reached out and pulled her back in.

"She's fine. Someone's with her."

"*Someone?!* You don't even know who's watching her?"

John gently tugged Maddy into his chest. "They have a schedule. They're taking turns sleeping in the living room with her. Remember? We talked about this."

Maddy began to settle into her husband's arms. "But I thought we agreed to try to have her in here with us."

"We did. But you stirred every time she coo-ed. I jumped every time you stirred. We need our sleep."

Maddy softened against him. "She coo-ed? What did it sound like?"

John sighed. "It sounded like she was resting peacefully and didn't need us waking and hovering over her."

"Oh."

"Maddy, we need our sleep. *You* need your sleep. You've been through a lot. Your body needs to heal. We have a houseful of capable women who are graciously willing, even anxious, to help us. Let them help."

Maddy felt the fatigue start to settle over her. "When do I get her back?"

John either chuckled or groaned - probably both. "As soon as she seems like she's hungry, whoever's on duty will bring her in here."

"Okay."

Maddy pictured her baby sleeping in the next room and smiled. "So, who's in there with her right now?"

A pause preceded John's answer. "Pretty sure it's Ed."

Maddy jumped, but her husband continued to hold her close while she processed his obviously not-funny-at-all joke. He leaned in to kiss her head. "Try to relax. She's in good hands. Sleep."

Knowing that John needed to sleep almost as much as she did, Maddy made an effort to calm down. "Thanks for the picture of Ed holding our baby. That'll help me relax."

"He'd do just fine. Likely anyone in the house would. *Sleep.*"

Maddy acknowledged that truth and nestled in.

"Where's Burt?"

Sigh. "Right next to the bassinet."

"Oh. Well, that's good."

"Mmmm."

"I guess he defected, huh?"

"Night, Maddy."

Maddy closed her eyes. "Night, John. Love you."

"You, too," he gently snored.

Sunday - 2:00 a.m.
Becky

A gentle rustling sound in the bassinet lifted Becky out of the doze she promised herself she wouldn't take. She quickly reached out and patted the squirming baby, trying to open her eyes and get oriented. Why couldn't she see Bella? She turned toward the kitchen, where she knew she'd left the light on over the sink.

It didn't take long to realize that the darkness of the room had nothing to do with her inability to wake up from a sleep she hadn't really slept. The room was completely dark, and it was starting to get chilly. They must have lost power.

Becky felt around for her phone and turned on the flashlight. Pointing it off to the side of the bassinet, she let just enough light touch her niece to confirm that she was still swaddled snugly, and had managed to keep her little knit cap in place. Relieved, Becky tucked her phone into her pocket so that it lit up the path to Maddy's room, a path conveniently blocked by a giant, sleeping wolfhound. Becky sighed and smiled. Burt apparently wanted to cover his bases, but even he finally had to sleep. She picked up her niece and held her close, giving herself a precious moment with the miracle in her arms, then made her way to her sister.

Burt woke in time to block her way. He stood as she reached the door, stretched his long body, then sniffed inquiringly at the bundle she held. There would be no entering the room without a confrontation Becky wasn't willing to have with a newborn baby in her arms.

"Maddy, John," she whispered.

Bella's gentle fussing intensified, and Becky didn't want the baby's cry, or Burt's reaction to it, to be the thing that woke the exhausted new parents. She heard stirring in their bed and breathed a sigh of relief.

"Maddy, I've got a delivery for you."

"Oh, wonderful. Thank you!" Maddy moved into a sitting position. "Please, bring her in."

"I can't."

"What? Why?" Maddy's tired voice raised slightly in alarm.

"She's fine, Maddy. I just can't get past Burt."

The wolfhound continued to stand in the doorway, nosing at Bella.

"Oh, Burt!" Maddy whispered with a half laugh. "Come. *Now.*"

Her dog tensed and turned his head. He looked back at the baby one more time, then opted for obeying the command. Becky followed him carefully into the room.

"Sit," Maddy instructed him, and he complied.

"Good work," Becky observed as she gently handed Bella to her mother.

Maddy's happy sigh almost made Becky forget the latest debacle. Her sister didn't even notice that her room was cool, or that her little nightlight wasn't doing its job.

"I think the power's out," Becky whispered, wondering if John had awakened during the last few minutes' commotion. A quiet snore indicated that he was among the unconcerned.

"Oh no, really?" Maddy looked around and seemed to process the lack of light. She leaned toward her husband. "John," she whispered gently.

He lay, unmoving, beside her. Becky resisted the urge to shine her phone light on his face.

"John." As she leaned, Maddy dislodged her nursing daughter, and the resulting squeal, tiny as it was, roused her husband.

"Everything okay?" he asked, waking and fumbling upright. He peered over Maddy's shoulder and stilled, smiling at the sight of his daughter. He leaned back against the headboard and closed his eyes again. It appeared that he might actually fall back asleep.

"Honey, the power is out," Maddy said. "Lights are out and it's getting a little cold up here."

An unmistakable groan accompanied John's subsequent exit from his hard-earned place of rest. "Generator should have kicked in," he muttered, finally standing and looking around, as though the offending machinery could be found somewhere in his bedroom.

Becky, supremely glad that her brother-in-law had worn pajamas to bed, said, "I'm sure Tank would be glad to help you."

John whipped his head around, clearly not expecting anyone else to be in the room. He ran a hand through his hair and eyed her with some confusion.

It would have been funny, and probably still might be at some later point when they looked back on this night, but in the moment, Becky decided to opt for apology over laughter. "I'm sorry to disturb you. I figured you'd want to know."

"Of course," John replied, looking around the room again.

"I'll let you get ready," she said, stepping back into the hallway. She figured he might want to wear something more than flannel pajama pants to go out into the storm.

A few minutes later, he emerged with a giant flashlight that lit up the living room with a thousand watts of illumination. Becky looked at her phone light with some disappointment and tucked it away.

John took a moment to check on his boys and then made his way to the front door. "Where's Tank?" he asked, pulling his coat on and stepping into his boots.

"Should be down in the Captain's Quarters. Want me to go scare him out?"

"No, that's okay. I'll grab him," John replied, regaining some of his more predictable gentleness. He turned to her. "Keep an eye on my girls?"

SSS

Becky heard the apartment door rattle way too soon. There was no way they'd had time to fix anything. Had John even found help? Would he mind that she had taken over his space and was snuggling in his bed next to his wife?

John walked into the room and paused. "Okay, that's not what I was expecting." He sighed, resetting. "I can't find Tank."

"He isn't in the Captain's Quarters?" Becky started the process of slipping out of the bed.

His hands on his hips and the tilt of his head indicated that John had investigated that possibility. Becky was rather glad that she couldn't really see his expression by the light of her phone.

"Sorry. Of course, you looked." She finished maneuvering out of John's sleeping space, straightening the covers as she went. "I don't know. The last I saw him, he was in my room, but ..."

"Ahh," John replied.

"No 'ahhh'," Becky sputtered defensively, straightening to face him. "He walked me to my room, sort of, and we were just talking when Liz texted me to come up here." She looked between John and Maddy, not sure why, after years of not caring what people thought about her choices with men, on this night, it mattered. She sighed. "I'll go find him."

Becky left the room and hustled down two flights of stairs. If Tank had stayed in her room, she wanted a moment alone with him to do something ... bad.

She didn't want witnesses.

SSS

She marched into the kitchen and through the door to the bedroom she often used, her insipid phone light guiding the way. She stopped short when she looked at her bed.

Three conflicting emotions raged at the sight she beheld. Tank Kimball, former NFL linebacker, the man who struck fear in the hearts of other linemen and not a few quarterbacks, was curled on his side on her twin bed, asleep. Curled was not the right word. Nothing about his frame seemed capable of curling. But he lay on his side with his legs bent, undoubtedly due to the fact that he wouldn't fit on her bed any other way.

Why was he trying to fit on her bed in the first place? He had access to a big, queen-size bed in the Captain's Quarters, and with inn space at such a premium, he'd better have a really good excuse for not using it.

That was thought number one.

Or more like number three. Thoughts one and two were more immediate, and conflicting. The man lying on his side hardly appeared small and helpless, but his very posture conjured up pictures of a younger, smaller Tank, who maybe had been just a bit vulnerable ... sometimes. That softened Becky's heart a little.

That was thought number two.

Far and away, the number one thought was that in less than twenty-four hours, she may very well find herself tucked in next to that unwieldy linebacker.

Hopefully not in that bed.

There was, however, no time to indulge the direction of any of those thoughts. "Tank!" she whisper-hissed.

Walking up to the bed and the impressive back facing her, she shoved his shoulder. "Tank! Wake up!"

He started to turn, and Becky thought he might tip right off the bed. She tried to steady him as he began to shift toward her, but her little act of kindness back-fired. He threw his big, heavy arm out and grabbed a hold of her before she realized that he was fully awake. It was fairly quick work for him to haul her over and into the bed next to him.

This tossing her around business was going to have to stop.

"You came back," he said sleepily, snuggling her next to him.

It took incredible effort to resist sleepy Tank and the exceedingly inviting spot she found herself in, her transit there notwithstanding. "No, Tank," she replied, which was kind of silly, because she did come back - just not for him - or not for him *for her* - for John.

Two in the morning was not a great time for clarity.

"Let me go," she wriggled in frustration. "I have elbows, and knees, and I'm not afraid to use them."

Tank tensed appropriately, and then wisely let her go.

Seizing the opportunity, Becky jumped to her feet and planted her hands on her hips, which didn't matter because he couldn't see her. "We lost power, and John needs you to help him with his generator. He was looking for you in the Captain's Quarters, because that's where you were supposed to be. Why are you in here?"

Hopefully, her tone communicated the terrifying visual Tank was missing. The bed creaked as he shifted, and Becky could actually hear the scratchy sound as he rubbed his hands over his face.

"What's with the generators around here?" He lumbered to his feet, and his phone lit up the room. He flashed it at her and she winced, covering her eyes.

"Hey! Watch it! Shine that on the bed so I can find my own phone."

"This is yours." He tossed it to her, or at her, and pulled his own out of his pocket. "Where's John?"

Being irresistibly drawn to someone who endlessly irritated her was exhausting. Becky threw her hands up and marched back into the kitchen. "Looking for you, remember?"

They heard the man in question making his way down the back staircase into the kitchen, his ferocious light preceding him.

"Hi John. I found your apprentice," Becky called out, more than ready to send Tank out into the storm. "He'd be happy to help you get the power back on."

Sunday - 3:00 a.m.
Grace

A not-so-subtle pound on the door had both Grace and Alex jumping out of a deep, very relaxed and happy sleep. Alex found his way out of the bed first.

"I hope everything's okay."

Grace was on his heels, burrowing into her no-longer-warm-enough sleeping shirt.

They eased open the door to a rather menacing-looking Tank. Grace relaxed a little, in spite of the unusual interruption. Tank didn't need an alarming reason to look menacing.

Becky suddenly edged in front of him. "I'm so sorry! I told him not to pound on your door."

"Is everything alright?" Grace asked, huddling into Alex for warmth.

"You said she didn't answer your text," Tank said to Becky.

"You texted me?" Grace asked. "I'm so sorry I missed it."

"It's really not a problem." Becky elbowed Tank. "I told him that, but, of course, he didn't listen."

"Why do you have your coat on?" Grace asked. Tank's coat was wet and his face was red, as though he'd just come in from the storm.

"Generator," he grunted.

"Is that why it's so cold?"

"Yep," Becky replied. "Power's out and the generator didn't kick in. John and Tank just fixed it or reconnected it or whatever."

She looked up at Tank, seemed to consider his wet state, then wisely took a step away from him. He grinned and closed the distance.

Grace looked around the hallway, considering the small lamp on an antique table, and the lights over the staircase. "So the generator works for the whole house; not just the furnace and certain appliances?"

"It has to," Becky replied, moving away from Tank again. "Just in case the power goes out and we have an inn-ful of guests." She cringed a little. "Like now."

Grace thought about her generator at the coffee shop, and figured she'd be revisiting its usefulness. The present moment, however, was more pressing, and she happily shelved that concern. "So, am I on for baby duty?"

"If you don't mind. John's getting a space heater going, so it should be toasty soon."

"Then I get to meet the baby!" Grace's sleepiness melted away as she warmed to the thought.

"Bella. They named her earlier this evening."

"Oh, that's beautiful!"

"Yep. I think that's what it means."

Before they could fully indulge this happy contemplation, Tank stepped up behind Becky and wrapped his arms around her.

Becky couldn't be blamed for squealing. She really had no protection from Tank's cold, wet jacket. "Get off of me, you big jerk! You're soaking wet!"

Tank grinned and nuzzled her neck, which didn't sit well with his bride-to-be.

Alex chuckled beside her, and Grace wondered how long it would take her parents to wake up and join the fray.

It wasn't long.

A door opened down the hall, and the four of them turned with a guilty start, Tank swinging Becky around in front of him.

Grace's parents appeared, tying their elegant robes in unison.

"What's going on out here?" her father demanded.

"Edwin, put her down!"

There was a beat of silence as Becky stopped struggling, and tilted her head to look up at Tank. "Edwin? That's your name?"

Another beat of silence.

"You're telling me you were planning to marry someone who doesn't even know your given name?" Grace's dad rumbled disapprovingly.

"Not someone. *Becky*. And not were. *Are*. Still planning." Tank awkwardly turned his forearm while keeping a hold of Becky, and looked at his watch. "Seven hours."

"What's wrong with Edwin?" Becky asked.

"There's nothing wrong with Edwin!" Grace's mother sputtered. "It's my father's name!"

"I love that name," Becky replied, apparently too taken with the reveal to worry about being clamped to Tank's wet chest. "My best friend in Kindergarten's name was Edwin."

Grace watched the whole exchange with wonder. Tank had never told Becky his name?

"Oh, well ..." Her mom could hardly continue the argument.

"Why wouldn't you tell me your name?"

"Don't like it."

"We never really called him 'Edwin'," her dad chimed in.

"You didn't. *I* did," Mom countered.

"When did they start calling you 'Tank'?" Becky asked.

"It was all I ever knew," Grace offered. "I remember asking Mom one day who Edwin was. I had no idea who they were talking about."

Grace's recollection broke the tension and everybody laughed. Tank set Becky down and she turned to him, hands on her hips.

"When were you going to tell me?"

"When we get married."

"So, Pastor Rob knows your name?"

"Yep."

Becky punched him. "You're a jerk."

"I agree."

They all turned in surprise to Grace and Tank's mom.

"I hope you take better care of her when she's your wife," she muttered. "I'm going back to bed."

The group watched, dumbfounded, as she walked back to her room. Grace's dad looked on for a moment, shrugged and followed.

The four remaining turned to each other. Before anyone could speak, Ed popped his head out of his room.

"Party out here?"

Sunday - 4:00 a.m.
Liz

"I'm so sorry to wake you. Are you up for baby duty?"

Liz blinked at the message on her phone screen. She'd meant to set an alarm, but apparently, it wasn't necessary. She'd heard the ping of the text through the layers of happy sleep.

"Of course. Should I just meet you upstairs?"

"That would be great. TYSM!"

Liz looked at the acronym for a moment and then smiled.

"You're welcome. Be right up."

She turned to look at her new husband, but of course, she couldn't see much of anything. Liz knew he was there, though, could feel his warmth beside her. She sighed happily, rested her hand briefly on his solid arm, then eased out from under the covers. The room was chilly, and she immediately regretted leaving the warmth. With a sigh, she made her way to her bag and found the next day's jeans and sweater. Apparently, she was starting Sunday early.

With one last, longing look at her husband, or at least in his general direction, she quietly opened and slipped through the door.

Sunday - 5:00 a.m.
Maddy

She couldn't make sense of the argument. Someone sounded angry, someone sounded sad, and someone sounded ... well, that emotion wasn't clear, but there was definitely a third someone in the mix.

Was she dreaming? Maddy tried to pull herself out of her fog of sleep. The sad one particularly held her attention. Was he or she hurt or frightened? The angry one wasn't loud, but there was no mistaking the emotion. The third one had a soothing voice, and Maddy might have relaxed back into sleep, if she wasn't there already, had that voice not suddenly changed.

It was louder. It was firmer. It was calling her.

"Maddy, I need your help."

Someone did need help! Maddy finally shook off the last dregs of sleep and swung her legs over the side of her bed, trying to get oriented. The nightlight didn't reveal much, but it did direct her attention to the doorway.

Why was Liz Michaels moving furniture in her apartment?

"Hi Maddy. Sorry - Burt won't let me through," Liz whispered.

Maddy's disoriented gaze fell to her growling dog. Of course, the angry one. And the sad one? Maddy jumped to her feet and stopped just as suddenly, her body reminding her that she was still healing. She drew a calming breath. Bella was safe; she glanced up at Liz again to confirm this. Yes, Bella must be safe in her bassinet. Maddy steadied herself, then slowly made her way over to the door.

"She just started to fuss," Liz explained. "But Burt wouldn't let me get by, so I thought I'd be able to muscle through with the bassinet. I figured that would be safer for Bella, anyway ..."

"And he still wouldn't let you pass," Maddy concluded. "Weird dog. What does he think you're going to do?" She patted Burt's head and then pushed him out of the way, which was only possible because he allowed it. "Let her in, Burt."

Maddy braced some weight on the bassinet as they rolled it together toward the bed. She smiled in wonder at her fussing daughter, itching to get her back into her arms.

"Why don't you get comfortable and I'll hand her to you?" Liz suggested.

Maddy happily did so, and moments later, her daughter was nestled in.

"Such a beautiful little girl," Liz said softly.

"Thank you," Maddy sighed. "Thank you so much for watching her and letting us rest."

"It's my pleasure. Truly," Liz replied. "Can I get you anything before I head back to the living room?"

"If you'd refill my water, that would be great," Maddy said, hating to ask more favors, but so grateful for the help.

"Happy to," Liz assured her, picking up the water bottle. "Anything else?"

"I think I'm good. Thank you so much for everything."

"You're welcome. I'll bring the water back and then wait for your call when you're done nursing. It would be good for you to get a little more sleep."

"Perfect." Maddy looked again at her daughter. "Do you ever get over the wonder of it all?"

Liz stopped in the doorway. "No," she replied softly. "It's an ongoing miracle of chaos and joy."

Maddy looked up and nodded. "And so it begins."

Sunday - 6:00 a.m.
Becky

"Happy wedding day. Can you come let this dog out?"
Wedding day.

Becky groaned. She didn't feel particularly bride-like and wasn't likely to get there any time soon.

Her phone buzzed again. Anita sent another message.

"Sorry, Liz isn't sure she can control the dog and he's getting pretty antsy. Left his post by Maddy's room and is pacing by the front door."

Wow. Burt meant business.

Becky rolled out of bed, considering her wrinkled shorts and T-shirt sleeping ensemble only briefly before heading out the door. She kicked into some slippers and stomped up the steps.

Happy wedding day, indeed.

§ § §

Burt lumbered down two flights of steps pretty quickly for a dog his size, and Becky followed as quickly as her tired legs could carry her. In the kitchen, she grabbed somebody's coat - probably Ed's - off the hook by the door and pulled it on. With a deep breath, she opened the door and let the dog out.

The dark, snow-covered scene was still and pristine for a moment, then Burt's momentary pause turned into decisive action. He forged a path through the snow-laden porch, down the steps, and out to the beach. Becky watched him for a moment, glad that the snow had actually stopped falling, then scuffled into the laundry room for a doggie towel.

She returned to the door, huddled into whoever's coat, and waited. Finally making her peace with being up for the day, she started a pot of coffee. She supposed there might be other early risers who would appreciate the effort.

The smell of fresh-roasted coffee brewing lifted her spirits considerably. The fact that Burt still hadn't returned threatened to dash them again. It seemed he had plenty of his own business to attend to on this fine, freezing morning. She opened the door and peered out. The sky was lightening some, but the sun wasn't due up for another half an hour.

Where had the stupid dog gone?

The taste of fresh roasted coffee made Becky feel like a human again. Had Burt returned like a normal dog, she might even start putting the long night behind her and begin looking forward to her wedding day.

However.

One more look outside gave her no new information. "Burt!" she called. "Come!"

She didn't have a lot of confidence in her ability to reel him in. They had a good relationship - she wasn't afraid of him - but she certainly wasn't the boss.

"Burt! Come! *Now!*"

The dog wasn't compelled by the addition of a time frame.

Moments turned to minutes and the sound of a dog collar jingling remained more embedded in Becky's imagination than reality. She sighed. There was no way she was going to bother Maddy and John when they might actually be sleeping. There was only one other person who had any kind of control over the wolfhound.

With a groan, she made her way up to his room.

$\int \int \int$

Like Burt, Tank didn't immediately respond. Unlike Burt, her groom-to-be was very likely tucked in bed, warm and comfy, and oblivious to the importance of the day.

Becky decided to enlighten him.

Because the door to his room was somewhat removed from the other doors in the hallway, she took the liberty of giving it several more, hearty raps.

Becky finally heard movement, and she waited, as ever, with her hands firmly planted on her hips, scowl in place. Tank sure was taking his sweet time while Burt wandered the neighborhood. She figured the dog would eventually return, but the storm added an element of uncertainty that had her a little worried. Tank's unresponsiveness to a problem that he couldn't possibly be aware of was as good a reason as any to be irritated with him, and since that was her go-to emotion with Tank, it was comfortable territory. Besides, he was tucked in, sleeping comfortably, again, and she wasn't.

He opened the door and Becky choked on her, *"It's your wedding day. Go find the stupid dog!"* speech.

Tank stood sleepily regarding her, garbed only in his athletic shorts, his bulky former linebacker perfection on full display. She stepped back, dropping her hands from her hips and tucking them into the pockets of Ed's coat.

She looked away from her fiancé and considered his. Tank belonged on the cover of a magazine, and she looked like somebody's grampa.

"Nice coat," Tank observed, the humor in his low, sleepy voice evident.

Becky couldn't respond. All she could think was that this picture of her - uncombed hair, make-up-less face, weird, shapeless parka, and fluffy slippers - would be burned into Tank's memory forever. No flawless wedding dress would ever erase it.

She sighed and looked up, lifting her chin high so that her eyes went higher.

"Aren't you cold?" she asked imperiously.

"Aren't you?" he asked, nudging her coat aside and revealing her own more-like-summer pajama wear.

"I have a coat on," she pointed out unnecessarily, whipping it closed around her.

"I'm plenty warm," Tank assured her, his voice matching his claim.

Becky refused to go there. "I let Burt out and he won't come back in for me."

She sighed again, realizing that she had no current reason to be irritated with Tank, so waking him up early and rudely wasn't exactly a wife-to-be kind of thing to do. With an effort, she softened her voice and her request. "Would you be up for helping me? You're the only one he'll listen to. Well, besides Maddy, and I don't want to bother her."

"Hmmm," Tank responded, running a hand over his stubbled jaw. He smirked at her concerted effort to look only at his eyes. "I guess I should get dressed first?" His normally hooded and scowly eyes danced a bit at her discomfort.

That look somehow became more distracting than his traps or his pecs.

Becky turned on her heels, trying to muster some irritation. "You can go out like that if you like," she said over her shoulder. "But you should probably find some boots. Snow's deep."

She heard him chuckle as she hustled down the stairs to the kitchen.

$\mathcal{SSS}$

Of course, Tank made quick business of finding and corralling Burt, and had him returned to the penthouse in less time than it took Becky to brush her teeth, make sense of her hair, and slip into jeans and her favorite, green, cable-knit sweater. Fortunately, by the time Tank returned to the kitchen to join her, she felt a little more composed.

That composure evaporated when he backed her into the refrigerator and kissed her. It wasn't really the response she expected or deserved for dragging him out of bed so early.

Responding with the enthusiasm such courtesy demanded, she was well on her way to forgetting her breakfast menu and all of the people who would likely soon be hungry, when he pulled slightly away.

"Marry me today?" he asked.

She smiled beneath his lips. "I guess," she replied. "But only because you found Burt."

He smiled and turned his attention to the kiss.

Becky made a rather uncommitted effort to pull back. "We're not married, yet," she reminded him a little breathlessly.

He stopped momentarily. "Yeah, but we're alone."

She managed enough space to put a finger on his lips. "We can wait a little longer, Tank. We've only got about three and a half hours to go."

"Ten o'clock," he mumbled. He groaned and leaned his forehead on hers. "I won't make it."

"Yes, you will."

"People will never leave."

"Sure they will," Becky replied, then reconsidered. "Well, maybe not your parents."

He groaned again.

"Gotta be tough, Tank," she reminded him playfully. "Gonna be a long day."

S. Jane Scheyder

Sunday - 7:00 a.m.
Grace

Her overdeveloped coffee sensors picked up the scent the minute Grace stepped out of her room. Who had made coffee? She'd hoped to get breakfast started before anyone else felt the burden of it. Becky had a big day ahead of her, and the Fordhams sure didn't need to be worrying about feeding people.

Grace hustled down the steps, hoping Alex would get a little more rest before starting the day. Her necessary path through the dining room - that design anomaly always confounded her - confirmed that someone was well on their way with breakfast preparations. The scones and muffins that she'd brought were laid out, and the coffee smell grew stronger.

Someone had been very busy, fairly early.

Her father's laugh brought her up short as she put her hand on the door to the kitchen. It had been a long time since she'd heard that sound, and it both warmed her heart and utterly confused her. What party was she missing this time?

She slowly entered the kitchen, drawing the attention of her father, her mother, and Becky. Their faces were relaxed, their smiles tentative, but sincere. Grace definitely needed some of whatever they'd been imbibing.

"Morning," Becky was the first to greet her. "I'll put some water on for tea."

"Thank you," Grace replied. She gave a little wave to her dad as she walked over to her mom and pecked her on the cheek.

"Good morning, Grace," her mom echoed quietly, her smile becoming a little more guarded.

"Morning. What have I been missing?" She tried to sound as though it were perfectly natural to find her parents enjoying a private joke with Becky.

Tank walked in from the sunroom, grounding the scene in a little more reality. Grace breathed easier as he walked up and gave her a side hug that only left her slightly bruised.

"Becky's ruining Mom and Dad's perfect impression of me."

Grace looked around with wonder. "About time."

Tank cuffed her head playfully and walked over to Becky, leaning against the counter and settling in beside her. Grace straightened her hair and considered the group. She was dying to know what they'd been laughing about, but the moment seemed to have passed. She regretted having interrupted them, but leaving didn't really make sense, so she opted for practical.

"How can I help with breakfast?"

"Well, thanks to you, we've got the baked goods all set to go with the coffee," Becky replied, tucking in next to Tank. "I figure we can put the egg casserole in for brunch a little later. You know, the one that Anita made sometime before or after she delivered Maddy's baby?" She grinned. "Good thing the Davidsons got in before the storm really hit. Can you imagine what we'd have done without her this weekend?"

"She's amazing. Who knew she had all those skills?" Grace walked over to make her tea. "I sure hope she can sleep this morning."

"She's already on baby duty," Becky reminded her. "She took over for Liz at six. Had to get me up to get Burt out. Then I had to get Tank up to get Burt in."

"Oh, should I go see if she needs a break?" It made Grace a little sad that her mother wasn't a part of the conversation, but they could only expect so much improvement in one weekend. The fact that the five of them were in the same room together having a non-combative conversation was victory enough.

Becky contemplated her offer. "You could try, but my guess is now that she's up, she'll be ready to go for the day."

"Probably true," Grace agreed.

"Oh, look!" Her mom was the one to direct their attention to the sun that was beginning to peek over the horizon. Everyone made their way to the windows, mugs in hand, to watch the display in quiet, shared awe.

Grace felt her throat constrict as she considered the couples on either side of her, united in their appreciation of the miracle before them. It was an inspiring sight, the sun being especially welcome after the long and overwhelming storm. They stood there for some time in companionable silence, an equally awe-inspiring miracle.

The door opened behind them and she turned, feeling her face light up at the sight of her husband. He hesitated in the doorway, no doubt feeling the tension emanating from her parents.

"You're just in time," Grace assured him. "Come watch the sun rise with us."

He nodded and walked into the room, coming to stand by her side. Tank and Becky greeted him quietly, then returned their attention to the horizon. Her parents gave him a wide berth, going so far as to return to their post at the island counter in the middle of the kitchen. Evidently, whatever healing process they'd begun with Becky didn't extend to Alex. Grace sighed and pulled her husband closer.

He kissed her temple. "What a way to start the morning."

"Amazing, isn't it?"

The four of them continued to enjoy the peaceful announcement of the new day, leaving her parents to make of it what they would.

"Well," Becky finally said, turning from the show. "If that isn't symbolic, I don't know what is." She reached up and kissed Tank on the cheek, then brushed at her lips. "You're going to shave that, right?"

Tank answered by rubbing his cheek against her face. Becky sputtered and leaned away from him.

"Nice, thanks." She lifted a hand to protect her face from further assault and addressed the others. "So, who's shoveling, and who's taking a long, relaxing bath and getting ready for her wedding?"

Tank growled and Alex and Grace smiled.

"I can help Tank clear the snow," her father offered, somewhat gruffly. "We'll make quick business of it."

Tank rolled his shoulders with a sigh. "There won't be anything quick about it, Dad, but it needs to be done." He scowled without rancor at his bride-to-be. "If we finish in time, maybe I'll make it to the wedding."

Alex laughed. "I'll help. Wouldn't want you to miss your big day."

"Not necessary."

All eyes turned to her father, and Grace cringed. What game was he playing?

"We can handle it," he informed the room, avoiding eye contact with Alex.

"No doubt," his son-in-law responded carefully. "But I'm happy to help."

Her father should have been pleased with the offer, but said nothing. Grace squeezed her husband's hand.

"I'm sorry," she whispered, "and thank you."

A tap on the outside door drew their attention, and Frank entered the room a moment later, stomping his boots on the mat.

"Did you see that sunrise?" he greeted the room with his usual cheer. "What a beauty!"

Tank raised his voice over the greetings and agreement. "Don't take off your coat. We're shoveling."

Frank pretended to be taken aback. "Who, me? A guest?" he protested. "Not before I have some of Grace's coffee." He kicked off his boots and made his way to the coffee urn. Filling a mug, he turned to the rest of the room. "Please, go ahead. I'll be right behind you." He grinned and sipped his coffee.

The mood of the room relaxed and Grace was grateful. Whatever issues her parents were currently processing with her husband didn't need sorting out on the morning of her brother's wedding.

Conversation continued comfortably while Frank enjoyed his coffee. When he poured his second mug, Grace said, "Okay, I'm going to take over in here. Becky, you run along." She waved her hand in dismissal, and then, breathing deep, said, "Mom, would you give me a hand with breakfast?"

Her mother looked momentarily surprised, and then, if Grace identified it correctly, slightly pleased. "Yes, of course I'll help."

There was no 'of course' about it, but Grace was relieved that the effort to connect was received by her mother. Tank punched Frank's non-coffee arm on his way through the kitchen.

"Coming?"

Frank grinned and made a show of protecting his mug. "All in good time, my friend."

Hearing lots of voices in the kitchen, Liz hoped that she and Christopher could enter the fray quietly and under the radar.

She should have known better.

The room grew silent as they walked through the door, every pair of eyes glued to them as they entered the room. It looked as though half of the group was about to head out.

If only we'd waited a little longer.

"Morning, newlyweds!" Frank boomed. "You missed some interesting inter ... discussion, while you were ... sleeping." He quoted with his fingers, making it easier to catch the missile Tank aimed at his head.

"Hey," Frank considered the wadded-up napkin. "This could have hurt me."

"Can't believe I missed," Tank replied. "Huge target."

Frank smoothed his hair back with a grin. "What can I say? Big head - big brains."

"I meant your mouth."

Frank guffawed. Tossing the napkin onto the counter, he mercilessly brought the attention back to Liz and Christopher. "Coffee, you two?" He set some mugs on the island. "Don't know how you like it," he wiggled his brows, "but I'm sure you need it. You must be exhausted."

Becky rolled her eyes and walked over to give Liz a hug. "Welcome to the ongoing insanity."

"Thank you," Liz replied. "It's everything I hoped for."

Christopher laughed quietly beside her, and Becky seemed delighted with her unexpected sarcasm.

"So, what are my chances of getting some cocoa?" Liz asked a little more gently.

"Better than average. 'Though it will take a few. I wasn't thinking you'd be up so early." Becky's eyes danced mischievously.

Liz sighed and glanced up at Christopher. "Suppose they have room service here?"

He absorbed the circus with his usual calm. "May as well brave it and get it over with."

Liz hummed her agreement. "Good luck getting your coffee." She glanced at Frank, hovering near the mugs he'd set out.

"I'm not afraid," Christopher replied stoically, squeezing her hand. "Stakes are too high."

Liz turned to Becky. "How are you feeling? Ready for your big day?"

"Who knows?" Becky replied, measuring out the cocoa powder. "We're down to two hours. Maybe it will really happen."

"It will," Liz assured her, happy for her friend, but distracted by how handsome Christopher looked in profile as he braved a conversation with Frank.

"He is one good-looking man," Becky observed.

"And you'll be married soon," Liz encouraged her friend absently, dragging her eyes away from her new husband.

"I was talking about Christopher."

"Oh." Liz accepted the cocoa Becky handed her and tried to sip, but it didn't work. She set the mug down and sighed. "He is, isn't he?"

"You'd better go rescue him. No telling what Frank's filling his head with."

"And who knew Frank could talk so quietly?" Liz observed with concern, picking up her mug. "I'm going in."

She walked over to join the two men, who seemed to be having a normal conversation until she approached. Evidently, she was the object of Frank's endless teasing. No real surprise there.

"How are you, Mrs. Harrison?" he asked, a twinkle in his eye.

Liz almost forgave him when he addressed her like that. "I'm well, thank you, Mr. Davidson. And you?" She took a chance and sipped her cocoa, daring him to say something that would cause her to spit it out at him.

"Just reassuring your husband here that the walls are nice and thick upstairs. I know from experience. We had to do some significant repairs on this place." He feigned an innocent smile.

Liz groaned inwardly. She was fairly certain that she hadn't interrupted a conversation about the structural integrity of Maddy's Inn. She repositioned her toasty mug, unwilling to put it down for the heat it offered her chilly hands. "Honestly, Frank, I'm so glad to hear that. I don't know how anyone else would have slept last night, otherwise."

Of course, the rest of the room quieted in time to hear her response. She felt Christopher's gaze and could only imagine what he was thinking. Before she could bring herself to look up at him, he slowly lifted his mug and clinked hers.

The group around them laughed, and Frank set his own mug down and bowed. "My work here is done."

Liz met Christopher's gaze and they shared a private smile that she felt down to her toes. Choosing distraction over throwing herself into his arms, she turned and watched the show continue as Frank directed his energy toward tormenting the groom-to-be.

Tank's scowl indicated that he knew it was coming.

"Time for me to shove this guy's head - and the rest of him - in a snowbank. Who's helping?" Frank called out cheerily.

Tank's father stood. "I'll get my coat."

The room stilled in surprise. The humor of his timing utterly escaping him, Mr. Kimball went to get his outerwear.

Liz hadn't even been aware of Tank's parents in the room. She noted that his mother was looking at her, a little perplexed. Liz smiled tentatively and sipped her cocoa.

"Better keep the princess in her tower," Frank moved toward the door with the rest of them. "No telling what this beast will do when we're done with him."

Tank growled, and Becky said, "Nonsense. I'm coming out to help."

"No," Tank replied tersely. "We're fine."

Frank grinned and watched the tumult he'd churned up erupt.

Becky got right up in Tank's face. "I shovel around here all the time."

Tank put his hands on her shoulders as though to stop her, then surprised everyone by leaning down and kissing her soundly. "Let us do it."

Becky considered her fiancé and smiled. "Well, if you insist."

His mouth quirked. "I do."

Time stood still as their surprisingly sweet exchange foreshadowed the day's big event.

Frank slapped Tank's shoulder. "We'd better get going, or you won't have time to shower before you say those words again."

He ignored the responding glower as the door from the stairwell opened and Anita entered the scene with the Fordham boys.

"I've got some hungry boys here, and I could sure use a cup of coffee," she announced, taking in the room as she closed the door behind her.

"Oh, I should have thought to send some up," Becky replied, getting Anita a mug. "These guys are going out to shovel, and I'll bet they could use some help when you boys have had a bite to eat."

Liz smiled as Becky affectionately rubbed Blake's shoulder. It was obvious they had a special relationship; he'd made a beeline for her as soon as he entered the overwhelming room.

"I'm ready to shovel now!" Parker exclaimed, running up to Tank and slamming him with a hug.

Tank absorbed the impact, staggering back appropriately. He ruffled Parker's hair. "Get something to eat first, Buddy."

"Aww," Parker's shoulders sagged.

"Come on over, Parker," Becky said. "Thanks to Ms. Liz, the cocoa's already made."

Parker slumped over to the bar stool. "Then can I play in the snow?"

Becky smiled. "You'll have all day to play in the snow."

"But church first," he grumbled. "Dad said."

"Church with your Aunt Becky and Uncle Tank getting married," Grace reminded him. "Won't that be fun?"

"So many weddings," he sighed.

"Get that boy some coffee," Frank suggested with a laugh as he led the shovelers out.

"Yuch! No way!" Parker replied, giggling and climbing up onto the stool.

Christopher set his mug down and turned to Liz. "I guess I'll help outside. See you in a bit?" He ran his hand down her arm, leaving a tingling path in its wake.

Liz squeezed his hand as it passed over hers. "Thanks for helping. I'll just stay inside and stay warm."

"Perfect."

She watched as Christopher made his way across the room and silently agreed.

Sunday - 9:00 a.m.
Maddy

"I hope Anita remembered to tell Becky to come up here to get ready." Maddy looked around and considered her room. "It's better than my going down there, right? I mean, that room behind the kitchen is so tiny."

"I'm sure she'll be up soon," John replied, focusing entirely on the beautiful little girl in his arms.

Watching her husband hold their tiny daughter, Maddy felt like her heart would burst. Was it really possible that she had already arrived and could attend her aunt's wedding? Could this weekend get any better?

"Bella can go to the wedding, right? She *has* to," Maddy mused. "And anyway, who would even miss out on the wedding to stay with her?"

"Uh-hmm," John replied, swinging Bella gently back and forth.

Maddy watched as her husband unapologetically ignored her and stared into the face of his daughter.

"I think the roof just blew off the house."

He looked up and chuckled quietly. "I can't think of anything other than the fact that I'm actually holding her." He continued to sway with her, then said, "After nine months, well eight, at least, of you holding Bella every minute of every day and night - adjusting your whole life, the way you moved and slept and worked, to accommodate her, I finally get to share the privilege, the responsibility," he sighed a little, "the burden." He turned to Maddy, a mixture of awe and humor on his face. "She hardly seems a burden now, does she?"

Maddy swallowed and smiled.

John walked over to the bed and sat down. Burt, firmly planted on the floor next to the bed and in front of the bassinet, looked up with concern. After a moment, he lay his head back down on his big paws with a resigned sigh.

"When I first met you," John continued, relieved that the dog hadn't challenged him, "I somehow knew I wanted you to be a part of my life, even though I couldn't imagine room for anyone but Blake and Parker." He shook his head and continued. "You moved into our little town, so determined to embrace your new life. And the boys were so drawn to you."

"The boys were," Maddy repeated with a smiling nod.

He grinned. "Yeah. That was a big deal. They'd been hurt, too. But the way you made me feel - like there could be hope again, and joy, and laughter ..." He looked at Maddy intently, and she felt the surge of whatever it was that had connected them when they first met. "All wrapped up in your beautiful Maddy-ness," he said, clearly remembering that connection, too.

"It didn't take long to hope for a life with you, but that God would give us Bella on top of it all," he looked down at their baby, sleeping quietly in his big hands. "And to deliver her safely ..."

He gave up trying to use words, and lay Bella gently on the bed. Leaning over, he cupped Maddy's face in his hands and kissed her.

She met the kiss with every bit of fervor her very tired body could muster. She was surprised at what she currently had in her tank for this man who expressed himself so beautifully.

John seemed surprised, as well.

Their kiss took on more of a 'before baby' feel than an 'after baby' feel, and Maddy was amazed at how quickly her head, at least, was ready to go there.

"Okay, well, I can go back downstairs and get ready, if that would be better."

John and Maddy jumped apart at Becky's voice. Burt lumbered up quickly, on alert.

"Seriously, I'll just take Bella - I'm sure I'll find someone to watch her ..."

Maddy laughed. "No, Becky. Stay. We'll behave."

John grinned at Maddy, kissed her once more on the forehead, then slowly stood. "I'll let you two do your thing." He glanced at Bella, who lay sleeping on their bed. "Do you want me to take her with me?" He looked half hopeful - half frightened at the thought.

"No, that's okay. Let's just move her to the bassinet."

John lifted Bella reverently and then tucked her in, Burt watching every move. After they'd stared at her for another moment, John turned to Maddy. "You'll be careful, right? You won't overdo it or anything?"

Maddy smiled up at him. "I'll be fine. Becky will help me get dressed and then I'll help her ... do something. We'll figure it out."

"Grace will be up when breakfast is done. Hope it's okay that I invited her. She needs to get ready, too," Becky piped in.

"Of course!" Maddy beamed. "The more the merrier."

John turned to consider his sister-in-law. "You've been awesome, by the way. Thank you."

Becky waved him off. "Please. We're all just doing our part." She considered him for a moment. "Your part is to lend Frank a clean shirt. And please, see if you can keep him away from Liz and Christopher. He's having way too much fun at their expense."

"Oh no," Maddy murmured, biting back a smile.

"Poor Liz," John commiserated. "I'll see what I can do."

"Actually," Becky reconsidered, "I invited her, too, so I guess if you can just keep him off the third floor, we're good."

John chuckled and looked out the window, his amusement fading. "We're going to have to shovel out and see about the power."

"Shoveling is covered," Becky replied. "Guys went out about half an hour ago."

John's shoulders visibly relaxed, and Maddy shared his relief.

"Even Tank's dad helped," Becky added, smiling at their mutual looks of surprise. "It's been some weekend."

ſ ſ ſ

"That doesn't fit so well anymore, does it?" Liz observed.

Maddy looked down at her dress, which hung rather oddly on her post-baby frame. Though she clearly had weight to work off, her figure had definitely undergone a transformation. She glanced back up at Becky, Liz and Grace with a grin. "Well, it fit a few days ago."

"Yeah, we were wondering if you were even going to be able to squeeze into it, and now look at you," Becky's disgruntled tone didn't fool anyone.

"Sorry, Beck," Maddy replied cheerfully. "I hate to ruin your wedding pictures."

"Really, Maddy, what were you thinking?" Grace asked, a smile in her voice.

"And leave it to my sister to find a way to become even more curvy on my wedding day." Becky huffed, circling her. "Seriously, Maddy, I'm going to look like a gangly teen-age boy standing next to you."

Maddy laughed, marveling a little at the parts of her dress that were straining and the parts that weren't - very different from a few days earlier. The parts that were straining were also a little tender. She'd definitely have to feed Bella before the ceremony.

Rolling her shoulders, she tried to settle into the dress a little better. "No one and nothing on earth could make you look like a gangly teen-age boy. *Ever*," she replied. "Now, how does this scarf thing go?"

"It's not a scarf, it's a drape," Becky corrected her with a sigh. "Like I'd ask my bridesmaids to wear a scarf."

Maddy grinned, allowing Becky to arrange the silk cloth around her. Grace marked and copied the effort. The silvery gray drape was stunning with their simple, crimson dresses.

"You two look beautiful," Liz said, snapping pictures with her phone.

"Thank you," they replied in unison, grinning.

"It's fun to have a reason to wear something other than a coffee apron," Grace continued, looking down at the dress, and spinning slowly in a circle. "My husband won't recognize me."

"It'll be good for him to remember just how gorgeous you are," Becky observed. "He'd just better keep his hands off you until the ceremony's over."

"Tell that to the groom," Liz added, snapping another picture of Maddy.

"Tank having trouble behaving?" Maddy asked, smiling for the camera. She'd obviously missed much of the drama unfolding on the floors below the baby wing.

"He's been such a child!" Grace happily filled her in. "Glowering at everybody one minute, then flirting shamelessly with Becky the next. He kissed her in front of everyone this morning. I almost fell over."

"He didn't!" Maddy exclaimed. She'd never seen that kind of display from Tank. Hugging, sure, or more like half squeezing the life out of Becky when he came home from traveling. She knew there was affection, but it was never gently expressed.

"It has been ... interesting," Liz agreed. "I didn't know him that well before, but I'm beginning to understand some of the challenges of fielding his ... intensity."

"Nicely phrased," Grace rolled her eyes. "You didn't grow up with him." She adjusted her hair in the mirror. "You might not put it so charitably."

Liz laughed quietly while Becky walked over to the closet door where her dress hung.

"When I think about how mad he made me when I first met him, I can't believe I'm signing on for spending the rest of my life with him." Becky held the dress up against herself and turned back toward the others. The off-white, strapless, satin gown was simple, but the lace overlay gave the dress an elegant, antique feel.

"If you'd have told me a year ago ..." She paused and smiled a little, "well, maybe more like fifteen months ..." She considered again. "Okay, well, for sure a year and a half ago, that Tank and I would be getting married, I never would have believed it."

"I had you pegged from the beginning," Grace pointed out with a knowing smile.

"You always say that," Becky replied. "I never saw it coming."

"Why do you think I had him stay here at the inn with you when he came to town?"

"You said you wanted to give Maddy the business."

"Instead, Tank gave *you* the business," Maddy delighted in the perfect set-up, even if the joke was lame.

"Ha ha," Becky smirked. "You fell for his ridiculous football player charm - if you can even call it that - way before I did."

"We all saw something in Tank that you refused to see," Maddy countered primly. There was no arguing that Tank was difficult at first, but once he got working with John and Frank, lending his woodworking expertise to the penthouse project, the whole family had pretty much fallen for him. The three men worked together almost seamlessly, and the boys loved Tank from day one. Becky had taken a lot longer to understand the nuances of Tank's appeal.

"And now you've seen the light!" Grace said, waving her hands in dramatic proclamation.

Becky rolled her eyes. "Oh, please. You're going to make me change my mind."

"Not happening," Grace said firmly, approaching the bride. "I worked too hard to see this through. You're not pulling out now. Let's get this thing on you."

Becky pulled off her robe and submitted to Grace's help. Maddy would have loved to have been the one dressing her sister, but knew she had to conserve her energy. She contentedly watched the display from the comfort of her bed. Grace, after all, was heartily invested in both the bride and the groom.

"*You* worked hard," Becky huffed, lifting her arms. "No one's worked harder than I have. A little credit, please."

Grace laughed as she slipped the dress over Becky's head. She zipped to the waist, and then started the process of buttoning. The dress fell into place over Becky's trim figure, and the women fell silent in admiration.

"You're so beautiful," Maddy said softly, not bothering to fight the tears that rolled down her cheeks. She wasn't sure she'd ever see this day, and there were simply no words to describe how happy she was for her little sister.

"Thank you," Becky whispered, a little mesmerized by the effect of the dress as it snugged up in all the right places. It wasn't just the fact that the dress was beautiful; it was the fact that she was putting it on for real. This time, Tank would see it. This time, she would wear it to her wedding and become his wife.

All frustration with the difficult groom dissipated as the women breathed a collective sigh.

Then a tiny baby's whimper became a squall, and a large dog's whine became a series of short, confused barks.

The spell broken, the women laughed and returned to their final preparations. Maddy, both giggling at and concerned by Burt's reaction, gave up on shushing him and lifted Bella out of her crib. He quieted as the baby did, which was good, because Maddy clearly had a challenge in front of her. Looking down at her dress and the drape, she couldn't help but glance at the clock.

"Ladies, I'm going to need some help."

ſſſ

Maddy slowly negotiated the first staircase in her slippers with Burt by her side. Liz followed with Bella, and Grace trailed them with Maddy's shoes. Becky would follow soon.

Becky had better follow soon.

For all of the excitement in those moments before the wedding that was finally happening, Maddy had seen that moment of doubt in her sister's eyes. Regardless of Tank's last-minute antics and his needing to prove himself groom-worthy, Becky still struggled with allowing herself to be a bride.

Under any other circumstances, Maddy would have stayed with her sister until it was time to walk into the parlor-chapel, but she needed to get Bella settled, navigating the introductions that hadn't yet happened. Becky was going to have to work through her last-minute doubts on her own, and Maddy had to trust that she'd be fine. Becky would remember and embrace the forgiveness they'd talked about so often.

If not, Maddy would march back up two flights of stairs and knock some sense into her.

They stopped at the landing so she could catch her breath, and perhaps, change the direction of her thoughts.

"How are you doing?" Liz asked, concerned. "You can rest, you know. Take as much time as you need."

Burt stood between them, conflicted about his role of protector when his charges were separated. He contented himself with leaning heavily into Maddy while sniffing at the bundle of Bella.

Maddy smiled and scratched his head. "I'm okay. Just a little dizzy. And I should probably sit before Burt pushes me over." She lowered herself onto one of the pair of chairs in the hallway which no longer seemed superfluous.

"Good idea," Liz replied. "I'm going to step into my room." She turned to Grace. "Can I hand off this little treasure?"

"Oh, yes," she smiled, setting Maddy's wedding pumps on the carpet and reaching for Bella. Burt glanced at the shoes, clearly in crisis. In the hierarchy of dog-sniffing, they ranked pretty high. His protector reflex won out, however, and he brought his attention back to the baby exchange.

Maddy smiled as the tiny bundle that she'd carried by herself for so long was now carefully passed between her friends. Grace tucked Bella into her side while Liz slipped into her room.

Another door opened, and Alex stepped into the hallway, looking fine in his probably very expensive but casual church wear. He paused as he took in the sight of his wife, looking rather dazzling, and holding a baby. It was probably a lot to take in, and Maddy couldn't help but watch his face process all of that information.

He finally found words. "You look amazing, Grace."

No doubt, his wife had heard that a time or two, but Maddy was delighted with the phrasing, and, of course, she agreed.

Grace acknowledged his compliment with an off-handedness she couldn't possibly feel in the face of his open admiration. "It's the dress, but thanks. This is Bella."

She turned Bella slightly for her husband's benefit, and once again, Maddy felt overwhelmed as her happiness spread through her friends. She was glad that none of them seemed too worried about her overgrown dog behaving like a nervous grandmother.

Alex gently patted the bundle. "Hello, Bella." He looked up at his wife and they exchanged a private smile. Maddy tried to pretend that something else in the hallway was worth looking at.

A moment later, Alex turned to Maddy. "I'm sorry to ignore you, but it's your fault for making something so beautiful and distracting." He walked over, reached out, and then reconsidered laying his hand on her shoulder as Burt bristled between them. He dropped his hand. "Congratulations. And you look radiant."

Maddy felt herself coloring at the compliment. "Thank you. I feel impossibly happy. Guess that shows." She extended a hand and let him help her to her feet. Burt watched, ready to pounce if Alex misbehaved. "Time to find my place in the party down there."

"They're definitely ready for you ladies," Alex replied. "And don't let the look on Tank's face fool you. He's happy."

Maddy laughed and then sobered as she breathed through her tummy's objection to the sudden movement. "So, he's going to wait for her, right? Becky's a little concerned that he doesn't know, or, more likely, will ignore wedding protocol, and not stay put until she comes."

"Well, John and Frank are close by. They make a formidable barrier, but I'm not sure they could stop Tank if he decided to leave the room."

Maddy tried to stifle another painful laugh. "They'd better not try in my parlor. That's where the nicest antiques are."

Alex offered her his arm, causing Burt to grudgingly move to her other side.

Liz stepped out of her room and assessed the situation with a nod. "I'll grab the shoes."

The group descended the steps and rounded the corner into the parlor, where everyone was gathered. John walked over to meet them as the rest of the room erupted in applause. Maddy smiled at their sweet welcome and gave them all a little wave.

"Hey everybody. Thanks for making do without me this weekend." She looked around in wonder at the happy gathering, then turned to Grace, who handed her daughter carefully into her arms. She turned back to the wedding party as Burt planted himself at her side.

"This is Bella."

Sunday - 10:00 a.m.
Becky

Becky considered her reflection, trying to reclaim the festive air that had permeated the room moments earlier while her friends were gathered around her. The dress was still perfect, the lace covering exquisite. She couldn't stop staring at its beautiful simplicity. She'd refused to try it on after the first fitting, which had, fortunately, proved sufficient; something about covering herself with something so beautiful and symbolic had seemed hypocritical.

A smile surfaced as she wiped at a tear, and it wasn't a smile for the camera. It was simply an acceptance of grace that forced joy through and around and over all of the doubt. She no longer tried to mask a past that she could never heal on her own. That past was in the hands of someone who was able to heal her in ways she'd never thought possible. God loved her, not because of how she looked, but because of how He looked at her. Locking that promise away with the other truths that had so powerfully healed her heart, she walked boldly up to the mirror and embraced Becky the bride. She marveled at her beautiful dress and gasped at the mascara smudging around her eyes.

Refusing to buy into the lie that she was simply covering up, Becky intended to make sure that her face reflected the joy she felt on the inside.

Two minutes with her make-up bag did the trick.

ʃ ʃ ʃ

Becky felt almost airborne as she floated down the steps, her dress moving with her like a silky second skin. Rounding the corner onto the second-floor landing, she came up short and stifled an un-bride-like squeal. Face-to-chest with her husband-to-be, she backed up and tried to shove him.

"Why are you here? You're supposed to wait downstairs!"

Unmoved, like always, Tank stood and regarded her, dropping his gaze to take in her dress, pausing on her legs, and then moving back up to her face. He reached out to touch her cheek.

"You look beautiful."

Becky wanted to stomp her fairly expensive taupe pump, but managed to swallow her frustration in the face of his uncharacteristically gentle endearment. "You're not supposed to be here. You're supposed to wait for *me* to come to *you*. You'd know that if you'd showed up for your wedding rehearsal." She blew at the wisp of hair that had escaped her up-do.

Tank gently touched the wisp, then drew his finger along her jaw. Becky tried to ignore the tingling as she waited for an explanation.

"Everyone was there, waiting. Maddy said you were coming, but that you were still upstairs."

"What part of that meant you had to come and look for me?"

Tank shrugged his big, stupid traps, which were no less obvious, even draped in an expensive suit. He looked amazing; Alex must have helped him shop. Becky wanted to drink in the sight of him, all decked out for her, but she was too irritated.

"I thought you might have second thoughts," Tank sounded a little uncertain.

"And then I'd what - just leave? Walk through the snow and go home?"

He raised a brow.

She wanted to argue his unspoken challenge, but she knew, and he knew that she knew, that he had a point. Ten minutes earlier, she might have done that very thing. The guys had shoveled, after all, and the path to her car was clear.

Her frustration abating in the face of his concern, she put her hands on his considerable chest, slid her fingers along his lapels and sighed. "Yeah, there was a moment." She looked up into his eyes. "But it didn't last." She tilted her head and eyed her almost-husband with real appreciation and a wave of gratitude. "So, as you can see, I was on my way to join you, to marry you. Will you please go back down and let me make my much-anticipated entrance?"

He eyed her for a moment and then leaned down and kissed her temple. His lips lingering, he said, "Don't keep me waiting."

Trying to keep her feet beneath her, she said, "Is Otis ready to do his job?"

Tank grunted. "Almost knocked him over on my way out."

Becky laughed. "Tell him I'm coming."

Tank took one more look at his bride. "You are so beautiful."

Becky sighed her thanks and watched him walk down the stairs with an easy grace, unusual for someone his size. She managed to hold her ground so she could make her own entrance. It wasn't easy to wait.

$$\int \int \int$$

Otis considered Becky with fatherly pride as he awaited her at the bottom of the steps. "You look lovely, Becky dear."

A camera snapped, and Becky looked to the side of the foyer, where Anita captured the moment. With everything that her friend had already contributed to the unparalleled success of the weekend, Becky had all but forgotten that she'd asked her to take pictures of the wedding. Well, she had pretty much asked everyone, but Anita was seizing the opportunity. No surprise there.

"What can't you do, Anita?" Becky smiled for the camera.

Anita grinned and clicked away as Becky turned to join Otis.

"Thank you for doing this, neighbor," she said, choking up a little. He'd been a true friend, and always a source of wisdom over the past year and a half. She was grateful he could fill this role.

Still, she ached to have her father beside her. For a few moments, the sadness that her parents weren't able to witness this remarkable day surfaced again. The images that she had often entertained through her childhood flashed before her: looping her arm through her father's to walk down a flower-laden church aisle, a crowd of family and friends looking on in awe.

But her parents weren't here, and as hard as it was, that was okay. This day was about Tank, about their new beginning. It was about committing to something for once in her life. It was about marrying this good man, not because she suddenly deserved him, but because she was willing to admit that she never would, and she accepted his love anyway. Looking at Otis, and blinking away the tears, she knew that this was exactly how it was supposed to be.

"It's an honor, my dear," he said, holding his arm out for her. "Ready? The crowd's chompin' at the bit in there."

Relieved that he opted for a light response, Becky stepped with him into the parlor.

In lieu of a wedding march, the waiting crowd erupted in applause, and Becky smiled at her friends as she entered with Otis at her side. That beautiful group quickly faded as she locked eyes with her almost-husband. She'd seen him moments earlier, but there was something mesmerizing about the way he stood next to Rob, his hands folded in front of him, serious and handsome, his eyes glued to her as though he could will her right into the room.

He could and he did.

She joined him by the fireplace, his stoic look of appreciation something she wouldn't soon forget.

They turned together to face Pastor Rob, who sported a clean shirt.

She really owed John.

"Tank, Becky, family and friends: I have to say that this is the first time I've seen a bride walk in - not to music - but to applause. Definitely fits the occasion. And the matron of honor," he smiled at Maddy, "received the same greeting. Can't imagine why." He winked at the new mother and turned back to the wedding couple. "You're surrounded by a remarkably supportive group of friends, a resilient bunch who would probably rather have me just start the vows, but you know I have to preach a little."

The small, familiar crowd shared a laugh and sat down to listen to his wedding message. Rob paused a moment while everyone settled back into their seats, then started in earnest.

"Look at you two. What a picture! You getting this Anita?" He leaned around the pair of them and acknowledged the photographer. "You could probably make some good money on these shots. This guy's got some notoriety."

Tank shook his head and Becky grinned at him. They'd made the paper when they'd first agreed to fake date a year earlier. She hadn't really given much thought to the press that Tank's wedding would generate. They'd thought about it enough not to care when they moved their wedding date back three months. That the press wouldn't likely keep up with the change of plans, especially in a snowstorm, was not a matter of regret for either of them.

"You're a beautiful couple," Rob acknowledged, "and that's both a blessing and a curse. Who wouldn't want to be like you?" He considered them both keenly. "But it comes at a cost, doesn't it?"

"In fact," he eyed the rest of the crowd, "we all make an effort to show our best side, don't we? Never mind our inner struggles or past heartaches, let the rest of the world think we have it all together, and look perfect, to boot."

He returned his gaze to Becky and Tank. She had a feeling that Rob had shared his more general, user-friendly sermon with Liz and Christopher the night before. He'd hardly had time to prepare something new. Was this message going to be completely off the cuff? Did she want to be the object lesson if it was?

"But none of us is perfect and we never will be on this side of heaven. And while you two could grace the cover of a magazine, and may, in truth, before this is all over, that's not what really matters, is it? Your commitment to each other, before God, is a holy thing. Not holy, like unattainable perfection, but holy, like, 'set apart'. God will bless it, but you have to treat it like the treasure it is - set apart, special.

"Right now, it's easy to look into each other's eyes and see the treasure in your faces. But let's be honest, that will change. The real treasure is the relationship that you commit to Him. One that lasts, no matter what happens to the bodies you're packaged in."

"Amen!" Ed called out from the back of the parlor.

Laughter bubbled up from the group, and, smiling, Rob continued. "Perfection is a false commodity. Nobody in this room is perfect. Not even little Bella over there."

Someone gasped, likely Parker, and Rob continued. "We are all flawed from the beginning, and not one of us improves the raw material we're given, on our own. But," he eyed the room meaningfully, "we are all redeemed, forgiven, made new; no matter what we've done, it's covered."

There was a murmur of agreement. Rob looked between Becky and Tank. "And by God's grace, we can treasure the raw material in each other, in ourselves, and in the relationships He blesses us with."

Becky glanced up at Tank. That she felt treasured by him was one of the most amazing gifts he gave her. She swallowed the lump in her throat and braced herself. Rob wasn't done.

"And that's it, isn't it? Marriage is about the miracle of improving on the raw material with a friend, a lover, a partner in life's often challenging journey. You're in it together, now, and this relationship, this treasure, while celebrating the individuals that make it up, is its own new thing. Today we set it apart and commit to build on it, to celebrate it, to hold onto it, no matter what life throws at you."

He paused and looked at them both intently. "Now, ready for those vows?"

Sunday - 11:00 a.m.
Grace

Grace watched in a kind of awe as her brother exchanged vows with Becky. He looked so happy. Well, *happy* was a bit much. Tank never exuded a particularly cheery vibe. He was just so utterly absorbed in the woman he was speaking to, promising her his faithfulness with an intensity that even a sister could acknowledge was pretty heart-stopping. For a private guy, he was looking at his bride like there was no one else in the room, or the house, or the county, for that matter. Becky was no paper doll, as Tank liked to call her, but anyone on the receiving end of his quiet and deliberate words of commitment would need nerves of steel to keep from swooning. If people even did that anymore.

Next to her, Maddy sighed a little, and Grace laughed to herself. She noticed it, too.

Becky followed, promising to keep Tank in line for the rest of his life. She only stumbled a little, using Tank's given name, probably for the first time. Grace would have loved a clear view of her friend's face at that moment. Tank blanched, but recovered quickly, the magnitude of the event overshadowing his momentary discomfort. The giggle in the back of the room was quickly muffled as the service proceeded. The exchange of rings was equally solemn; everyone seemed to understand that for this marriage to get locked in, silence and complete focus were necessary.

Grace was actually a little surprised; she had expected the event to be a little more light-hearted. For a wedding that had been haphazardly moved up, almost canceled, then postponed and rescheduled at the whim of a snowstorm, it had the unexpected ambience of an affair of state.

The rings exchanged, the inhabitants of the make-shift chapel held their collective breath while they awaited the prayer that would seal the union of these two head-strong and almost comically lovesick adults. The absence of Rob's normally easy smile contributed to the general aura of gravity.

A surprisingly piercing wail changed the mood decidedly, and the matron of honor jumped. Everyone turned to the source, alarm turning to smiles at Bella's determination to remain the center of attention. Liz walked over to Maddy, somehow side-stepping Burt as she handed the baby to her mother. Maddy tried to quiet her, but Bella had found her voice and continued to explore its impressive boundaries.

Rob, determined to bring closure, yelled a closing prayer and benediction over the group, and then invited Tank to kiss his bride.

With a baby crying, a dog whining, and a roomful of people expectantly waiting, Tank took Becky's face in his hands, and simply leaned down and touched his forehead to hers. The look that passed between them was for the newlyweds alone, and then Tank drew his wife into an unexpectedly gentle, but very thorough embrace.

The room once again erupted into thunderous applause.

§ § §

Congratulations flowed freely as the snowbound group toasted each other with glasses of champagne for the second day in a row, in and around the kitchen of Maddy's Inn. Grace could hardly remember a time when she was happier, except for her own wedding less than a year before. She smiled at her husband, wondering if he was remembering, as well. His fond gaze suggested that he was.

He made his way to her side and clinked his glass with hers. "Good memories, hmm?"

She clinked, then kissed him. "The best. Seems like yesterday."

"So, what are we doing for our anniversary?"

"Dry-walling the basement?"

"Sounds romantic," Alex replied. "Maybe if you weren't drinking orange juice, you'd be more creative."

Grace laughed. "I have to keep my wits about me to get this brunch on."

Alex turned to take in the crowd. "What a great group of people."

"They've sure weathered more than a storm together." Grace smiled as Anita continued to take pictures of the post-wedding festivities: Blake and Parker toasting each other with gingerale-filled champagne flutes, Maddy rocking her little one, looking tired but oh, so happy, Otis leaning in to say hello to Bella, Frank and John laughing at something Rob was saying, accompanied by strangely-flailing arms, Ed chatting with the other newlyweds, who sipped their champagne with matching dreamy smiles, and Becky holding court over them all with her ever-looming groom.

Grace sighed. Her brother was married. Her brother was happy. What more could she ask for?

The door from the dining room opened, and her parents entered, apparently having missed the initial toast. They approached the counter where Grace and Alex manned the champagne.

"Hey, Mom and Dad. Champagne?"

"I'll have half a glass," her mom replied, smiling carefully at Grace and nodding at Alex.

He poured a glass and handed it to her. "Mr. Kimball?"

Grace's father looked from her to her husband, obviously still reconciling the information they now had, with the Alex they had rejected over the past year. There was no easy way to transition, and the struggle in her father's eyes showed it.

Alex handed him a glass. "To new beginnings."

Her father received it, considering the champagne as though it held all the answers. He looked up and nodded. "To new beginnings."

Grace and her mom chimed in, and they all clinked and sipped their drinks. Fighting the tightening of her throat and the tears that threatened, Grace smiled and sighed and leaned into her husband. He slipped his arm around her and pulled her close, as pockets of laughter continued to erupt around the room.

"How about Hawaii?" Grace suggested quietly.

Alex pulled her even closer. "Now, you're talking."

$$\int \int \int$$

Grace sat back with a smile as she finished the last of her artichoke and egg casserole. She hadn't really expected to sit down to eat, but after Maddy's family had taken their meal and a fussy Bella upstairs, and Rob had hit the road to get back to his family, the rest of the group had managed to squeeze in around the dining room table. Although very cozy with twelve, it was nice to make use of the formal room for the wedding lunch. It was the first time Grace had ever eaten a meal in there, and she guessed that it wasn't used very often.

Conversation quieted as Tank stood. He and Becky had been nestled at the head of the table together, looking very cozy, though Becky seemed to have nowhere to go with her shoulders. It didn't seem to bother her, however, and she looked up with an ethereal smile as her husband began to address the room.

"Becky and I want to thank you all for sticking it out with us this weekend, not that you had a choice," he acknowledged.

A few laughs quickly quieted, since Tank didn't often take center stage to speak, at least not in a personal setting. Grace was riveted along with everyone else.

"I'm sorry that I worried you and kept you waiting on Friday. I'm sorry for the … uh … difficulties that I caused." He turned to Becky. "I'm sorry I gave you reason to doubt me. It won't happen again."

His intensity was evident, even in profile. Grace glanced at her parents and noted their softening expressions as they listened to their son. Swallowing, she returned her attention to her big brother. She knew this weekend was a big deal, but had not expected such an emotional ride. Alex squeezed her hand, following the direction of her thoughts. She squeezed back as Tank turned to the group and continued.

"Thank you all, for everything." He looked around the room. "The meals, the clean-up, the maintenance and shoveling, the party," he narrowed his eyes at Frank, "and the uncontested winner," he zeroed in on Anita, "bringing Bella safely to us." He paused, seeming to fight his own emotion, then nodded and lifted his glass, first to Anita, then to the room in general.

Becky stood and joined him. "Thank you, Anita, and thank you all so much for making this the best wedding day - weekend - ever."

Grace silently applauded her for giving Tank a minute to catch his breath. His look of admiration, in return, was a sight to behold.

The door from the kitchen opened as the Fordham family began squeezing into the room. Blake and Parker maneuvered to the head of the table with Tank and Becky, then John entered cradling Bella, almost unaware of the crowd around him. Maddy followed, taking in the whole group and beaming like only a new mother and proud inn-owner could.

"And to my sister," Becky continued, hardly skipping a beat, "who's put up with me …" she faltered a bit, then continued, "and has never given up on me." She raised her glass, her voice catching. "Thank you."

Maddy smiled and blew her a kiss.

Tank pulled his wife close. *His wife!* Grace didn't know if she would ever believe it.

"Maddy, John, thank you for hosting this circus." He raised his glass to them, and everyone cheered.

The room finally quieted again as Bella cooed, John rocked, and Tank cleared his throat.

"You are the best friends a couple could ask for."

Another round of quiet cheers followed, every bit as sincere, but this time factoring in a sleeping newborn. Tank raised his glass a final time.

"Hope you've enjoyed your weekend." He nodded at the window. "Storm's over. Roads are clearing." His eyes glinted mischievously. "Checkout's at noon."

Sunday - Noon
Liz

Liz waved with the others as Ed, Anita, and Frank pulled out of the driveway. It was something to think that she was standing on the family side, waving the visitors off; amazing how quickly she'd been made to feel part of their clan. She'd be on the other side of the good-byes soon enough, but then she'd be heading off to start her own new family. Suddenly overwhelmed - but also enthralled - with the prospect, she checked a laugh that definitely would have alarmed the rest of the group.

Christopher sensed something, because he pulled her closer as they stood on the porch. "Shall we get packing before Tank kicks us out?"

"I told Grace I'd help clean up the kitchen," Liz said as they filed in behind the rest of the family. "She took Bella back up to the penthouse so Maddy could mingle. It won't take me long after that."

"I'll help," he offered, being useful certainly among his motivations.

She reached up to kiss his cheek. "What a guy."

They walked through the dining room, and everyone picked up something from the table or sideboard. Liz then urged Maddy and Becky out of the kitchen so they could chat in the family room, and found herself settling in with her new husband to finish the clean-up. It was rather symbolic, and more fun than she'd ever had doing dishes. The loaded glances he shared every time they brushed by each other, or he dried a dish that she handed him, probably factored in. By cleanup's end, they were ready enough to give Tank and Becky the space they needed, and reclaim some of their own.

Otis was saying his good-byes as they entered the sunroom.

"I'm so delighted for both of you," he glanced with fatherly affection at Maddy and Becky. "Can't believe I got to be on the front lines for all of this happiness."

Their replies were consumed by their respective hugs, and Liz and Christopher held back a bit, allowing for the poignant moment to pass between friends. Liz hadn't met Otis before this weekend, but she could see why he'd left a mark on the Jacobs sisters with his gentle, calming presence and unwavering support.

Otis waved to the rest of the group as he stepped out onto the porch. "Sure was nice to meet you," he called out to Liz and Christopher. "And congratulations to you, too," he added with a grin.

"Thank you!" Liz called back.

As the door closed behind him, she turned to the rest of the group. "I'd like to echo his sentiments; it was so nice to meet you all, and it was an honor to be a part of this - these - celebrations." She glanced up at Christopher. "We're going to pack up and head out, ourselves, but I figured we'd make our good-byes official while you're all still gathered."

"You don't have to rush," Maddy gently objected. "Whenever you're ready, we'll give you a proper good-bye from the porch."

Liz fought the urge to gauge Tank's response to this cheerful invitation to hang around. She smiled as Maddy continued.

"Thank you so much for cleaning up after us, and for all that you did for me and this crew this weekend. I hope you'll come back when you can be a guest, again."

Liz returned Maddy's hug. "It was a pleasure, on all fronts, and I do look forward to coming back soon." She took Christopher's hand. "Give us about ten minutes and we'll be ready for that proper goodbye."

∫∫∫

Liz zipped up her bag and looked around the room. "I'm good to go." She glanced at the unmade bed; it felt strange to leave it like that, but someone would be following up to clean. That someone would have their hands full after this weekend.

Christopher followed her gaze. "Nice work with Frank today, by the way. Pretty gutsy."

Liz loved how humor showed in his eyes even when his smile was minimal. She walked up to get a closer look. Dropping her bag, she wrapped her arms around his neck.

"Well, it threw him off, anyway. They were going to think what they wanted; might as well play along."

Christopher pulled her close. "It does put the pressure on for tonight." He leaned down and kissed her, communicating anything but uncertainty about what lay ahead for them.

Liz enjoyed the moment immensely, but finally pulled back. "I am cleared for Tuesday, so we've got a couple days."

He nodded. "We've just witnessed what can happen in forty-eight hours. Apparently, it's plenty of time."

Liz laughed. "I'll take a little less commotion and a little more ..." she looked up at her new husband with a raised brow, inviting his thoughts.

"Rest? Relaxation?" he finished for her.

"Sounds wonderful," she agreed.

"When do we see Kelly again?"

"She said she had no time for me before tomorrow," Liz replied with a knowing eye-roll. "Which is her way of giving the newlyweds some time alone."

"I really like Kelly."

Liz laughed again. "Let's go home, shall we?"

Sunday - 1:00 p.m.
Maddy

"I can't believe I missed half the weddings that happened here this weekend," Maddy observed as the Kimballs and the Fordhams found their way back into the sunroom.

The sunlight reflecting off the snow was beautiful but blinding, so she settled into one of the recliners facing the fire. Burt plopped down in front of her with a sigh. Fumbling for the footrest handle, Maddy paused when a hand covered hers.

"Hold on, Honey. I don't want to catapult you into the kitchen."

Maddy immediately regretted laughing at John's warning about the comfortable, but unpredictable chair.

"Burt, you gotta move," John said. The dog looked up at him briefly before putting his head back down on his paws.

Maddy braced her tummy as she bit back another giggle. "Go ahead, he'll figure it out."

It was John's turn to sigh as he did his best to ease the footrest up and the chair back without jostling her too much. Burt got up with a groan, casting a doleful glance over his shoulder as he shifted to accommodate the footrest. Maddy released her own happy moan of contentment at the simple, but profound comfort of having the weight off her legs.

She observed with satisfaction that Becky nestled with Tank on the couch across from the in-laws. "I'm so glad Liz and Christopher went through with it," she was saying. "Neither really strike me as risk-takers, and yet, less than two months from the time they met, they're married." She sighed happily. "It's so romantic."

Maddy stilled at this revelation. *Two months?* That was half the time it took her and John, and she thought *they'd* set some sort of record. She glanced at her husband, now seated in the recliner next to her.

Sometimes, you just know.

"I wondered about that," Mrs. Kimball said, somewhat cautiously. "We went to bed early last night and this morning we knew that we had missed something."

"Yep. They got married before we did."

Tank grumbled beside her, and Becky reached up to stroke his cheek. "Poor Tank. Gotta show up for your party if you want to keep first billing."

He nipped at her fingers, and she tucked them around his side as she snuggled into his chest, decidedly unconcerned about showing affection in front of his folks.

"Where do you think they'll live?" John asked.

"Good question," Becky mused. "I think Christopher had a job offer in northern Vermont. Maybe he can still take that."

"Doesn't he have a farm or something in town?" Maddy asked.

"Yep. Just north of. It's been in the family for years, I guess. Maybe he'll rent it out?"

"Well, good for them," Maddy replied. "It's not easy to uproot yourself mid-career. I hope they're really happy."

"Me too," Becky replied. "You know," she said, her mind obviously working in a new direction, "you could really sell your inn as more than a romantic get-away. Market it as a destination wedding place."

Maddy considered the thought. "Interesting. May have to think about changing the name." 'Maddy's Inn' had been a temporary name that ended up sticking. They'd have to call it something more romantic to sell it as a wedding venue.

"Love Inn," Becky suggested, drawing out the words. "In love, Love Inn - you could have fun with that."

Maddy picked up on her energy. "That's so cute. Think it's too hokey?"

With a sigh that might as well have been an audible "yes", Mr. Kimball turned to Alex, who stood near the fireplace. "As long as we're talking business, I'd love to know more about what you did to turn Goldhearst around."

Alex straightened and turned to his father-in-law. Despite her own absorbing conversation, Maddy couldn't help but notice how he brightened at the prospect of discussing his business world. As he launched energetically into his reply, she turned back to Becky.

"So do we go with Inn Love, or Love Inn?" Maddy asked, grinning as Tank rolled his eyes and turned toward the other conversation, undoubtedly hoping for a little less frill.

"Love Inn, Inn Love," Becky tested them both. "Where do you want the verb?"

"Could be a modifier," Maddy pointed out thoughtfully.

"No," Becky's eyes lit up. "Wherever you put it, it's definitely a verb."

$$\int \int \int$$

The business conversations ebbed as Grace entered the room with Bella. Burt immediately stood at attention.

"She started fussing, so I decided to come down, but now she seems to be sleeping again."

Maddy was itching to hold her daughter but knew it would be better if she waited a little while to nurse. She was about to suggest that John take her when Tank released Becky and slowly stood. He walked over to his sister and looked down at the sleeping baby. Everyone, including the dog, stilled as the biggest and tiniest forces in the room truly met for the first time.

"Want to hold her?" Grace asked, peeking over at Maddy for approval, which she readily gave.

Tank looked at the little bundle, hardly bigger than the footballs he'd spent his career playing with, and finally nodded. Grace lifted Bella and gently placed her in her uncle's arms. Maddy's heart warmed at the sight. She'd probably seen a gentler side of Tank than most people when he dealt with John's boys, but watching him now was something to behold. He stood motionless, looking down at the ball of blankets in his arms.

Maddy glanced at Becky, whose eyes shown as she watched.

It was Bella, of course, who broke the spell with her tiny cry. Tank stiffened and all but dumped her back onto Grace. Maddy's heart skipped several beats as she watched the exchange, but Grace smoothly retrieved her daughter and brought her over. Burt eyed the transaction with concern, but was good enough to make room for Grace to approach.

"Bella needs her Mama," she said.

"Thank you," Maddy replied, impossibly relieved and happy to be holding her daughter again. Bella settled in for the moment, content to be close while Maddy rocked her gently. When she remembered that she still had guests in the house, Maddy looked up to see that Grace had joined Alex in front of the fireplace. They stood together, their heads close, as they tried to manage a private conversation.

Good luck, Maddy smiled to herself. Nothing about this weekend had been private for anyone, though so much good had come of it all. There was more to celebrate than any of them could ever have imagined.

Given that her own privacy had been thoroughly compromised in the course of the weekend's happy events, Maddy had no problem enjoying the sweet picture that Alex and Grace made as they finished their conversation and Alex leaned in to kiss his wife on the cheek. She wasn't the only one watching them; they were center stage as they stood in front of the roaring fire, with the two sets of Kimballs on either couch, and John and Maddy in the recliners.

Tank, safely tucked in beside Becky again, and apparently having recovered from holding a crying newborn, looked up at his sister. "Well, Gracie, you received that hand-off pretty well. Practicing for a reason?"

Maddy shook her head. *What a football player-y way to ask about starting a family.* Her breath caught as Grace's face lit up and Alex beamed beside her.

"Well, Tank, as a matter of fact ..."

§ § §

All eyes turned to the older Kimballs. While Maddy acknowledged this reaction to be terribly unfair, she couldn't help but join what remained of the crowd in gauging their reaction to the news. Both of them sat with mouths agape, neither one close to forming words. Maddy quickly turned back to the parents-to-be, delighting in the fact that they only had eyes for each other.

Becky was the first to respond, jumping to her feet and hugging both Grace and Alex, her words of congratulations lost in her squeals, which were muffled in their necks.

Tank stood as well, clapping Alex on the back when he could be relatively sure he wouldn't smack his wife in the process. "Way to go, man. Great news." He turned to his sister and hugged her. "I couldn't be happier for you, Gracie."

Maddy held her Bella and watched the hugging and celebrating unfold in front of her. After squeezing her hand, John got up to add his congratulations. Burt watched, trying to figure out how all of the noise and commotion might affect his charges.

The Kimballs finally found their feet and their voices, in that order, and joined the celebration. Maddy looked on with a little bit of wonder and a whole lot of satisfaction. While she hadn't had much interaction with them over the weekend, she'd been sure that there was a good side to this couple. She caught Becky's eye and nodded at them, hoping her sister understood the important message: *I've been right about them all along.* A raised brow was the only discreet way she could drive her point home, and it was met with a rather emphatic eye roll.

Maddy considered this less-than-gracious response, and looked back at the older couple as they somewhat awkwardly patted backs and shook hands. Mrs. Kimball just kept saying, "Oh my," but in a more happy than alarmed kind of way. Whatever their reactions, and she was sure that she and Becky would discuss them at length at some point, relations had improved at least somewhat over the course of this eventful weekend.

Maddy waved her sister off with a smirk and focused on the future parents, who were delighting in the well wishes of the group, in whatever form they were given.

♫ ♫ ♫

Becky found her in the parlor a little while later. "I thought you might have come in here. Can't imagine why you didn't want an audience." She plopped on the settee beside Maddy. Burt had lifted his head as she approached, then settled back into his spot at Maddy's feet.

"I'm still figuring it out myself. I haven't mastered the subtleties of baring my breast discreetly in public. Might take a while."

Becky giggled and peered down at her niece. "It's so amazing, isn't it? She just knows what she needs."

Maddy marveled right along with her. "I'm so glad she knows what she's doing."

They sat for a moment in happy, contemplative silence.

"I'm so happy for Grace and Alex," Becky said, echoing the thoughts that had been expressed repeatedly since the announcement. It had been a beautiful ending to an amazing weekend. To see the Kimballs finally embracing their daughter, and their son-in-law, with such warmth and happiness was something they'd all be contemplating for some time to come.

"And I thought I couldn't get any happier," Maddy observed.

"I know!" Becky replied with feeling. She settled her slippered feet on the coffee table, which was never allowed, but would certainly escape comment on this particular day. She leaned her head on Maddy's shoulder. "It's all so complicated, isn't it?" she finally observed. "Having the responsibility for this tiny new life must be so terrifying, and yet, the most natural thing in the world."

Maddy nodded at Becky's astute understanding of her present emotions.

"And yet, it obviously doesn't come naturally to everyone," the assessment continued. "Grace has never been particularly close to her mom or her dad, which is really sad. But right now, they're all in there, celebrating their happy news together." Becky played with the soft edge of Bella's blanket. "I've been so mad at them for so long on her behalf, which really doesn't help my daughter-in-law status," she pointed out, "but now, I could cry over the transformation. It's like they finally realized what they've been missing, and they're not going to waste any more time."

Maddy felt a little choked up, herself, her emotions readily accessible, given the nature of the weekend. "That's wonderful," she agreed. "I'm so happy for all of them."

The fire crackled quietly as they sat together, lost in thought.

Becky's reverie about the complexities of parenthood wasn't over. "I sure didn't make it easy for Mom and Dad."

"I'm sure we both gave them a run for their money in one way or another," Maddy replied. "My defiance may have been less obvious, but it played out in lots of subtle ways."

She felt her sister's eyes on her as she considered this rather general and safe confession. Now that Maddy held her own daughter in her arms, she had the beginnings of a new understanding of a parent's love and patience. She supposed she'd be learning a lot in the years ahead.

Bella squirmed, demanding the end of the too-serious conversation. The Jacobs sisters, neither of whom were Jacobs anymore, delighted together at the happy distraction.

"It was so fun to hear their reaction when you called them yesterday," Becky said with a smile. "You could hear how choked up Dad was, and I think Mom wanted to jump in the car and just start driving."

Maddy smiled at the thought. "After she calmed down about the whole birth-at-home thing."

"That was a little rough," Becky agreed. "Well, you can't blame them for being worried and feeling helpless, all those miles away."

Maddy hummed her agreement.

"When will John's family be over?" Becky asked. "Oh, they'll probably want to come over today, won't they?"

Maddy quickly put her sister and herself at ease. "His mom and sister are both anxious to meet Bella, but they know we need our rest, so I think they're going to check in tomorrow. His sister said she's serious about doing the cleaning and laundry, so I say they're more than welcome!"

"I love John's sister," Becky said with feeling.

The quiet moment that followed was unceremoniously interrupted when Tank stormed into the room. He reared back when he realized why they'd tucked themselves away and tried to back-pedal his overlarge body through the antique-ridden room. Burt stood, alarmed; again conflicted over the fact that his second favorite human was the source of potential danger.

Maddy laughed, and cringed at the twinge. "Burt, sit. You don't have to leave, Tank."

When he was at a safe distance, which essentially meant back at the entrance to the room, he said, "Sorry. Just looking for Becky."

"Well, you found me." Becky waved, but didn't move. "What's up?"

Tank gripped his hips and sighed. "Party's over. Let's go to my place."

Maddy bit back a smile at his open plea.

"I thought power was still out all down the beach," Becky replied nonchalantly.

"Can't hurt to check," he replied stiffly.

"Well," Becky said thoughtfully, "could you check and just text me? I really don't want to get all bundled up and then find out we can't stay when we get there."

Maddy could hear Tank's growl across the room and decided to have compassion before his mood transferred to her dog.

"Are the others ready to leave?" she asked. "I thought Grace was going to check in at her shop."

"Yeah, I think they're heading out soon."

"Oh, well, that's good. I mean," Maddy quickly qualified, "I'm sure everyone's ready to get back to their lives and all. How about your folks?"

"Grace is trying to get them to leave with her and Alex," Tank replied, not looking nearly as happy as he should with that bit of news.

"But?" Becky entered the conversation again, newly concerned.

"But they want to stay here," Tank ground out. "Spend some time with us."

"Ohhh," Maddy replied, chagrined for both of them.

Becky stiffened noticeably beside her. "*Now*, they finally want to spend time with us?"

Tank drew a big breath and sighed. "They say they want to see my workshop; check out the renovations on the house."

"I see," Becky replied. She stood slowly and walked over to her husband, still looking radiant in her wedding dress, though she'd exchanged her stylish pumps for the fluffy slippers along the way.

She placed her hands on his chest and Tank covered them with his own. "Maybe they could do that another time?"

Maddy smiled as she watched them work through their problem. Tank had lost his jacket and tie, but still looked imposing in what was left of his suit. He ran his hands down Becky's satiny sides, apparently now oblivious to Maddy and her nursing daughter.

The return of his infamous scowl indicated that he hadn't forgotten about his parents. "Another time when they decide to visit?"

Becky stepped closer and reached up to soothe her husband's very tense shoulders. "Should I give them a reminder of how much they dislike me?"

Tank huffed a humorless laugh.

Becky patted his shoulders and dropped her hands. "I'll talk to Grace. I think she'll be able to convince them to take a drive out to her new place, maybe stay the night."

"Don't count on it," he grumbled.

Becky laughed and pushed him, though he didn't budge. "I can hardly wait to be alone with you."

Maddy caught the admiration as Tank watched his bride leave him to enter his family fray. Becky would find a way to empty the inn, or more of it, before the day was over.

Epilogue
Becky
Sunday - 2:00 p.m.

Back in the penthouse, Maddy tucked Bella into her bassinet, then straightened and watched her for a moment. Becky tried to imagine what her sister was feeling as she looked at her daughter, but she had her own head full, contemplating the fact that *she* had a husband. He'd stuck pretty close since the ceremony, but had finally peeled himself away long enough to take his folks down to his house to show them how the renovations were progressing. Grace and Alex had said their good-byes and accompanied them, planning to take the Kimballs to their own home afterward. Becky was happy to catch her breath for a few minutes.

"I'm guessing she's okay, Mama. We'll just be here in the living room. Door's wide open, Burt's on guard. Doesn't get much safer than that."

"I know." Maddy glanced at Bella again, then walked toward the door, leaving Burt to man his post beside the bassinet.

"I'm kind of surprised he didn't want to play in the snow with the boys," Becky said as she and Maddy sat down on the couch together.

"Yeah, I think he was a little torn."

John, Blake, and Parker had called to the dog from the winter wonderland on the beach, and he'd quivered in anticipation before looking at Maddy and slowly sitting down at her feet. She laughed in recollection, then held her stomach with a groan.

"I really have to stop laughing. It hurts."

"Oh, I'm sorry," Becky said, wishing there was something she could do. "Do you think you should go see your doctor now that the storm's over?"

"Wow, you really are trying to clear the house out, aren't you?" Maddy tried to look serious.

Becky laughed. "Busted." She considered her sister more carefully. "You do look a little pale." She raised a hand to Maddy's objection. "Seriously. You've been through a lot. You've been great, but you don't have to keep being brave. It's just me, now."

Maddy sighed. "John said the same thing. He's probably on his phone lining up six different appointments for me while he's out 'playing in the snow'."

Becky smiled. "He just wants to take care of you."

"I know. But nothing's open today, and my doctor's on call at the hospital. I don't want to go to the ER if it's not an emergency. I just need a good night's sleep. We can sort it out tomorrow."

"Hmmm," Becky replied. "We'll see about that. I guess you're off the hook until John comes back in."

Maddy smiled her relief. "Well, so let's debrief. Grace seemed really happy when she left. How did she ever keep that secret all weekend?"

"She could have yelled it out in the middle of the kitchen and been completely ignored, there was so much going on. Maybe she did."

Maddy giggled at the thought. "I'm glad she's in a better place with her folks."

"Please. Between the baby news and Alex's new status? It's almost comical how they're behaving." Becky grinned. "And I can't believe they thought he was a barista. He's a nightmare behind the counter."

"Really? It's hard to imagine him not being competent at anything he tries."

"Don't ever order from him if he's helping at the store." Becky paused for a moment, then shuddered. "I'm glad Grace kept him out of our kitchen this weekend. At least I think she did."

Maddy held her tummy as she bit back another laugh. "Don't! Please." Looking toward the window, she drew as big a breath as she could, and blew it out slowly. "So, Liz and Christopher," she changed the subject. "How sweet is that? I wish they'd stay here in Clairmont. I'd like to get to know Liz better."

"I'm hoping they'll spend summers here," Becky mused.

"Our busy season," Maddy pointed out with a sigh. "Well, I hope they're happy. I love that they're taking a chance like this. Life is too short not to."

"Says the woman who changed careers and moved across the country all by herself."

"I'm still a little surprised at that."

"That was so brave." Becky marveled again at her sister's bold move from one coast to the other several years earlier. "You had no idea what you were getting into with this place."

"It was a gamble," Maddy agreed. She locked eyes with Becky. "Couldn't have done it without you."

"Oh, please," Becky brushed off the compliment. "I only got in your way at first." She shifted as she considered the woman she admired so much it almost hurt. "But you never gave up on me."

Maddy took a hold of Becky's hand and squeezed it. They sat for a moment, processing the memories, and then heard the unmistakable sound of two energetic boys in the stairwell. Burt began to whine from the bedroom.

"I'd close the door, but I don't know what Burt will do," Maddy looked a little concerned.

Becky got up and moved toward the bedroom. "Do you think he'll bark?" She peeked inside at the giant, pacing baby guard.

"He usually doesn't, but all bets are off," Maddy replied. "I guess we'll find out."

Becky winced and pulled the door gently closed, as the boys burst into the apartment.

3:00 p.m.

"When will they come back?" Parker asked, climbing on Tank like he was a set of human monkey bars. Becky was glad her new husband had changed out of his suit, though she wouldn't mind seeing him in it again. Still, it wasn't hard to make her peace with the way his crew-neck sweater hugged his healthy frame in all the right ways. The way he wore his jeans wasn't hard on the eyes, either.

A knowing look from this fine specimen as he grappled with their nephew reminded her to respond.

"They're just making sure your Maddy-mom and the baby are okay. Shouldn't take too long. Don't kick your uncle in the face."

Parker had scaled one side of his newly official uncle and was on his way back down the other, so Tank braced him with one hand and backed toward the couch, bent at the knees, and shook him off. Parker landed giggling in the pile of pillows.

Becky walked over and wrapped her arms around her husband. "Thanks for rolling with all of this on our wedding day."

Tank grunted, but smiled. "I'm glad they're seeing the doctor."

"Me too."

Maddy was not happy about it, but she couldn't argue the wisdom of getting little Bella checked. Having finally won her over, John had packed up his girls and taken them to the ER. Hopefully, it was a slow day at the medical center, and Maddy's doctor would be able to see her and put all of their minds at ease.

"Are you gonna kiss some more?" Parker giggled from his pillow throne.

"Maybe," Becky threatened. "Or maybe I'll kiss you, instead."

"No!" Parker jumped off the couch and ran into the kitchen.

Blake smiled and shook his head while he tried to concentrate on his video game.

"Hey Buddy," Tank said, releasing Becky. "You got room for another player?"

"Sure I do, Uncle Tank!"

Becky smiled as she watched the giant uncle settle onto the floor next to the little nephew. She glanced at the clock, hoping it really wouldn't be too long before they heard from John. Her need for time alone with her new husband hardly registered while she waited to hear that her sister was okay. She was glad Tank seemed to be of the same mind.

Becky looked at him with a sigh, and then glanced out to the kitchen. "Hey Parker, I'm coming for you!"

She heard a shriek as he bolted toward the dining room door. "Stay out of the parlor. You know the rules."

He giggled and ran, and Becky set off after him, fully appreciating the irony that whatever terrible beast he was imagining her to be this time around, it was likely the last image she wished to project on her wedding day. However, this day was proving to be full of surprises, and filling the time until her sister came home with a good report took top priority. Hopefully, they'd have news before she fed the boys some dinner. She offered a prayer for her sister and then gave chase to her nephew.

4:00 p.m.

Becky would never have guessed that she'd spend her wedding day playing Hide and Seek. Regardless of how she arrived at this moment, the visceral fear of being discovered by her husband was very real. Turning off all of the lights on the main level of the inn, or, more accurately, not turning them on once the winter sun had set, was probably not a good idea. The boys had better obey the no parlor rule. She was not about to come out of hiding to enforce it.

She folded herself into the space behind the high-back Victorian chair in the front office, her flexibility allowing her to fit if she eased her backside between the credenza and the wall. There'd be no quick escape, and the attempt would be nothing short of humiliating. She was determined to emerge on her own terms when Tank finally gave up looking for her. No attempt would be ventured before that.

At least she'd changed out of her wedding dress.

Becky held her breath, listening as her husband moved stealthily through the lower level in search of his quarry. His whereabouts were only evident when his prey squealed in response to being discovered. Parker had been the first one outed, and Becky heard him holler from the general vicinity of the kitchen. She'd found him first during her turn as well, mostly due to the fact that he couldn't help but giggle when discovery was imminent. She was determined not to make the same mistake.

Tank had been relatively easy to find because he was just too big to hide anywhere. It helped that he had grabbed her calf when she'd circled the couch in the sunroom in search of him. Becky had been the one to yelp in surprise when she found herself toppling into his lap in his *are-you-kidding-me-this-is-no-hiding-place* spot. He had silenced her objections effectively, and she'd almost forgotten to go look for Blake.

Luckily, Parker had stayed engaged in the game, and he found Blake tucked in the depths of the dark kitchen. Blake didn't feel so lucky, but Tank quickly distracted him by offering/threatening to be the next seeker. The boys had scattered, of course, and after one look at Tank hovering ominously in the shadows, Becky had quickly followed.

She snorted a laugh at the ridiculous situation she found herself in, and immediately regretted her carelessness. Burt came trotting into the room and began sniffing around. She wanted to hiss at him to leave but she didn't dare make another sound. He stood snuffling at her chair, and she waited, resigned, hardly hoping he'd get bored and leave before Tank found his way into the room.

Two giggling boys in the hallway confirmed that Becky was now the focus of Tank's search. She had a ridiculous urge to call out and give up before he found her, but quickly quelled it. Hunkering down, she held her breath as his footsteps approached.

"Guys, go check the sunroom for me."

His little soldiers raced off, and Becky's heart pounded as she heard Tank enter the office. She could just make out his hulking form with the last of the gray twilight finding its way through the windows. It was nothing short of terrifying.

"Hey Buddy," he rumbled to Burt. "Find something for me?"

The dog made a racket in his excitement to greet Tank, and Becky let her breath out quietly. How long had it been since he'd seen him, two minutes? The dog was unhealthily obsessed, though it may have had something to do with his being relieved of baby duty for the time being. Becky took advantage of the commotion and dared to breathe again when they headed back to the doorway.

Tank stopped then and turned, and Becky could feel his attention riveted on her corner. Once again, she fought the urge to cry, 'uncle', or whatever kids did to throw in the towel when the big, bad opponent was closing in. Holding her breath, she shrunk into her hiding place, marking every step as he slowly approached her lair. He stopped in front of the chair, taking in what he could see of her corner by the disappearing light.

Becky was sure he heard her heart hammering in her chest, because the chair started to move and Tank started to chuckle.

"Gotcha," he whispered, managing to sound both lighthearted and predatory at the same time. He pulled the chair away completely and hunkered down to her level. "Any last words?"

She could see him in relief against the window but wasn't really sure what he could see of her. Hopefully, the fact that she was pretty well stuck escaped him.

"You had help," she pointed out, trying to divert his attention while she shifted to dislodge herself. Not only was she stuck, her feet were falling sleep. Even if she did manage to get upright, she'd probably just fall over.

This wasn't going to end well.

Tank stood as though in anticipation of her pending humiliation. "Need a hand?" he asked, crossing his arms and rendering the offer moot. He watched or listened to her fumble in the dark, and Becky could all but hear him grinning.

"Why don't you go grab the boys? Tell them it's supper time. I'll be ... along," she grunted.

"No. This is more fun."

"You're a jerk. Help me up."

"You're stuck."

"My legs are numb. Are you going to help me or not?"

"I'm gonna take a picture first."

She heard him fumbling with his phone. "Don't you dare."

"Oh Becky," he laughed. "I have to, now."

A flash lit up the room just as she twisted and fell forward onto the ground, her ever-compassionate husband simply moving out of the way to accommodate her tumble.

5:00 p.m.

"Then Aunt Becky got stuck in the wall," Parker giggled, "and then she fell over and Uncle Tank took her picture. Show my dad and Maddy-mom!" he turned to his new uncle hopefully.

"Maybe later, Buddy," Tank grinned.

"Ha-ha, yeah, we had a great time," Becky rolled her eyes. "So, I think we've pretty thoroughly covered what happened here. How did it go at the medical center?" She turned the conversation back to Maddy. "I know you said you're fine, but I'm looking for 'stuck in the wall' details."

Maddy laughed and held her tummy. "There's not much to tell. We really are both good. Doctor just wants us to get some rest."

"And lots of fluids, *and* you need to eat," John added, moving her plate a little closer.

Maddy smiled at him. "Right, that, too."

"So how long did it take for him to be able to see you? And was he amazed at how perfect Bella is?"

"I guess it took about an hour before he came in?" Maddy glanced at John, who nodded. "And yes, he agreed that she's perfect. He had the pediatric doctor check her out and they were both really impressed with her weight and her color, and her lungs."

They both smiled. Bella must have let the doctor have it.

"Well, that's a relief," Becky said with feeling. She looked at Maddy's half-empty plate. "Can you try to eat a little more?"

"I'm stuffed, really," Maddy replied, pushing away from the table a little. "Thank you so much for feeding us." She smiled at the boys. "Sounds like you had fun here. I used to play Hide and Seek with your Aunt Becky when we were growing up."

"Back then I fit places. I'd have stumped her if she'd looked harder."

"That was one time," Maddy objected with a laugh. "And in my defense, I had a really good book."

"You left her hiding?" Blake asked, apparently considering new dynamics to sibling playtime.

John shook his head. "And I thought I knew you."

Bella squirmed in her car seat and all attention turned to the middle of the table, where she presided over the gathering.

"Well, I'm going to escape with Bella while you all continue to defame my character," Maddy smirked, undoing the buckles and lifting her daughter out.

"I'll carry her upstairs," John offered.

"Okay, I'll count, and you guys hide!" Parker exclaimed, running to the corner of the kitchen and covering his eyes.

Becky slid her gaze to Tank and he grinned back.

"Come upstairs, guys. Movie time," John said over his shoulder. "Take your plates to the sink and come on up."

Parker came out of his corner with a sigh. "Okay, that'll be fun, too." He grabbed Tank's hand. "Come on."

Tank grinned. "Plates, first. And Parker?"

The hopeful look he turned toward his uncle almost had Becky suggesting they delay their alone time for a movie adventure in the penthouse.

Tank squatted down to look into Parker's eyes. "Remember I married your Aunt Becky today?"

Parker's face fell a little. "Yeah?"

"Well, I'd like to spend some time with her."

Parker brightened again. "Oh, she can come!"

Becky bit back the laugh that threatened. "Thank you for inviting me, Parker." She put her hand on Tank's shoulder. "But I think we're going to do our own thing for a while."

Parker's shoulders sagged. "Kissing again?"

Becky's smile faltered a little as she considered the look Tank directed at her. She hoped no one else was paying attention.

She turned back to her nephew. "Yeah, kissing." She ruffled his hair. "You can come if you want."

Parker shrieked, "No way!" and started toward the door, before he stopped, turned around, and grabbed his plate off the table. He hustled it to the counter and then peeled up the steps as though Becky and Tank were about to give chase.

Maddy laughed and held her stomach. "Ow. I gotta get out of here. Come on, Blake. Let's go watch a movie." She beamed at the newlyweds, then quickly ushered Blake up the stairs.

A beat of silence followed as Becky and Tank considered the closed door and then turned to each other.

"Well," Becky said, fighting an unparalleled rush of nerves. She found it impossible to meet Tank's gaze, and yet, what was her new husband, if not a source of comfort? She squared her shoulders a bit and let her gaze travel up that nicely fitting sweater to the slightly stubbled jaw, paused for a moment on those very inviting lips, and then, feeling much braver, looked up into Tank's intense green eyes.

"Okay, I'll count. You hide."

Becky stumbled back. "Funny."

"One."

She studied his face. "You're not kidding."

"Two."

"I'm not playing Hide and Seek. I'd rather go watch the movie." She took another step back.

"Three."

"Come on, Tank, this isn't funny." Becky backed toward the door to the dining room.

"Four."

"You'll never find me, and I won't come out." She fumbled the door open.

"Five."

"This is no way to start a marriage." She ducked into the dining room, breaking the unnerving eye contact. His voice was still loud and clear.

"Six."

A wave of panicked determination propelled her through the house. "You won't like me when you find me!" she called out, considering the front door briefly before opting for the stairway.

"Seven," was definitely closer.

"You're cheating!" She called, scrambling up the steps.

"Eight," was in the hallway.

"We are *not* doing this," she said severely from the top of the stairs.

"Nine," was loud and clear as her husband came into view.

"Edwin Kimball!"

"Ten," faltered a bit as Tank came to stand at the base of the steps.

A beat of silence followed as they considered each other from opposite ends of the staircase.

A slow smile spread over Tank's face. "Oh Becky Kimball," he said, taking the stairs two at a time, "I have to now."

The End

S. Jane Scheyder

Acknowledgements

Many people have been acknowledged and thanked throughout this series – friends who provided a place to write and watch the sunrise in Maine, friends who fleshed out characters, who helped me understand the renovation process or tea and coffee varieties, and always those who prayed me through the writing process. My heartfelt thanks goes out to all of you, yet, again! For this final book in the Inn Love – Clairmont Series, I want to especially thank my beta readers. Some of you know Clairmont and its characters well, some of you were asked to get to know them for the first time. Your wisdom and insights were invaluable, and you made the final product so much better. Thank you for your time and honest feedback!

Jessica – I dedicated this book to you because you've always been at the heart of these stories. You brought Maddy to life in the first book, and continued to give thoughtful, challenging input whenever I asked you for it. You hold my characters to account in a way that only someone who really believes in Clairmont can understand! Thank you for giving my sister dialogue joy and depth and reality!

Hannah – the time and love you put into your observations will always have a special place in my heart. Thank you for your uplifting comments and for being merciless with my smiles and grins! You made important feedback fun and palatable, you made Becky more stylish, and you made my kitchen smell better. Your understanding of character interaction made your input pure gold.

Jenn – You bravely took on my novel with very little notice and you gave me some of the most profoundly important technical feedback, for which I am so very grateful! This book flows better because of you, and it was a bonus to have a few laughs on the side with you! I hope we get to work together on future projects!

Ann – You were another brave soul who took on reading something out of your normal genre-zone and gave me valuable input about the story's ability to stand alone. Thank for your time and support!

Linda – You have been a faithful reader and have prayed me through every book in this series. I will never be able to thank you enough for your sharp eye and for your enthusiastic support for my writing. You are a treasure of a friend!

Jacob – As always, you make my readers' first view of my work inviting and beautiful. I am so grateful for your talent and your vision and your willingness to share them with me. Thank you, too, for your brave redirect in the final hours of this book. I can hardly put words to how important that was and how grateful I am that you are invested enough in the characters to know when a difficult change needs to be made. Thank you!

Jan – My continued thanks for your prayers and support in our writing and publishing efforts!

More titles in the Inn Love – Clairmont Series

Cafenova
Maddy's Story - Where it all begins ...

You Smiled, a novella –
Grace's Story *(available only on Amazon Kindle)*

Done With Men Forever
Becky's Story

Mistletoe, a novella
Liz's Story *(available only on Amazon Kindle)*

About the author

S. Jane (Susie) Scheyder grew up in the Midwest, lived for years in the South, and now calls New England her home. She graduated from Valparaiso University with a degree in Music Merchandising, though writing has always been her favorite artistic outlet. Having dreamed of renovating and running her own B&B, she found the theme of her first novel, *Cafenova*, the first of the 'Inn Love - Clairmont Series'. Susie's first children's book, *One More Thing*, about a boy who puts off bedtime, was released in 2014, followed by *How Will You Change the World?* in 2016. Susie and her husband raised five children and live in Connecticut.